What People are Sa[ying about]

Wooing the L[...]

With so many derivative and poorly written supernatural stories out there, Lee Morgan's debut novel is as refreshing as summer rain. Those in the know will enjoy a tale about the initial twists of the real Crooked Path; the uninitiated will glimpse worlds and possibilities that mainstream religions have desperately tried to hide.

Gavin Andrew, author of *Paganism & Christianity, A Resource for Wiccans, Witches and Pagans.*

This book lays hauntingly vibrant foundations for a promisingly potent series. Morgan opens the reader to an Otherworld peopled with individuals who are endearingly complex and connected with a Fated unfolding that seems to sing of bleeding stars and bright shadows. I am utterly transfixed with Christopher Penrose and his world.

Gede Parma, author of *Ecstatic Witchcraft*

Wooing the Echo

Book One of the Christopher Penrose Novels

Wooing
the Echo

Book One of the Christopher Penrose Novels

Lee Morgan

COSMIC
EGG
BOOKS

Winchester, UK
Washington, USA

First published by Cosmic Egg Books, 2013
Cosmic Egg Books is an imprint of John Hunt Publishing Ltd., Laurel House, Station Approach,
Alresford, Hants, SO24 9JH, UK
office1@jhpbooks.net
www.johnhuntpublishing.com

For distributor details and how to order please visit the 'Ordering' section on our website.

ISBN: 978 1 78099 896 1

A CIP catalogue record for this book is available from the British Library.

Design: Stuart Davies

Printed and bound by CPI Group (UK) Ltd, Croydon, CR0 4YY

We operate a distinctive and ethical publishing philosophy in all
areas of our business, from our global network of authors to
production and worldwide distribution.

Dedication

For my life partner Brett Morgan, you were there through the journey around England during which this novel was conceived, and through the years that gave birth to it. Nobody knows all the stories from those times any more like you do, and nothing I do could have been done without you.

What is Love?
It is grief in the heart,
It is stretching of strength beyond its bounds,
It is the four quarters of the world,
It is the highest height of heaven,
It is breaking of the neck,
It is a battle with a spectre,'
It is drowning with water,
It is a race against heaven,
It is champion- deeds beneath the sea.
It is wooing the echo.
—The Wooing of Etain

1

'The twelvemonth and a day being up,
The dead began to speak:
'Oh who sits weeping on my grave,
And will not let me sleep?

'Tis I, my love, sits on your grave,
And will not let you sleep;
For I crave one kiss of your clay-cold lips,
And that is all I seek.'
—English Folk Tradition

Christopher sat on the deep windowsill of his room. His legs were drawn up, his arms around them and his face was in profile against the blanched sky. Like a bird of prey in a dizzily-placed eyrie this was where he perched and watched things pass. There was a stillness in his gaze. It was like the lung-burn of a suspended breath, or the heavy crush of a low, gathering storm that will not break. A room had been closed up and locked behind those eyes and to open it would be to disturb fragile and intricate patterns in the dust.

The intuitive observer, could they stand like a spectre in that room and watch without being watched, would be able to taste the salty tension in the air around Christopher's body, a smell, like the ozone after lightning; sense there was something behind that stillness that was coiled and crouched ready to spring, something pungent and animal.

But of course the average observer would not see such things. Physically Christopher was what one might call a well-made man, tall and hard-bodied. He possessed the sort of natural muscles in his shoulders and chest that many men work hard for at a gym. His hair was blond and still cut in a schoolboy cut that was just beginning to become unkempt. There was something a little distant about his blue eyes. The abstracted quality to his gaze was perhaps created by the fact that his eyes were slightly asymmetrically placed, one a little higher than the other. His smile, when it came, was stunning for its sudden brightness and the dazzling white teeth. He was attractive. He should have been gorgeous but somehow wasn't.

On that day Christopher was sitting in his windowsill, watching the midday sun strike the wet ground with violent illumination. A Westerly had just bustled away the watercolour of greys and luminescent fog that the sun had made with the rain clouds. Christopher sighed to himself. He traced the descent of a raindrop on the glass pane with his finger. Sometimes something aching swelled in his chest like an ocean and he couldn't explain it or release it. He would realise then that he had been holding his breath, waiting… Waiting for something that he could not name, waiting for something to happen that did not happen. Slowly he exhaled his breath.

Getting up Christopher ran his fingers through his hair and reached for his coat that was slumped over a chair by his bed. The house had come to seem too small. As he grabbed his coat a framed photograph on his desk caught his eye. The picture had been there for years, and yet somehow today the inquisitive blue eyes of the boy in the photograph seemed to cut right through Christopher. He turned the photograph over face down on the table.

Christopher's family home was in West Kennet, Salisbury. Their house was situated on a narrow leafy, lane called Gunsite Road. It backed onto the fields where the Neolithic earthwork of West Kennet Long Barrow stood and was just down the road from Silbury Hill. If one continued along the main road in that direction it was easily possible to walk to Avebury, something he did regularly to get to Irene's house.

When he arrived he let himself in at the front gate and closed it behind him. A sluggish wind moved the rusted wind chimes

2

and they gave of a creak and a few more musical tones. No matter how many times he'd come here it always seemed too quiet.

'Hello, love,' Irene said as Christopher approached her. He bent down and kissed her on the cheek. Back when they were boys she had been the mother of his best friend but somewhere between her son's death and now, Irene had become Christopher's friend. She had the kind of face that always looks happy, even when she clearly wasn't. It was her turned up nose and heart shaped face, he always thought, that made her seem girlishly cheerful. This effect only increased the pathos of her gaze, from which all the sorrows of the world seemed to seep at times.

'Hello, Irene. I just thought I'd drop in on my way by.'

'It's always lovely to see you dear, why don't you come in and I'll make the tea?' Christopher smiled at the repetition of their ritual and followed her. The teapot ritual had begun when Eugene was still alive and the boys were probably not really old enough for caffeine. It had seemed an exciting adult privilege to Christopher then, sitting up for tea. Irene had read them poetry, which had all gone over Christopher's head at first.

Now it was like a guilty secret, the teapot and its tattered tea cosy, the chipped china and the refusal to forget. Irene would lay a third teacup for Eugene. Neither Christopher nor Irene ever said anything about that cup. It just sat there brazenly white and empty, like a wide unearthly eye. They never stopped laying it and at the end it was packed quietly away.

Village gossip said that Eugene's room had never been packed away and was still as it had been the day he died. The door to that room was always closed and Christopher didn't want to know if it were true. Only in his nightmares was that door ever open. In those dreams he'd be moving toward it through no choice of his own, forced to see what was within.

Even though Christopher had heard all of Irene's stories

3

before he didn't interrupt her. He was too keenly aware that he had told his own stories about Eugene at least twice. But there were some stories he didn't share with Irene; some that were just too strange for words. They were locked away, in a wordless, airless room inside his psyche; dust gathered on them and nothing else changed. Christopher always enjoyed hearing what Eugene told his mother when he got home from school on the day they met.

'And then he declared, "Mum, I've met someone who's a freak like me."'

Eugene had died at thirteen from a congenital heart abnormality. Christopher knew all the details. He'd been there for his friend through open-heart surgeries and attempts to find a matching donor organ for him. Christopher had watched and felt the waves of hope rise and fall until there was just an ache at the centre that hope no longer touched. But despite all he saw, the medical explanation paled beside the one that Eugene himself had given him.

'When babies are in the womb they have a hole in their heart. It's like a link to our mother's circulation, but it's also a door. It's a gate to the Otherworld. Because when we are in the womb we are neither alive nor dead, and the gate means that in our hearts we can still walk between the worlds. At birth in those few disastrous seconds when we are cut loose and we breathe the air of the living, this signal goes through our system and slams the door shut. Bang! We are shut out from the world of the dead.'

Christopher had jumped and then smiled. 'And...' he started tentatively, because it appeared that Eugene had finished speaking.

Eugene raised his eyebrows looking significantly at Christopher. 'And with me, it never happened. The door didn't close, the walking back and forth never stopped. So every day a little death seeps into my life's blood and I hear footfalls.'

'Hi, what have you been up to?'

Christopher looked at his sister Millicent for a moment as he took off his anorak and hung it up, then he looked down again. He couldn't seem to leave the house without attracting a range of questions these days.

'Why don't you get one of those little plastic tracking devices and tag my ankle so that you never have to lose track of me?' he suggested, only semi-playfully.

She sighed and her brow creased. 'I'm only trying to show I care about you, all right? There's no need to be so defensive. It makes people worry about you more. What are you doing that's so secret you can't tell us about it?'

He walked past her into the hall as she spoke, intent on heading straight up to his room.

'I'm shooting up,' he muttered.

'Don't joke about stuff like that.'

He turned back around, leaning on the banister.

'I'm sorry, Milly. It's just a bit like the inquisition around here lately. Can I go now?' he asked quietly, his voice showing something vulnerable for a moment.

'Sure,' Millicent responded. 'You can't keep pushing everyone away though,' she said, when he reached half way up the stairs. With a sigh he stopped on the landing.

'All right, you want to know? I was at Eugene's mum's house, okay?' There was a short silence. He looked down at her, her sensible tied back blonde hair, her pale thin face and her furiously working lips. She opened her mouth but didn't say anything. After a moment he took pity on her.

'Why don't you come up to my room? Let's not have this conversation on the landing.' With a nervous but grateful smile Millicent followed him up the stairs. When they got inside his room he closed the door behind her and sat down on the bed. She pulled out the wooden chair at Christopher's desk and sat down. For a moment she twiddled with the globe of the world on his desk. Christopher just sat there, knees apart, his elbows leaning on them, supporting his chin in his hands.

'Why don't you say what you want to, Milly?'

Millicent felt uncomfortable with her brother at the best of times. It seemed he became a man without her noticing, while she was trapped in some perpetual cardigan-clad girlhood. Not only that, he was the sort of man that intimidated her. It had been the popular good-looking people, the physical, sporting types who had ridiculed her at high school. She was plain, not unattractive, but plain in the literal sense. Not only was her brother, she grudgingly admitted, good-looking, he was one of those muscular sorts. She had to sometimes remind herself that Christopher wasn't popular or sporty; at least not any more. He had given up water polo around the time Eugene died and not done any sport since. He was bookish and weird. His body seemed an obtrusive accident of nature now.

'Christopher, I know we never talk about it but I want to talk about Eugene.'

'Okay.'

She was surprised. She had expected some resistance, at the very least some sarcasm.

'Is that all?' she couldn't help asking.

'I'm just pleasantly surprised that someone is actually asking me rather than talking about me behind my back.'

She disliked the slightly amused smile on his lips; it suggested some hidden self-confidence that did not comfort her. It was as though he were somehow above the petty matters that interested his family. She thought she saw a faint sadness under the cool amusement, but she couldn't be sure.

'Eugene has been dead for four years now—'

'Five,' he corrected quietly. 'Five years and two months.'

'Yes,' she replied, 'Yes, quite some time. Do you think maybe you're not coping?'

'Oh come off it, Millicent,' he said, turning his back to her as he looked out into the front garden. 'What's the point here?'

'The point is I think it's unhealthy!' she blurted out.

'Okay, why?'

'It's been too long.'

'Too long for what?'

'Too long for it to be healthy.'

'We're going in circles,' he said.

In desperation she found herself blurting out exactly what she was really thinking.

'Christopher were you and Eugene...' She stopped herself when she saw Christopher's face darken. Something made her want to retract her question.

'What? Were we what?'

Millicent could feel the colour rushing into her cheeks. She stammered.

He groaned, smacking his hand down onto the window frame. 'Is that what all of this is about? Is that all? Something as stupid and unimportant as that?'

'I hardly think it's stupid, Christopher! This is West Kennett after all, not London!' she yelled back, getting to her feet.

'That's what you're so worried about? What people think? That's what really matters?' There was another silence, 'You really want to know!' he yelled.

'Yes!' Millicent found herself yelling back, 'Yes I want to know!'

'No!' he shouted, turning to her. 'No,' he said more quietly, his brow furrowed. He shook his head with a look of hurt confusion. 'Why don't you go down stairs now?' he said very quietly.

'Are you dismissing me?'

He turned back to the window. 'No. I just thought you could go tell Mum and Dad the good news.'

'Christopher—' she started to say before he cut her off coldly.

'You got your answer.'

It felt as though some very delicate aspect of his love for Eugene had been exposed to the glare of neon lights, damaged by it, like an old manuscript assaulted by light and air. What the hell difference did it make? He didn't want to say 'why did she want to know if we were sleeping together?' It was not that the idea revolted him at all, it just seemed irrelevant under the circumstances. With Eugene dying so young the question seemed to mock them. As if there'd really been time to figure things like that out, he thought.

Sitting at his desk now Christopher was gazing into space without actually seeing what was in front of him. Then slowly, in a gradually dawning kind of way, he realised he was looking at the photograph of Eugene. It was a photo that had been taken during their school camp in the Lake District, and one of his favourite pictures of his dead friend. It wasn't unusual for Christopher to look at it. What was unusual was that he had turned the photograph over on its face before he left. Christopher frowned and a feeling of clammy cold began to form on his skin.

Forgetting his irritation with Millicent he got to his feet and opened the bedroom door.

'Millicent? Did you touch anything when you were in here?'

'No, of course not!' she shouted back from her room, irritation in her tone.

Coming out onto the landing Christopher loudly repeated the same question to his mother down in the kitchen.

'Of course not, honey. I haven't been in your room.'

Despite being flanked by a lot of thatch and ancient stone the Penrose home was a relatively new two-storied place with a carefully well-maintained lawn and hedgerow. Whilst the home was new, the family's occupancy in the area was not. Christopher's mother Jane had been born just up the road in the same farmhouse that her Mother before her had been born in. They had been farmers so being an only child Jane stood to inherit land. Jane would not have thought of leaving the area, but had been happy to marry a well-paid engineer whose income supplemented her inheritance and made farming no longer a necessity. So the Penrose family built a new home on land already in Jane's family and settled a stone's throw from where she was born.

Sometimes Christopher fancied that the ultra-modern interior of their home was some kind of defence against the numinous presence of the stone-age monuments that dotted the landscape around them. The rubber-sealed and double-glazed windows could block out the sound of the wind coming off the haunted stones and whistling through the barrow, but there were some uncanny things that they couldn't keep out. And while Christopher was meant to be talking to his father his mind was still on the photograph of Eugene that appeared to have moved.

Christopher's father Rodney sat in front of the television and flicked it to the cricket channel. He turned the volume down so he could keep an eye on the scores as well as have an important conversation with his son. Christopher's mother sat quietly off to one side in an armchair, perched on its edge.

'Have you thought any more about what course you'll accept, son?'

'What do you think I should do?' he asked.

His father sighed and put down the remote control. Christopher stared at the object, it seemed funny to him suddenly. The remote control completely summed up his relationship with his father. Rodney was a man in his early forties with mid-brown hair beginning to grey. He wore metal-framed glasses and when he smiled it was possible to remember that he was once handsome and happy.

'This isn't about what I want son, it's about what you want.'

'Oh,' Christopher murmured quietly.

'What was that?' his father asked sharply, quick to jump on this sign of defiance that would take the conversation to comfortably familiar ground.

Christopher looked at him. Rodney's need for authority over his son seemed to hang like a tangible presence in the air between them. Christopher sighed after a while and heard himself speak, but did not feel like a real participator in the conversation.

'Dad, I don't want to do science or computers or accounting. I'm not that kind of smart.'

'Rubbish,' his father quickly asserted. 'See Jane? It's attitude. He keeps underestimating himself. If he won't strive how am I meant to help him?'

'Rodney please, let him speak. You have to stop pummelling him with your point of view. Go on, Christopher.'

'I was just trying to say I think I'm more right-brain smart.'

'That's a fallacy you know,' his father interjected.

'Rodney!' Jane cried.

'I'm just saying, Jane. That whole thing about the left side of brain controlling reason and the right brain creative thought, it's a gross simplification.'

'We're here to talk about Christopher,' she reminded him.

'I think I'm artistic,' he said quietly.

'See, this is that bloody Steiner school you sent him to causing this, Jane! You scored in the eighties for your Maths exam! You're no idiot, Christopher. I can't help feeling this interest in literature or whatever it is, is about your lack of self-esteem. You think you're not capable of taking on anything but a soft subject.'

Christopher rolled his eyes and looked away out the window.

'Is that Millicent's psychoanalysis of me?' he said after a moment.

'Millicent does say that she thinks self-esteem is a problem, and that you might be leaning towards the arts because it's easier and you're depressed.'

Christopher snorted with disgust.

'What do you expect? Millicent has absolutely no imagination.'

'That's unfair,' his mother said.

'Perhaps it is unfair, but it's true. That's why you both prefer her. Because she's boring and reliable and she likes all the same boring, reliable things you do.'

Mr Penrose shook his head and got slowly to his feet with his remote control, pointing it at the television he switched it off.

'Young man, you are eighteen years old and if you're not going to start thinking and acting like an adult then I wash my hands of you!'

'Rodney!' Mrs Penrose cried, jumping to her feet also. 'This is not what I asked you to do! He doesn't need this on top of everything he's already going through.'

'Would you stop defending him, Jane? Maybe if you would dislodge the boy from your breast long enough for him to become a man...'

'So now you are blaming me!' she yelled back.

'Would you both just stop it!' Christopher cried. Despite his manly appearance his youth was obvious suddenly. He turned away from them both and walked over to the windowsill. For a while he looked out into the front garden but didn't really see it. 'I'm going to take the offer to study Arts at UWE, and I'm going to take English as my major,' he murmured.

'And what are you going to be at the end of that?' his father sneered.

'Educated,' he replied quietly, 'if that still means anything.'

'Not a damn thing in this day and age.'

Mrs Penrose gave her husband a glance of such distilled cold fury that he fell silent.

'It does, Christopher,' his mother said. 'There are places, circles, in which education and culture still matter deeply. Unfortunately your father has never moved in any of them. It doesn't mean they don't exist.'

'I suppose you could always be an English teacher or a librarian or... or something,' his father muttered, obviously looking for a way out of the conversation and the room. Having switched off the cricket he now appeared distinctly uncomfortable.

'Or something,' Christopher said to himself.

'Your mother and I want the best for you boy, that's all,' his father said as he walked past, giving Christopher a conciliatory slap on the shoulder. 'And we've spent a damned fortune on your education.'

But Christopher didn't hear or notice. He had disappeared out through the window and down over the lawn, out along the horizon where the reddish sunset was turning to purple behind some pine trees. Far out into the distance where the watery black of his pupils fixed themselves, his soul wandered. Back with his body his mouth smiled strangely and his posture softened, lost its defensive edge. He never knew what was said that triggered a memory, a memory that was capable of transporting his being, but suddenly he was sitting beneath that row of alpines and he could hear Eugene's voice reading aloud to him from a book.

'Some say the world will end in fire, some say in ice. From what I've tasted of desire, I hold with those who favour fire.'

He had looked over at Christopher and closed the edition of Robert Frost's work. Eugene had tended to make eye contact that went on for ages and his gaze hadn't let Christopher off the hook that day. In the half-light Eugene's strange, widely spaced blue eyes had had a sudden feral gleam about them. 'What do you think? Ice or fire?'

'I'm not sure,' Christopher had said.

'I am. I want to *burn*.'

Christopher shook his head to clear his thoughts. After the brief abstraction his clarity was startling. He almost felt light-headed, like he'd taken on too much oxygen.

'That's what I'll do,' he murmured to himself. But he was no longer talking about university. He simply knew that he had two choices: *fire or ice*. He could numb out into a white quiet, pedestrian death, the same type that so many living people he knew had already succumbed to. Or he could burn. And unlike at the time when Eugene had asked him, he was now old enough to know which one he wanted. He heard again those words of a dead man in the mouth of a dead boy, and they told him more about life right then than anything his father had to say.

Seeing Christopher immediately after exercise Jane took pity upon the visible quiver of his muscles under his clothes and the aggravated heat of his cheek. Something about the vulnerable flesh of his earlobes seemed to move her inexplicably. Feeling foolish she came over to speak to him.

'I found out something interesting today at the PACT meeting,' she told him as soon as he came in through the front door.

The 'Pewsey Area Community Trust' was a group where some of the locals got together to launch schemes to improve the economic and social life of Pewsey. Christopher's mother liked to feel she was 'contributing', being someone who had never needed to struggle much economically in life.

'What's that?' Christopher asked, pulling off his Wellingtons and leaving them in the foyer.

'There's a team of archaeologists following up on the Stanchestor Hoard. I had a good conversation with one of the Masters students who are assisting in the dig for practical experience. Apparently they found human remains a layer down under the Roman villa.'

'Yeah?' Christopher said, helping himself to a glass of water. It didn't particularly surprise him that they had dug up human remains from around here. West Kennet Long Barrow had been a tomb after all, with numerous skulls and long bones once inhumed there. Christopher tended to assume that the chalk of the entire region was one-tenth human bone.

'I took the liberty of inviting her to dinner,' Jane said quietly.

Christopher didn't say anything so she added: 'You're not angry are you? I'm not trying to orchestrate your social life or anything it's just—'

'Not at all. It's just what I want. I need to socialise with someone. It's as good a place to start as any,' he said, bending and kissing her on the cheek.

Fending him off gently she wiped at her face.

'You're all sweat, boy,' she protested to cover her joy.

'It's a brilliant co-incidence. I've just been thinking that I need to meet people. I'm just going up stairs to have a shower.'

2

*'Our deepest hungers are not for food and drink, not for amuse-
ments and recreations, not for property and wardrobes, not for
notoriety and gossip. We hunger for truth, we thirst to drink
beauty, we yearn to celebrate, we stretch out to love and be loved.
This is why anything less than everything is not enough.'*
—Fr. Thomas Dubay

Christopher began peeling off his soiled and damp clothing in
the bathroom. The room had brown tiles and a large mirror
surrounded by numerous electric lights, as was the fashion
sometime in the mid-eighties when they were fitted. The room
itself, like everywhere in the house, was excessively warm.

Stripping completely naked he leant against the washbasin
and looked at himself. This was something that it had never
really occurred to him to do before. He had hardly noticed his
body, nor paid attention to its many changes since Eugene had
died. The hair near his forehead was now dark-blond and
clumped with sweat. When he gazed into his own eyes they
shocked him, much like they were the eyes of a stranger. There
was something uncomfortable about staring into them for too
long. He saw them as two vital blue flames that seemed to dance
back at him from the mirror like they were laughing at him. They
looked like a man's eyes, slightly deep-set and full of vigour and
adult humour.

The man's face smiled at him without Christopher's conscious
decision to do so. It seemed that both his eyes and his smile
possessed an innate knowing that he himself wasn't aware of yet.
He had not thought of himself as a gendered, let alone sexual
being, until Millicent's questions had forced him to.

Christopher looked at his broad shoulders, turned to look
also at the even more unfamiliar muscles in his back. He felt
more a sense of curiosity than pride. As he saw himself there in

the mirror, he found he was thinking about his ancestors and the genes that had made his body, and why. *Look at it,* he thought, *those genes formed me with a function in mind and it probably wasn't reading dusty books.* It was an unavoidable conclusion, although it was not a comfortable one: His body was designed for action. He would have been some sort of hunter or warrior in any other culture in the world. *No doubt this body is a direct throwback to some swordsman or another who lived a thousand years ago,* he thought. Somehow this thought made his skin begin to prickle coldly again, as those ancestors suddenly came to seem like ghosts living under his skin.

Curiously Christopher leaned closer still to his own reflection and looked deeply into his own eyes. The feeling that they were a stranger's eyes became more and more intense the longer he stared, but he forced himself not to look away. A tension gripped his stomach, a feeling somewhere between excitement and rising dread. For a moment the surface of the mirror seemed to morph, just a faint shimmering, as though it were made of water rather than a solid substance. Christopher acknowledged the shift from his own eyes looking alien to consciously thinking: *those are not my eyes.* The blue was not the same shade as Christopher's eyes. The expression was faintly ironic. And then his reflection winked at him.

In a sudden clumsy rush of movement Christopher took several fast steps back from the mirror and collided with the bathroom wall. His breath was coming fast and all the hairs were standing up on the back of his arms.

When the doorbell rang Christopher had been talking to Millicent about the university course that he planned to accept. He desperately wanted the sound of voices, the movement and the bright lighting to drive away the lingering sense of unease he felt.

'I'll get that,' said his mother. Jane was glowing with excitement, and also a little with Scotch. She was dressed smartly in a black slim line dress, and with a dust of blusher on her cheeks she looked very young and pretty. Too young to have Millicent as a daughter, Christopher thought, Milly looks a bit like Mum's older sister at times. He felt unkind for the thought, but it was, nonetheless, true. His mother clicked her pair of spaghetti strap high-heels to the door and opened it.

'Hello, dear, do come in.'

Jane ushered in a young woman a little taller than herself, with long dark hair that fell around her exposed shoulders in glossy curls. Her lips had that impossible sheen-lipstick that advertising promises will not even be smudged by kissing.

He noticed her exposed skin, the sense of fashionable and sexual display that she gave off, and the way she moved in her platform heels. Despite her appearance there was a sadness in this girl's eyes that Christopher found quite explicit, and it drew him to her as like attracts like.

'Put your eyes back in your head, Christopher,' Millicent snapped.

Christopher smiled almost wistfully.

'I guess she's just not what I expected from an archaeologist.'

The young woman put down the small bag she'd been carrying as she looked around herself.

'Hi Jane, it's great to see you again!' She leaned over and kissed both of his mother's cheeks. 'I love your place!' she enthused as Jane showed her into the sitting room. 'It's so quaint with all those hedges leading up to your cute little street. Hi!' she said, spotting everyone else and greeting them like she already knew them.

'Everyone, this is Sophia Kallis, she's doing her... what was it? A Masters in Osteology and Funerary Archaeology? Did I get it right love? Sophia's at your future university, Christopher! Sophia, this is my husband Rodney.'

Rodney got to his feet and held out his hand.

'Pleased to meet you, Sophia,' he said smiling as she shook his hand warmly. 'Can I get you a drink?'

'Oh yes please, that would be smashing.'

'What would you like?'

'A dry red if you have one open, but don't open anything especially, I drink everything.'

Rodney laughed. 'My daughter drinks dry reds so we have one right here.' He went over to the cellaret and poured her a drink.

'This is my son Christopher,' Jane continued after Rodney had handed Sophia her glass of wine.

Christopher got up and held out his hand. 'Hi,' he said.

'Hello, Christopher. It's lovely to meet you at last. Your mother was telling me you're going to accept an offer to study Arts at the university this year. Good for you,' she said, shaking his hand energetically. Sophia's behaviour was exuberant and extraverted but still when she looked at Christopher he sensed the same sadness.

'And this is my daughter Millicent. She works in a solicitor's office.'

'That must come in handy, having someone who knows the law around,' Sophia said, shaking Millicent's somewhat limp hand so vigorously that its limpness was visible.

'I don't know that much about the law. I just shuffle papers for people who do and make appointments. It's hardly exciting here in little Wiltshire anyway,' she replied coolly.

'Oh,' said Sophia, seemingly put off for only a moment before smiling again. 'So tell me a bit about what the local area is like. It's obviously fascinating historically, but what's it like to live in? For young people?' she said, looking at Millicent and Christopher. 'There wouldn't be a lot of night life here...'

'My brother and I don't really get into night life,' Millicent replied.

'But I'd like too,' Christopher interjected, 'I'm actually only just old enough for nightclubs this year. I haven't had a chance yet.' He sipped his Scotch.

'Oh, wow, I took you for older! But I should have realised with you about to go to university. You should come out with my friends and I some time. Would you mind that, Jane? Me taking your son into Salisbury one night?'

'Not at all. Christopher's eighteen, he's a man now. It's up to him where he goes.

'I just have to go and check the dinner. Rodney could you go and get some wine out of the cellar for me? You kids stay in here, help yourself to drinks and get acquainted.'

As though at some mutually agreed upon cue the two parents exited the room, leaving Sophia alone with Christopher and Millicent.

'Can I top up any one's wine?' Christopher asked.

'Thanks ever so much, that's plenty. Cheers.'

Millicent took the bottle from Christopher to refill her own.

'So,' Christopher said, seating himself across from Sophia. 'What era is this dig you're working on?'

Sophia smiled. She folded her legs and leaned back in her chair.

'It's a pre-Roman burial site but its occupation was continuous until up to the Roman invasion. Afterwards it was abandoned and a Roman villa was built nearby and farming occurred over the top of it. It's a really valuable find, very rich in ritual deposits. Most exciting for me is that there's been two fully articulated skeletons.'

'What sorts of ritual deposits were with them?' Christopher asked.

Millicent sipped her wine in chilly silence.

'We found some weapons mainly, and the female skeleton had some clear stones and shells and piece of animal bone in what was probably a pouch worn at the neck. We think it might be a hasty burial, a war cemetery maybe. I'm taking a module in Biomolecular Archaeology this year so I'll get to observe as they attempt to extract DNA from the adult male's jaw.'

Christopher was leaning forward listening intently and nodding.

'And what sort of things will you be able to know about them from it?'

'Oh everything! Well practically, if you take it from the osteology perspective and the genetic we'll know about childhood diseases, age, social class, facial appearance, if he has living descendents, if his diet was poor or good.'

'And how does this help us?' Millicent blurted, and then paused colour rising in her cheeks. 'I mean... I just meant... How do these kinds of discoveries affect our lives?'

Sophia smiled knowingly and nodded.

'Ah huh. I know exactly where you're going. What I always say is this, as a science we're not exactly out there curing cancer. We're just trying to understand things, to keep records. I think it's a natural human activity. Everybody hopes that they will be remembered when they are dead. And in some ways I think the long dead have their own legacy that we don't always appreciate. When we recognise where we have come from, I think that helps us to appreciate what we have now.'

'What do you mean by that: 'appreciate what we have now'?' Christopher asked.

'Do you know how tough life was for a man in those days?'

'Not as well as you do, I'm sure. But...'

'At your age you would have been fighting for years, if you weren't dead already. You're thinking about things like going to university. Back then you'd be lucky to still be alive! My adult male that I'm working on at the moment, our DNA candidate, he wasn't much older than you. His body was hacked with a sword so brutally it nearly severed his spinal column. He may not have even died immediately, and there was no morphine in those days...'

Almost as though to give her the last word when Christopher

was full of questions and queries her mobile phone went off.

'Sorry about that,' she said, taking out a silver coloured phone. 'But I better take this.' She got up and walked out of the room and into the hall. 'Hello?' they heard her say.

'Do you like her?' Millicent asked quietly.

'I think she's fascinating,'

'And totally out of your league baby brother,' she said, going over to refill her wine glass. After a moment Sophia appeared.

'Your mother says dinner is nearly ready.' She turned and walked back towards the dining room. Despite himself Christopher couldn't help noticing the slight sway of her slim hips under the short skirt. He got up promptly to follow.

After dinner Christopher picked up his laptop and changed the playlist. While he did he detected Sophia looking at him intently.

'What?' he asked, smiling. 'You're looking at me oddly.'

'You're a strange young man.'

'Freak' was Eugene's preferred word, Christopher thought. *But from him it was a term of endearment.*

'What's so strange?'

Sophia flopped onto the couch.

'Let me put it this way, what are your interests, what do you like to do?'

Christopher thought about it for a moment.

'Poetry is probably my main interest. Other than that I like history, art, music, walking. I used to play water polo when I was younger. I like driving my car. And I like... well I want... conversation. Real ones.'

Sophia nodded like this had somehow confirmed her worst suspicions.

'See, the water-polo thing, that's a bit nerdy but almost normal. Driving your car, that passes,' she said, leaning forward as though confiding something.

Christopher's eyes were involuntarily drawn down her

cleavage. *Well there you are,* he thought ironically, *there is something else 'normal' you've just discovered you like. Mum and dad will be stoked.*

'The rest though,' continued Sophia, 'is like something out of a nineteenth century novel. Back before we got electronic entertainment. Freaky freaky freak freak. Nice. But freaky.'

There's that word...

'Oh. That would be the 'Waldorf Factor' as we call it. I went to a Steiner school. If you know what that means it will explain a lot for you.'

'Aren't they the ones where the kids don't learn to read for ages and paint lots of watercolours?'

Christopher laughed.

'These are probably two things they are known for yes. But there's more to it than that. Some people describe it as an 'arts education' others as 'holistic.' My Dad was not that into the idea but Mum had read all these articles about the performance of Waldorf kids, and Dad agreed to send me there until I finished year eight. After that they sent me on to Bishops for the 'status' part.'

'Okay... Steiner schools are the 'no TV till you reach a certain age' people as well, aren't they? I guess this kinda makes sense.'

'Yep, that's the ones. I didn't keep a life-long love for finger-knitting but I did hold onto the creative side of things.'

'See with most people, they talk about liking poetry to try and show how smart they are.' Christopher looked taken aback and Sophia added, 'And I can see you're not like that. That's the weird-arse part.' She took a small sip from her port and laughed. 'And I don't know, I really don't know whether that is really uncool or really, really romantic. I dunno.' She took another drink and slowly blinked her dark dreamy eyes, 'Shit,' she said getting up as though some kind of spell had suddenly broken, 'I can't believe you're only eighteen!' Walking over to where Millicent was standing like a guard by the lounge door Sophia said, 'Where

22

is the bathroom from here, hon?' Millicent pointed it out. As soon as Sophia was out of sight Millicent turned to Christopher.

'I'm going to bed.'

'Okay Milly, good night.'

Millicent rolled her eyes.

'That'd be right, you're just dying to get rid of me aren't you?'

Christopher frowned in confusion and shook his head slowly. 'I only said goodnight. I didn't tell you to go.'

'Well you may as well have,' she snapped before turning and storming out. Christopher shook his head in bewilderment and went to get himself a glass of water. He felt maybe everyone needed to start sobering up.

When he returned Sophia was back. He took the time now to seat himself slowly and have a good look at her face. Judging by her name he guessed that she was half Greek. But he felt that one of her parents was probably English, her skin was a smooth, clear, pale shade of olive that required no foundation. Her nose was straight and fine-boned, and her bottom lip was pouty and sensual. The black defined arch of her eyebrows had obviously been painstakingly shaped.

'Sorry about racing off like that,' she said, patting at the corners of her dry looking eyes with a tissue, 'I've just had a bit to drink and I've been having problems with a boyfriend. He keeps texting me all the time.' She sniffed and dabbed carefully trying not to disturb her mascara.

'What sort of problems?' he asked. He was not at all surprised she had a boyfriend, or too concerned about the fact. But he did welcome the confidence as a sign that they were making friends. It was hard for him to really know what people did when they were making friends; it had been so long since he'd had one.

'Oh, he's a prick. He's an ex boyfriend really, just he can't get it through his head. Someone gave him my new mobile number. I'll have to change it again now. Just glad it wasn't my address or something, that's harder to change. Oh! I've gone and made a bloody fool of myself. Look, I'm really sorry about this.'

'No!' he said, 'No, please, go on.'

'Okay,' Sophia sniffed. 'Well. We started out as fuck friends I guess.'

Christopher spat his mouthful of Scotch back into the glass.

'Are you okay, sweetie? Are we old enough to be having this discussion? Yeah? I thought so. Now, anyway, the sex was great, but then things got a bit heavy. Before I knew it he started to want to know where I was going and with whom etc etc. If I went out he'd start calling on my phone and I got scared. Then things got *really* heavy... I could tell you some stories!' She sighed. 'A girl just can't get safe, relaxed, casual sex these days.'

Christopher stared mutely at her for a moment before he stammered,

'No... I... guess not.'

She laughed and slapped his knee. 'Jane is a lovely woman, Christopher, and I hope you don't take this the wrong way, but she's really kept you living in Never-Never hasn't she?'

Christopher sighed, looked down and then looked back at her with a rueful grin. 'It's not her fault. It's mine,' he said with quiet conviction. 'I think I belong somewhere else.'

'But where?' she asked.

'I don't know. Sometimes I think if I had to fight for my life maybe I'd feel more alive.'

'We live in a virtual Utopia, Christopher.'

'Yes, virtual,' he said frowning. 'That's the perfect word for it isn't it? We've got stuff, possessions, coming out of our ears and every second person I speak to is depressed, medicated, or knows someone who topped themselves. Even my bloody mum's been medicated for years...' Christopher noticed how Sophia was looking at him and felt compelled to stop. She sat and looked at him in silence for a long time. After a while he said, 'What?'

'I'm just thinking that I will take your father up on his offer for another visit after all.'

'You weren't going to?'

'Not on your life,' she said without breaking eye contact with him. 'I was planning on running out the front door and making a lot of excuses about why I would be busy forever.' Suddenly she got up and headed for the door.

'But where are you going now?' he asked, getting up and going after her, 'You haven't told me what you think, or argued back...'

She stopped in the doorway and turned to face him.

'Honey,' she purred, her eyes looking languid and full of sensual promise, 'I've had a lot to drink and I'm feeling a bit emotionally available right now. I'm going to get out of here before I pervert your sweet innocence.' She turned and headed for the door, picking up her handbag and coat before letting herself out. It was only after she'd stepped out the door that he recovered enough to follow her and call after her,

'Sophia?'

'Yes?'

'I don't want to be innocent.'

He heard her laugh echo back out of the darkness. It had a husky quality to it that was both gentle and sexy. She closed the car door.

3

'How dull it is to pause, to make an end,
To rust unburnished, not to shine in use, —
As tho' to breathe were life!'
—Tennyson

After running and doing some chin-ups Christopher headed indoors to take a shower before his mother began to complain that he was sweating on things. The endorphin rush from the exercise made his head feel light and his fingers tremble on the door-handle. He was pretty sure that 'self medicating' for depression with exercise was working for him. And as a remedy Christopher figured it sure beat his back-up plan of putting Portishead's *'Wandering Star'* on repeat and cutting his wrists.

'Christopher? There's a telephone call for you.'

'Who is it?' he asked, walking towards his mother who was holding out the phone to him with a mildly irritating smile on her face.

'Sophia,' she said, turning her back quickly.

'Thanks,' he murmured. 'Hello?'

'Hi, it's Sophia here...' there was a moment's pause. 'I was wondering if you'd like to do something.'

He smiled.

'Your kind of 'do something' or my kind of 'do something'?'

'What? You mean stay in or go out?' She laughed. 'I don't know. I guess we could spend half our time in and half out.'

'I'd like that,' he said. 'Tonight?' he suggested, realising he was gambling a little and risking sounding desperate.

'Maybe,' she said doubtfully. 'It's just... No, fuck it. I'm over so much stuff right now. You know what I mean? No point letting life slip by is there?'

'None at all.'

'I'll see you tonight hon. What time then?'

'Seven-thirty?'

'Sounds great.'

'I'll see you then.'

'Okay sweetie, bye-bye.'

As Christopher went to make his way out of the hall to go up the stairs his mother was loitering.

'Let me guess?' he said smiling reluctantly. 'You want to know about my phone call. Or were you comfortably eavesdropping?'

She feigned shock and offence, placing one hand against her chest. 'How could you suggest?'

Christopher laughed and ran upstairs to shower.

'Well I guess you won't be interested then,' he called down.

'Is she coming around or not?' His mother called up to him, her voice sounding desperate. He smiled to himself and shut his bedroom door without replying.

As far as Christopher was concerned the one good thing about the degree of interest his parents took in his friendship, was that they kept out of the way when Sophia was there. The moment the doorbell rang there was no one else around. He opened the door to find Sophia dressed to go out.

'Hi, Christopher.' She smiled.

She was wearing an orange crop top and a short black pleated-skirt. Her legs were bare down to a pair of tiny open toed orange high-heels.

'Come in,' he said, holding the door open. 'How have you been?' he asked, as he showed her into the sitting room.

'Don't ask!' she said, sitting down. 'It's been a nightmare. My ex left about five messages on my phone while I was here. He assumed because I didn't pick up I must be with a man.' She made a snorting noise to indicate how ridiculous the whole thing was. Christopher smiled and nodded, sharing the joke. 'No offence,' she added with a flick of her hand, 'You know what I mean 'with a man'.'

'I knew what you meant,' Christopher said.

'But let's not talk about him.'

'Would you like a drink?'

'Is the Pope a Catholic honey? I would kill for one.'

'Wine?'

'Not if you've got Vodka. I don't like to mix when I go out.'

'We've got every spirit and heaps of wine. My mum's a serious lush, dad and Millicent aren't much better. It's the middle class heroine. Have some! We all will. What do you want with yours? Anti-depressant chaser?'

Sophia laughed.

'You're kind of Mr Social-Commentary aren't you? Orange juice thanks hon.' He went and got her a drink and then poured a Scotch on the rocks for himself.

'Does your Mum wash down her anti-depressants with it? Is it Valium? She so looks like a Valium girl.' Sophia asked, taking a long sip of her drink and settling back into the chair.

'I think it is actually. I've only recently started realising that my family *drinks*. I mean I knew that they drink but I'm starting to realise that they *drink*.'

'Ah ha, it's like a fish not noticing it's in water, honey. You'll need to watch that.'

'I've been thinking a lot about the conversation we had last night,' he said, aware of how much of an understatement this was, and how it didn't really follow on from what they were talking about.

'What in particular?' she asked.

'About what you feel about modern life and ancient life. I know it was a hard life in the past but life must have been very... intense and immediate. Now everything is so... cheap and flippant and I hardly know anyone who is happy. Really happy, I mean.'

Sophia shook her head and exhaled slowly.

'You sure are one idealistic kid.'

Christopher looked away, both surprised and dismayed by how much this slight to his manhood stung. He reminded himself that a week ago he thought he was still a kid too and turned back to her.

'So you think my take on the past is overly romantic then?'

She sighed.

'No. Not essentially. I would agree with what you're saying theoretically. But it's one thing to just say 'oh yeah and I know it was a hard life' and another to live it. You've never really suffered and neither have I. You've never had to kill a man or grapple for your life in freezing mud. I just think it's all very well in theory.'

He was already nodding.

'I know exactly what you're saying,' he said, 'But I guess I just question whether 'ease' and 'happiness' are the same thing. I guess maybe I'd be willing to suffer a bit to know my life had been... real.'

'Real,' she murmured. She crossed and then uncrossed her legs before picking up her drink. '*Real*,' she said again, and then she looked at him very intently. 'What do you mean?'

'I don't know!' he said breathlessly fast, 'I just know I've felt it, in moments. And when those moments are over everything around me feels artificial.'

'Like poetry?' she asked with an ironic twitch of her eyebrow.

'I don't think poetry is artificial,' he retorted.

'You don't see animals reciting soliloquies from *Hamlet*.'

He grinned, appreciating her response as much as he desperately disagreed with it.

'But we're not like other animals. I see poetry as one of our most real things. It's a spontaneous outpouring of our inner nature.'

'Yeah, spontaneous once you've learned the necessary language skills and prepared your writing equipment.'

Christopher smiled again, leaning forward in his enthusiasm.

'But that's just the thing, Sophia. Don't you think language is natural to homosapiens? We all have it... I mean I'm not the one with the degree in anthropology, but why can't that be our form of barking or chirping? Plus in iron-age culture poetry was oral, like in all preliterate societies. Once you've memorised something it becomes a part of you.' 'That was great back then,' she replied. 'But we don't need that sort of oral culture now. We have cinema and the internet and MP3 players that serve the same purpose. Why go backwards?'

He shook his head.

'Because they can't replace the human breath. Let me prove it to you!' he said suddenly.

'Prove what?' she asked, putting down her drink.

'What the breath in words can do.'

'Okay,' she agreed. 'But this is weird. What are you going to do, read some?'

He shook his head dismissively.

'I'm going to recite it.'

'You know poems off by heart?' she asked, as though this were one of the strangest things she'd ever heard.

'Dozens of them,' he whispered with a smile, as if he was telling a terrible secret.

Then he thought about it, scanning desperately for the perfect poem. It had to be the right one. He knew that from when Eugene had shown him. There was only one chance, and maybe even only one poem for any one person.

'Okay,' he said, settling mentally on one with a smile, it could be *nothing else* in Sophia's case. 'But you're going to have to lean forward.'

'Lean forward?' she asked.

'Yes.'

'Why?'

'Lean forward, close to me, and look at me while I'm speaking. So it's...intimate. Poetry is meant to be intimate. It's like...' he searched for an appropriate analogy, 'it's like the whisper of a lover.'

'Cool,' she said, shuffling forward rather excitedly like a child about to listen to a bedtime story. He began, staring deep into her eyes, reciting in a quiet but perfectly modulated and rhythmic tone.

'There will be time, there will be time
To prepare a face to meet the faces that you meet;
There will be time to murder and create,
And time for all the works and days of hands
That lift and drop a question on your plate;
Time for you and time for me,
And time yet for a hundred indecisions,
And for a hundred visions and revisions,
Before the taking of a toast and tea.

'In the room the women come and go
Talking of Michelangelo.

'And indeed there will be time
To wonder, 'Do I dare?' and, 'Do I dare?'
Time to turn back and descend the stair,
With a bald spot in the middle of my hair-
(They will say: 'How his hair is growing thin!')
My morning coat, my collar mounting firmly to the chin,
My necktie rich and modest, but asserted by a simple pin-
(They will say: 'But how his arms and legs are thin!')
Do I dare disturb the universe?' He paused for a moment as if the words spoke personally to him and he was seriously considering the question.

Her eyes flickered away from his as though the intimacy was making her uncomfortable. *Disturb it!* He thought to himself. And without hesitation he reached out for her hand and took it in his.

'In a minute,' he continued, his voice a little hushed, 'there is time

For decisions and revisions which a minute will reverse.

'For I have known them all already, known them all,' he declared with such conviction that it seemed that he alone knew what it was that he had known.

Sophia closed her eyes for a moment, leaning closer to him as though lulled or hypnotised.

'The eyes that fix you in a formulated phrase,

And when I'm formulated, sprawling on a pin,

When I am pinned and wriggling on the wall,

Then how should I begin

To spit out all the butt-ends of my days and ways?' he murmured, looking down for a moment.

'And how should I presume?' he asked with simple poignancy.

'And I have known the arms already, known them all-

Arms that are braceleted and white and bare

(But in the lamp-light downed with light-brown hair!)

Is it the perfume from a dress

That makes me so digress?

Arms that lie along a table or wrap about a shawl.

And should I then presume?

And how should I begin?'

Christopher's voice died away in the empty quiet room and they both suddenly became aware that they were touching. Both of them pulled their hands back and sat up further in their seats. 'Wow,' said Sophia, getting quickly to her feet. 'I... that was like...wow.'

She rubbed her face with her hands, and then the hairs on the back of her arms. 'Okay, you win,' she said quietly. Then without looking at Christopher she went over to the bar and refilled her own drink. She stood there for a while drinking and readjusting her hair.

'Tell me what it means,' she said abruptly.

Christopher looked at her for a long time.

'It's part of *The Love Song of J. Alfred Prufrock*. It's about a timid guy who hasn't really lived his life and he gets into this situation where he wants to take a chance, but he doesn't know if he dares. He's too caught up in how the world sees him, wanting to appear decent, ordinary and not pitiful. But in the end it's full of pathos anyway because underneath he's really passionate. And the older he gets, the more afraid he is to appear ridiculous.'

She nodded for a long time, hugging herself unconsciously.

'But more than anything it's like a spell. You cast it over someone and suddenly they can imagine what it's like to *be* that guy.'

'Do you relate to him?' she asked. 'I know you're not old, but you know what I mean.'

Christopher smiled.

'No. He is what I want to make sure I never am.'

Sophia nodded but didn't look up.

'So you want to disturb the universe do you?' she asked.

He smiled again. 'Damn right.'

I want to burn.

She downed the rest of her drink and turned to him, her eyes looked glassy all of a sudden.

'Trust me hon, get out there and live a bit. Once you've been burned a couple of times you'll see that the real world isn't like poetry. You're not going to want to disturb anything, you'll just be thankful that it's not any worse.'

Christopher pressed his lips together tightly. His whole body seemed to resist what she had said. But she had evoked her superior experience and he couldn't argue.

His heart wanted to say 'I watched the person I love most in the world die'. But he didn't. Christopher had an innate dislike for people who throw up their personal tragedy to win an argument. He felt it was indecent, and also a little like using an atom bomb to crack a nutshell. *At the end of the day*, he told himself, *I am still living at home with my mum and I've never had a girlfriend.* Before Christopher could think of something to say to concede this point Sophia changed the topic.

'All right, so what's your bloody story?'

'My story?' he echoed, taken aback.

'Your story. You've been living at home all your life. You've never been in a serious relationship. If I'm any judge of it you're as virginal as my twelve-year-old cousin. Where does a virgin who lives at home with his mum get that kinda...' she flailed her hand and then finally declared, 'passion. This passionate, sexy thing you've got going. Not to mention the confidence. And where the hell do you get this memorising poetry thing from anyway? Your mum and dad are charming but dull. Your dragon of a sister is about as poetic as groceries, and your mum says you have no friends!

'So you went to a school where people crochet their own coloured hats! It still doesn't add up. What's the go, Christopher?' she demanded almost accusingly, as though these anomalies in his character had somehow hurt her personally.

'I had one,' he said.

'A friend? Where did he go?'

'He died,' Christopher said quietly.

He hadn't meant to reveal it, but it was the key she was looking for and he knew it. He looked down. It was such an exposing feeling, hearing the involuntary quaver in his voice. *Why didn't I hold back?* He thought. It was as though the poem had opened a door between them and it was too late to shut it.

'Recently?'

'When he was thirteen. We met at primary school. He died shortly after I turned fourteen.'

'And that was your last friend?' Her voice was fairly gentle but there was puzzlement in it too.

'Yes, my last *real* friend. He was also the one who introduced me to poetry. He was a very... unusual person.'

'I imagine,' she said, in a way that said that she couldn't possibly.

'Okay,' he said, getting to his feet. 'Why don't we do your thing now?'

'All right,' Sophia put down her empty glass. 'First things first, do you have any clothes suitable for clubbing?'

Christopher rolled his eyes.

'Tons. I never wear them. Mum bought me all this clothing when she thought I was gay. It was her way of saying it was all right with her if I wanted to just, 'come out' already. For some reason she seemed to think that if I was feeling the urge to sleep with other men I must be wanting lots of shirts made from shiny stuff.'

Sophia laughed.

'What on earth made your mum think you're gay? I mean sure, you haven't got laid yet and you like poetry. But really, other than that there's nothing particularly gay about you.'

'It was because of my friend,' he said, his expression neutral.

'Cause you were close as kids?'

Christopher smiled faintly. There were so many emotions, they flickered secretive, mercurial and brief, beneath the surface of his smile.

'We were *very* close,' is all he said, before ascending the staircase to go and change.

What a weird but cool guy, Sophia thought. *The poetry thing is sexy, but what's with this boy friendship mourn forever thing? I mean I guess it's a bit of a turn on in a metrosexual sort of way, all that sensitive, walking the bi-line stuff... Fuck Sophia, you're being such a cynical cow. Something amazing is happening here. This could be a great friendship. You're not jealous of this dead kid are you? Plus, this guy is eighteen and you are twenty-four. He was in year eight when you were at university!* But she still couldn't help finding something fresh and utterly disarming about Christopher's lack of worldliness.

Sophia shook herself to clear her head. As much as she wanted to fight it she was intrigued by the mystery Christopher presented. But she had a belief that sex ruins great friendships, and should only really be done with people with great bodies for whom you have either no feelings, or a mild contempt. So with her mantra firmly in mind she resolved to keep Christopher as young as possible in her mind.

'Is this all right?'

She looked up. Christopher was standing on the stairs in a pair of very well fitted and very nicely cut black trousers and a short sleeved black shirt made out of a shiny material. Both items of clothing fit him snugly without being too tight. The colour looked striking with his blond hair and the whole thing showed off his lovely build. *Damn*, she muttered mentally, *how old did I say he was again?*

'Great.' She managed, without sounding too enthusiastic.

He smiled in that irritating way that was so attractive. *It's like he knows I find him maddeningly attractive but he's not too hung up about whether I do or don't, she thought. How the hell is he not in love with himself?* Every good-looking guy she'd met practically pashed their own reflection in the mirror at the gym. She doubted Christopher had even seen the inside of a gym.

'Well let's go then, we'll take my car,' she said, grabbing her handbag. He picked up his wallet and keys at the table in the foyer. 'When we get drunk I tend to get a taxi home and hunt the car out the next day.'

'Okay,' he said, and followed her out into the night air.

Her aqua blue sporty hatchback was parked at the bottom of the driveway.

'Hop in,' she said. Christopher got in beside her and she started the engine.

'Where are we going?' he asked, as they drove along the A4.

'We're starting at the Moloko Bar to teach their vodka a lesson.

I'm meeting a couple of friends. But The Chapel is our ultimate target.'

'I like how you make it sound like you're on a mission.'

Sophia laughed.

'That's because I am, honey!'

They drove on with the music blaring and no conversation until they reached Salisbury. Sophia parked the car in an off-street car park and opened her drop down section. She took out a packet of tobacco papers.

'What're you doing?'

'Rolling a spliff,' she said, beginning to heat the little block of hash over her lighter. 'You know what this is, right?'

'Yeah. I went to high-school.'

She glared at him. Whether it was there or not, she sensed disapproval.

'What?' she demanded, running her tongue along the sticky strip of the paper 'Shocked?'

He shrugged in a non-committal sort of way.

'It's not like you're shooting up.'

A little disappointed somehow, Sophia pouted and put the joint to her lips. She lit it and inhaled, holding it in for about ten seconds before exhaling a long column of smoke.

'Want some?' she asked with a mischievous grin.

'Okay,' he replied, to her surprise.

She passed it to him and he took a drag of it. She waited expectantly for him to cough. But he didn't. He leaned his head back as though unaware she was watching and exhaled the smoke.

'So what are your friends like?' he asked, taking another drag.

'Like me I guess,' she said, even though she knew that wasn't quite true.

Christopher and Sophia didn't leave the final pub until the wee hours of the morning. They poured out into the street with the other laughing and talking patrons, the music still thumping in the background. Sophia still held a plastic cup with vodka and orange in it. Christopher stood talking to one of Sophia's male friends named Geoff while the women talked amongst themselves. Justine, a slim blonde girl whose makeup was traced with glitter leaned close to Sophia.

'So are you seeing him then?' she asked, elbowing Sophia gently in the arm.

'Who? Christopher?' Sophia giggled and slugged from her drink in reply.

'Come on,' said another of her friends whose name was Rachel. 'You've been holding out on us, girl.'

'I have not! There's nothing to tell. Trust me!'

'He's hot,' Justine said.

'He's a child,' Sophia protested.

'Yah, right. He's a child. And my arse fits into size eight jeans,' put in another friend, Becky, flicking back her dark hair derisively.

'He's eighteen. Like, as in 'barely-legal', get it?' Sophia attempted to explain. 'Plus I'm friends with his mum. The kid's a virgin and I'm taking him out for his mum, guys.'

'Oh! I love a virgin! Get them young, train them up,' said Rachel, who continued to go on to tell the others some lewd story about some younger man she had 'trained up.'

'Would you mind if I get his phone number then?' Justine asked with a coy little smile. Sophia involuntarily found herself glancing at Justine's extra thin frame that she considered more fashionable, and therefore more desirable, than her own.

'Back off you tart! I told you, he's too young,' Sophia tried to joke but her friends jeered her.

Sophia downed the rest of her drink and looked for Christopher. As she walked towards him he was in animated conversation with Geoff and smiled when he saw her.

'Are you ready to go?' she asked.

'Sure,' he said, 'I'll just say goodbye to the others.' She watched him go over to her friends. Their conversation was not audible but Sophia could see the girls giggling and Justine flicking her hair. For a moment she didn't like her friends very much.

As she watched it became more than that. Justine's already slim face morphed slightly until it looked starved and sharp, her eyes were the hungry eyes of a predator. The cacophony of laughs suddenly had a hyena-like quality to it. She frowned. *God, she thought, Justine likes his vulnerability, it makes her feel powerful. They all do.* She looked away. How ugly it all was when you could see what was going on behind their painted on faces.

This happened to Sophia a lot when she went out drinking. Smoking in particular made it hard to stop it happening. The façades that people put up would just suddenly drop, allowing her to glimpse a second of their inner nature. It was written in every gesture, in the very stance of their body, even in the way they laughed. But these were her friends. She knew each of their stories; which ones had been raped, which ones interfered with as children, which ones had been in abusive relationships, the ones that had eating disorders. In fact all of them fell into one of these categories. *Christopher just has no idea about the sea he's swimming in. I think he thinks girls are nice.*

Sophia burned with impatience to get him away from her friends. What had she been thinking bringing him here, where she could be recognised? What if Josh had actually worked out where she was now? And that was not even to mention releasing her friends on Christopher. She shook her head. Better than anyone she knew what all these girls had gone through in their own ways, and Christopher looked at them like it hadn't even occurred to him that they might be predators. It was really no wonder they were all chaffing to fuck him, she thought. The poor sod doesn't even realise he's hot.

'Did you have fun?' she asked as they walked back to the car.

'Yeah it was cool. I enjoy music, and your friends are nice,' he paused, and then laughed to himself. He looked over at her briefly as though about to make a confession. 'I could do this scene, for a while at least. But I don't think it's going to save me or anything.'

Sophia raised her eyebrows, and then stumbled a little. She looped her arm through his for support.

'What do you mean?'

'You know, what mum wants. Her introvert son turned into a nice, normal, party-going teen, preferably asserting my hetero-sexuality with numerous female conquests.'

'You think that's what your mum wants?' she asked, feeling pretty drunk and only able to word simple questions.

'Something like that. What the other mum's sons are doing I guess. Don't get me wrong, that might be fun for a while. But it would never satisfy me.'

'Wow,' she murmured. 'You know what would satisfy you... I'm twenty-four and I still don't know. So tell me, Christopher Penrose.' She laughed, turning to walk backwards and look at him. 'What would satisfy you?'

He smiled. 'That's what I'm trying to figure out.' He reached for her arm again then and said, 'Right now I just feel drunk and strange. I'm half melancholy and half something else I don't even have a word for. And I like words.' He laughed. 'You've probably noticed. I just know I don't want to go home right now.'

Involuntarily her heart skipped in her chest and adrenalin washed through her. *What a fool I can be,* she thought.

'Can we divert and walk through the cemetery?' he asked.

She glanced at his eyes to see if he was serious.

'Why would you want to do that?' she murmured, holding a little tighter to his arm. But they were already beginning to ascend the steps that were cut into the stone wall of the cemetery.

'You sound dubious. You're not afraid of dead people are you?' he joked.

For a second her heart tightened in a different, less pleasant way. The moment of discomfort was replaced after a while by a bitter little smile.

'Me? Dead people are my life. I work with them too. It just seems a bit odd, that's all. We go to a club, get pissed and wander round graves.'

'I like cemeteries. They're peaceful.'

Sophia snorted. She thought of cemeteries as anything but peaceful.

They took the path through the headstones and looked out over the lights of the city. The wind picked up a little and Sophia became aware that her hair was probably messy from dancing. She pulled out the clip and took out the pins. It fell down around her shoulders and she gave it a good shake. Christopher stopped and turned to look at her with a soft smile on his face. 'You look beautiful like that.'

She didn't know what to say. He was still looking at her.

'In this light I can't see your clothes and you look like you belong in a Pre-Raphaelite painting.'

'Thanks,' she muttered and turned to keep walking slowly along the path. To let him know she wasn't walking off on him she reached for his arm. 'You're going to be one hell of a lady killer one day, Christopher.'

He just laughed like her statement was intended as a joke.

Sophia took a joint she'd rolled in the toilet and lit it, cupping the flame with her hand, protecting it from the wind. After she'd taken a lungful of smoke down she added, 'The only thing I remember about the Pre-Raphaelites is the picture of Ophelia drowned. I liked that one.'

Smoking seemed to expel her anxiety with every outward breath, that's why she still took the risk, despite its *other* effect on her.

Sophia's eyes scanned around the darkness of the tombs and gravestones but the shadows were empty. The cemetery was full, home to the bones of thousands. So there were no new burials.

She wandered a little as she smoked and when she came to the last drag she stopped under the ancient yew tree that Christopher was looking up into.

'Wow,' she murmured, dropping the joint and stubbing it out with her shoe. There had been a light rainfall earlier and the tree was spangled with droplets of water that caught the light from the streetlamp and refracted tiny rainbows from it.

'It looks like fairyland,' she whispered to herself. She stood on tiptoes to try to touch the droplets but her fingertips were a couple of inches off touching them. She felt Christopher's hands under her arms and he lifted her up so that her hands slid through the boughs and water ran down her arms. She gasped at the thrill of the cold and at him lifting her like that. With her fingers she burst the little bubbles of water and let it rain down all over her. He set her down. Sophia turned to him embarrassed suddenly by the gesture. Quickly she looked away from him.

'I should get you home before your mum murders me,' she said and turned to walk along the path towards the car.

'Why do you keep doing that?' His voice came quietly from behind her.

She turned around. She didn't want to because she could feel 'it' was going to happen. In the half darkness for a terrible moment she saw the cruel brambles snaking around his skin and the blood running down his face.

Quickly she shut her eyes, waiting for it to be gone. But in her mind the images rose again unbidden, blood coming out of wounds in Christopher's chest, blood running down his face as though he were crying blood.

'I can't do this,' she mumbled, staggering blindly off the path. Christopher's hands caught her. She could vaguely hear him speaking.

'Do what, Sophia? Are you all right?'

'You think you want to see him but you don't! Everyone thinks they want to see *them* until they do...' she snapped suddenly.

The hot feeling was coming up her spine near the base of her neck and baking her brain. If she didn't stop soon things would be said through her that she could not recall or control. Through her bleary eyes she could see Christopher's mouth move but couldn't hear him speak.

'You don't know what's around you...' But her voice was only a whisper. She was subsiding into his arms.

'Everything's going to be okay,' he told her.

It sounded like he meant it. It sounded like he knew somehow what he was talking about.

4

'But oh for the touch of a vanished hand,
And the sound of a voice that is still!'
—Tennyson

The cemetery was deserted that day. Christopher preferred it that way as he came there to talk to Eugene and he didn't want an audience. Usually he would tell Eugene what had been happening in his life, simple things. But he would never say Eugene's name. Today was different. Christopher didn't sit down, he stood facing the head stone as though in confrontation with another sentient person. Sophia's words to him a few nights ago in the other cemetery in Salisbury went around and around in his head. *You think you want to see him but you don't!*

'What is it, Eugene?' he demanded loudly. This was the first time he'd dared to say Eugene's name out loud here, or to phrase a question that might require an answer. Christopher wondered if Sophia was right. Was he afraid he wouldn't be answered, or afraid he *would*? Or was he just afraid of the black wave of grief that one word conjured?

'Is there something you want to tell me? Is there something I needed to say to you? Are you... Are you still... still here, somehow?'

Silence.

Christopher looked down at the impassive gravestone. Suddenly he felt angry. If Eugene had actually been before him rather than the stone he'd have wanted to shake him to extract an answer. Approaching the headstone Christopher stood staring down at it for a long while, as the silence seemed to brew and boil with unbearable tension. In a sudden burst of frustration Christopher brought his fist down on the stone, hard enough to draw blood. The delayed rush of pain was oddly satisfying to him.

He was about to walk away when a soft gust of air caressed the back of his neck. The cool breath of air made the hairs on his neck rise and he shivered. It was that same feeling again, that clamminess he'd felt when he realised the picture was standing back up, and when his eyes had changed in the mirror. For a moment Christopher sniffed at the air very intently. It had only been there for a moment but the smell was immediately evocative. Christopher felt he could *smell* Eugene; the way his skin had smelled, mingled with the softener his mother used on his clothes...

Without meaning to Christopher clamped his other hand down harder over his bloodied knuckles and shook his head. *What is going on? What are we when we die? Are we just a huge absence that haunts the living? Or something else?*

'How come you don't seem scared?' Christopher heard himself whisper to Eugene in his memory. It had been near the end and Eugene had often frightened Christopher with how fearless he seemed.

'Because death isn't real, Christopher,' Eugene had murmured back, his eyes still glimmering with so many secrets that Christopher had yet to untangle. Secrets that he ran out of time to ever untangle...

Christopher headed rapidly for the car. He hadn't even brought flowers that day and he left just as unceremoniously, almost fleeing from Eugene's grave-side.

By the time he reached the car he was thoroughly shaken and paid no attention to the speed limit as he pulled out of the cemetery. He was almost half way home when, without explaining to himself why he was doing it, Christopher slowed the car to a stop at the side of the road and prepared to do a U-turn.

Although he didn't know why or what he meant to say when he got there, he was going to see Sophia. If anything could cleanse that feeling that something cold and slippery had climbed under his skin via his bleeding hand, if anything could lift this sense of dread, it would be Sophia's presence.

Almost as soon as he'd murmured 'fuck it' to himself and headed off along the road to Salisbury the rain began to pitter-patter on the windscreen. He switched on his windscreen wipers. *What do you intend to tell her?* He asked himself. *That you're falling apart because your best friend's ghost refuses to talk to you? Or crazier still that you think he's been fiddling with things in your room?* It didn't matter, he concluded, he would know what to say when he got there.

Christopher was speeding on the wet roads but that didn't seem to matter either. When he spotted cars banked up for the turn he needed to make and realised that one lane was closed due to the Kennett River flooding he impatiently turned down a less well-used road to try and go around.

When he reached about the same ground level as the main road he saw that the water was up a bit on that road as well. Swearing quietly to himself Christopher slowed down a little. The water splashed up onto the windows until he reached about half way. Beginning to become concerned that the water was too deep he revved harder on the accelerator. The engine struggled and the car lurched forward abruptly only to putter to a stop.

'Shit.' Christopher murmured to himself, winding down his window to get a better look at the predicament he had gotten himself into. The water was higher than it had looked, almost past the top of his tyres. In frustration he attempted to start the car again. The engine made an unhealthy sound and conked out. Christopher leaned back in his seat. 'Perfect. Just perfect,' he said to himself.

Before he could recover from his anger at himself there was a thump on the car's boot. He swung around in time to see something disappearing over the top of the back window and then heard it step across the roof. After a moment the rather agile form of a man appeared on his bonnet, crouching and giving him a quick, strange smile. The dark-haired man leaned around to Christopher's open window and said, over the sound of the rushing water.

'May I suggest you stop trying to rev the car?'

'Okay,' Christopher complied.

Automatically he put the hand-break on and leaned back in the seat.

'Now if you want to get out and help me, we'll push the car out of the water,' said the man.

'Is the water shallow enough?' Christopher asked, but seeming not to hear him the other man lowered his legs down, shoes and all, into the water. In a moment he was standing by the car door, holding onto it to avoid slipping. Christopher barely had time to look at him, but he did take in the fact that the other man's shirt was laced together with string through the button-holes where buttons were curiously absent and that in contrast he was wearing sunglasses. Christopher would have liked to have had more leisure to examine the proud, strangely Neanderthal make of the other man's face and his odd clothing. But the stranger was saying,

'You'll have to climb out the window.'

'Right,' Christopher said, gaining composure and taking off his seat belt. Grabbing hold of the roof Christopher used his upper-body to pull himself out of the car until he was seated backwards on the doorframe, then he swung his legs out. He had been going to remove his shoes but noticing that the other man had left his on he suddenly realised the impracticality of such an action. There also seemed something almost laughing under the other man's scowling black brows, as though Christopher's practical incompetence amused him. But Christopher could really only catch glimpses of his eyes.

Christopher lowered his legs into the icy floodwater. At first he drew his breath in at the feeling of the river water running into his boots and soaking through his socks, but he also got a satisfaction from it. When he was safely grounded the stranger grunted,

'You take this side, I'll take the other. You did take the hand-break off right?' Christopher grinned, feeling really stupid.

'I'll just get that.'

After leaning back through the window and releasing the break, Christopher watched the dark-haired man wade through the water toward the back of the car as though he hadn't noticed the current or the temperature of the water. Christopher followed.

'All right.' The man said. 'On the count of three.' He counted to three and they pushed the car. It was difficult to get footing on the slippery riverbed. It took considered muscular effort just to stay planted but the car lurched forward.

'You okay?' The stranger asked, as they gathered a bit of momentum.

'Ah huh,' Christopher managed to get out.

As they neared the bank Christopher's foot slipped into a hole in the riverbed and he nearly let go. With what seemed like extremely good reflexes the other man managed to slam one hand down over Christopher's forearm to grab him. With the other hand he seemed to prevent the car stopping completely for a moment while Christopher got his footing. Smiling rather maniacally as though having a good time he reapplied his shoulder to the car as soon as he saw Christopher was all right.

When the car was safely on dry land they both stood dripping and wiping the sweat from their brows. They laughed a little without speaking, in the strange camaraderie of mutual physical exertion. Then Christopher became uncomfortable. This man had just helped him out immensely. It seemed awkward to have to ask his name.

'Thanks for helping me,' he said instead, to break the ice.

The other man reached into his top pocket and pulled out a still dry packet.

'Cigarette?'

'No thanks.'

The man leaned on Christopher's mud-splattered car and smoked thoughtfully for a while, not speaking.

'So.' He said after a time. 'You in a hurry?'

'No,' Christopher answered, taken aback and quite forgetting that he had indeed been in a hurry. 'Why?'

The other man just looked at him just over the top of his sunglasses, with a dark glittering amusement in his eyes.

'You couldn't wait for the traffic diversion? Or you thought you could get through that in a little city car like this?' he said, gesturing toward the car.

Christopher smiled sheepishly and shrugged.

'I haven't had my license very long,' he heard himself explaining to his own mortification.

'You looked in a hurry.' The man commented. 'Like you were on a mission.'

Even with the sunglasses he still makes an unusual amount of eye contact for a man, Christopher thought. Somehow it reminded him of Eugene. But that thought was too painful, so he ruminated instead on why on earth someone would be wearing sunglasses on such an overcast day. The sky looked like evening was coming on and it was close to midday.

'Yeah, I guess I was. The cold water sort of knocked some sense into me.'

The man smiled, not looking at Christopher but away through the trees and past the river.

'It does that,' he said. 'What's your name?'

'Christopher,' he said with relief. 'What's yours?'

'Seth.' He blew out a long, slow stream of smoke. Then he turned to look at Christopher. He looked at him very blatantly then like he was reading him. 'Your car should start again after a while. But don't try it yet.'

Seth looked like he might be about to go. Christopher's heart hammered desperately like it had when he had wanted to secure a repeat visit with Sophia. For some reason he didn't want them to part company yet. There was a strange feeling that had been growing since he'd first laid eyes on the other man. A prickling feeling at the back of his neck, which he somehow knew was the feeling of being in the middle of a strongly fateful event.

And it looked as though this strange man might just slip back into the woodlands without any normal salutation, just as he had come. Somehow he knew that this situation, with this man, was not a situation where keeping within socially proscribed boundaries was going to help.

'You're interesting.' He blurted out, sensing that honesty would hold Seth's attention better than small talk.

Seth turned around to look at him, bluntly surveying Christopher again.

'Why?'

Christopher liked him then, liked him immediately, for his lack of pretence and for his lack of fear. He smiled faintly.

'I'm not sure. I think it's your low bullshit factor.' The other man smiled but said nothing. 'And maybe that I can't even imagine what sort of environment or background created you.'

'Can't you?'

'No. You seem like something from another place...' Still Seth didn't say anything. He just smoked his cigarette. Christopher flailed against Seth's silence. 'Am I offending you?' he asked.

'Not at all.'

'Do you want to leave?'

Seth turned back to look at Christopher in that same blunt fashion, straight into the eyes in the way grown men seldom do to one another except in threat.

'No,' he said again. 'Otherwise I would have.'

'It's just that you don't say much.'

'I'm not used to it.'

'Talking?' Christopher asked, unable to imagine how that

could possibly be.

'I live alone,' he explained. 'I haven't spoken to anyone since the day before yesterday.'

'Wow,' Christopher exclaimed. 'That must be odd.' Seeming to regard this as small talk Seth did not pursue it. Christopher searched for the right thing to say. 'Why are you talking to me if you shun human contact so much?'

Seth's eyebrow twitched ironically. 'You're interesting.'

Christopher smiled.

'Why?'

Seth just looked at him in that odd way with his eyebrows slightly contorted.

'You're like something from another place.'

'We should see each other again,' Christopher said.

Seth nodded.

'We should.'

Sophia sat with her legs up on her bright blue couch. She was watching television and using a fork to conduct pieces of a broadly 'Asian' stir-fry into her mouth. She picked up the remote control to change the station. There was nothing much on. Sighing she flicked the station back to a game show that she left on for the noise even when she wasn't watching it.

Sophia wondered what Christopher was up to. She had felt anxious and unsettled since her night out on the town with him. Several of her girlfriends had left messages on her message bank or her phone but she didn't feel like answering them. They were all questioning her about her drama with Josh getting her number, they were all saying: 'Don't worry you've got the restraining order. If he shows up just call the cops.' Or: 'You are so shagging Christopher aren't you?' Sophia let them leap to their own conclusions about her reasons for not calling.

The light had begun to fade in her apartment. She got up, moved an orange inflatable lounge chair with her foot and switched a light on. Half of her wanted to turn the phone back on in case Christopher was trying to ring. The other half of her felt petulantly toward him. Somehow it seemed as though he'd made a fool of her, though she wasn't quite sure why or how. There was just some lingering feeling of embarrassment and exposure that clung around the edges of her memories of Saturday night. It was as if she had done something she couldn't remember. *Shit, did I make a move on him?* She thought. No, she was sure she hadn't. Best not call him or he'd start thinking she had it for him. Especially as she just wanted to call to let him know she wasn't sweet on him but could he please come around? With a sigh she picked up her phone and punched in the number, hoping that Jane or Millicent wouldn't pick up.

'Hello,' said a weary female voice on the other end.

'Hi hon, Sophia here…'

'I figured. Shall I get my baby-brother?' Millicent all but snapped.

What is it with this chick? Major fucking issues.

'No that's fine darling, I'm looking for your mum,' Sophia lied.

'Oh.' There was a short pause. 'I'll get her.'

'Fucking Hell,' she murmured to herself. 'Just get laid bitch.'

'Hello, Sophia,' Jane's voice said, obviously glad to hear from her.

'Hi, sorry if I've interrupted something. I just wanted to chat for a sec.'

'Sure,' Jane said. 'I'll just take something off the stove. One moment love.' Sophia bit her lip during the pause, embarrassed by this mention of having interrupted Jane's dinner preparations. 'Okay, I'm back. What would you like to chat about?'

'Oh, it's just about Christopher. He was telling me that a friend of his died when they were kids…'

That's it Sophia, she thought, *just leap bluntly into it.*

'Oh.' Jane sighed in a manner that told Sophia that this turn of the conversation was not a pleasing one. 'Yes. Eugene.'

'How did he die Jane?'

'Eugene was ill, he had multiple holes in his heart. He was on the transplant list but he was hard to find a match for. They tried some surgery on him on more than one occasion but his heart was so weak. Christopher knew Eugene was dying since the first day they met. Literally. He came up and introduced himself to Christopher saying "Hi, I'm Eugene and I'm dying. I just like to get that over with."'

'Christopher is still talking about him then?'

Sophia frowned to herself, pushing the phone to her ear with her shoulder. Something about the tone in Jane's voice wasn't sitting right with Sophia, she found herself defending Christopher.

'He only mentioned it once, only after I asked him if he had any friends. I pushed him really.

'What was he like, Eugene?'

Jane sighed again.'Eugene was a very gifted boy. Very charming too I suppose, rather odd.'

'Gifted as in brilliant?' Sophia asked.

'I think it would be fair to say Eugene was a creative genius, Sophia. He played two instruments beautifully. He was topping the county in English and writing some very mature poetry. Eugene was like a walking advert for Waldorf education really. He was winning poetry writing competitions and all sorts. He was... it's hard to explain, gifted socially, abnormally mature. Sometimes I thought too mature, for Christopher I mean. I think he made Christopher grow up too quickly.'

Sophia raised her eyebrows.

'You think, hon? He seems quite socially... well you know what I mean. He doesn't have a lot of friends.'

'I think that's almost part of it. Eugene made Christopher expect so much from friendship, from other people, from life even. Eugene was such an all or nothing person. Every friendship had to be dedicated to as though it was the passion of the ages. And his personality seemed to totally dominate Christopher's.' There was a short pause.

'Sophia, can I ask you a personal question, just between us girls.'

Sophia rolled her eyes. 'Sure.'

'Has Christopher... well you know... I know he's far too young for you, but has he shown any interest to you? I mean in an intimate sense.'

What part of the nineteenth century did they dig this lady out of anyway? 'An intimate sense?'

'You mean has he made a move on me?'

'Or any sign...'

'Not really Jane. Why do you ask?'

'It's just that I...'

'Do you think he's gay?' Sophia blurted, unable to wait any longer.

'No! Goodness no. I mean, not... gay as such. It's just—'

'Just what? Christopher seems quite heterosexual to me. What's concerning you?' There was another pause. It was clear that whatever Jane was going to say bothered her deeply.

'It's silly. It's just something I saw once when Eugene was alive... I mean it was probably perfectly innocent. I was in the kitchen and I looked out the window into the front yard and Eugene was leaving. I remember it so clearly, Christopher was sitting on the garden seat near the conifers and Eugene was standing in front of him. He bent down and kissed Christopher, and then he left.'

'Like what kind of kiss?'

'Romantically, on the mouth.'

'Are we talking tongue here or what?'

'Heavens no! I mean, I don't think so. It did linger a bit... it was innocent seeming. But abnormal nonetheless, don't you think?'

'Well... 'Abnormal' if you think being gay is abnormal, for

54

sure. It's not platonic average 'buddies' type behaviour.'

'Yes, and that's the strangest thing, they were barely even teenagers. Not even old enough to have romantic feelings.'

Sophia found herself raising her eyebrows in doubt again.

'How old were they?' she asked.

'They can't have been more than twelve or recently thirteen. Eugene died when they were thirteen.'

'And how did Christopher react to Eugene kissing him like that?'

'Like it was totally normal. Put up his hand to touch the side of Eugene's face. Christopher smiled at him and Eugene backed away slowly still looking at him, then he went. There was something... disturbing about it,' Jane confided.

'Did you dislike Eugene, Jane?' Sophia asked.

'That's the thing. No one could dislike Eugene, not as such. He was so charming, sweet, talkative, well mannered, a very, very mature little man. Barely came to my house without an, "Aren't you looking lovely today, Jane?" Or a, "Can I help you with that?" But there was always something unnerving about him, like he was almost too aware.'

Sophia got up suddenly and began walking around turning on all of the lights. The more they talked the more Sophia thought she understood exactly what it was Jane was talking about. Yet somehow, despite the disturbing sensation that had almost risen to dread now, she couldn't stop speaking about it.

'See I'm not an old fashioned person, Sophia,' Jane continued. 'I lived through the sixties. I'm not homophobic. If he were gay I would support him. It's not that...'

'No,' said Sophia quietly, slowly turning around and scanning the corners of her living room.

'It just felt like Eugene brought something uncanny into our lives. It will sound ghoulish of me to say this, but it was almost like the boy was too comfortable with his own impending death, it wasn't natural. He was never *scared*. And now he is dead it seems as though his hold over Christopher is even stronger.'

There was a protracted silence before Sophia eventually spoke.

'Do you think I should try and broach the topic with him?' Sophia realised even as she said it that there was no logical reason to poke her nose into this area of Christopher's life. There was something drawing her to the topic, and her curiosity seemed perverse.

'Perhaps with you being closer to his own age he'll talk to you where he won't to me. Shall I tell him you called for him?'

'That would be great.' When Sophia put down the phone she rubbed her naked arms vigorously. Sitting back down in front of the television she turned the volume up a couple of notches.

5

'What an antithetical mind! tenderness, roughness, delicacy,
coarseness, sentiment, sensuality, soaring and groveling, dirt and
deity—all mixed up in that one compound of inspired clay!'
—Lord Byron

It had rained in the night and the public footpath was awash
with mud. The slipperiness of Christopher's descent from the
Whitehorse Walk slowed his progress but he had learned his
lesson about trying to rush in wet conditions. Luckily
Christopher knew exactly where he was going. The vague direc-
tions Seth had given him were to an old World War Two military
building that had long since been a ruin. Christopher and
Eugene had played in it as boys and told ghost stories there.

Christopher couldn't imagine why Seth would tell him to look
for him there. It wasn't as though it was near anything. As
Christopher crested the hill the shell of a stone building could be
seen amid bushes and choked with brambles. It had a half
crumbled chimney, two holes for windows and a door hole. The
roof had long since fallen away.

Christopher paused a moment before descending. The place
had changed since he had been there. The bushes had grown up
around it and someone had boarded up the door and windows.
A makeshift roof had also been added, cobbled together out of
wrought iron and old pieces of old thatch. *Don't tell me he lives
here*, Christopher thought, as he began to walk down towards it.
He didn't know what to say to this strange man. The whole thing
seemed even more intimidating suddenly when he realised that
Seth might be a squatter. Far from the disdain that some people
feel toward people squatting, Christopher was filled with a kind
of respect bordering on awe.

Despite the door being boarded up Christopher still
approached. There was an old iron horseshoe nailed to the door.

Christopher felt that was suggestive of occupancy and knocked. From within he heard something move. As he looked through the slats in the wood he saw the flicker of a candle flame flare up in the darkness. A shadow was cast for a moment and then a very dark eye showed itself close to his. Christopher nearly jumped.

'Come around to the window and I'll let you in,' said the deep, gravelly voice he remembered.

Christopher walked around the cottage. The wooden board on the side window slid back revealing an empty window cavity. Christopher figured this was the door, bending down he climbed inside. It was dark, even by comparison to the intensely overcast day. Christopher blinked for a moment until he was able to focus on Seth.

The man before him looked to Christopher to be about twenty-five, maybe a few years older than that at most. He was wearing a black overcoat and his dark brown hair hung around his face in slightly wavy clumps. With his sunglasses gone Christopher was able to see the dark eyes that gleamed in the light of the candle. Once again the primitive qualities of his face, the bold hollows of his strong but high cheekbones, his prominent chin and dark, dramatic brow line impressed Christopher. He imagined that this was what Emily Bronte meant her Heathcliff to look like.

'I'm glad you came.' He gestured for Christopher to come into the room.

Christopher saw a half a forty-gallon drum that sat in the spot where the fireplace once was. Inside it kindling had been laid but not lit. Beside the fireplace was a neat stack of wood and an axe. Just off to one side was an old spring bare bed with a thin mattress, a pile of blankets and a pillow or two. Next to the bed was a tree stump with a glass of water, a pile of books and a candle. By the old hearth stone was an enormous cooking pot and tripod stand, a broken bird's cage and a few barbequing utensils. Without really meaning to, Christopher found his voice coming out hushed with awe. 'This is amazing.'

Seth gave a slight flash of his teeth in a smile. They were oddly placed teeth, Christopher thought. It was an odd smile all up.

'One second,' he said, disappearing into the other room. He came back carrying a large tree stump to act as a second seat. As the other man was somewhat shorter and less obviously well built than he was, Christopher was impressed by Seth's obvious strength. 'Sit down.' He offered.

Christopher did so and Seth sat down on the other stump, both of them facing the hearth even though the fire wasn't going yet. In front of the two men, on the stone remnants of the old mantelpiece was a large pair of stag-antlers, some stones with natural holes worn through them and a bone-handled blade.

'I don't often receive guests,' Seth said with a certain irony.

'Well, thank you for inviting me. I really mean what I said before. I think it's amazing you living like this. It's inspiring to think that people can really live... simply, naturally I mean.' Christopher felt a little silly suddenly and added, 'I guess I just want to meet people who don't live like my family.'

'What does your family live like?' Seth asked quietly.

'Just like everyone else.'

Seth looked at him, regarding him pensively for a moment.

'But how's that? What if I don't know how 'everyone else' lives, Christopher? I want you to tell me.'

There was something so stark about the way this man said things that it put Christopher off balance. He wanted to protest that his life had not been interesting and that he would much prefer to hear about Seth's life. But the sincerity of Seth's question was too obvious.

'What are you? Working class? Middle class? You've got no county accent so you went to a good school.'

Christopher felt utterly taken aback at this brutally honest discussion of class, something that he'd always experienced as a kind of taboo subject.

'Yes, I went to Bishops after a Steiner school, so I guess we are very middle class. I live in one of those newer houses near the Long Barrow. It's two storied with plush carpets and air-conditioning. It has three bathrooms and even the towel rack is heated. Everything I wear smells like fake lavender from my mum's fabric softener,' Christopher declared with a passionate hatred that even he hadn't expected from himself.

Seth surprised him then by laughing. It was a genuinely happy sound, a new softer sound that was endearing to Christopher.

'And you're not happy with your environment then?' he asked, beginning to roll himself a cigarette.

Christopher smiled. 'You could say that.'

'For someone who's had such a fill of all things modern you sure aren't anything special with cars.'

Christopher laughed.

'I've never been the car kind of boy.'

'You bookish?' Seth asked, licking the edge of his cigarette paper.

'Yes, intensely.'

'You don't look bookish.'

'No, that's part of my dilemma.'

'Ah,' said Seth. With a smile he placed the cigarette between his lips and lit it. 'I thought there was a dilemma. What is it?'

'I suppose that it's just that I'm bookish, and weird. But my body wants to do other things. I feel all out of place.'

Seth nodded to himself as he smoked. 'Are you a virgin?'

Christopher tried not to show his shock or his sudden embarrassment at something that had not previously embarrassed him. 'Yes.'

'Ever killed anything?'

'No.'

'Ever seen anything born, human or animal? Eaten anything

you saw die or made anything you use from scratch?'

'No for all.'

'Simple case of 'Male, Middle Class and White Syndrome'.'

Christopher winced; Seth's words were so true they were painful. 'What's your accent?' he asked, wanting to change the subject a bit.

'It's a Nottingham county accent that someone with a much posher one once put a good effort into curing to little effect. What's your real dilemma?'

Christopher was taken aback. For a moment he had to shut his eyes. The idea that Seth could see his deeper dilemma so clearly seemed unbearable all of a sudden. Did he walk around with his broken heart hanging out like an untucked shirt? Quickly he composed himself and opened his eyes. He had already discovered that bald-faced honesty was the only way to talk to Seth. Taking a deep breath he committed to the idea of total revelation.

'The only person I've ever really loved is dead... And I can't let go.'

Seth smiled, oddly and enigmatically. He stubbed out his cigarette and threw it into the fireplace. Turning to Christopher he stopped smiling and looked very serious.

'*Now* I want us to be friends.'

Christopher stole a rapid glance at his watch as he tore up the driveway. He had stayed with Seth longer than he had meant to, unwilling to return to his own world. There was only time to let himself into the house and have a glass of water before he heard Sophia's car pull up in the driveway. *Thank God she didn't arrive when Millicent was here on her own,* he thought. It had occurred to him that Sophia might never have spoken to him again if that had happened.

When he opened the door to her Sophia looked concerned but tried to hide it with a smile and her usual vivacity.

'Hi, honey,' she said, standing up on her tiptoes to give him a sisterly kiss on the cheek.

'Come in.' he said, and she followed him into the foyer.

'Are you okay?'

'Yes. Why?'

'You sounded, like, really weird on the phone. Urgent.'

By this time she had followed him into the sitting room and he had shut the door behind them.

'It was,' he said, turning to her and suddenly grasping her hands in excitement. 'But not in a bad way. I met this amazing person I want you to meet.'

Sophia was confused. After hearing the way Christopher's voice sounded on the telephone she had come over as quickly as she could. She had been agitated for the entire car trip, thinking to herself that there were only two options. One was that Christopher was terribly depressed and needed her, possibly something to do with his dead friend was about to be revealed.

Or secondly, that some new and disturbing element of their relationship was about to come to the fore. *What if the poor kid's fallen for me?* She thought. *How would I let him down gently?* She had played the whole thing out in her mind; him telling her, her gentle but firm rebuff, her explanation that he was too young. But now it appeared that his urgency owed nothing to her but to someone else, who appeared to be a man, and a homeless man at that.

'So let me get this straight, you met some hobo-'

'He's not a hobo,' Christopher insisted, too excited to be annoyed, 'He's just this guy who's rejected all society's bullshit and he's living in this way that... I don't know, plumbing the primal depths of what we are. He kills his own meat and stuff.'

Sophia nodded for a couple of seconds.

'Right. So you've met some hobo who plumbs and shoots stuff, I get it. It's like *Fight Club*, dried venison on an abandoned highway etc etc; I'm feeling the vibe. I guess it's easier to get in

62

contact with primal depths when you're covered in your own filth.'

'Sophia!' Christopher objected with a smile, accepting the teasing. 'Seriously though, you should see the stuff he reads.'

'That's all well and good Christopher, but what does it have to do with me?'

Christopher just looked at her for a second. She seemed more attractive then than he'd ever seen her. She'd come straight from work in jeans and flat shoes. Her white shirt was flimsy and a little see-through. Her hair was down and she was wearing hardly any makeup.

'You look so gorgeous,' he said, half way through his thoughts.

'Yeah, right, and I guess I'd look even better if I was out in a mud hut covered in cow dung, like I ought to be in the state of nature, huh?'

Christopher laughed with real humour. He liked that she made him laugh. He couldn't remember when he'd laughed like that.

'I'm not talking about returning to a state of nature. I just mean I like how your face really looks, that's all.' His voice didn't hide how *much* he liked her skin and in that moment he didn't mind.

'I look terrible,' she said self-consciously, dragging her fingers through her hair in sharp angry strokes, 'I came straight from work because I thought you were in trouble.'

Christopher felt a sharp stab of tenderness for her in her unprepared state. 'Thank you,' he said, putting his hand on her shoulder.

She looked up at him for a second. 'Oh no, that's quite all right really. I mean, getting to meet your tramp will square it, I'm sure.'

He pretended to hit her but he was laughing again.

She smiled.

'So is this some sort of social experiment? Neanderthal man meets late homo-sapiens female, just to see what happens?' she asked, taking a seat.

Christopher sat down across from her. 'I don't know what it is exactly. It's just a feeling,' he said. 'And I guess with my parents gone I wanted to—'

'Your parents are gone?' she said abruptly. 'I... I just hadn't noticed.'

'Yeah. Well, they are, and I thought I'd take advantage of the situation. I wanted to invite you both to stay with us over the weekend.'

Sophia looked thrown off balance. 'Sure, I guess. Weird, but okay. So tell me about this guy.'

Christopher smiled and leaned forward. 'He's about your age. He was born on a farm where his family worked for generations. He was home schooled and seems to have no surviving family, as far as I know. But he's got this tattered little copy of Rimbaud's *Season in Hell* that sits by his pillow like a bible.'

Sophia appeared to consider this for a moment, crossing her legs and playing with one of her loose tresses. 'Who was Rimbaud again?'

'He was a French poet, only fifteen when he started writing immortal work. He was a mad, drug-fucked visionary who just trampled all over the social conventions of his time. He was like a late nineteenth century Jim Morrison.'

Sophia smiled. 'You make it all sound so exciting.'

'It was. It is! Eugene taught me that. He showed me this complete other world...'

'Didn't you say Eugene died when he was thirteen?'

Christopher paused painfully. He wished he hadn't said Eugene's name. 'Yes. He did,' he said.

'That is amazingly young to have such a good knowledge of poetry.'

'Yes. He was very, very clever.'

She leaned forward a little. 'Are you okay, Christopher? You seem upset.'

Christopher shook his head slowly, not because he meant to answer no, but because he struggled to find words

'I'm not a shallow person, Sophia,' he murmured, looking away from her and out the window. 'I can't stop being sad because people think I should.'

'No, of course not, nobody would expect-'

'But they do,' he snapped uncharacteristically. 'They all do, mum, dad, Millicent.'

There was an uncomfortable pause where he thought bitterly that Sophia was probably wishing she hadn't brought the topic up.

'Eugene must have been very special.'

'Yes,' Christopher said impatiently. 'Special, musically gifted, child prodigy. Yes. All of those things.'

'But fundamentally?'

'Fundamentally I loved him! He was *everything* to me. Why do people seem to need that explained?'

She looked down at her hands that she was wringing in her lap. When her voice came again it sounded very raw. 'Maybe because they haven't experienced it. Maybe we need you to paint a picture.'

'All right,' he said looking at her. 'But I hate those words. That's what everyone said at his funeral, all that special, gifted shit. They played a recording of him playing the cello so everyone could talk about how talented he was and shake their heads at the waste. But he would have laughed at them! He was always amused by platitudes and anything that people say because it's 'expected' or the conventional thing to do.

'Eugene was the kind of person who cut through everything you expected and left you in shock, even when you thought you knew him and knew what to expect—' Christopher stopped, noticing that Sophia appeared uneasy. 'What?' he asked.

Sophia appeared to be staring past him into the space behind him. She looked quickly back at Christopher as though she'd been caught doing something wrong.

'Nothing,' she mumbled. 'Please go on.'

'You've gone pale. Even your lips are pale...'

'I'm fine... Christopher. What did he look like?'

Christopher frowned. 'Why do you ask?'

'I just want to know.'

'Okay. He had brown hair, blue eyes, kind of big, widely spaced blue eyes, a turned up nose, high cheekbones, dimples, very expressive eyebrows, a cheeky smile. Adults called him 'cute'.'

When Christopher said the word 'cute' it sounded like an obscenity, but Sophia didn't smile, she just nodded soberly. After a moment she cleared her throat and seemed to regain her composure.

'Your mother talked to me about you and him.'

Christopher smiled. He was pleased that she had told him.

'I thought so.'

'Why?'

Christopher shrugged. 'Because that's mum?'

Sophia kept looking at him with the air of someone who was about to be very upfront.

'She told me about spying on you and him.'

Christopher looked unsurprised. His eyes scanned the distance out the window and then looked back at Sophia.

'No surprises there.'

'She said she saw him kiss you.' Christopher didn't answer. After a few moments she said, 'Christopher?'

'What?'

'Are you going to say something?'

'What do you want me to say?'

'Well I just told you what your mother told me, I thought you might respond in some way.'

Christopher shrugged again.

'Like what? Do you want me to confirm or deny, or to say it wasn't what it looked like or something?'

Sophia blinked several times then shook her head. 'Christopher you must realise how unusual you are?'

He rolled his eyes. 'Unless I was a retard, yes. I just can't imagine what you want me to say about kissing someone. A kiss is irreducible isn't it?'

Christopher jumped back a little in shock when Sophia leapt to her feet and began to pace. Suddenly, almost violently she swung around. Her brown eyes seemed cavernous for a moment. As though where there had once been surface gloss and shine there was now a terrible depth. He was almost frightened of her. For some reason it reminded him of the alien appearance his own eyes had taken on in the mirror.

'Tell me how you did it!' she demanded. 'How the hell did you feel all this stuff and not want to act on it when there was so little time!' The words seemed to erupt from her without her conscious consent. Already she knew they weren't fully her words. She shut her eyes and they seemed to flicker under the surface for a second, 'I mean... do you know... Did you ever ask him? What if I had wanted ... My God,' she whispered, opening her eyes. 'Forget I said that. I'm being crazy.'

'No,' he said abruptly, getting to his feet. 'No, you're not. I want to hear this, what you're trying to say. Do you mean touching him? How did I touch him like that and feel what I did and not want to do more?'

Sophia just nodded swallowing hard.

'I was young,' Christopher said quietly, and his voice was as raw as hers. 'We were on the threshold between boyhood and manhood. I loved him entirely, so... so... I don't think I'd have known what to do anyway. I suppose there is more to passion than just sex, Sophia.'

Unexpectedly Sophia laughed with real humour. 'How would

you know, you haven't even had sex yet! You shouldn't knock what you haven't tried honey, I'm telling you.'

Both of them could feel the openings between them close. Christopher's whole body seemed to recoil and flinch back. With an ache he realised he could actually feel his heart close to her. He didn't want to let it happen but he didn't yet have the courage to show to her what she was denying him.

'We should stop nattering on like this and go and talk to your poor bore of a sister before she starts sticking pins in a hex doll of me.'

Christopher nodded his agreement, but he couldn't smile.

6

'Between the idea
And the reality
Between the motion
And the act
Falls the Shadow.'
—T.S. Eliot

'Hi, Seth,' Christopher said, as he opened the door, 'Thank you for coming.'

There was a familiarity and genuine quality in what Christopher said. It came from the fact that his words were far from being platitudes. And he could tell the other man knew this. Seth didn't seem to feel any concern for the usually socially awkward moment of standing on a threshold. He seemed to be taking his time looking at the house and at Christopher.

'It's very new and warm,' Seth said, with a mischievous hint of a smile.

'Yes,' Christopher replied. 'Are you going to come in then?'

'You haven't asked me to yet.'

Christopher grinned and looked to the side in bemusement. It seemed such an oddly formal request. 'Well, come in then.'

Seth stepped into the well-lit foyer and blinked for a while in the glare. He took off his overcoat. Underneath it he was wearing the same shirt he had been wearing when Christopher had first seen him, still fastened with the piece of string.

'Your friend is here already?' Seth asked.

'Yes, she's just through here in the sitting room.' Christopher let Seth into the room where Sophia was seated. The lighting was dim, as Seth had explained he preferred, due to being accustomed to candle light.

Just as Sophia set eyes on Seth and Christopher was about to introduce them, Sophia shot up out of her seat as though a spider had been dropped down the back of her neck.

Christopher stared in shock at Sophia for a moment, and then looked to Seth. He was about to ask if they knew each other. But Seth had taken a step back and was breathing rapidly, regarding her like an animal with its hackles up.

Sophia had put the coffee table between them and was panting too, wringing her hands and opening her mouth occasionally to try and speak. Both of them seemed like wolves of a foreign pack, circling one another, trying to decide which of them was the prey and which of them was the predator.

'Do you two know each other?'

'Not in so many words,' Seth replied, not taking his eyes off Sophia.

Sophia regained her composure quickly, and dusting herself down as if clearing away cobwebs, she sat.

'I'm sorry,' she murmured, rubbing her temples. 'I don't know what came over me. You guys must think I'm such a flake. You reminded me of someone... I think.'

The whole time she spoke she didn't look at Seth. Seth seemed to relax immediately.

'It's quite all right, Sophia, really, I'm not offended.'

'How did you know my name?' She blurted jumpily.

Seth smiled his odd half-smile. 'Christopher mentioned it.'

'Well, do you want to sit down, Seth?' Christopher asked.

Seth seemed comfortable enough now, and took a seat across from Sophia. Sophia was still visibly shaken. Christopher moved to her side and sat beside her putting an unobtrusive hand on her back and rubbing it.

'I'm just really sorry,' she said, her voice sounding thick as though she was about to burst into tears. Christopher couldn't fathom what was wrong, but the depth of her distress concerned him. She had never seemed this upset before.

'Really,' Seth said slowly and meaningfully. 'You're not the first person to have that reaction.'

'Why is that?' she asked, dabbing at her eyes with a handker-chief.

Seth sighed and looked away for a while. He looked up at the ceiling as though making an important decision. Then he drew in his breath to reply. It was at this point that the door opened and Millicent entered. She stopped for a moment.

'Oh, Christopher, I'm sorry. I didn't realise you were in here. Hello, Sophia,' she said, warmly. 'And who's your other friend?'

Seth just looked at her, his expression neutral.

'This is Seth. Seth this is my sister Millicent.'

Christopher passionately wished he was dead. He watched in disbelief as his perfume scented sister swept past him and offered her hand warmly to Seth. He shook it and Millicent sat down next to him. Christopher who had been imagining scenes of hideous snobbery watched in amazement.

'So where did you two meet?' she asked. 'Christopher have you offered drinks?'

He shook his head.

'Oh well,' she said airily. 'We'll get to that. Where did you say you and Christopher met each other?'

'I didn't say,' Seth replied quite seriously, as though he didn't even understand the figure of speech. Millicent just laughed as if Seth had intended a joke.

'No seriously, Seth. Where?'

'I met Christopher when he got his car stuck in the flood water.'

Millicent nodded as though this were something great.

'So what do you do, Seth?'

'Lots of things. But I suppose you mean for money?' Millicent laughed again and nodded. 'I carve things in wood and sell them at the market.'

'Oh really? What sort of things?'

Sophia had recovered enough by this stage to make signif-icant eye contact with Christopher. Her eye contact mutely conveyed the message of 'what the fuck is going on?'

'Drink?' he asked Sophia.

'Yes please. Double Scotch.'

'I think I'll have a triple,' Christopher muttered under his breath.

'I'll have a red, thanks,' Millicent said.

Christopher waited while Seth spoke to ask him what he wanted to drink.

'...statues of gods, handles for reworked dagger blades, leather pouches. Craft bits and bobs for the people who come to look at the Long Barrow and Avebury.'

'What kinds of people come to look at the barrow? I never pay the tourists any attention. Haven't walked out there for years,' she said.

'The kind of people who tie ribbons on the ribbon-tree at the sacred spring and leave the charms there, Millicent. You're living right next to a major holy site.'

Millicent just stared at him, lost and fascinated, as though she were unable to look away and had forgotten not to stare. It disturbed Christopher for some reason. She looked drugged and placid like an animal mesmerised by headlights.

Sophia broke the silence. 'I've noticed the ribbons on the trees out near our dig. I do archaeological work around here and we're practically fighting our way past people with dowsing rods and people charging crystals and all that. You don't seem like them, Seth.'

Seth nodded slowly. 'Nah, I'm old school.'

When nobody replied Christopher took the opportunity to say, 'Did either of you two want a drink?'

'I'll have red wine thanks,' Millicent said, still sounding dreamy.

'Do you have ale?' Seth asked.

Christopher's dad occasionally had Hobgoblin ale in the cellar so Christopher went to look for some. When he returned,

Millicent was speaking.

'I guess you never realise how fascinating the place you live is. When all these things are right in your backyard you tend to take them for granted.'

She was sparkling and her cheeks were flushed. Christopher noted that her glass was already close to empty. Sophia was sitting back with her legs crossed and her dark eyes regarding the proceedings with quiet interest.

'I've always been interested in magic though,' he heard Millicent tell Seth, as he handed an ale to him.

This was news to Christopher. He just wished he could grab Seth and take him somewhere else. After taking a seat next to Sophia he made eye contact with Seth and subtly conveyed his apologies for his sister. As he watched Millicent come back with her next drink Christopher handed the can of ale to Seth.

'So Seth,' said Sophia, who seemed to want to steer the conversation down an altogether different route, 'Christopher said you were home schooled. I've heard a lot of negative things about home schooling, but you seem so knowledgeable. Was that your parent's doing?'

Seth smiled. 'I don't know if my parents could read actually. But I had a guardian later on who took over my home schooling. He was very learned. The rest was all my passion. Passion tends to find a way.

'So... you disturb the remains of our ancestors and study them?'

Sophia laughed for the first time and Millicent, either because she was no longer holding Seth's attention or because of the topic change, began to look a little sullen.

'Yes, I suppose I do.'

'Does it bother you?' Seth asked.

'No. Why should it?'

Christopher watched. Seth sipped his ale and looked at Sophia in that penetrative way of his. Christopher loved the fact that he never knew what Seth would say next.

'Because they're somebody's bones.'

'No, I'm fine with bodies as long as they're all dried up.'

Christopher already saw that Seth preferred Sophia as a person but that Millicent might be interesting to him for other reasons. It surprised Christopher that he felt quite ambivalent about the fact that he could sense Seth's sexual interest in his sister. He was too interested himself in seeing where the night would lead to be worried.

'But what about the people to whom the bones belonged?' Seth asked.

'They've been dead forever,' Sophia said, as though surprised that anyone would bother about them.

'But they have spirits still.'

'That is assuming I believe in spirits?'

The conversation seemed to suddenly have a cat and mouse feeling about it. Christopher wasn't sure why it felt that way but he was practically holding his breath.

'Well, do you?'

'I try not to.'

'Why?' Seth asked.

Sophia smiled in a knowing way and then got slowly up to refill her glass.

'That, my dear,' she said, in a mysterious sort of tone that matched her little Mona Lisa smile. 'Just encourages them.'

Millicent laughed in an odd strained way, assuming another joke had been made, even though no one else was laughing. She got up jerkily, stumbling through the tense atmosphere to refill her glass again.

'Feeling like a couple of drinks, Millicent?' Christopher said through his teeth.

'Well, mum and dad are away Christopher and while we're getting up to a few things we wouldn't normally do, I thought I'd join in.' There was laughter in her tone, but there was an edge to the comment.

Seth had just watched Sophia pour her Scotch in an odd half-amused way that hinted at a shared understanding that Christopher wished he could access. But he was afraid that if he tried to steer the conversation back to where it had been going his attempt would be clumsy or intrusive.

'So have you found anything more about your skeleton, Sophia?' Christopher asked.

'Nothing interesting,' Sophia answered quickly, a little too quickly. 'It would take another archaeologist to be interested by a thorough analysis of pollen samples.'

Seth smiled and sipped his ale.

Millicent downed some more wine and turned the conversation back to Seth.

'Do you live with anyone, Seth?'

'No.'

'Do you have anyone special in your life?'

'It's been some time since I've been seeing a woman, if that's what you mean.' Christopher thought Seth seemed annoyed by these questions, or maybe uncomfortable. It seemed to him Millicent was being tactless, but he acknowledged to himself that he was probably being hypersensitive to Seth's loss because of his own.

'I'm in the same predicament,' Millicent went on while Christopher quietly died of embarrassment.

'One just doesn't meet interesting men where I work.' As Seth didn't enquire where she worked Millicent continued on, 'I work at a solicitor's office. They're such... you know 'suits'. So dull!' She giggled and sipped her wine.

Good God, Christopher thought, *why doesn't she just rip her clothes off right now and leap on the poor man?*

'Where's your toilet?' Seth asked, standing up.

'I'll show you,' said Christopher with desperate speed, relieved at the chance to get Seth alone.

As soon as he closed the door behind them he said,

'I am so sorry about my sister. She isn't normally like this.'

'It's okay. You don't need to apologise. People react strangely to me.'

He went up the stairs and walked straight towards the bathroom without Christopher showing it to him.

Christopher smiled. *It is fairly obvious*, he thought, *mum has a pretty sign on the door.* He figured Seth had wanted to get him alone too. Quietly Christopher grabbed himself a drink of water from the kitchen and loitered.

'Mind if I get another ale?' Seth asked, on his way down the stairs.

'Sure,' Christopher said, 'I brought a few up from the cellar, they're just there, help yourself.'

'Tell me something, Christopher.'

'Yes?'

'How would you feel if I fucked your sister?'

Christopher looked at Seth for a moment as he thought about the question. 'I guess I'd wonder why you'd want to.'

'I would have thought that was pretty straight forward, it ain't love at first sight.'

'It's just hard to see my sister as sexual. But I suppose I don't really feel anything if I had to be honest, except a morbid curiosity.'

Seth nodded. 'Well I'll be sure to tell you all about it,' Seth said with a grin, before taking a slug from the can.

Christopher laughed and hoped that Seth was joking about that last part.

'So why haven't you had Sophia?' Seth asked.

'We're friends. I haven't thought seriously about 'having' her at all. I mean I've *thought* about it of course. Just not seriously thought about it. It's not like that.'

'Little secret, mate,' Seth said, putting his arm around Christopher's shoulders and pulling him nearer. 'She wants it to be,' he whispered. Then he hit Christopher on the back. 'Trust me,' he added, 'I have the Second Sight.'

'Really?' Christopher asked.

'Really,' Seth replied in all seriousness.

As they walked back into the other room Millicent was drinking from yet another fresh glass of wine, and telling Sophia about something perfectly uninteresting that happened at work. Christopher refilled his own drink and took a seat.

'I should drive back and pick up my stuff before I get too drunk if I'm staying the night,' Sophia said, addressing Christopher.

'You can borrow my clothes,' Millicent said, not noticing Sophia's thinly disguised horror. 'No!' Millicent declared drunkenly, 'I insist. You can't leave now; we're having such a good conversation. She's lovely Christopher,' she said, getting up and stumbling over to sit on the arm of his chair.

'I was wrong about you, Sophia. I have to say. My little brother is a bit sweet on you I think,' she said, draping herself over Christopher. 'And I wasn't sure about it, but now I think you're lovely.'

Christopher cringed and pushed her knees together to prevent her exposing herself any further. He wasn't embarrassed by Millicent's comments about him liking Sophia, who wouldn't like Sophia? It was more that Millicent was embarrassing herself and she was his sister.

'Thank you, Millicent,' said Sophia.

Christopher smiled at her apologetically. Sophia, however, seemed more uncomfortable about what Millicent had said than he was. She began to drink her Scotch more quickly and when she was finished she refilled it immediately. Christopher remained silent while Millicent redirected her attentions toward Seth. Seth drank his ale and answered her questions where necessary. He wasn't overly polite or overly rude. He just did his own thing. Christopher had to smile. *If he really is thinking of sleeping with her he obviously doesn't intend to work for it.*

But what was really worrying Christopher was Sophia. He desperately wanted to get her alone so he could ask her what had happened before and what was still bothering her now. Millicent poured herself another wine but Christopher refrained from commenting, even though he felt she'd had more than enough. She took a few more sips and then went to get up to head for the bathroom. It only took two steps before she slipped and stumbled on her high heels, pitching forward toward the coffee table. Christopher jumped up to catch her but Seth was already there before he'd even reached his feet. Seth caught her easily and picked her up like a child. Millicent lay draped across his arms giggling.

'I think you need to go to bed,' he said, with a suppressed grin of amusement.

'Me too,' Sophia said.

Christopher opened the lounge room door as Seth carried Millicent to bed. As they rounded the doorframe Millicent's thigh lolled to one side briefly exposing her lacy underwear. Christopher pulled her dress down.

When they reached the top of the stairs Christopher flicked on a light and opened the door to Millicent's room. Christopher seldom ventured into it and he felt slightly intrusive about doing so. Seth on the other hand seemed to have no such compunctions. The room seemed to represent his sister for Christopher. It was decorated in white and lilac and smelt of her Violets perfume. It was also meticulously neat. This image that he held of her was vastly different to the one she presented now as Christopher pulled back the bed sheets and Seth lay her down.

Sophia stood in the doorway, watching and saying nothing as Christopher slipped off her high heels and Seth pulled the cover over her.

When they had switched out the light and closed the door

Sophia remarked, 'She can't hold her alcohol can she?'

'She doesn't normally drink like that,' Christopher replied, as they headed down the stairs and back into the lounge room. His concern was evident in his voice.

Sophia laid a reassuring hand on his shoulder. 'She'll be okay in the morning. She just got a bit over excited.'

'Mmm,' Christopher replied.

Christopher watched Seth lean back in his seat and cross his arms.

'Mind if I get straight to the point?' Seth asked, addressing them both.

Christopher smiled. 'There is nothing I would rather.'

Seth turned toward Sophia, who seemed to have frozen into her earlier posture of wary expectation.

'You know what I am and I know what you are. Do you want to talk about it?'

Sophia was silent for a moment and then she was on her feet again, going toward the alcohol bottle but not doing anything with it.

'I don't know what you're talking about, hon,' she said. 'But I'm sure you and Christopher are going to get on like a house on fire with your sense of drama.'

Seth stood up, a lot more slowly than Sophia had and moved into the path between Sophia and her seat. 'Don't fuck about, Sophia,' he said quietly, 'it doesn't suit you.'

Sophia stopped. She looked terrified and all of Christopher's instincts told him to protect her somehow, to make it stop, and yet he was spellbound.

'Okay, you win,' she murmured.

'You want to sit down?' Seth asked.

She nodded mutely and Seth stepped out of the way, letting her sit back down next to Christopher.

The protective urge felt physical in Christopher's body now, it was like a spasm in the pit of his stomach. It flashed adrenalin to his arms and legs and made his groin feel strange. But there was another instinct, or maybe intuition. What was coming he couldn't protect her from, because it was the truth. He knew both things with complete certainty in those moments. He knew he'd have fought for her, shed his blood for her. And he also knew he couldn't throw punches at what was frightening her.

'Sophia,' Seth said, taking a swig of his ale. 'Tell me what you saw when I walked in?' She was shaking her head immediately in a convulsive denial. 'I don't know. I just don't know. Don't question me on it, Seth. I don't understand the shit that happens to me sometimes, okay?'

'I can help you to understand it,' Seth said calmly. 'Christopher, is it okay if I smoke in here?'

Christopher nodded, though nobody normally smoked in his parent's home. Seth took out an already rolled cigarette. 'Tell me about it.'

'Cold,' Sophia blurted. 'It was cold. Deathly cold. You sent chills running up and down the back of my neck—' she stopped there, shaking her head and beginning to choke back tears.

Christopher tentatively put his hand on her knee, offering it to her to hold. She accepted.

'What else?'

'My hairs rose.'

'And?'

'I felt the floor dropping away, a sense of vertigo. What is this in aid of?' she asked.

'You know what I am, Sophia.'

'So you keep saying!' she snapped. 'I don't know anything right now.'

'You see things,' he prompted.

She nodded then and as soon as she did she began to really cry.

'I'm crazy!' She wept.

'She has The Sight,' Seth explained, taking a drag on his

cigarette and blowing it casually into the air, as though all of this were a normal evening for him. 'In times past we would have called her a "witch".'

'Now we have new words for it,' she cried. 'Complete–fucking–fruit bat' is popular!' She let go of Christopher and covered her face with her hands.

'So she's psychic?' he clarified.

Seth nodded.

'More or less. She can see and speak to the dead, foretell events and she can probably tell when you're lying to her. Though in Sophia's case I would say her full potential is pretty much untapped.'

Christopher stared at Sophia with blatant fascination. She looked up at him.

'Oh God, don't look at me like that, Christopher. I'm not the prize act in the travelling Freak Show.'

'No,' Seth said quietly. 'That's probably me.'

Christopher couldn't tell whether there was irony in Seth's tone but he turned to look at the other man. 'What do you mean?'

'What does he mean?' Sophia said. 'He means if we had some fucking crucifixes and garlic hanging about the place tonight might have panned out differently. That's what he's saying Christopher!' With a last hysterical throwing up of her hands she added, 'I can't believe this is even happening.'

Christopher looked at Seth who took a drag on his cigarette before stubbing it out.

'Now you're wondering what she means,' Seth smiled, and blew out his smoke. Christopher realised as Seth's teeth caught the light in a white flash that this was the first time he'd seen them. 'I'm what used to be called a 'vampire', Christopher. Though it's a much abused term today, so I don't expect it explains much in itself.'

There was a moment of silence during which Christopher noted with amazement that Sophia hadn't batted an eyelid.

'A…a vampire?' Christopher repeated. 'Are you serious?'

Seth just nodded. 'That's why I reacted as I did when I saw Sophia. I knew she'd know because there was a time when her kind used to root out my kind in the villages. Hand us over to the authorities because they alone knew which one's we were.'

'What…what do you mean when you say you're a vampire? What are we talking here? You can't come out in the day? Something like Anne Rice or something?'

Seth laughed. 'Not even close. I can come out in the day if it's overcast, as you know. I am quite photosensitive though, yes. The sun gives me a rash. I'm not immortal, I can't fly…'

Christopher's mind flashed on the image of Seth as he'd first seen him and remembered the sunglasses.

'So you drink blood… but you're drinking beer.'

Seth snorted again as though in disgust. He smiled again allowing his teeth to show. Christopher was surprised to feel the instinctual jump-start that his heart got from the sight of Seth's sharp canine teeth.

'I told you, this ain't Bram Stoker, this is the real thing. I eat food like everyone else. But sometimes I crave blood if I don't go out in spirit-form for a bit. If I don't have it for long enough it starts to send me a bit bolshy. I can control it with animal blood, and if I always go out at a certain time and do certain things. That's about it.'

'Yeah, right,' exclaimed Sophia. 'Like that's the whole of it. Look at the trance your sister was in!'

Christopher had to admit he'd noticed that it was hard to break eye contact with Seth, but he'd put it down to straight charisma rather than an occult power. He certainly didn't find it an irresistible force. But his sister…well, Christopher found that a little more difficult to explain away. He had no idea why Millicent had been so susceptible. After a moment he frowned and moved closer. He realised that he had been examining Seth like he was some exotic specimen, rather than someone he'd considered a friend a few minutes ago.

Christopher was shocked and chastened when he picked up on the mild hurt in Seth's eyes when he saw the way Christopher had been looking at him. This time when he looked at Seth it was with a new humanity.

'Would it make you uncomfortable if I looked more closely at your teeth?'

Seth gazed at him for a long time without speaking. Eventually he said, 'Come here.'

Christopher got up and went over to kneel in front of Seth's seat. Seth took Christopher's hand in his and drew back his top lip as though in a snarl. Carefully he ran Christopher's fingertips across the tips of his canine teeth. Christopher felt the sharp tips that could have cut him if he pressed any harder. He noted that they were a bit longer than the other teeth, and stronger than most people's teeth. But the teeth next to them on the outsides were another set of canines that came in from higher in the gum as though jostling for space. Even the set of teeth inside the normally placed canines looked a bit sharper than normal. All the while as he did this Seth's eyes were settled on him from above the impressive weapons in his mouth.

'Believe me then?' Seth asked when Christopher removed his hand.

Christopher squeezed Seth's arm briefly. 'It wasn't about belief,' he said quietly.

'They're a bugger when you bite your own lip, I can tell you that much. And they're a pain when you feel really happy and want to smile and you freak out small kids.'

'Nothing has changed about how I see you. You can smile around me,' Christopher said.

Seth nodded in acknowledgement and leaned back in his seat.

'That's why I told you,' he said, 'I tend to avoid those who will treat me as a monster or want to drag me off to a psych-ward. Or worse still, suspect me of having had implants because I'm some try-hard little emo wanker. And then of course there are witches, where I don't get a choice,' he said, looking over at Sophia.

'Yeah, well, I'm sorry, Seth, but where I come from, fang teeth, blood drinking, big monster thing.'

'Where do you come from?' he asked with understated irony tingeing his strange straightforward manner.

She glared at him for a moment. 'Look buddy. So I see spooks and I know stuff about people. I'm not a patch on you.'

'We're going to get on so well,' said Seth, leaning forward with a malicious smile burgeoning around his mouth. 'Spooks really like me. So I'll be able to have all your old favourites swarming about you trying to get into your head and say stuff through you in no time. That freaky suicide that used to bother you as a kid…'

'Stop it.'

'Why? Come now Sophia you must have missed that little girl who drowned in the bathtub.'

'That's not even true, there was no such little girl. Just stop it or…'

'Or what?' Seth asked with one raised eyebrow.

Christopher felt a strange feeling from Sophia; it made him want to move away. He couldn't explain it but it was like being in the same room with someone who keeps staring at you or standing too close to you when they talk. Something she was doing was just making him inexplicably uncomfortable. But Seth seemed to be enjoying it.

'You wouldn't be trying to cast the Evil Eye on me Sophia, surely? That's the sort of thing freaks do.'

'You smug bastard.' She murmured, opening her purse to search for another joint.

Seth just smiled slightly and reached for his own cigarettes. 'Just get comfortable with your place in the circus troop. We really don't need to be enemies these days.'

Seth got up and looked at Christopher. 'Christopher, I have to go. I'll come back in the evening tomorrow. Thank you for this, really... I've been quite lonely.'

Christopher got up too. He was moved and thrown off by this sudden display of vulnerability. 'Can I see you out?'

'Of course.' Christopher touched Sophia briefly on his way past. It was just a light touch on her shoulder, but it was full of his concern and affection for her.

'I'll only be a second,' he said, 'are you okay?'

She nodded. He followed Seth out into the hallway where Seth put on his overcoat. Christopher unlocked the door and followed him out into the semi-dark. There was only the light of a few stars and what electrical illumination found its way through the curtained windows of the house.

'That's better,' Seth said, very quietly, as though to himself. They both stood there enjoying the darkness and the stillness. Christopher loved that stillness because it was pregnant with possibility and in those moments his whole world was shaken up and rearranged. And he was glad, relieved even, that it had been disturbed. 'Are you afraid of me, Christopher?' Seth asked.

From Seth's tone it was difficult to tell how he would feel about the answer.

'Not at all,' Christopher replied, still looking up at the stars.

'Why not?'

'I really don't know. I believe you utterly. '

Seth nodded. 'What if I took this opportunity to bite you?'

'I guess I'm not afraid of bleeding.'

Seth laughed quietly. 'I like that answer,' he said thoughtfully, looking up at the sky. 'I like people who aren't afraid. I like you.' He looked at Christopher, 'As it happens I would never bite you against your will. I don't do that. Not to anyone. I just wanted to know.'

'Were you always this way?' Christopher asked, 'Since you were born?'

Seth nodded. Without further formalities he walked away into the darkness, his hand stuffed into his pockets against the cold.

Christopher shut the door quietly behind him and went to Sophia who was standing by the heater shivering.

'Are you all right?'

He hadn't made a decision to, yet he found himself reaching for her, and to his surprise she came quickly into his arms. He closed them around her and shut his eyes. This was the first time he'd really held her. He could feel the warmth of her body up against his. In his stomach he felt those little clenches again and a warm rush. To his delight that warmth flooded down and down until it suffused his groin. Something in that feeling reminded him he was indeed alive in a way that brought deep relief and comfort.

'You and Seth are the only people in the world who know,' she said.

'Why didn't you tell me?'

'I didn't think anyone would believe me, did I?' she said, pulling back a little to look at him. Her dark eyes were red-rimmed with crying. Tentatively he reached out and gently stroked her cheek with the edge of his hand. His hand twitched a little as he touched her and she pulled back suddenly.

Christopher was shocked speechless by how much he didn't want to let her go and how close he'd been to crying out in protest. She put the coffee table between them. It seemed to Christopher that her face contained some sort of defeat that he couldn't understand the source of.

'I guess you've got what you wanted then. All that passion and intimacy business, or whatever you call it. I suppose this makes you my best friend.'

Christopher smiled. It was like a sudden burst of sunlight, from his eyes but also from his heart. The hurt he'd felt when she pulled back was soothed by her words, and the spreading warmth filled his torso like an inferno.

'Come on, let's get you to bed. You look exhausted,' he said.

He showed her up the stairs and into the guest room. Turning on the light he indicated the double bed. 'You can sleep here. Is there anything you need?'

She shook her head. 'No, I'll just sleep in my shirt, I'm too tired to change.'

'Okay, well... good night.' He realised he wanted to kiss her. He wanted to kiss her the way he used to kiss Eugene. It was the first time he'd felt that urge since Eugene's death. He almost felt it, him pressing his lips down over hers and lingering like that with her lip between his, gently tasting before opening his mouth more... 'I'll leave you to it,' he murmured.

'Christopher!'

'Yeah?'

'Don't leave... I'm scared.' Her voice came out tight and unnatural sounding. Christopher wished he had some words to tell her how relieved he was that she'd spoken. 'Do you want me to stay till you're asleep?' he offered.

'I feel dreadful putting you out like this, you must be—'

'No, I mean, I'd like to do that.'

'Okay,' she nodded, her expression still sheepish. 'If you don't mind.'

'I could do with the company too after tonight.'

Sophia got up and began unbuttoning her jeans. For the first time since her comment about casual sex on the night they met, Christopher was suddenly uncomfortable. He looked away quickly. 'Do you want me to leave?'

She waved the comment away absently. 'It's only my underwear, I'm sure it's not the first time you've seen a woman in her...' Sophia shut her eyes and hit herself in the forehead. 'God, I really didn't mean...I keep forgetting you're a... I'm just a wreck tonight.'

'It's okay.'

'No, really. I totally forgot. It sounded like—

'No, it didn't. It's okay.'

'It's just that I keep—'

'Sophia, seriously, I'm not offended. Other than my mum and sister it is the first time I've seen a woman in her underwear.'

She slipped under the covers while Christopher looked at the carpet pile. 'Shall I leave the lamp on?' he asked.

Sophia smiled and nodded. 'Thank you.'

Christopher sat down in the chair by the bed and pulled the rug over him that usually sat on the chair.

'And how are you, Christopher?' she asked quietly.

'A bit shaken,' he admitted. 'A few hours back I wasn't even sure I believed in life after death.'

'That changes everything for you doesn't it?' she asked, and there was something strangely hollow about her voice.

'Yeah,' he replied softly. He sat thinking for some time while she was silent. Something was welling in his chest, a pressure that was turning into pain. It was a pain he didn't yet put into words, didn't know how to. Then Sophia put words to it for him.

'I've seen him,' she said suddenly.

A chill went through Christopher. He wouldn't have been surprised if his teeth started to chatter. *Aren't you happy Christopher?* He asked himself. *Isn't this exactly what you wanted?*

'Did you ever feel him?' she asked gently.

He wanted to say that he felt Eugene all the time, in his head, in his heart, in his bones. That was the cause of his protracted mourning, his inability to stop *feeling* Eugene everywhere. Yet he didn't know if that was the kind of 'feeling' Sophia was talking about. Even when he tried to ask her the words seem to hurt his mouth, tighten his throat.

'I don't know,' was all he murmured. He feared he was being unsympathetic to Sophia's own anxieties so he forced himself to talk about it. 'Were you afraid when… when… you saw him?' It occurred to Christopher that he should maybe be more sceptical. Yet somehow he felt he had always known these things, somewhere in the back of his head. Try as he might he just couldn't explain away the picture in his room and his certainty that his reflection has winked at him without him moving his eye.

Or maybe it was in his blood where this knowledge hailed from, deep inside him where his ancestors lived. His ancestors who were probably some of the old piled bones from the Long Barrow, or had become part of the chalk beneath the grass of his home. Anyone who saw Sophia's eyes when she spoke about her Sight would know she was telling the truth, he thought.

'Yes,' she said, her voice sounded afraid even then. Her face was so pale she looked unwell. 'He's strong, Christopher. Unusual. And... and I'm afraid of you and me... when we get close, cause that's when Eugene comes.'

Christopher frowned and suppressed a shiver. He sat thinking about it for a long time while Sophia began to doze off. Eventually he turned the light off and lay down beside her. He didn't get under the blanket but he pulled the rug over him. Before he went to sleep he whispered into the air as softly as he could.

'Don't be jealous of her, Eugene. You've no reason to be. My heart is yours always.'

It seemed to Christopher that the atmosphere seemed lighter and the room felt warmer. Sophia seemed to sleep more peacefully after that too. At length Christopher also slept.

7

'And indeed there will be time
To wonder, 'Do I dare?' and, 'Do I dare?'
Time to turn back and descend the stair...'
—T.S Eliot

Seth's blood seemed to stir as though in answer to the cold sound of the wind whistling in the chimney. He felt a kinship with that wind. He thought of himself as one of the goblin people of the Black Huntsman, who some call 'The Company of the Wind'. He felt a brotherhood with its hollow sound, it was calling to him, telling him that tonight he would need to fly. It felt so right, this aloneness with the elements. It made the night before seem strange to him. The beautiful latent power in Christopher haunted him. He had never met someone like that. Christopher and he were total opposites. Seth wondered if Christopher would even be able to see in the darkness of Seth's life. And the archaic creature from beyond the hedge, with the voice and demeanour of a modern woman that was Sophia... How strange. How exceedingly strange, in this quiet little town that he should find two like them.

Simply because he knew that these connections were powerful and some spirit of perversity was with him, Seth had considered not going back. But that was before he got into bed and listened to the wind. By midmorning that wind would blow all the clouds away and let the sun through. But for now... It was helping him to make sense of things.

Christopher seemed so full of fiery vitality and yet that very same young man was in love with a dead boy. And that very vitality, well, it was only part of what Christopher had within him. So far the other part belonged to Eugene. *What Christopher needs is the skills to be able to control that precocious little savant before Eugene eats him alive*, Seth thought. But how to convince

Christopher to walk the path he would need to in order to find that control? He knew Sophia would offer Eugene no competition at this point, but it didn't help Seth to know how to put the offer to Christopher.

'Honesty,' Seth murmured to himself, 'and a little dash of what his heart most desires.' He smiled to himself. As far as he was concerned these were the things that made the world go around.

Realising she was speeding Sophia eased off the accelerator and took a deep breath. How could she tell Christopher what she was seeing when she didn't even want to acknowledge her own abilities? She already hated the way he looked at her like she was the eighth wonder of the modern world when she told him anything about it. But to Sophia it was perfectly obvious that the coming night was going to change all their lives forever and that no one was going to escape it. What she couldn't predict was in what ways. The encounter with Seth had already left her shaken, it seemed that him putting a name to what she was had just made it stronger.

Unbidden thoughts about Christopher came next. She remembered in a rush every look of concern, every hand squeeze or hug, him staying with her all night, and most of all how he had held her right up against his body. 'I think my brother's a bit sweet on you,' she heard Millicent's voice say in her memory.

'No Millicent,' Sophia said out loud in the empty car by way of an answer, 'I think it's me that's sweet on him. That boy is just too innocent for words.'

After they had walked around the hills and it had rained on them Christopher had come inside and taken his shirt off. Talking to her all the while he had unbuttoned his long-sleeve shirt and thrown it near the heater to dry. She had stared openly before he threw a towel around his shoulders. Looking up quickly he had caught her looking at his body and looked somewhere between surprised and embarrassed. His lack of ego touched her. The masculine lack of self-consciousness with which he wore his looks, and then that sudden boyish shyness...

'Damn,' she murmured to herself. *But God damn he has a body,* she thought. 'Maybe I should fuck him after all.'

She was instantly ashamed of this thought. She knew it cheapened what was developing between them, and at the same time she knew that's why she'd thought it. The hollow feeling in her breastbone and the quivering in her stomach both spoke of presentiment. She knew those feelings were sadness and fear. She didn't want to look at Christopher and have her Sight open up again. After all she had seen him bleeding and anyone she had ever saw bleeding like that...

When she reached home she packed her clothes, had a shower and dressed. With an odd smile she threw a handful of condoms into her handbag. *What the Hell,* she thought, *if not with Christopher why not Seth?* She shrugged. What did it matter anyway? *If not Seth why not a lesbian fling with Millicent, she'd be up for anything at the moment.* Sophia laughed bitterly at herself. When she saw the light starting to fade, she got up reluctantly and went into the bathroom to make her face up and put the last touches on her appearance.

'Hey, Christopher,' Millicent's voice said, as she breezed down the stairs and into the kitchen.

'You're looking surprisingly fresh this morning,' Christopher commented looking up from his laptop.

'Thank you,' she said, ignoring any other implications that the statement might have carried.

Christopher watched her put the kettle on, quietly observing her painted nails and the unfamiliar perfume that had wafted in with her. Watching her hum to herself as she made coffee he had to put his book down. There was something about it that disturbed him. He couldn't help thinking that she seemed in some kind of trance.

'Okay. Now is it just me or is something weird?'

'How do you mean?' she asked, pouring water into her cup.

Christopher suddenly lost the will to explain. He shrugged and went back to his reading. She seemed happier than usual after all. 'No, right you are. Everything's normal. As you were.'

Seth brings the force of catastrophic change in his wake indeed, Christopher thought. He smiled to himself and his pulse accelerated at the thought of the night that was coming. Whatever was coming with Seth, Christopher felt incapable in that moment of regretting it. He was ready to embrace change, if it came with fear and even pain, as most change does, then all the better.

As he had said to Seth, he was not afraid to bleed. What he did fear was a conflict of interests. If there was anything monstrous about Seth Christopher felt it would have nothing to do with his canine teeth or his light sensitivity. He didn't want to see Sophia scared. Yet the things Seth brought with him were what Christopher longed for. And he, personally, was ready for whatever was in stall for him.

Christopher met Sophia outside. She was wearing a short electric blue dress with shoestring straps. It was made from a satin-effect material and she had her knee high boots on. He smiled. As flashy and modern as her tastes were he had to admit she looked sexy.

He now knew that she was wearing a push-up bra, but somehow, knowing it was an illusion didn't decrease its effect on him. What really confused him was just how many pairs of shoes and handbags she owned. He didn't think he'd seen her with the same ones twice.

'Hi sweetie,' she said. 'Sorry I was gone for so long but my hair took forever. How did Millicent pull up?'

'That's the really weird thing,' he said, following Sophia towards the door. 'Millicent looks like drinking to excess and passing out does her the world of good. She's in there glowing, looking better than she ever has and getting around in a new perfume.'

Sophia laughed. 'Wow, you notice when a girl wears a new perfume. She's got it for Seth something shocking hasn't she?' she said, slapping Christopher's arm for emphasis.

'Ah huh.'

'Oh well, tonight will be interesting,' she muttered. 'Do you think he'd even be interested in her? I couldn't tell.'

'I think he'd sleep with her. I don't know if I'd call it 'interest'.'

'I see,' Sophia replied, as they headed up the stairs to put Sophia's bag back in the guest-room. 'You're looking handsome as usual, in your understated kind of way.'

Christopher laughed. 'In my better pair of jeans and one of my half-dozen white shirts? I wouldn't have thought 'understated' was your cup of tea?'

'On men it is. I've had that many clotheshorse boyfriends where I practically had to fight them for bathroom mirror space. It's really pathetic when your man is prettier than you.'

Christopher smiled. 'I don't think that would happen to you very often.'

'Don't smooth talk Christopher Penrose,' she said, punching him lightly in the arm. 'It doesn't suit you.'

'I wasn't. I'm obviously not great on the old pick-up lines am I? Anyway, I've just got to check something in the oven. Do you want me to fix you a drink?'

'Sure,' she said. 'Can I just get juice for now? I am so dehydrated.'

He headed downstairs with Sophia following him.

'Hi Sophia!' Millicent called from the other room. 'I love that dress, where did you get it?'

Sophia explained she'd bought it at *Next*.

When he came into the room he found Millicent was wearing their mother's clothes because she had nothing revealing to wear herself. She was dressed in a relatively short black skirt, a red blouse and a pair of rather 'seventies' heels.

'I turned the heater on in the sitting room,' Millicent said, when she saw Christopher. I figured we'd take our drinks in there again.'

They all went in and sat down. The conversation between Millicent and Sophia continued, but Christopher all but blocked it out. All he could think about was when Seth would arrive. When he got up to get the pies out of the oven he cast glances out the window at the gathering dark. Everyone had nibbled on the food. Millicent was on her second drink and Sophia had switched to alcohol before the doorbell rang. Although Christopher had been waiting for it, he could not possibly have beaten Millicent to it. She was on her feet in a second.

'I'll get it. Why don't you guys pick some music?'

Sophia felt much calmer tonight. She knew what to expect. When the sinking feeling in the pit of her stomach came and the cold clawing sensation began to make its way from the base of her spine to the hair at the back of her neck, she accepted it. On the first night it had been like some half-forgotten figure from a childhood nightmare had somehow penetrated into her adult waking hours. Understanding was quickly replacing cold terror. Seth winked at her when he entered. 'Sophia,' with a nod of his head.

Sophia was a little ashamed of herself for it, but she was glad Millicent was there. The other woman provided a welcome buffer. Sophia just didn't imagine Seth would be so brutally honest in the presence of Christopher's sister. Millicent's inane chatter had a soothing quality for her, it seemed to bring normality into the room and promise some predictable shape to the evening.

As Christopher greeted Seth and got him a drink Sophia watched Millicent playing with her top and showing Seth most of her cleavage in the action. Seth noticed Sophia rolling her eyes and smiled at her in quiet acknowledgement. *He's shameless,* she thought, *he includes himself in my scorn and yet he's still happy to look down her top.*

As Christopher re-entered the room Seth's attention was diverted away from Millicent again. There was a kind of mutual interest in one another between Christopher and Seth that Sophia couldn't fathom. She recognised sexual interest between people whenever she saw it, but when the interest was something else — Well, it went out of her realm of experience. It became mysterious. She found herself paying attention to it because of that mystery. Wanting to silence Millicent for Christopher's sake, so that he might speak to Seth himself, Sophia reached for her handbag.

'Spliff anyone?' she asked, pulling out a cigarette case and opening it.

'What's that?' Millicent asked.

'Marijuana,' Christopher answered, 'Seriously Millicent? I can't believe we went to the same primary and middle school. By the time I was twelve I knew that parents of friends were growing it under lights.'

'Oh, Christopher! Must you tell everyone about our hippie school experience? It was embarrassing enough while it was happening,' she said. 'You're seriously going to smoke drugs here?'

Sophia laughed, noting the pleasure that both men were taking in Millicent's sudden discomfit. She surprised herself then by allowing a little more of her own cleavage to show, consciously taking their attention away from Millicent.

'I was planning on it. Anyone?' she offered.

'Thanks,' Seth said, helping himself.

Christopher declined and poured himself another Scotch instead. Millicent looked back and forth between Seth and Sophia and seemed to read from them that she was being challenged.

'What does it do to you?' she asked nervously.

Seth had a slight smile playing about his mouth as he exhaled the first lungful of the smoke, almost into Millicent's face. 'It just relaxes you. Has analgesic effects as well.'

With the lascivious intent his words seemed to convey it didn't surprise Sophia at all when Millicent agreed.

'Okay. I guess there's a first time for everything.'

Sophia leaned over and passed her a joint, but it was Seth who took out his lighter to light it for her.

'You breathe it back and hold it for a little while before you let it out.' Sophia instructed, feeling for the entire world like she were back hiding behind the school and smoking in secret.

Millicent did what she was told and tried to repress her coughing.

'So what did you intend for tonight, Christopher?' Seth asked, his tone ambiguous.

'I don't know, I was going to wait and see what happened,' Christopher replied.

Seth smiled at him in his slow, knowing way. He even showed his teeth a little, but Millicent didn't seem to notice.

'You're very fond of that aren't you?' Seth said.

Christopher only smiled.

Millicent seemed uncomfortable then. 'I've got an idea,' she jumped in. 'Let's play Truth or Dare.'

Sophia looked at her scornfully. 'Truth or Dare?' she echoed.

Seth merely exchanged a glance with Christopher.

'Well it would help us get to know each other, plus it would make for an entertaining night.'

Bimbo! Sophia thought, *in your prize stupidity you've stumbled onto something these guys will love.*

'All right,' Christopher agreed.

Seth smiled when Christopher said it.

That would be right, she screamed at Seth in her head, hoping he could hear her. *You love it. You're like a whore doing a striptease.*

You like to play with what you reveal and what you conceal. And if you feel like living on the edge a little that night everyone else has to expose themselves too.

Seth looked up abruptly as though she had said something to him. For a while she held his unreadable gaze but was the first to look away.

'Are you up for that, Sophia?' Christopher asked.

She sensed the genuineness of his question. *Whoever said men aren't intuitive had never met these two, she thought.* His protective comment gave Sophia such a warm sensation that she nearly blushed. *What the fuck am I,* she asked herself, *sweet sixteen and never been kissed or something? I'm going nuts.* As though someone had challenged her Sophia found herself drawing her posture up a little straighter,

'Yeah, I'm up for it.'

'Excellent,' said Millicent, excitedly sitting forward in her chair. 'Now everyone must agree implicitly to answer truthfully or to go through with any dare that's judged reasonable by the majority of us. If anyone refuses they're out of the game.'

'Fair enough,' Seth agreed.

'Okay,' Christopher said.

Sophia just nodded.

'I'll toss a coin to see who goes first, then that person can pick someone, then they pick for themselves whether its truth or dare.'

'This is so juvenile,' Sophia murmured to herself, stubbing out her spliff.

She really didn't want to smoke any more if they were going to be playing this.

'Okay,' said Millicent, having found a coin. 'We'll do it between Christopher and I first, then the winner out of us can go against the next person. Heads or tails?' she asked Christopher.

'Tails.'

She threw the coin and turned it over on her hand,

'It's tails.' She handed the coin to Christopher. 'Now you go against Sophia.'

'Heads or tails, Sophia?' he asked, looking at her with a smile.

'Heads,' she replied.

He threw the coin and turned it over onto his hand.

'Heads it is,' he said, handing her the coin.

As she turned to ask Seth if he wanted heads or tails he was grinning at her with his dark eyes glittering maliciously.

'Do you want to win Sophia, or do you want me to?' he asked.

'I want to.'

'Heads then.'

Unable to look away she threw the coin and looked down at it on her hand.

'Tails,' she murmured.

'Damn,' he said, reaching for his beer.

Sophia's focus shifted from the outside to the inside. It felt as if she were swelling and expanding, almost to fill the room. It seemed that her mind had tentacles that could reach into any mental crevice and detect the energies around her. There were a hundred things she wanted to know. It was truth she desired from them most, and perhaps the urge was sadistic. Truth was, of course, what she most feared.

'Go on,' Seth prompted. 'It's a child's game otherwise, like using monopoly money to play poker.'

You're so fucking smug, she thought. She almost hated him in that moment. She extended her mind aggressively and let the hot pulsing in her forehead spread to the top of her skull. The heat in her seemed to lick at the darkness of Seth like a tongue of flame. A deluge of voices tumbled over her, rocked her and shook her, made her fear they would pull her apart. The fear almost shut her down but she steeled herself and let herself sink deeper into the maelstrom. Just when she thought she'd be pulled over, tugged off course and lost there, she clearly saw a girl there, standing behind Seth but some distance off.

'So is it truth or dare, Seth?'

'Which do you want from me?'

'Why don't you tell me, I imagine you know exactly what I want,' she shot back at him.

'Truth would be your poison I'd imagine,' he replied.

'Okay. Who was the girl with the dark eyes and hair and the little mole above her mouth on the... on the right side... and...' in the flush of power she felt no sense of Seth's feelings, or whether it was a low blow, '... and scars on her wrists.' She saw the pain flash through Seth's subtle being. She saw it as clearly as if his skin had just turned blue and his eyes had turned to blood. At the same time she knew he'd let her see his response, and she felt immediately ashamed by the fact.

'Her name was Lucrece,' he said, slowly and succinctly.

'What's going on?' Millicent asked, looking back and forth between Seth and Sophia.

'Sophia can see things,' he said, leaning forward with eerie tenderness as though he were speaking to a little child who happened to be in the room.

'Seth!' Sophia protested through gritted teeth.

'Well she's going to have to know if we're going to play this game,' he said, turning back to Millicent.

'What do you mean 'see things'? Like ghosts or something? Are you serious?' Millicent's tone sounded incredulous but it was Seth talking so her eyes were wide and accepting.

'Perfectly, my dear,' he said. 'That's how she knew that about me,' he said, looking at Sophia over Millicent's head. 'That is how she knew the appearance of the love of my life who committed suicide five years ago. She knows all our secrets. You should be afraid of her.'

Sophia scowled at him. His smile made her wish to claw it off his face.

'This is scary,' Millicent said.

Seth placed a soothing hand on her shoulder, as she was

sitting leaning up against the couch he was sitting on now. 'I'll protect you, Millicent.'

Sophia noticed Christopher shake his head almost impercep- tibly.

So even my sweet Christopher is too under his spell to protect his poor dumb sister, Sophia thought. *Great, he's going to eat her for breakfast, probably literally.*

'I'll go next,' Seth said. 'What would you like, truth or dare?'

'Dare,' Sophia replied.

'Thought you might. Okay. I dare you to throw that bloody mobile phone into the river.'

'My mobile?'

'Yes. Chuck it. Do people really need to contact you on a twenty-four seven basis? Does it warrant interrupting just about every important moment in your life?'

Sophia smiled ruefully. 'Some of us prefer important moments to be interrupted. But, yes, all right, I'll do it when I leave here.'

Seth nodded. 'Who's next?'

'I'll go,' Millicent said quickly.

Sophia noticed that the colour in her cheeks appeared unnat- urally flushed. It wasn't like the general flush from alcohol but instead two hectic spots of colour had appeared in her cheeks. Her eyes had a manic glimmer. It was disturbing.

'This is for, Christopher. Truth or dare baby brother?'

'Dare.'

'I dare you to have sex with a woman,' she declared triumphantly.

Sophia looked up in shock to see Christopher's reaction.

'Why?' he demanded.

'Well, you told me you're not gay, but you're still obsessed with Eugene. Until you've had sex with a woman how will you really know?'

Christopher flinched visibly at the mention of Eugene's name.

On his face Sophia could see irritation but with her other sight she saw Millicent's words wind him like a punch to the stomach. She hated Millicent for so casually wounding him. Christopher's reply was cool and didn't show what Sophia knew was there.

'Well I can't exactly do that right here and now. It's kind of not up to just me, with it involving a woman and all that.'

Millicent went to open her mouth to deliver her coupe de grace but Sophia heard herself speaking. 'I'll do it.'

In the brief moment that she had had to think about it, all Sophia could remember thinking was 'they're going to get him a prostitute or something.' Seeing the twinkle in Seth's eyes she wasn't ready to put it past him, and she knew that if both of them agreed to it she'd be out-voted. Christopher had agreed to the terms, she couldn't imagine him backing out.

The concept of him losing his innocence in such a way, a sleazy sort of way, much like how she'd lost hers, was alarming to her. It didn't occur to Sophia to even think about what the others would think of her, she just leapt to Christopher's rescue.

Sophia fiddled with her hair in the bathroom mirror. She had told Christopher to meet her while she fixed herself up. In truth there wasn't that much to do. She had showered and applied her makeup impeccably only an hour or so earlier, going into the bathroom was just an opportunity for Sophia to get her head together. *God, I bet Millicent thinks I'm such a slut.* The next instant she realise that Millicent probably wouldn't care if she jumped Christopher on the floor in front of them, so long as she got her go at Seth while they did it. One last time Sophia looked at herself in the mirror. She couldn't believe how her heart was pounding. *This is so weird,* she thought.

As she came out of the bathroom she started to think about Christopher. *I bet the poor kid's nervous as Hell.* Sophia was just glad that she'd had so much experience and would have no trouble setting him at his ease, showing him what to do and making sure nothing got uncomfortable. She knocked on the door as a formality and then walked straight in. Christopher was sitting in the deep windowsill. He was in profile to her, his legs drawn up on the ledge, leaning against the sill looking out. She was surprised by how casual and reflective he looked sitting there in his beaten up boots and his hair needing a cut.

'Is it cool if I turn these lights down to dim? If I'm getting my gear off I like the light flattering.'

Christopher didn't answer. He didn't really get the chance to before she turned the switch down to the lowest setting possible without plunging them into darkness.

'You just need to relax hon,' she said, sitting down on the bed to unzip her boots. 'We're good friends and you know how much I care about you. Who better to have your first time with?'

Still he hadn't spoken. Sophia went barefoot across to him, wearing only her blue slip of a dress. She wanted to reach out to him but his silence and motionless prevented her.

'I hope you don't mind, I'm a major safety girl. I'm so unready for children it's stupid. I'm on the pill and I have never had sex in my life without at least one condom.'

She pulled out some condoms from her handbag and started throwing an assortment onto the bed. 'I've got ribbed, they're my favourite. Ultra-thins, they should be your favourite. Then there are the novelty ones... but you don't look like the novelty kind of...'

Before she could finish he got up, walked over and in one sweep pushed all of the condoms onto the floor.

She looked up at him in confusion. His hands closed around her arms and pulled her close to him. There was a moment where she just stood there, even more confused by their sudden proximity than by his recent action. Then she felt his fingertips against her cheek.

'Why are you doing this?' he murmured.

She felt his breath against her skin and his words carried such a tender sincerity that it constricted her chest for a moment.

'Doing what?' she managed to get out.

'This,' he whispered, looking at her with pain in his face. 'This... I don't know... this bullshit.' Now her heart was absolutely thundering. She realised she had never seen Christopher ruffled like this before, never seen him display so much obvious emotion. 'You said you're on the pill.' She nodded. 'And you've always used at least one condom?' She nodded again. She didn't understand what he was getting at or why the expression of pain and frustration on his face.

'And I'm a virgin. So why do you want to use a condom?'

'Are you seriously suggesting we have unsafe sex? What if...' she cut herself off because she couldn't think of a plausible reason. Without warning Christopher took her face between both of his hands and raised it so he could look into her eyes.

'I want to be inside you. Not through latex. I want you.' He touched her face in a slow almost experimental sort of way. To her disbelief she could feel herself yielding to him, to his touch, to the passion in his voice and to his request. He leaned slowly down and touched her lips with his. His kiss was soft at first and hesitant but it quickly gained in pressure.

He drew her bottom lip into his mouth first. Then his lips pressed down on hers and she opened her mouth naturally to admit his tongue. The touch of his tongue sent an electric shock wave through her that left her disorientated. Her arms went up around his neck of their own accord.

He kissed her so skilfully her head reeled. He might be a virgin, she thought, but if I'm any judge this is *by far* not his first kiss. By the time he broke the kiss off she was dimly aware that she had never felt anything like that before. Before she could gather her self-possession he started kissing her neck. The unmistakeably male sensation of stubble grazing her skin made her tense involuntarily. Everything seemed out of control and she didn't know how it had happened.

Christopher's hand stroked her arm reassuringly. 'Are you all right?' he murmured.

She nodded, feeling silly. *Why do I feel so nervous?* She asked herself. *He's so much more of a gentleman than any other man I've slept with, and it's him that's meant to be nervous.* But in the moment when Christopher pulled aside the tiny straps on her dress and let it fall from her shoulders, she suddenly knew what it was. *He's not natural,* she thought, *this isn't natural. How can he be so confident and so inexperienced at the same time?*

'Do you really want me, Sophia?' he asked and she could hear vulnerability in his voice then, just for a moment.

'Yes,' she said quietly, 'I think I really do... a lot.'

He smiled at her. 'Can I please take your dress off?'

She nodded and gasped as she felt the material slide down around her waist. He pulled it down over her hips until it fell to the carpet leaving her only in her underwear. With one hand he pulled out the clip in her hair allowing it to fall down around her shoulders. Slowly he lay her down on her back on his bed. She had imagined she would be on top so she could show him what to do. Instead Christopher seemed to have a fair idea of what he wanted to do.

He knelt beside her, paused to undo the buttons on his shirt and take it off, followed by his singlet. Having removed half of his clothes he came down over her, eagerly kissing her mouth. She responded to him passionately, opening her mouth for his tongue and parting her legs so he could lie between them. His hand closed around her breast and she gasped at the unexpected feeling. There was a growing hunger in her to feel his hands on her body. She could feel his erection pressing against her pubic bone, it felt urgent and possessive, but Christopher himself seemed surprisingly unhurried. The heat between her legs was growing and she was shocked at the effect it had when he touched her. She had never felt her fluid gush out of her like that before. With a sudden touch of a man's impatience Christopher fought with her front fastening bra.

'Thank God, you *are* human,' she whispered, her voice husky.

He just laughed and pulled it back to reveal her naked breasts. She hadn't expected him to draw back and pause to look at them. His eyes looked warm. His expression showed he appreciated what he saw. But even in the dim light she felt uncomfortable. Normally Sophia was more than happy to show off her gym-toned, waxed, tanned body. But now... she was, for the first time, so desperate for the man to be pleased by what he saw that it made her shy.

'I've done that a couple of times in my imagination,' he whispered as he reached out his hand and caressed her naked breast. He gasped quietly when he felt it in his hand.

'Really?' she couldn't help quietly asking.

'I am a man, Sophia.'

He smiled as he ran his hands over her. It felt like he was learning the territory of her and at the same time enjoying her too much to care whether he was doing it right. She moaned as his mouth found her nipple. Closing her eyes she felt like she was going to burst into tears or something equally silly. She was so full of desire and so full of words she wanted to say to him, but she didn't dare. As he kissed and sucked her breasts she felt him press between her legs. Those little, almost involuntary presses that a man does when he really wants to enter you. The thought made her smile.

'Touch me, Christopher, hurry,' she murmured.

'I thought I was meant to go slow?'

'You are. But don't,' she said, not even trying to be rational. 'Take them off.'

Kneeling up Christopher obliged, leaving her completely naked. Before she could grab him as she had intended to he was back on the bed again his mouth seeking her breasts. She could feel his fingers between her legs. She parted her thighs eagerly, desperately wanting that touch, and completely amazed at how well he was doing it.

'How do you know how to do this?' she gasped, looking up at him as he rubbed her right where she wanted him too and began seeking to fill her with his fingers.

'Reading about it,' he said, breathless too. 'Nothing mysterious.' Then she felt his fingers in her and she moaned. He was kissing her stomach, running his tongue over her skin. He just seemed so into her that it was a turn on in itself. Never before had she really wanted to please a man like she wanted to please Christopher. She thought about throwing him off her and going down on him. But she couldn't move to stop him as he parted her legs further and kissed her lower and lower until his mouth was between her legs. When his tongue found her clitoris the last of her thoughts and her tension left her. She writhed under him, gently pressing herself against his tongue. The most exciting thing of all was the sounds of enjoyment he made as he discovered and explored the crevices of her. When she was so hot and slippery with wetness that she could hardly lay still he kissed his way back up her body until he was looking down at her.

'I love you,' he whispered, with such a sincerity that she could not doubt he meant it. She closed her eyes, squeezed them shut tight. She heard him undo his jeans; she felt what she had been waiting for, his cock pressing into her. Never had she been penetrated so easily. He went into her in three partial thrusts, looking down at her for reassurance at first, and then squeezing his eyes shut.

Sophia knew what it felt like to have a flesh and blood erection inside her for the first time. And it was beautiful. She nearly laughed with happiness as she looked up at him and she relished the pleasure and pain of his eager thrusts. When she saw his mouth open with the shock of the pleasure, his eyes turn unfocused with it, she had to kiss him. It seemed such a privilege suddenly to be introducing him to these feelings, almost holy. He pressed his forehead against hers for the last few thrusts. Then she felt the tension go out of him and the warm unfamiliar sensation of being filled with a man's semen. He lay panting on her for a couple of moments. She didn't want him to move. Really it hadn't lasted very long at all, but it seemed timeless, as though they were one before the beginning of time.

After a moment, he rolled off her and they lay there in silence. Their breathing sounded so loud to Sophia in the new stillness. Then he turned to her and kissed her.

'Thank you,' he said quietly, 'I just want you to know I want to do that again. Now. And that that was... something very amazing.'

Sophia turned her head away so he wouldn't see she had tears in her eyes.

8

'And the dead leaves
Come to cover the dead
Dead children now and then speak with their mother
And dead women now and then long to come back
Oh! I do not want you to return
The autumn is full of disembodied hands
No, no these are dead leaves
They are the hands of the dear dead
They are your disembodied hands.'
—Apollinaire

Sophia went for a walk afterwards 'to think', as she put it, leaving Christopher alone in his room. He sat in the chair beside his bed in only his jeans and the boots that he had not had the presence of mind to remove earlier. Images of Sophia made their way back and forth in his mind and every now and again he would smile slightly. It felt strange that it had really happened. It was such a cataclysmic change in their relationship, and yet in a way it had been so gradual, that he had fallen in love. Of course he'd thought about it. As he'd told Sophia 'he was a man.' But the thoughts had only been dreams, fantasies, not thoughts with intent or seriousness behind them.

'My God,' he murmured to himself, as he let his head fall back against the chair. He shook his head slowly. It was surreal, he decided—that was the word for it. He hadn't felt nervous, he had just known he wanted her and he wasn't prepared to try and hide it. And then when it happened, when he felt himself moving inside her, it had shocked him.

He had never been one of those boys who joined in when the other boys went mad about sex. Christopher's desire had always been manageable, rational. But then he had not known how it would feel. He remembered her naked body beneath him, her breasts in his hands, his body between her legs that wrapped around him in passion. Nobody could have prepared him for how it made him feel when she moaned. Knowing he was pleasing her... It was some kind of crazy drug. Shutting his eyes he replayed every movement of her body, every gasp, in slow motion.

Yet something subterranean in him hurt. He couldn't quite word to himself what it was, but he knew it was connected with Eugene. In his mind, as he sat there, he came right up to the door of asking himself if he'd liked to have done something similar to that with Eugene, but he didn't enter the room. He lingered outside the threshold of that place, savouring the strange mixture of sweetness and sadness that the loss of his virginity had left him with. The question of whether it should have happened some other way seemed to hang in the air but never settle. As right as it had felt to be with Sophia, there was sadness so deep, underneath that feeling, and he could not fathom how far down it might go. If he began to explore it, he feared he'd drown. It was better to linger on the warmth of finally understanding what it felt like to be fully alive below the waist.

As soon as she had closed the door to Christopher's room Sophia felt it. Immediately a sick coldness coiled in her stomach. Someone was there, and it wasn't Seth or Millicent. And yet the physical presence of another human breathing in the darkness with her was so strong that it could have been.

When she reached the landing Sophia stopped and closed her eyes for a few breathes, trying to get her rising fear under control. Before she even looked she knew there was someone on the stairs. Finally, like a frightened child peeking through their fingers Sophia forced herself to open her eyes. Even though she expected it she jumped when she saw the shadowy figure of below average adult height that stood about half way down the stairs. Her heart accelerated even faster. Nothing petrified Sophia more than the children...

But it wasn't quite a child, it was something much worse and it was waiting for her. She hesitated at the top of the stair one foot suspended in the air about to descend. There was something of mute implied challenge to the boy's stance. Like heat haze on a pavement in summer, the stairs began to swim and she felt that where she wanted to place her foot was no longer solid.

'Let me past, Eugene,' she said with as much confidence as she could muster. But her voice didn't even fool her. It came out thin and reedy in the still, close air. Sophia couldn't see Eugene's face but she knew it was him. She had seen him a good few times now; this pale, silent creature with those strange, preternaturally intelligent eyes that would fix her with their bottomless stare, his form entirely still. She knew it was Eugene because his presence was so strong it made the darkness feel like sackcloth held over her nose and mouth and there were few ghosts she'd ever encountered who were that powerful.

'No,' he replied, full of self-assurance. His voice was not yet fully broken but was deeper than a child's. It held a throaty adult complexity that both intimidated and intrigued her. 'I have a better idea,' he whispered. 'Why don't you never come here again?'

'Why don't you get the hell out of my way?' Sophia flared up at him. Forgetting for a moment she was speaking with the dead, whose knowledge and powers she did not fully know. She simply took umbrage to being spoken to like that by a thirteen year old boy.

'Make me.'

Sophia swallowed hard and forced herself to take a step toward him.

'I might not be able to make you. But you can't stop me coming down these stairs.'

'Can't I?'

The shadowy form shifted slightly and she felt a swelling in the air and a pressure in her temples. Gripping the banister tightly in her hand to avoid falling Sophia tried not to give him the satisfaction of seeing her stumble.

'You can't do anything to me unless I'm afraid of you.' Her voice had that reedy sound again and she cursed herself inwardly for her cowardice and bad acting.

Eugene laughed then. It sounded cheerful and bubbly, but the sound of childish laughter in the darkness froze her blood down to its very innermost wellspring.

'That's an interesting theory. But irrelevant, as you *are* afraid of me.'

'I am not afraid of you,' she said it as an affirmation, with all the determination she could muster. 'And I'm not leaving him.'

'Why don't you come down then?' He continued to stand in the very middle of the stair. Sophia hesitated. 'Come on, Sophia,' he prompted. 'If you're not afraid of me you won't mind coming down here and squeezing past my cold body.'

Sophia sucked in her breath and held it. It was like he knew how to conjure up the dread of every terrible encounter of her childhood.

'But that's it isn't it?' she managed to say. 'That's the only power you have isn't it?'

'If it was it would suffice, would it not?' Eugene mused, leaning against the wall.

As he moved into this posture, one pale hand caught the light from a window. Sophia's mind flashed on an image from her childhood. It was of a fish's pallid under-belly in the moonlight when her grandfather had taken her night fishing. She shuddered.

'Human dread is a powerful force,' he whispered.

Sophia blocked out this disturbingly adult comment and continued to walk steadily toward him. As she got closer she kept telling herself, he died of a heart abnormality it's not going to be horrific, he's got no massive head wound or anything up his sleeve. But it didn't stop her pausing when she was standing only a stair above him. *Jesus, the light doesn't pass through him.* She flattened herself to the wall and slid past him. For a moment she was, back to the wall, facing Eugene. His face was half obscured but the pale light caught the contours of it. He was strange, ethereal. He might have been pretty if he wasn't so pale. And so dead... He was just staring at her steadily, waiting. It was as though his eyes had their own faint light source behind them. And then the electric light above their heads flicked on, plunging Sophia's darkness adjusted eyes into retina-shocking brightness.

Sophia yelped in shock. Before she covered her eyes with her hands she caught a flash of Eugene's pale face, dark under the eyes and blue at the lips only inches from her face. Still half blinded by the light she ran clumsily down the rest of the stairs. Behind her she could hear his boyish laughter.

Christopher got up, pulled on his shirt and headed downstairs to see Seth. He sensed that Seth understood about this sort of thing, and he also felt that in that moment there was some kind of window of opportunity during which intimacy might emerge between the two of them.

As he stepped out onto the landing Christopher experienced a slight prickle on the back of his neck, even though someone had left the light on. The air seemed unnaturally still and almost viscous. He lingered there for a moment sniffing at the air like a curious puppy. It had seemed for a moment like the landing and the stairs smelt of hospital disinfectant. The smell disturbed him; it tugged painfully at deeply buried sense memories.

This feeling in the air, this phantom smell, these things that Christopher would have once considered to be his imagination now held the possibility of truth. He considered whispering Eugene's name. Christopher paused on the stair. For a moment he was quite overcome by how close Eugene felt. It made him catch his breath and then his heart began to hammer with a mixture of dread and a thick, deep desire that he had no words for. The feeling had no name and yet it welled up from his core like viscous black blood.

Leaning against the wall, half way down the stairs, Christopher closed his eyes. He was trembling a little now and yet he wanted to get closer and closer to that feeling, no matter how cold it was.

'Eugene?' he whispered.

As usual the utterance of Eugene's name seemed to skin Christopher and make the air feel as empty as the darkness of space. Then he heard the distinct sound of the light switch flicking and the stairs were plunged into darkness. Christopher gasped quietly, his heart pounded and he swallowed hard, and yet he had no intention of running away. Yet to Christopher's intense frustration it felt like the light flicking off had somehow exhausted the building energy in the room and he now knew he was utterly alone.

When Christopher entered the room Seth was leaning on the window sill looking out. Christopher had come in very quietly. He was about to speak to avoid startling Seth when Seth without turning around said,

'Hello, Christopher.'

'How did you know it was me?'

'I can see your reflection in the glass,' he smiled as he turned to Christopher. 'How was she?'

Christopher had to think for a moment before answering the question. For a moment he was confused by what Seth meant because what had happened with Eugene on the stairs was still rioting through his consciousness. When he finally collected his thoughts Christopher wanted to say something about the wonder of it and the sadness all at the same time. He didn't want to say something trite.

'Quite amazing,' he replied, taking a seat.

Seth came and sat down across from him.

'Good,' he said. 'I really don't think we could be really close unless you'd done it with a woman you were insane about.' Christopher wanted to deny he was 'insane' about Sophia but instead found it was a pretty apt description. 'Or a *person* you were insane about, as the case may be,' Seth added.

Christopher looked up at Seth then and nodded thoughtfully in response to this qualifier.

'I don't know what to say about it,' Christopher said, changing the topic.

He wanted to be 'real' with Seth. But there was simply a depth he couldn't go to yet, he couldn't talk in detail about other things he was 'insane' about. If he gave words to that then he feared he would never be able to push it back inside him.

'Did you see visions Christopher?'

'Visions?'

'Yeah, did you see things? Did you get a little look at the ecstasy of death?'

Christopher smiled. He loved Seth for being able to ask a question like that. But at the same time this mention of death prickled the surface of his skin.

'Yes. For a moment,' he began. 'It was like my mind was compressed to a bubble, and it was bobbing on the sea. A wave swept over it and burst it and my mind was dispersed across the universe. Everything was unutterable blackness.'

Seth nodded.

'Have you ever heard the term 'petite morte'?'

Christopher nodded.

'It's a French term for orgasm isn't it? "The little death."'

'Indeed. Only thing is there ain't a thing 'little' about it when there's love, and when there's magic. And yet at other times... it can just be fun. I fucked your sister and drank her blood. That was just fun.' Seth held eye contact all the while as he spoke and waited impassively for a reaction. 'Are you angry with me?'

Christopher blinked a couple of times and searched inside himself for what he felt.

'Maybe I should be,' he said quietly.

'But?'

'Is she all right?'

'She's bruised and tender in a couple of places, but she'll be fine tomorrow. She really enjoyed it actually. She kept begging me to bite her again. I love it when I find one like that.'

He was still looking at Christopher as he lit up his cigarette. There was a brief silence and extended eye contact between them that held a deepening tension. Christopher could see there were many layers to what was going on between them in those moments. There were questions of ethics, of trust, or how far they could go together and when it was too far. Christopher took a deep breath,

'Truth or dare?' he said.

Seth smiled.

'Truth,' he replied, exhaling his smoke in that long meditative way of his. Christopher leaned forward in his seat with the urgency of what he wanted to ask. His heart hammered.

'Tell me about *her*, Seth. Tell me all and anything you can bear to, about her, about you, about all and only the stuff that really counts. I want to know what you think about at night. What your pain is, when you lived most. And if you want me to, I'll tell you anything you want to know about Eugene; things I can barely speak of, things I've never told anyone.'

Christopher shocked himself by adding that offer to the end. In a way he hoped Seth wouldn't take him up on the last bit, but it seemed only fair if he was asking for an equal revelation.

After a moment Seth nodded.

'All right,' he said quietly, and there was an unmistakeable rawness in his voice. 'I hope you're not embarrassed easily, either by sex or emotion, because I promise you neither decency or stoicism.'

'I'm not too easily embarrassed,' Christopher said. 'But if I can be, I want you to embarrass me.'

'As you wish.'

And so Seth began to tell his tale. Even while he was speaking and letting Christopher hear the words of it, he was lost in it himself. The images rose before his inner eye as though they were all happening again. To tell Christopher was to live every sensation, to be racked by every utterance, to give birth to the narrative of it. The words let his pain crackle across the air between him and Christopher and ripped apart the space between them. Seth knew there would be no turning back the deluge now. Her face was inexorably before him, as beautiful as his doom, as certain as the fact that all things pass...

...Her white throat thrashed with breath. The voice of her father faded into the background of things, along with the song of birds and the aeroplane that passed overhead, on that day. All he was aware of in the universe was the pendent that lay at the base of her throat, in the little hollow there, and the pulse behind it that moved it slightly. Then he was being moved on. She smiled surreptitiously.

Later, through a hedge he had time to feast voluptuously on the sight of her. His body had prickled hot all over with the voyeurism of it, seeing into that closed garden through the tangled hedgerow. He, outside that hedged space and yet penetrating it with his gaze. Her, sitting there under the tree, her skirt spread around her on the grass, her book resting on her knee. Seth studied her hungrily. He knew the dark sweep of her thick eyelashes, the ivory line of her jawbone, the tiny mole above her mouth on the right side and the tapered fingertips of her pianist's hands. He knew she could play. He had listened to her, standing on upturned buckets to look through windows, half way up workmen's ladders, crouching on tree branches in the darkness. Shutting his eyes he would drink in her playing as though it contained her soul, as though it were a secret message. In silent despair, in unutterable, inexplicable agony he watched her. But more than anything else he knew that 'other thing' about her. The thing that made her smell different to other people, made her music even sound different to when other people played. Only he noticed these differences in her it seemed.

At night, he couldn't explain any of it to himself, as he lay awake in his family's cottage. He felt no immediate relationship between this emotion and anything he'd ever heard about love in a song or a poem. There was nothing in his experience that prepared him for it. He told no one of his pain, not even his father, with whom he shared a great, though unspoken, bond. In her vague sort of way his mother would smile when she noticed him off his food.

'You're in love dear, tis common.'

She didn't think to question with what girl Seth was in love. But it wasn't common for Seth. Maybe it never is. Perhaps Seth could have confided in his father. The deep silences of Seth's father, Heath, were unfathomable and felt as ancient as the land he'd lived on all his life. Heath had spent too much time alone in the woodlands, or so Seth's mother said. Spent too much time in a green space, thinking of nothing but the ways of animals, tales of Robin Hood and faeries, she said. Seth's mother was a fragile sort of woman who appeared strangely traumatised by life. Seth blamed his sickness for her anxieties. Heath was the one that Seth could talk to about his sickness. His gift, his curse, his secret. It had been Heath with his gnarled woodsmen's hands that first gave him the fresh blood of a rabbit when he was suffering with anaemia as a child. Seth remembered those hands of the earth, silently offering him the forest's sacrament that had brought back his health.

Maybe that is why it is different, Seth had thought. Maybe that was what caused this scorch across his brain, this dark thumping ache behind his breastbone. Maybe he felt like this because he was a 'vampire'. He didn't know. Nobody had yet given him that word for what he was. He just knew that when her eyes, almost ebony under her brow, had looked up unbidden as though she sensed his gaze and searched the gaps in the hedge till they almost fell into his, he burned. And he knew they were *alike*.

Lucrece was the daughter of the man his father worked for, a man who trusted Seth's father. He and his wife only had one daughter, Lucrece. Her mother seemed a Romantic and impulsive sort of woman. She seemed to enjoy the sound of her own speaking voice and always spoke for her daughter in public. Seth knew deep in his bones that Lucrece and he were each other's doom. It seemed obvious somehow. And he headed toward her accordingly, as any young man of passion seeks his destruction. He had no romantic conceptions about this; he did not find the disaster alluring. It was just unavoidable. The dark face of Mother Fate.

It had started with a crawling sensation in his guts that had prickled its way up his spine. It raised every hair and made it vibrate minutely in each follicle. It was a recognition. Whatever it is in nature that draws the moth to flame, that force was at work in Seth. It was Nature, and yet it was nature intensified by the eye, by his human eyes that had behind them the great reptilian expanse of the lower cortex, topped by the angel-machine of the neo-cortex, shedding bright light on the mechanisms of the reptile within. It was busy, highlighting, emphasising flesh, form, and movement with a dream-like aura. His higher mind wrapped a glamour around her image, an erotic haze like the fading significance of a dream from the night before as the day wears on. Except that the glamour never faded. Lucrece remained totem like, dominating his imagination with an atavistic fervour.

As the days wore on the torment had been this: their glances, her music, her reading, all gave him tantalising glimpses into what lay inside that englamoured casing, yet he could not get close enough to her. And if he could get close to her what would he say? Lucrece's father had allowed Seth to use his extensive library for some time, but Lucrece never seemed to be in that part of the house when he was. All he could manage to find out was that she was nineteen, a year younger than him.

He broke in the afternoon one spring day. He had been reading poetry. Staring at the ticking clock and seeing the light curtain billow with the breeze, the book he was holding slid, almost noiselessly, to the floor. It didn't matter, he sensed in the throbbing in his temples. Seth sensed it in the surge of his arteries. None of the consequences mattered if he could... If he could, like in his dreams. In his dreams he did not know the difference between having his erection inside her and his complete submersion in her. It seemed mystical. In his dream he was thrusting between her legs and also within the beauty of her dark eyes, the place he couldn't reach. Stars glittered there beyond that darkness. Those stars seemed to spin so fast afterwards that he knew it must be the chaos of ultimate destruction he was witnessing. Finding himself awake in the warm confines of his narrow bed with his spilt seed on him, this death felt like emptiness, a hollowness in his stomach.

And now in that moment as he watched the wind play carelessly with the curtain, and a bee droning on a flower, he felt himself dying again. All of Nature's unheeding movement was churning around him in the quiet. For the first time in his obsession with Lucrece he heard a phrase of poetry echo in his psyche with which he could relate. It was a few simple lines from Yeats' *An Irish Airman Foresees His Death*:

'The years to come seemed wasted breath,

A waste of breath the years behind

In balance with this life, this death.'

As soon as he thought it Seth went for the library door and

threw it open. Without thought or fear he charged up the stairs to her room. He knew where it was from looking through the windows with his binoculars. When he reached the door he had grabbed the handle and went to storm into her room and say or do he knew not what. But as he tried to enter she had been coming out and they collided.

The girl gasped, coming up hard against Seth's body. Seth would remember that moment for the rest of his life. It had been ever so brief, yet so full of the most intense agony and mad excitement. Neither spoke. Their eyes locked and their breathing was a tumult. She smiled... Smiled a full smile that showed her sharp teeth. She grabbed Seth's arm and dragged him into a run. They raced down the stairs, him following suit, with no under-standing but not caring where or why she was running.

They raced out into the garden and then beyond its confines into the woods and they kept going. Lucrece stopped only when they were in a clearing. She turned to him with her eyes wild and her hair dishevelled. Another mental snapshot, her, there, her strange pale face flushed in the cheeks and nose. She had stopped and spun in the dappled sunlight, and as he watched her he saw her shut her eyes against the faint light as though it hurt her. He had heard it all of course, the local gossip.

'Of course she's not right, never has been,' they would say. 'God knows it's probably that father of hers who's to blame.'

'I think the mother,' another would say, disagreeing with the first.

Lucrece had looked at Seth almost evilly from under her brows and beckoned to him. Her eyes seemed unnaturally wild.

'I mean, the Denison boys said they were the ones to rescue her the night she climbed the bell tower. They found her up there on a winter's night in nothing but her underpants. Not even a bra! And God knows what happened before they took her to the Police Station.'

Seth saw it almost in slow-motion: Her turning and running

to the boundary fence of her father's property and then climbing under it. Him climbing through after her and them lying in the dirt holding hands... He saw them lying there while the gentle rain started, laughing at intervals but not knowing why.

'The family is embarrassed that's all. I think it's just a weakness of mind. The mother's a bit soft brained but all in all they're all right folks. The whole town was out by the time the ambulance took her away after all.'

'What did she do?' Someone had asked.

Seth hadn't been able to bear doing anything that felt so tawdry as to gossip about her.

'They had a sheet over her, nobody knows.'

But Seth knew. He knew then as he kissed the long, elegant white scars on her inside arms. Almost as though this gesture catalysed something between them they were suddenly against each other. Lucrece was gripping his face, digging her nails in slightly.

'Do it to me, Seth,' she said fiercely. 'You have to, or I'll die.'

'So will I,' he told her, as he half undid half ripped her dress off.

'Hurry,' she cried, tearing at his shirt. They started kissing and her tongue was in his mouth and his hands found her naked breasts. She was moaning, half hysterical. But it made a kind of sense to Seth. He figured he would probably do the same if he could speak. The desire to be all through her system, to run in her veins, to drink her in, it was almost too much for him. She was dragging down her panties, frankly offering those secret parts of herself to him. Opening herself with her fingers like a Sheila-na-Gig fertility idol.

'I'm yours, Seth,' she declared passionately, with an almost menacing intensity. 'Do it. Do whatever you want.'

He didn't have to think, he put his hand straight between her legs. But he couldn't stand it for long. He dragged her up onto her knees. There she was before him, her breasts bare and her hair full of bracken fern. Holding her face between his hands he looked at her for a moment. She just smiled in that crazy way of hers and nodded ascent to his unasked question. He unzipped his trousers then and gently drew her down towards his groin. Still smiling she went down on her hands and knees and began to suck him. As he went into her mouth he saw stars dancing behind his eyes. He ran his hands through her hair and caressed her breasts. It made him tense every time he felt the light but careful touch of her sharp teeth. Satisfied by the feeling he pulled her back and laid her down. She pulled him down on top of her.

'Break me quickly, Seth.'

And there it was, the beautiful nightmare of it, the tight, wet little opening that gave beneath his passion. How he moaned then to feel her push back and drive him into her by wrapping her legs around him. She alternated between chanting,

'Ow, ow, ow,' and 'Oh, oh, oh,' depending on whether pleasure or pain was dominant at that particular moment.

But Seth did not dare slow down or be gentler, as her thrusts back were as strong as his into her. After a while she cried for it to be deeper and he had pulled her legs up against her chest and gone into her again. This time he made her eyes roll back in her head. But then he wanted something else. He wanted everything. He pulled himself away from her and pulled her panting onto her hands and knees,

'Hurry!' she cried again. Seth rubbed her wetness up into her backside and began to enter her there as well, gently at first, his hands holding a fistful of her dress at either hip. She moaned and wriggled and when he was all the way in, he began to thrust. 'Harder Seth, hurt me a little more,' she murmured.

Seth did as she asked. He understood. She wanted to know that he'd fucked her. She wanted to know it everywhere, just like he wanted to be everywhere. When she felt his seed go in she moaned. He came down over her for the final convulsion. They both lay in the dead bracken and dirt for a few moments, breathing hard, wet with sweat and light rain.

'There's more that you want,' she whispered. He hesitated. It felt so exposing because she was right and he was terrified to answer. 'Don't be afraid, Seth. Do it all.'

Seth took her in his arms. He took her in his arms with guilt and shame and tenderness. And then he bit her hard and fast. Not the seductive precision piercing you see in vampire movies, but a hard driving of a canine into flesh. She cried out and arched back, choking a little. He had expected this even though he'd never done it like this before. And oh the ecstasy of it... His mouth filled with her blood slowly and he drew at the wound hard, demandingly. Lucrece was trembling in his arms but she was moaning. She pushed back her head offering her throat. There was no control; he ravaged her throat as he had ravaged the rest of her. And the most intoxicating thing of all was that she loved it.

Seth never knew how he got away with what he did to her. However, he would wonder, did she get back home, her clothing torn, hobbling with his invasion of her virgin orifices, her neck bruised and blood in her tangled hair. But at the time he was intoxicated. He would have taken any risk to do it again. And he, they, did take any risk, over and over again. It was almost too painful to remember the beauty of the first time he'd let her drink his blood. Seth remembered them sitting in the woods both wearing sun-hats and sunglasses on an overcast day. He rolled up his sleeve and showed Lucrece his veins. She stared at them the same way he tended to stare at veins. As he took out the scalpel he'd brought with him and slowly cut a gash in his own forearm it seemed exciting rather than painful because he could see the flash of hunger in her eyes.

'Here you go, baby,' he whispered, tenderly bringing her face and his wound together. He had pulled in his breath hard at the pain and the thrill of her demanding sucking. For a moment he'd closed his eyes and let his head drop back. But then he wanted to watch her while she did it. He had not been disappointed.

Smouldering black and hot with hunger her eyes were also slightly unfocused from enjoyment. Just watching her his erection felt so rigid and throbbed so hard he thought he might climax right there and then. The empathy with her was total. He found himself whispering things to her while she drank from him like, 'I know. Oh, I know.' He knew the hunger. He knew also how she had been made to feel ashamed, and what it was to be asked to do it, to be given it.

All thoughts of whether Seth could ever be Lucrece's social equal seemed irrelevant when they were together like that. Yet when it happened, Seth knew what a shock it must have been to Mr Hanson-Stoke to find them in the library. Her hands were on the windowsill, her knees on a chair and he was taking her from behind, while she moaned loud enough to summon all their dooms from Hell.

The backhand across the face didn't even stun him back to reality. He was too full of the drug of her. It had drowned out all sense of duty or obligation, all sense of social propriety or nicety. Even when he saw her stand before her father defiantly, her breasts still exposed.

'Go to Hell,' she told him. The man's shock and fury had been palpable, so much so that he had not been able to stop her from delivering her last blow. She knelt before Seth and began to lick the blood from off his face, as it ran out of his mouth at the site of her father's blow. 'Surely you understand? He's just like we are.'

As Seth took his first good, up close look at Lucrece's father, he knew that this was true. But he did not have long to continue to make sense of things and there were so many things left undone. He wanted to go after her as her father dragged her away, he wanted to open an artery for her and let her have anything he could bleed out. There was no chance to make sense of the chaos behind her eyes or the ache she had created between his legs, for he was never to see her alive again.

Village gossip was his epilogue to her, just as it had been the prologue. According to the whispers of ghoulish local gossips and the Newspapers, from which he cut out her photo whenever he saw it, it had happened two nights after they were separated. It was to be that elapse of two nights that was to haunt Seth most as he tried to piece together the events that led up to her death.

Lucrece was found down by the river. She was down-river of the county bridge, about half a mile, naked and lacerated in several places. The cause of death was judged to be suicide, and her underwear was recovered on the bridge, along with her ripped dress. The dress was stuffed with torn pages from her diary that had apparently contained lovesick mania about some boy and some very depressive and mentally ill rants.

There was nothing, as far as Seth could find out, that alluded to her suicide directly or to her previous attempts. Nor was there any word of the secret they had shared. Why had they shared it? Through what infidelity or wild coincidence it had happened he was never to know. His Mother had become hysterical when she found out that Seth was with Lucrece. He had known it would be bad but could never have imagined she would consider the idea so awful. Was he really so very inferior to Lucrece that their love was such an abomination? His mother told Seth he would have to leave or his father would risk losing his job and their home.

'…And that my friend, was that,' Seth said.

Christopher did not know what to say. Tears streamed silent and unwiped down Seth's face.

'My God,' was all Christopher could find to say. He wanted to touch Seth and offer some kind of comfort, but it seemed suddenly in the silence that to move towards him would be to retreat from the truth in his story. So he just nodded slowly. Seth leaned his head back against the chair; he still didn't bother to wipe his face. Christopher hated his own discomfort. He wished he were less embarrassed by this emotional intimacy, this intimacy that he paradoxically wanted so much. Seth's throat convulsed with the force of swallowing down his emotion for a moment.

'But I still see her Christopher, she's haunted me ever since.'

'Her ghost?' Christopher murmured.

Seth nodded.

'But not as you might imagine. Lucrece was... as I am. So her spirit... it's more potent. She was never staked to her grave so she is undead. I have a dead woman for a wife.'

Christopher shuddered involuntarily. Seth's words conjured images of Seth living in that cold ruin with the wind whistling in the chimney, with a silent pale woman. Christopher imagined her as a cold ghostly companion in Seth's bed, or in the shadows, keeping him with one foot always in the world of the grave. But he didn't want to ask *the* question. It was almost too macabre and too private at the same time. When he did it was because he was unable not to ask.

'Can you... well is she... does she have substance in...'

'Can I touch her?' Seth interjected abruptly.

Christopher could only nod and for a moment he had trouble swallowing.

'Yes. But only at certain times.'

'At what times?'

'It requires sorcery,' Seth said. 'And great outputs of my life-force. My blood usually, is what she wants.'

Christopher leaned forward. His body almost lurched forward with the urgency he felt. It was out of his control, for he too was sensing his own doom looming, as Seth once had.

'Would you teach me, Seth?'

'I thought you might be about to ask that,' the other man replied.

9

'It is like this
In death's other kingdom
Waking alone
At the hour when we are
Trembling with tenderness
Lips that would kiss
Form prayers to broken stone.'
—T.S. Eliot

Millicent stretched on the bed and winced as she began to feel her body. Her neck was sore and she felt the unfamiliar tenderness between her legs next. But the feeling was not of concern to her. She began to drift back into sleep. The dream seemed to rise back up in her mind as though it were a movie screen that began to play again the moment she shut her eyes.

She was in a mossy old growth forest lying on an enormous tree stump. It looked like it must have belonged to a thousand year old oak and the way she was draped on it, it felt like an altar. The shadows of a fire moved quickly in the wind, but they seemed to part around her and never touch her skin, as though the shadows of the firelight were dancing around her. She could see that she was naked on the rock but felt no shyness. Out of the flying forms of darkness that massed and cavorted above and around her, moving the way horses gallop when they're out of control, there came shadowy figures dressed in rags and bits of skins and masks. The clothes they wore looked like they had been shredded by the winds, as though their wearers had been wandering in the forest for hundreds of years. Millicent looked up at them with no fear. Some wore the mask of the wolf's head, others cloaks of crow's feathers.

There was one figure she recognised. The woman looked like Sophia. Yet there was something so alien about her that she somehow was not Sophia. The woman's hair was dread-locked and dyed by clumps of clay or woad. Her face and breasts were painted black and around her waist was a loincloth of feathers. Below the loincloth, instead of normal legs were the feathered and clawed feet of the owl. Then the company of wraiths parted. For a time the only sound was the howling of the spirit wind. A male figure came forward.

It was Seth, and unlike Sophia she knew it was him in soul as well as body. He wore tight fitting leather pants and his upper body was naked but strangely it was black, as was his face. Not negro-black but black like the night-sky is black and there was hair upon his body that was not there in real life. There was something strange in his gait and when she looked down she saw that one of his feet was the cloven foot of a beast. A bone that hung around his neck on a leather throng bobbed just above her in the air. It moved with some mysterious force more gentle than the wind. It swung like a hypnotist's watch over her face. Millicent's soul recognised everything that was happening and felt no surprise. A red haze fell across her vision.

A seeping wetness and coldness stole its way into her awareness. The heaviness of her body against the icy sheets and her hair sticking to her face woke her. Millicent smiled. It doesn't really matter what it is that's going on, Millicent thought, because this is it, this is the real thing. This is life. She took a deep breath and let it out in a prolonged sigh. At last...

'Will you?' Christopher prompted when Seth's reply was not forthcoming.

Seth smiled and leaned back in his seat. Finally now, he wiped the tears from his face with the back of his hand.

'You do realise, of course, that you have no idea what you ask of me?' Seth replied after a moment.

'Of course,' Christopher replied quietly. 'Could you tell me?'

'No. That is the problem you see,' Seth said. 'Magic is

something you can never prepare someone for. Magic will make you, Christopher. It will find all the secret empty places of longing in you and fill them more surely than any other love. And magic will break your heart.'

A slight, rather sad smile crossed Christopher's face for a moment.

'I know what you're thinking. You think your heart is already broken, you think that this crooked and winding way is the only path left for you now. But you're wrong. The heart breaks like every wave on the beach and there's a darkness you'll have to pass through that you can't even see from where you are now. '

Seth's gaze settled over Christopher, drinking him in, pondering the nuances of expression in his face.

'I want it still,' Christopher said at length.

'I had a feeling you might say that too.' Seth sighed. 'Well, you'll have to earn it.'

Christopher merely nodded as though he'd expected as much.

Seth quietly liked the boy even more. *He's got heart,* he thought, *but will he be able to face the darkness when the time comes?*

'I don't doubt your courage,' Seth said.

'It's thoroughly untested,' Christopher replied with a candid smile. 'At the moment it just consists of high ideals.'

Seth rolled his eyes heavenward. 'Gods, save us from high ideals,' he said under his breath.

'We'll start as of this moment. The magic begins testing you from the very first moment you ask for it. So think of my conditions as the beginning.'

'What are they?'

'If you want the magic, you have to come to Her. You need to come with nothing but your need and your readiness. I don't know any other way to teach it than the way I learned.

'Come to me tomorrow at dawn. Bring nothing with you except your clothing and books.'

Christopher took a long slow breath.

Seth watched him and waited. Come on boy, he thought to himself, come to me, leap the fence.

Christopher looked up suddenly. Seth could see both his urgency and the rising energy of readiness in his eyes.

'Can I ever come back?' he asked.

'You can. You may do as you wish. But nothing you ever see or do will ever look the same or feel the same.'

Christopher nodded gravely.

Good, Seth thought, *he understands; he's afraid.*

'And Sophia... Can I see her?'

'Not until you're trained. I want nothing from the outside distracting you. And I warn you that you may not want her at the end. These are my conditions, accept them or reject them.'

Seth watched Christopher staring down at the floor. He could see the tension in every fibre of the other man. As he had before Christopher looked up rapidly.

'I'll do it,' he said.

Sophia didn't get far due to the fact that the night was so dark. She leaned against the Penrose's front fence shivering in the light rain. The occasional high beam from a car passing along the A4 interrupted the blackness. But as soon as they were gone it was back to the smell of wet thatch and the macabre presence of elder trees.

It had been years since she had been out in the darkness on her own. And it was because of people like Eugene. At first as she stood there, she took comfort in the faint silver sheen of the cars slicing the blackness. But then it stopped helping. There was the darkness. It was a darkness that seemed to cave in her skull and pour into her like black water. A torrent of lost voices and sadness... She could feel it all now. The landscape around her was sodden with memory, soaked with blood and stacked whiter than a bone-yard under the green grass with Britain's fallen.

Her archaeologist's brain had been developed as a way to sort those impressions, give names to them, stick tags around things and bag them up. Double bag them. But those traces, those ghosts, seemed to brush against her in the touch of light rain. What has Christopher done to me? She thought. *He comes along with all this fire and passion, almost convinces me he understands what he has, what he is, what I am. But it's all innocent. He's like a child playing with matches. He just walks in and blows open this floodgate, blows my fucking mind and says, 'oh, by the way, I love you.' Like that's a perfectly normal thing to say before inserting your penis into someone. He doesn't even realise life's not like that. He doesn't know shit.*

'Sophia.' She cried out in shock and spun around.

Christopher was there, standing on the lawn behind her, smiling. He stood in the rain-curtain that the light made, and the droplets spangled his hair. He was wet-through looking for her, his hair was plastered down. It gave the whole thing poignancy. Sophia's heart ached. Silently Christopher draped his coat about her shoulders. She wanted to shrug it off but she knew it would hurt him. She hated the gesture in that moment. It seemed like ownership, as if he was claiming her as his. Yet she knew it wasn't meant that way and that he was beautiful. Somehow she just didn't want that to be true.

'Are you all right?' he almost whispered. At least he was respectful of the atmosphere. She shut her eyes and shook her head slightly.

'All right?' she murmured thoughtfully. 'You know, I don't think I know, Christopher. Am I all right? I'm not sure about that one. But d'you know what I can tell you?'

'What's that?'

'I'm fucking terrified,' she cried, her arms flapping up uselessly at her sides and falling back down against her thighs with a slap. 'Of this, of having this, of losing this, of the whole thing. Let me tell you a thing or two about relationships,' she said, her voice rising with a hysterical edge to it. Bending down she picked up his coat off the grass where it had fallen and handed it to him. 'I don't know what you think you know about love, but it just ain't that easy! People don't just give it to you like that. I've had a heap of guys say they love me. Some of them meant it for a while, some of them meant they were going to start stalking me, some of them just thought I'd believe it and let them get their leg over. Some of them say it after they get drunk and hit you or even threaten to kill you for speaking to another guy. Oh God, Christopher,' she sighed. 'Don't look at me like that. Don't go off on some righteous anger thing now.'

'I wasn't going to.'

'Good, because this Knight-in-Shining-Armour thing is lovely, but here in reality it just involves you beating someone up or them beating you up. Either way I'm not impressed.'

Christopher looked at her.

'I'd get hurt for you, if needs be,' he said simply. 'But I'm not an idiot. I'd rather help you now than beat people up for things I can't change.'

She wanted to hit him. *I hate this I'm so wise bullshit!* She thought. At the end of the day she knew that he was as desperate to prove himself as any drunk in a pub brawl.

'Great, well help me then!'

'In what way?'

'Well you seem to have all the answers. Why don't you tell me?'

Christopher just looked at her again. He seemed quizzical, wistful even, but not angry. She wasn't used to this kind of quiet, thoughtful response from men.

'I was planning on loving you. I was hoping you would talk to me and I'd listen. If you'd let me I'd like to keep having sex with you for... well, for a long time. I don't have any answers. As you're so fond of pointing out, I don't have any experience with women. But I'll give you everything I have to give.'

She sighed and looked away from him. The last thing that she wanted to see was the sincerity and simple honesty in his eyes.

'And what's that?'

'My heart.'

'I don't think you have that in your possession to give,' she murmured, turning back to him.

There was a moment of sad and open acknowledgement between them. He didn't deny the truth of the statement, he couldn't.

'Well,' he said, reaching out his hand for her. 'If you'll take the pieces of mine I'll take the pieces of yours.' He smiled. 'I think it's a fair deal.'

She didn't know whether to be furious or fall upon him kissing him madly for saying that.

'You're a prick you know that?'

He just continued to smile at her and took her hands.

'Do you love me?'

She could hear the ache in his voice, the need to hear her say it. It was a gulf she could have fallen into, his broken heart. She reached among her own debris to try to gather up the pieces with which to make her offering to him. It seemed she cut her hands against them but she still managed to look up at him.

'I love you, Christopher. Yes.'

There was a moment where she could see the effect of her words moving through him and then he spoke.

'Will you do something for me? Something really important that I wouldn't ask you to do unless it was really, really important?'

She looked up at him with incomprehension. *What planet does this guy live on?*

'What?' she snapped.

'Wait for me.'

'Wait for you?' she echoed incredulously. 'During what?'

'I can't tell you,' he said with a smile that made his eyes twinkle.

He drew her into his embrace with a gentle kind of force and kissed her on the mouth.

'What do you mean you can't—'

He kissed her again, holding her up against his body. *If I could lose myself here, she thought, if this was it, this was all he wanted I'd sleep with him again right here and now on the lawn.*

'Will you have me when I come back?'

She could feel her body answer before she did and she was sure he would feel it too. She nodded.

'Go and do whatever it is you're doing, Christopher. Take as long as you need to take, and come back when you feel like it and I'll wait for you and we'll get it on. Are you happy with that you consummate bastard?'

He burst into a radiant smile.

'Completely.' He picked up her hand and kissed it before closing her palm around his kiss. 'Thank you,' he whispered. 'I'll make sure you don't regret it.'

10

'We are such stuff as dreams are made on
And our little lives are rounded with a sleep.'
—Shakespeare

Christopher was bruised deeply by his mother's response to his news. Whatever his father said about him leaving could never really matter by comparison. It would be an after-thought. His mother's pain and confusion had gotten under his skin like a shard of glass. As if her emotions were a north wind that sneaks in between cracks in walls and under doors, filling a house with draft. He and his mother had gone somewhere together that they had never gone before, a raw and painful place, and it had frightened him, changed him. When Rodney yelled at Christopher he looked unflinchingly at his father while he demanded answers.

Somewhere in his heart Christopher knew the source of his father's anger. He knew the incomprehension of his son that gave rise to this frustration. But it did not come from the bloody soul wound as his mother's yelling and crying had come. So it could never be so terrible.

'Well? Are you going to say something?' His father bellowed.

'There's nothing else to say.'

His father ranted on, and Christopher endured it.

'I'm your father, damn it! I will be shown some respect. We've put a roof over your head these eighteen years and now I want a bloody answer!'

'I'm sorry,' Christopher said quietly, 'I can't. I don't expect you to understand. I just ask that you trust me.'

Rodney shook his head in bewilderment.

'I'll never understand you! I never have! Why can't you just be… normal.'

A sad smile crossed Christopher's face for a moment, but he

didn't answer.

'Huh? What are you smiling at?'

'I don't know, Dad! I don't know why I can't just be normal!' Something in those words caused Christopher to raise his voice unsteadily when he said them. The vulnerability they pulled out of him made him feel like a child again.

Rodney looked defeated. His rage had burned itself out. He slumped and turned his back. He seemed to grope then for something, a prop to distract himself. Anything to avoid looking at the stranger who live under their roof and was called his son, Christopher imagined.

'Do you realise what you're doing to your mother?'

'Yes,' Christopher all but whispered, his voice choked slightly but his father missed the catch of emotion in the word.

'Well! How can you do it to her?'

'Because I'm not normal, Dad! I'm... something else. And I need to find out what that is or I may as well be dead.'

'What do you mean?'

Christopher shook his head in obvious frustration.

'Dad... I don't think I can explain that to you.'

'Don't be so arrogant.'

Christopher just shut his eyes then. The chaos of the situation seemed a little unreal.

'You do whatever you want then, but don't expect to be able to come back. If you don't tell me what you're doing you'll never be welcome under this roof again.' Rodney was ready with more words he probably would have regretted but then he noticed Jane on the stair.

'Leave him, Rodney,' she murmured. Her eyes looked glazed and she didn't seem to blink a lot. 'Some people have a destiny that the people around them won't understand. Christopher is one of those people. I knew it when I was still carrying him. With Millicent it was all different, I knew she was mine. Christopher...' she murmured his name like it was something from long ago. Like it was something already lost. 'He never was.'

Rodney, confused and oddly humbled by his wife's words and manner, looked over and saw to his shock that his son was crying. Defeated, the older man shrugged.

'You do what you feel you have to, son.'

Christopher could always feel the coming of dawn like a welling up of warm power in his chest. Even if he was in bed in a shuttered room, whether he had tossed and turned away a sleepless night or stirred just before the sun. He didn't even need to hear the twitter of birds to know it was coming. The pressure in his solar plexus told him. This morning was pure and raw. He felt it through a mist of sadness almost too terrible, mixed with exhilaration so great it seemed to betoken a completely new life.

The night before Millicent had come into his room after all the lights were out. The only illumination had been the outside light through the window. She had been wearing a long white nightgown and for a moment he'd thought she was a ghost. Amid the chaos of Christopher's revelation nobody had enquired into the band-aid on the side of her neck.

Christopher had been sitting on his bed in the dark, his bag packed at his feet. Millicent drifted quietly in and sat down on the bed beside him. She placed her hand on his hand where it lay on his leg without saying a word. Nothing about it surprised Christopher. He felt beyond surprise now. The world he used to know had been smashed to pieces and all the old patterns and paradigms lay smoking in the wreckage.

'I understand,' she whispered, as though they were co-conspirators in some unmentioned plot. 'I just want you to know that.'

Christopher nodded.

'That means a lot to me,' he said. And it did. As they sat in that moment of real intimacy, neither of them was uncomfortable.

Christopher knew all the things that she didn't need to say. He knew that Millicent had glimpsed with Seth what he had seen with Eugene, all those years earlier, the beyond, the something more, the ineffable. He knew that, like him, she would never be able to stop thirsting for it now. They were both doomed and liberated. Maybe that was the truth behind the myth of a vampire's kiss, Christopher mused.

It was in that same mood that he stood on his family's back step and watched the sun come up. It happened so very gradually. The dew began to settle, and the world seemed to exhale quietly in the hush. He looked out over the landscape his home was built on and felt his skin prickle. Half bathed in the first orange rays of the sun, was the shadowy tumulus of Silbury, framed against the pale sky.

Christopher felt his night accustomed pupils contract as he stared into the heart of the sun. The light spangled the frosty grass across the fields leading to the Long Barrow. There was a strange feeling in his guts then, as though the ancient, brooding land were stirring awake and galvanising its inhabitants. For the first time he thought he knew what people talked about when they spoke of the 'energy' of the place. He imagined people coming out of their homes by the dozens, electrified by this feeling, to come and bow down to the sun. All through this vision, these feelings, he could hear an insistent dark whisper: 'Come to me Christopher, jump the fence.' Christopher looked down at the ground at his feet. He picked up the knapsack that now contained all his worldly goods, and set off toward the sun.

When Sophia left Christopher's place she stopped on the bridge and threw her mobile phone into the river below. It dropped into the running water with a satisfying 'plop', but it hadn't really meant much to Sophia. She knew that all her contacts were on her home phone as well and she had planned to update her mobile soon anyway. The whole gesture seemed a little insignificant by comparison to the other changes.

Afterwards she didn't want to go back to her flat so she went to the lab instead. Sometimes Sophia liked to work to stop herself thinking. She especially liked to work when no one else was there. And it was only her and Subject Twenty Two that night. 'Twenty two' was the male skeleton from the dig, giving an initial assessment of him was part of her practical assignment. Meditatively, Sophia rolled up her tape measure and said into her Dictaphone,

'Subject Twenty Two is a five foot eleven male, between the ages of twenty and thirty. Sex was clearly determinable by width of the pelvic opening, which is extant, and by skull size and shape. The wear and tear on the teeth is consistent with other agrarian finds that have lived to a similar age. The low incidence of cavities would suggest a good diet and therefore a higher social status. This data is consistent with the subject's comparatively tall stature. The assumption that this individual was of aristocratic birth is born up by his grave goods and by the half-inch greater development in the right arm. Differences of this nature are often indicative of sword use. Military activity is made more likely by the presence of two knitted bones where wounds have occurred prior to death, wounds which have touched the bone and were administered by a sharp object.'

Sophia took her finger off the button for a moment. Somehow what she had just been about to say had left her. After looking at the skull for all this time it was starting to mesmerise her. Some bones were different to others, she already knew that from experience. Some bones would begin to reveal, if she looked at them for long enough, what their owner's face had looked like in life. This find fascinated her. It was an almost perfectly articulated skeleton.

But it wasn't his perfection that attracted her. Sophia rationalised the attachment, telling herself it was because of the tiny collection of personal items that had been found with him. Such things were so rare in the damp world of Britain, so precious and historically significant. But it was more.

With her trowel, tweezers and tiny paintbrush she had worked tirelessly to clear away the debris that time had covered him with. Along with her supervisor and their sieves they had found even the smallest bones of him, knucklebones, feet bones, missing teeth. It was the best find of the dig.

'The cause of death is apparent in multiple wounds,' she cleared her voice a couple of times before continuing, 'He... Subject Twenty Two... suffered two compound fractures. It can be conjectured that these wounds caused his death, as they show no signs of knitting.' She paused again, looking down at the noble, yellowing old skull. His strong cheekbones and jaw, his high-forehead and deep-set eyes, she could almost see him. His stunning smile, full of perfect, strong, white teeth could be easily imagined.

'The cause of death was the slicing of the upper vertebra also cleaving the humerus... The sword used was very sharp, obviously fine iron, which may help with dating the find if necessary.' She took her finger away from the button again.

Reaching down a tentative hand she ran her fingers over the smooth surface of the forehead. Without really thinking about what she was doing she slipped off her plastic glove. Closing her eyes she laid her palm flat against him. The cranium felt round and cold in her hand, the smell of peat and chalk were still upon him. Then she saw it, just for a moment, the flash of the assailant's blade as it glinted in the sun. With a gasp she pulled away. The speed of the blow had been dazzling, almost incomprehensible. Sophia gazed down into the empty eye-sockets.

'You must have not even had time to realise you were about to die,' she whispered affectionately. The adrenalin pumped through her now, as though it had actually been about to happen to her. Her hands shook. The man hadn't had time to make peace with death, or to say goodbye to all he'd loved in life. Maybe that was why she was drawn to him. It was like he knew…

Shaking her head she put her Dictaphone into her lab-coat pocket. She leaned against the cold metal table for a moment to steady herself.

'What the hell is going on with me?'

Sophia had always felt things, and seen things, but not like this. She went to walk out, just leave it all behind for the night. But as she headed for the door she thought she heard someone say her name. She hurriedly exited the room, shut the door and locked it behind her.

The dawn was a golden spectacle that morning, gilding the land and caressing it into arousal. Christopher shared in the excitement and newness of it, this rising of life. Yet Seth's ruin was a thing apart from the morning. A thin light moved inside, shadowy and uncertain. The interior spoke of secrets and mystery.

Christopher smiled to himself.

'Hello, Seth,' he said through the crack in the wall.

'So you came,' Seth's voice said from the darkness inside. 'Come in then.'

He entered through the hole in the wall that he had used on his first visit. When he stood up he found Seth wearing that same black overcoat, and indeed Christopher soon realised it was cold enough inside the ruin for a coat.

Christopher felt for a moment that Seth somehow knew what he had gone through to get there and how it had changed him. *Maybe he anticipated all of it*, Christopher thought, *maybe it was my first lesson*. He liked the fact that Seth was looking at him and not saying anything. The other man's behaviour seemed to allow the profundity of the situation to be acknowledged in the quiet. After a time Seth sighed and turned aside, taking his candle with him into the main section of the ruin, beckoning for him to follow.

'We are creatures of different times of day you and I. You

wake when I prefer to retire. What do you say we do about that?' He said this with a kind of sad irony, as though Christopher and he faced some kind of age-old dilemma, a mythic dilemma of light and darkness, risings and settings.

'I'll become nocturnal,' Christopher replied.

'Lovely,' Seth said. 'Then we shall see each other. I wish that Romeo would die, because apparently "then all the world would be in love with night and pay no worship to the garish sun", but till then? What can I do?'

Christopher smiled. This off-hand Shakespearean reference thrilled him. How he had longed to again know someone who talked about things like that as though everyone should know them.

'Would you like to sleep?' he asked Seth, realising he was probably imposing. Seth nodded, staring into the little coal fire in the grate. 'Soon.'

'I suppose you hate summer, where the nights are so short.'

Seth nodded. 'I love the depths of winter. I love to sit alone here, getting vitamin D deficiency and depression in the dark.'

Christopher laughed incredulously. 'You enjoy being alone in the dark and getting depression?'

'I said I love it, Christopher. It's not always the same thing. Do you always find love enjoyable?'

Seth stood up and took off his coat. Without explanation he lay down on his back on the bed. 'Do you remember what you dream?' He asked.

'Sometimes.'

'Do you need to dream? Do you find your dreams encroaching on your waking hours if you don't?'

Christopher smiled, he felt entranced by Seth's quiet rhythmic speaking and the lack of barriers between them.

'Sometimes, when I dream of Eugene,' Christopher said quietly. 'I... I... in those dreams I don't want to wake up.'

All except for the one about Eugene's bedroom, and the one

about his funeral, where the casket was suddenly open, in those ones Christopher was always struggling to wake but couldn't.

'You didn't sleep last night,' Seth told him.

Christopher wondered how he knew, but didn't ask.

'No,' he replied without elaboration. Somehow he didn't feel he needed to tell Seth about what had happened with his parents.

'Lie here,' Seth said.

Quite suddenly Christopher realised quite how exhausted he was. He lay down on his back next to Seth and they both looked up at the ceiling for a long time. Christopher felt a deep bone weariness and the beginnings of a relaxation more intense than any he could remember since long before Eugene died. The last thing he remembered was the cool but gentle press of Seth's hand on his arm.

'Welcome home, Christopher.'

Christopher stirred out of sleep like a trance was lifting from him. It was a pleasant feeling that contained no awareness of time or place. Where he had been it had been warm and comforting, waking from it was a sweet sort of pain. For a moment he was aware of something eerie about where he was. It felt like the old ruin had thousands of eyes in every stone.

As he turned his head he saw that Seth was sitting up. Seth's back was against the wall and his legs were crossed, his head slightly back. He took a cigarette from his shirt pocket and lit it as Christopher sat up. The flash of light illuminated Seth's face and the stone walls for a moment, then faded into the softer coal-like glow of the cigarette's tip. Afterwards came the characteristic upward blown cloud of smoke.

'Read me a poem you love,' was the first thing Seth said. 'Any poem, so long as it means something to you. And I want to know what it means to you.'

Christopher bent, picked up his bag from the floor and began to look inside. There was never any hurry with Seth, he knew that

already, so he took his time. Seth smoked meditatively. Life held
no deadlines for him. Christopher waited to feel guided. It was
something Eugene taught him. To say the right thing at the right
time was a subtle and a terrible art. You had to wait for inspi-
ration. It was not the type of art where you could screw up the
piece of paper and throw it out. If you made a mistake the conse-
quence might be the failure to achieve a connection with
someone.

He opened the well dog-eared page of a much-loved volume.
When he began to read his voice came out as a whisper,

'After great pain a formal feeling comes—'

Before he could continue he noticed Seth's mouth twitch with
a smile of recognition and approval. Christopher knew he had
passed.

'The nerves sit ceremonious like tombs;
The stiff Heart questions—was it He that bore?
And yesterday—or centuries before?
The feet, mechanical, go round,'

He looked up at Seth briefly who was looking at him intently
as he read.

'A wooden way
Of ground, or air, or ought,
Regardless grown,
A quartz contentment, like a stone.
This is the hour of lead
Remembered if outlived,
As freezing persons recollect the snow—
First chill, then stupor, then the letting go.'

'Why?' Seth demanded.

Christopher sighed and stopped to give his answer proper
thought.

'Because that's what it feels like when your heart breaks.'
Christopher shrugged. 'That first pain that you think you'll

never endure, and then that daze you enter like slowly freezing to death... The hour of lead.'

Seth nodded. 'Yes. The hour of lead... I remember it well, as it tends to be remembered, if out lived,' he murmured, still nodding his head slightly.

'All right,' he said, disposing of his burnt out cigarette by flicking it into the corner. Completely unexpected and unexplained he began to speak.

'I tell you, hopeless grief is passionless;
That only men incredulous of despair,
Half-taught anguish, through the midnight air
Beat upward to God's throne in loud access
Of shrieking and reproach. Full desertness
In souls, as countries, lieth silent-bare
Under the blanching, vertical eye-glare
Of the absolute Heavens. Deep-hearted man, express
Grief for thy Dead in silence like to death:-
Most like a monumental statue set
In everlasting watch and moveless woe,
Till itself crumble to the dust beneath.
Touch it: the marble eyelids are not wet;
If it could weep, it could arise and go.'

Because Seth knew the poem by heart he said the whole thing without looking away. Christopher couldn't breathe until he was finished.

'Why?' Christopher asked him quietly. The question had more than one meaning. He almost wanted to know why Seth would make him listen to that, so deeply had the stark despair of it gone with dry, scratchy fingers over the surface of his soul.

'Did you cry?' Seth asked in return.

'At the time, or later?'

'Either.'

'Not at the time. I couldn't. I was hyperventilating.'

Seth nodded.

'I just started running and ran till I fell down, and then got up and ran again. But I've never really sobbed. I think when you really cry your heart out then it's over. And it's not over. I don't accept it. I'll never accept it.'

Christopher nodded. 'I suppose we are at war with Heaven,' he said.

Seth grinned. 'That we are, Christopher, that we are.' He got up and began to stoke the fire. 'But when you think about it for what else were hearts given to us? If they were made breakable then we were meant to be broken and we were meant to cry out against it? 'Heaven' must like it when we put up a fight. This is the only viable conclusion. I must teach you how to live now, Christopher, seeing that no one has taught you yet. You need to learn how to feed and look after yourself. I have a lot to show you.'

11

'Poetry is the blood-jet
There is no stopping it.'
—Sylvia Plath

Christopher watched Seth skin a rabbit in the shadows, against the well-worn slaughter-block of the hearthstone. Ritualistic with his boning knife, Seth was crouching before the fire, the totemic antlers above him, with blood up past his wrists. There were so many questions coursing around in Christopher's mind. For a start he wanted to know what the antlers represented and why Seth gave them candles and blood. He wanted to know why Seth's crude statue of the Virgin Mary had a black face and why he gave her rose thorns. And most of all he wanted to know why Seth had a small cairn made of weasel bones and raven's feathers right next to his bed.

'Always take out the heart,' Seth murmured, scooping his fingers into the little creature's chest cavity. 'You must do that first, to free the spirit. I'd say it's as old as this land is, doing that.' Seth grabbed Christopher's wrist with the blood sticky between them. 'Hold it,' Seth told him.

Christopher took the luke-warm, slimy little object in his hands. Seth left his hand over Christopher's hands. 'This is what it's all about. This is where the magic is, in this, in blood, in the flesh, in the breath, in birthing, killing and dying.'

Christopher could smell the iron in it.

'Does it make you thirsty?' He asked, his tone curious but gentle.

'Yes,' Seth murmured. 'But it's old now, so not as much. The heat of life is so transient. If I teach you nothing else, fill yourself with the urgency of that fact till nothing else beats in your heart. The hunger is so very short lived in most people. And for those of us who feel it, it's a fire that torments us. And yet, without it there is no spark, no spark to kindle wisdom from.'

Taking the heart from Christopher he squeezed it slightly as he picked it up, making it leak thick, black blood onto Christopher's hands. It pooled in the centre of his palms, viscous as though he had been wounded. Christopher couldn't stop staring at the little black puddles there.

'It's not so very different being a vampire. The blood hunger is the hunger we all know somewhere, or knew once, when youth was hot in us. It's just for us, we feel it when we see blood.'

Christopher nodded slowly, he understood.

'You're here for the same reason. Millicent wanted me for it. The same thing I wanted her for, to fulfil my hunger. You want Sophia for it, a higher kind of hunger than Millicent's, but still the hunger. Sophia wants to take you inside her body the same way I want to take blood.

The hunger brought Lucrece and I together to our destruction. You hunger to be back in the presence of your friend Eugene, in some deep and mysterious way.

It's the hunger. It's why vampires fascinate people. Why people can't get enough of novels and movies with us in them. They give us all of their repressed urges, even their fear of their mortality. But really what they're staring at isn't an undead corpse that came back from the grave. What was buried was *them*. Their own hunger, buried in a thousand other things that they 'kind of wanted', that took the edge off the memory of real desire. That's why we can mesmerise and the idea of us can mesmerise people. It's not us you're staring at, it's your own desire. A vampire is just a blank space, a black hole. People look at some movie about vampires and get a little thrill out of thinking what it might be like to desire something so much it hurts, to be awake enough to remember what it feels like to almost lose control because you feel such need for something. Modern people need us to be their largely forgotten, satiated and dulled hungers for them,' he said with a smile that showed his savagely made teeth. 'So they don't have to.'

Everything was slow and dark and unformed. Only the snippets of poetry gave shape to the amorphous blackness. Christopher had entered the domain of Seth's soul, the realm of night. The poetry of it was a labyrinth of words and gazes, and it was also the method by which to traverse that labyrinth. The poetry did not consist only of poems.

Seth made cooking the soup a ritual and life itself a form of poetry. They crouched around the pot like witches brewing a spell as the rabbit meat and vegetables simmered and bubbled in the ancient hearth. Christopher was beginning to realise that getting away from electric lights, computers and televisions had already heightened his imaginative capacity.

'Don't ever make the mistake of limiting what magic is, that is the first thing.

'It is grief in the heart,
It is stretching of strength beyond its bounds,
It is the four quarters of the world,
It is the highest height of heaven,
It is breaking of the neck,
It is a battle with a spectre,'
Most particularly that part Christopher. But it is also,
Drowning with water,
It is a race against heaven,
It is champion- deeds beneath the sea.
It is wooing the echo.
Remember that always, for it will unfold and unfold the deeper in you go. Do you understand?'

'Not with my brain,' Christopher replied, staring into the coals that were reflected in Seth's dark eyes. 'But in my guts.'

Seth nodded. 'Don't listen when people say you feel it in your guts. That's not the deepest sort of knowing. We know things in our balls when they are beyond reason. Learn to listen to your balls and you'll start to understand a thing or two you don't know.'

'Is that sort of knowing connected to the hunger?'

Seth paused in stoking the fire. 'Just about everything happens because of hunger my friend. But if there were a part of your body that can teach you about the hunger, it's your cock and your balls. You just need to learn to listen. That's why I brought you out here. You can't hear the knowledge your body has, surrounded by all those modern distractions. You have to listen to the undercurrents out here. There aren't any over-currents. In this darkness, this silence, everything from the depths rises up. Eugene will be no different in time and everything else from your life with him. Are you ready for that?'

Christopher laughed. 'I doubt anyone is ever ready for that.'

'Indeed. But it's always a beautiful disaster.'

Sophia didn't go straight home. Instead she found herself taking a detour past her work. The keys to the university lab were on her key ring, so she decided to go in. She convinced herself that she was only going in to check and see if she'd left some paper work. But deep down Sophia knew that she didn't really need the paper work immediately.

As the laboratory door closed behind her she was instantly aware of something different. Flicking on the overhead lighting Sophia approached her skeleton. Everything looked in order, the only difference was that it seemed to draw her eye the way movement does in our peripheral vision. But the skeleton certainly had not moved.

'Maybe you'll understand,' she said, under her breath as she looked down at the bones. Her tone was a mixture of irony and poignancy.

The skeleton lay on a metal table, fully articulated and labelled. As she pulled up an office chair to sit down next to it she couldn't help smiling. *To think I accused Christopher of being a freak for the poetry thing,* she thought, *at least he doesn't spend his Friday nights with human remains.* She shook her head in a bemused manner and reached down to touch the surface of the skull. Sophia knew she shouldn't touch him with her bare hands. He had been dusted for pollen samples and his DNA had already been taken. That was how she had rationalised it to herself. But deep down Sophia knew she was overstepping a professional boundary.

'What sort of man were you?' she whispered, 'were you rough or gentle, smart or dumb? Were you as old as I am when they killed you? Or were you younger?'

'*Younger.*'

Sophia started in her seat but did not spin around. The voice had come from behind her. Her breath began to come more rapidly and the back of her neck prickled. With a sudden burst of panic she leapt up and went to race for the door.

'*Sophia.*' The voice was masculine and deep, strangely accented, but very real, and very close.

Steeling herself for what she would see she turned around. Just out of the glow cast by the lights that illuminated the table for study, was a figure. Sophia swallowed and took an involuntary step backward. This was the first time she'd seen one of her work subjects like this.

'Who are you?' her voice constricted in her throat as he stepped forward.

He was dressed in worn buckskin trousers and his upper body was naked except for tattoos and scars. His hair was wrought in wind-blown braids that were almost dreadlocks. He smiled at her and she saw those strong white teeth she was used to seeing in the skull on the table. His eyes were blue-grey and piercing, and his face was rather hard and angular. There was something of a worn quality about him as though the elements had battered him continuously for his full twenty years.

'My name is Artyn,' he said, before moving closer. 'I have to speak with you, Sophia.'

She glanced down at her notes as though they were a talisman that could protect her, and slowly backed away. He took a step towards her, still smiling. But the step was a confident one. He stood with his arms folded, his feet apart, balanced and squared off in a way that only bouncers tend to stand today. There was still a sword in his belt.

'Don't run,' was all he said.

Her fingers dragged down over her notes. Durotriges male, 18-25...

'How can you speak English?' she managed to ask.

He said something in his ancient tongue, which was reminiscent of Welsh but wasn't quite. Then he shrugged, and said no more. He's so solid, she thought, how is he supporting a manifestation like this? It was stronger than Eugene... The light seemed to glint off the golden torc around his neck and show the layer of dust on his clothing. Sophia wondered how his killers got the torc off him, as it had not been in his grave. The torc marked him out as an aristocrat and a warrior; it would normally have been part of his grave-goods.

'Why are you here?' she asked.

'You asked me to come.'

'I didn't ask anything.'

He just shrugged again.

Sophia's adrenalin wouldn't stop pumping. She knew he was right, she had asked him to come. He took a step toward her, and it put him within arm's length. He reached out to her. She looked down at his hands, strong, calloused hands with a manly nobility about them.

'Sophia, I came to tell you what you are.'

At that Sophia pulled away, spinning around she ran for the door.

'Leave me alone!' she yelled, slamming and locking the door behind her.

Without pausing she raced down the stairs and out into the night air.

When Sophia reached the street outside she stopped to catch her breath. She wasn't sure what had made her panic so deeply. There had been many ghosts that had tried to touch her in her life, many of them hostile, or half crazed. A lot of them had appeared in a horrible manner and Eugene had certainly been much more psychologically terrifying.

Artyn was in fact very seductive to her. When he told her he could tell her what she was, she believed him. The prospect was alluring, but also filled her with an inexplicable dread.

I've been running the hell away from who I am my whole God-damned life and I'm not going to stop now! With this resolution in her head Sophia headed rapidly for home, wrapping her coat close about her. The route that she took back to her flat went past Chicago Rock. The bowling alley with a bar attached had endeared itself to her in the past by doing free sample drinks. She looked inside and saw a vacant seat at the bar that seemed to have her name on it.

Walking in Sophia placed her handbag down and ordered a Vodka and lemonade.

'Hey Sophia,' said a fellow over at the pool table.

'Hey Robbie,' she replied reluctantly.

Robbie was wearing ripped jeans and a bandana around his head, a cigarette hung out of his mouth while he bent over his pool-cue to make his shot.

'Haven't seen you in a while, sweetheart,' he said, after taking his shot, as he sleazed over to her and briefly touched her backside. It was one of those light, almost non-existent touches that are so small that very few women will call the man to account for it. Robbie was an expert at those touches.

'Yeah, and I've been living, hon,' she said, taking out her own cigarette which was gently laced with hash and lighting it. He laughed and went back to his beer and his game, 'I can't believe I fucked him,' she murmured to herself under her breath. Rolling her eyes at her past, she thought about the time she'd slept with Robbie. She remembered drunkenly laughing and stumbling into the side street where his car was parked.

'You've got great tits you know,' he had murmured in her ear as he rubbed them. She had been leaning against his car like she was being frisked and his hands were up underneath her top. She could almost hear her own drunken giggling. 'Is right here okay?' he said, as his fingers groped inside her underwear.

'Anywhere's okay, sweetheart,' she had purred, moving herself against his fingers. 'As long as you use a condom.' And so he'd opened the backdoor and bent her over the seat with her mini-skirt up around her waist.

Sophia shook her head as she thought of it, and downed more of her drink. Anyone could have come along at any time! She hated how this man, how so many other men she'd been with, compared to Christopher. They seemed childish, juvenile. *But then am I really any different? She thought, I probably deserve someone more like Robbie.* She downed the rest of her drink.

The knocking at the front door became gradually more obvious. Sitting bolt upright Sophia grabbed for her bathrobe.

'Coming!' she yelled.

Pulling her robe on she muttered indictments under her breath against people who come around before ten on a Saturday morning. Trying to brush her hair a little with her fingers she fumbled with the door keys with the other hand.

'Just a minute!'

Finally she opened the door. It took her a couple of moments to process what she saw on the other side.

'Millicent?'

'I'm sorry to disturb you,' she said.

Sophia stepped back to allow her to enter, too taken aback to reply immediately.

Millicent entered, wearing a charcoal grey trouser suit with her hair plaited down her back. 'I just needed to talk to you.'

Finally Sophia's mind caught up with the situation and she nodded.

'Sure, come into the kitchen. This requires coffee, and so do I.'

When both women were seated at the kitchen table with their steaming coffees in hand, Millicent took a deep breath as though readying herself for something.

'I guess I just wondered if you know where they are. Christopher left us no forwarding address.'

'Me neither.'

'And I know Christopher will be okay. It's just...'

'You want to see Seth.' Sophia concluded to prevent elaboration.

'Yes,' she said, with a smile and a slight blush, adding quietly, 'I think he needs me.'

'Seth?' Sophia questioned, as gently as she could. 'I don't know about that. Seth's like a cat, he's a solitary creature. I'm not sure he needs anyone.' Sophia was trying not to hurt Millicent's feelings, but it appeared the effort was unnecessary as Millicent only nodded philosophically.

'And I know that. I'm not trying to be Seth's wife. I understand that he already has one. I'm saying I'm willing to be his whore.'

Sophia got up to refill the coffeepot. It wasn't even empty but she needed to get up and do it to buy some time to cope with what Millicent was saying.

'See Sophia, I'll be honest with you.' Millicent leaned back in her seat, her arms folded and looking steadily at Sophia. 'I know what Seth is... don't say anything,' she said, holding her hand up when Sophia opened her mouth to speak. 'I don't need any further explanations, I know everything I need to know about him here,' she said, placing her hand on her lower stomach. 'I believe people know these kinds of things sometimes. I get it from Mum. She's always known about Christopher, known he was different. And I know about Seth and how he's different. I don't expect him to love me. I just want to know where he is. I feel like I need to, for his sake.'

Sophia nodded and then sighed. 'So I take it you slept with him then?'

Millicent merely nodded. 'And you know something about a man when you do. We didn't use a condom and I guess it's his energy. You must understand what I mean, after being with my brother.'

Sophia nodded but looked away.

Millicent sat up in her seat, 'But see, you're different too. I'm not. I'm just an ordinary girl.'

Millicent leaned forward. Her eyes that Sophia had previously found wishy-washy now burned like blue fire the way her brother's could. 'But I'll tell you this much. This world that I've seen through Seth, that you're just naturally a part of, I want it.'

Sophia got up in disgust and paced to the window. She wanted to say 'nobody likes a tourist', but restrained herself. She knew it was unnecessarily bitchy.

'What do you mean?' she snapped instead, her dark brown locks trailing over her white satin gown, 'I'm not a part of anything, and I certainly don't do, or possess anything 'naturally.' I'm the most artificial person in the world. And even if I did, which I most emphatically do not, how would you know that you would want to be in that world? How would you know what it's like?'

'I *know*,' Millicent declared with a shocking confidence.

Sophia almost shuddered. She said it with such emphasis it could have had multiple meanings.

Millicent jumped to her feet and pulled down the neck of her polo-neck shirt to reveal a bruised wound just where the shoulder joins the neck. 'I'm having dreams, Sophia, strange dreams. And I know what you are.'

Sophia froze. 'What did you say?'

Millicent didn't repeat herself and Sophia started to wonder if Millicent had really said it or whether she had just heard someone say that. Millicent just stood there, seeming almost to challenge Sophia.

'If I find anything out,' Sophia said, staring Millicent down. 'I'll give you a ring.'

After a long moment Millicent looked down.

When she was gone Sophia wandered back to bed and pulled the covers over herself.

Sophia couldn't see the man in the dream but she knew it was Christopher. Something was cracking open inside her as his thrusts gently severed her aloneness. Hermetically sealed... there had been a tight silence and stillness in her soul and then the sensation of bursting light and rushing air. The scene changed rapidly. A blade flashed, catching the sun's light, fell and rose again in bloody light. Then she was inside a temple. Pungent incense filled her senses. There was a sound of chanting and the flickering of a fire. Then she saw herself distinctly, in her white lab coat, picking up the tiny finger bone, looking to see if anyone was watching, and slipping it into her pocket...

In the dream Christopher was on his back looking up at her. Sophia was kneeling over him, straddling him. He was about to penetrate her. Shadows gathered between her legs, and behind her head a sun disk glowed. Her eyes seemed to gleam with the mystery she represented. Christopher saw her above him, felt himself inside her and something beginning to stir in him, a power rising...

Christopher rolled over in bed. His hairs were standing on end, and his erection ached. The wind whistled in the old masonry and it was almost completely dark. Rolling over onto his back he looked up at the roof. He knew now that he had never felt real sexual longing before. It was almost like his grief over Eugene had somehow delayed this crucial part of adolescence. Although he had dreamed of Sophia he had not spilt his seed, but woken instead with a painful erection. The skin on his penis felt so aggravated and dry that he couldn't even bare to touch it to relieve his frustration. Shutting his eyes Christopher took some deep breaths and hoped for the feeling to go away. While he was doing this the heightened awareness that had settled itself into his groin began to spread all around his body, until he felt minutely and painfully aware of the skin all over him. He shivered. Before this new sensitivity had awoken all over he hadn't even realised how cold he was.

There was only a second or two of feeling cold before Christopher realised he couldn't move. He couldn't even move his lips or tongue to cry out. The sensation of sudden paralysis was alarming and for a few heartbeats Christopher was close to panic. Yet the sensation of physical hyper-awareness was still with him. He felt the very slightest movement of the covers that lay over him, as though an unseen hand had lightly tugged it. He couldn't open his eyes so he could only assume that as he'd heard no one enter the room, that the hand was unseen. The state of near panic and arousal melded together smoothly for Christopher into one heightened state where it seemed that the silence screamed, the darkness boomed, and every slight movement of the sheet against his inert body felt as strong as a blow.

Just as suddenly as the paralysis had come Christopher's system was flooded with an immense sense of well being, greater than any joy he'd felt since he was fourteen years old. It was a weightless levity, mixed with comfort and just tinged with a sharp edge of thrill. The paralysis released Christopher then, his eyes flew open and he started moving and panting for breath like he'd just come up from under water. It took a few moments for him to realise that he was wet with sweat and his own semen.

The rabbit struggled pitifully. Seth's hands freed it carefully. He held the terrified, injured creature as though it were his first-born. And then he held it out to Christopher. Christopher swallowed hard as he took it. Until this moment he had had absolutely no idea about death, about what it meant to eat the flesh of another animal... The animal's pain was agonising to him. He felt ashamed and guilty for its predicament even though he hadn't caused it.

'What do you feel?' Seth asked.

'Guilt. Pity. Helplessness.'

'But you're not helpless.'

Christopher felt its blood running out onto his hands. The meaning of Seth's words took slow root in him. At once he was aware that his hesitation was drawing out the creature's suffering, and just how much he didn't want to kill it. The rabbit gave a few courageous kicks but Christopher gently subdued it. The animals bulging frightened eyes shone in the moonlight. And Christopher felt that image burn into his deep mind.

With a deep breath Christopher placed his hands around the fragile neck and squeezed. Nothing could have prepared Christopher for the fragility of that little life, for how easily the neck broke in his grip. Nothing could have been harder than the ease of it. Christopher felt the vibration of the snap in his fingertips, and all the way through him, down to his feet. It clenched in his stomach on the way down, and was remembered by his loins. He screwed his eyes shut. He hated it.

The rabbits eye that had seemed to watch Christopher, slowly glazed over as he stared down at the animal in his hands. Seth let these moments pass in profound silence while Christopher crouched there with the creature in his hands, watching as the nerves twitched. The rabbit's panic began to pass forever, as its nerves unwound never to rewind.

'*It is breaking of the neck,*' Seth quoted quietly. It was from an ancient Celtic poem about what love is.

Christopher silently appreciated the reference. He was fully aware of the love that had been involved in his action.

'In the old days that made you a man. Did you hate it?'

'Yes.'

'Good, because that's the point. It's not the killing that makes you a man. A boy who thinks that, lingers forever between the world of boys and that of men. It's the *knowing* that matters.'

'The knowing of what?'

'Death, suffering, taking. The fact that all life takes from other lives to live, that there is no life or creation without destruction. And of everything that was involved in really *knowing* that for you.

'The boy's innocence dies with the animal. And knowledge is reborn in the place of it. The knowledge a man has of Death and sacrifice.' Seth got to his feet while he spoke and brushed down his knees. 'Without it, there is no knowledge of Life.'

He bent down and wet his fingers with the cooling blood. Silently he anointed Christopher forehead with it between the eyes, one long thick gash in the middle and two lines beside it, made with Seth's three middle fingers.

That night they sat by the fire again. Seth had asked Christopher to leave the blood on his hands and forehead. They sat eating and talking. Christopher had not seen himself in a mirror for over a week. But if he could have he would already have had trouble recognising himself. His hair was dirty and tousled and his face was grubby and stained with dried blood. But he was not filthy. Seth owned a bucket and soap from which water could be applied, cold, to the body.

Christopher had taken a perverse pleasure in this ritual after his hatred for his mother's plush bathroom and lavender softener. His face bore three-day growth. Seth and he shaved from time to time with a piece of reflective glass and an old cutthroat razor. The first time Christopher had used it he had cut himself so badly that Seth had to excuse himself from the room telling him where to find a towel. Christopher secretly coveted a disposable razor after his injury, but Seth had a hatred for anything disposable.

'Our ancestor's buried valuable objects in the body of their Mother as gifts for her. We bury garbage; think about it,' Seth told him.

Christopher's face was changing too. His bone structure was more visible, his veins, sinews and Adam's apple were more obvious and his eyes had taken on an extra depth. In the silence and darkness Christopher felt his senses becoming more acute; his mental chatter was dying out. He was developing an ability to focus on something for so long he could almost bore holes through it.

'Did you feel your ancestors with you when you did it?' Seth asked.

They spoke about it now while they were eating the rabbit. Christopher thought about it, or more properly, his body thought about it. He was learning to answer questions from his body now, not just from his mind. Sometimes the answers surprised him.

'When the neck cracked,' he replied, his voice meditative, 'it sent a tremor through my bones. It was like an echo went back through time, bounced into something and came back on me. My body remembered killing, yes, I think my ancestors remembered through me. And maybe even I remembered doing it before...'

Seth nodded. 'That's right Christopher. You've done it before. We *are* our own ancestors. Everything on this earth is recycled, DNA, water, air, and your subtle body. What other people call souls are a form of matter too, Christopher, don't make that mistake. They are a subtle 'second skin'. You need to realise that for what we intend to attempt the Otherworld is completely real. Its consequences are just as real, though not always quite so immediate or obvious at first.'

The fire crackled and spat, as raindrops began to find their way down the chimney along with sharp gusts of cold air. Christopher shivered. The two men sat facing each other on the two tree stumps near the fire.

'Okay. I can accept that. What I don't understand is how come so much of it sounds like psychology?'

Seth smiled slightly and leaned back. 'Ah we have come to this already, the questions of truth and trust.'

As though the topic was going to be taxing, Seth reached immediately for his cigarettes. Christopher couldn't help watching with interest. Seth's smoking was a form of communication in itself. He knew that Seth would not begin to speak again till his cigarette was lit and he had exhaled the first lungful of smoke.

'What you need to understand,' Seth said, while the first puff of smoke found its way up to the ceiling, 'is that magic is not the airy-fairy thing you think it is. It mingles insidiously with everyday things, things we think we already know about. Things like psychology and charisma or 'chemistry'.'

'But how do we come to know the difference then? I mean, in my case, how do I know that the things that are happening to me aren't just some wish-fulfilment thing?'

'Don't skip ahead to that yet,' Seth cut in.

'But surely the question of truth has to be pretty fundamental?'

'Does it?'

The question so shocked Christopher that there was only the sound of the rain for quite some time.

'Yes,' Christopher said after a while.

'Why?'

'Well if truth doesn't matter, what does?'

'What do you think truth is?'

Christopher sighed and shook his head.

'I don't know. I mean if you don't believe in truth what's the point of all this?'

'I didn't say I didn't believe in it.' Seth got up and walked over to his stack of books.

Seth's back seemed to present some impenetrable barrier to Christopher's understanding in that moment and he felt frustrated.

After rifling through his books for a while Seth turned around. 'You like to think of yourself as pretty reasonable don't you?' Seth stood there in the shadows, smoking his cigarette and looking at Christopher.

The rain hammered in all around them. In a few places the roof leaked and Seth kicked a bucket a few inches to the left to catch a new one. It was also very dark in the ruin, even with the fire. Sometimes Christopher felt lost in all the darkness.

'I suppose so. I don't want to be unreasonable.'

'What have you got against unreason?'

Seth seemed to be a little closer to him now but Christopher couldn't remember seeing him move, though he knew he had. The wind howled in an almost human manner, rattling the roof and making the leaks drip furiously.

Christopher shivered again. It was like the spring had suddenly disappeared and plunged the land back into winter. He was cold to the bone and the fire didn't seem to be producing much but smoke. While he sat there he allowed Seth's words, Seth's ideas, to penetrate him drop by drop, like the rain that leaked through the roof. After a while of thinking about it he smiled ironically.

'I think I'm a bit in love with the idea of being a good person.'

'Why?'

Christopher turned himself around to face Seth, he could see the dark glitter of the other man's eyes beyond the cloud of tobacco smoke. Trying consciously not to hunch and shiver in the cold Christopher took a deep breath and allowed himself to embrace it all, the place, the questions, Seth's differences, even his own fear.

'Because I don't want my emotions to cause pain to others.'

'Why?' Seth shot out again, almost aggressively.

'Because... because I hate hurting people.'

'Why?'

Christopher's mind swam. For a moment he felt dizzy, as if he might actually be about to lose consciousness.

'I don't know. It's not a rational thing. I don't know.'

'It is unreasonable?'

'Yes,' Christopher said. 'It is an unreasonable thing, a thing of unreason.'

Seth sat back down. 'But it's still real.'

'Yes.'

'One of the most real things about you, isn't it Christopher? Your unreasonable compassion.'

'Yes.'

'Then magic,' Seth said, with a slight smile through which he exhaled the last of his cigarette smoke. 'Is a bit like that. You've never seen your compassion. Any psychologist could argue you to a standstill on it, tell you it's all self-interest in disguise. They would say it wasn't real. Maybe it isn't, in the way they define it. But you still feel it, you still experience it so strongly that it produces a physical reaction in you.'

'It's who I am,' Christopher said.

'Exactly. But perhaps who you think you are isn't real?'

Christopher smiled crookedly and continued to look into the fire, looking deep into the coals and wondering if fire ever feels the need to ponder how real it is to burn.

'I would never know would I? The way I feel seems real to me.'

'And I'm a magical being my friend. If magic isn't real then neither am I. That's about all I can tell you about it.'

Christopher nodded.

'You'll know soon enough if it's part of your nature. And if it is, as I suspect it is, there will be no other explanation for you that'll fit. Nothing else that'll fit at all.

'My god,' Seth said, gesturing at the stag's antlers on the mantelpiece, 'is a creature of shadows and secrets. He doesn't leave his mysteries in the places that just anyone looks. And yet at the same time his mysteries are only hidden by the fact that they are seen so frequently that nobody notices them anymore.'

Suddenly Christopher's mind flashed on the dream about Sophia. He saw her kneeling above him again with the golden sun disk behind her head and the shadows that seemed to obscure the cleft between her legs. Something made sense to him and it was impossible to say how. Seth had told him to use his hunger and that concept seemed, in that moment, the most crucial thing he'd learned.

'I want to know Him,' Christopher said. 'I don't understand what kind of god he is but when I see the flame up there between the antlers, it stirs something in me.'

Seth only smiled. 'Good. Because you won't get far with dealing with the dead without Him.'

'Why's that?'

'You might say that the Black Huntsman, Old Skrat some call him, holds the keys when it comes to who comes and goes from the Underworld. He's the guardian of our mutual obsession.'

Christopher raised his eyebrows slightly.

'Death.'

'I've never thought of it as an obsession.'

Seth laughed heartily. 'You should start thinking about it, Compassion-Boy.' Seth slapped Christopher hard on the back. 'Cause you're going in there, down to the underground. And if you don't think you're doing it out of an obsession, I'd back out now.'

'I'm past the point of backing out,' Christopher murmured.

'You're like the Sun, Christopher. You're the light of all lights.

This is your test, your descent into the Underworld, your harrowing of hell. Just like when Jesus did it, but with a fuck load more heresy. It just remains to see whether you can handle the blackness of True Midnight. Because the death mystery ain't something out of Victorian sentimental poetry.'

'I know that,' Christopher said quietly.

'Don't be too fast to say that. You've no idea what you're saying yet.'

12

'I shall be telling this with a sigh
Somewhere ages and ages hence:
Two roads diverged in a wood, and I—
I took the one less travelled by,
And that has made all the difference.'
—Robert Frost

Sophia sat on her inflatable couch looking at the finger bone that she had stolen. *I must be going crazy,* she thought. It would never have occurred to her before to take something from a find. It was stealing from the nation, from a dead guy... But in a way Sophia didn't *feel* the way about it that she *thought* about it.

The world seemed to be going crazy around her and by comparison the action seemed almost normal. Almost as if it was abnormal that some people didn't feel anything toward the people whose bodies they studied. Her own insistence on rationality was starting to seem ridiculous to her. She turned the bone over in her hand. Looking down at this fragile relic of someone's lost past she wondered which finger the digit was from. She couldn't remember. But it was part of a real person's hand that hurt when he hit something, that he ate his food with, pleasured his woman with, and maybe played an instrument with. It was certainly used to wield a sword.

Sophia found herself slowly shaking her head. She frowned. *People like Seth exist. Everywhere, every day, we are surrounded by ghosts, by seers of ghosts, and people with secret otherworldly lives. They pass us every day in the street, looking normal, looking like me. All the while our eyes see only their mundane identity, when all around us is magic, mystery, horror and heartache, love and redemption. There are stories that would amaze us, if we could see the half of them written on the faces of those we pass in a crowd.*

All her life Sophia had been trying to be normal, trying to

concur with what she assumed everyone else thought. Then she met Christopher and everything seemed different. Now she felt as though she were standing on the abyss of abnormality, about to take a plunge that could make her a permanent exile. Somehow she knew that if she took that leap she could never recall it.

Images passed through her head while the TV and radio played at the same time. Another game show mingled with the Top 40 chart as she looked at the bone in her hand and thought. Thoughts flashed through her mind of different men she'd gone out with and how much they hadn't understood her, and her friends and how they hadn't understood. Then she thought of her family who loved her but hadn't understood, didn't understand and would never be willing to understand. She thought of the luxurious intimacy of having people *know*. After the initial fear of exposure had come the warmth of shared secrets. Christopher. Christopher who did understand. And even Seth, who was a pain in the arse, but who also understood. Suddenly she found herself nodding very adamantly.

'Bloody hell,' she murmured, reaching for the remote control to turn off the television. 'All right then.' She got up and went over to the radio and turned that off also. Silence fell over the room with an air of ponderous expectancy. Quietly Sophia exhaled and began to switch off the lights. When it was done and there was only the dim light from the street outside she sat down on her couch with the finger bone. For the first time in a while she was aware of her breath, of the sound of her heart beating. *All right,* she whispered inwardly, *come and get me.*

It was like vertigo, the sudden drop in her stomach, like going to ground level in an old elevator. Her head swam and for a moment she thought she was about to lose consciousness or even be sick. A strange heat pulsed in her temples. It was coming from the swimming feeling at the back of her head as it crested up in a great tingling wave to the front of her head.

Slowly she opened her eyes. Before she did so she knew there would be someone there. She braced herself. Silhouetted against the light from the window was the finger bone's owner, Artyn. Unlike Eugene the manifestation didn't completely block out the light, he mingled with it, forming an indistinct image that swam like heat on a pavement. When he moved Sophia felt the static in the air like someone had run a plastic ruler across her hair.

'You are ready to talk then, yes?'

Sophia swallowed hard and nodded.

'Thank you for coming,' she whispered.

There was a faint sound of laughter.

'There is much to say. This is hard for me. Will you help me?' he asked.

Sophia found herself reminded of Christopher by the man's simple openness and relaxed masculinity.

'What can I do?' she asked.

'Lie down on your bed and come over the wall into my world.'

'How do I do that?'

'Lie down on your bed, I shall show you.'

Sophia got up and walked into her room. She was acutely aware that Artyn was close behind her. She couldn't help thinking of the tales of incubi and women who were raped by ghosts.

'I will not hurt you, lady,' he said. 'You are in my protection.' This was said like a man for whom honour was lived and breathed rather than put on occasionally like a suit for weddings, as it is for most modern men. She felt ashamed of her mistrust.

'Don't be,' came his unobtrusive voice. 'Pardon my intrusion.' But instead of feeling her mental privacy violated Sophia was filled with a sense of comfort and trust. The feeling came from the man's energy as he had reached out to her to read her mind. Sophia lay down on the bed and Artyn came to stand beside her. His proximity felt as strong as a mortal man's, even though the visual image of him was not.

'Close your eyes,' he murmured. She did so and almost instantly she felt that dropping sensation again. It made her a little nauseas and she wasn't sure she liked it. Then a rising feeling followed it. Her eyelids started to flutter. In fact it felt like she was fluttering all over and she knew that whatever was happening it was Artyn doing it. A pulling sensation began, an odd insistent tugging, like someone trying to pull a tight glove off their hand. As she forced herself to relax and not become afraid the nausea gave way to a sense of euphoria, a shimmering release before she was lifted like a child. At first she thought the spirit had somehow lifted her off the bed, or caused her to levitate, but when she opened her eyes she realised this was not the case.

Not only was she not in her body, she was standing in another place altogether. Looking around her Sophia saw that she was in a dimly lit, circular hut with a central fire. She could smell hay and smoke. Looking at Artyn in amazement Sophia saw that the now alive and solid looking young man was smiling at her.

'Welcome to my home,' he said, inclining his head slightly and briefly touching his brow with his fingers. 'Would you sit lady?'

'Where am I?' Sophia whispered, staring around her at the weapons by the door and the human skull that was worked into the wall near the entrance.

'The Otherworld. It just looks like my home because I projected it from my mind for you to see.'

He gestured toward the rush mat. She moved towards it and sat. As impolite as she knew it was she couldn't help staring at him. In the flesh like this, or in the perfect illusion of the flesh that it was, he seemed even more foreign to her. His way of moving and sitting, his cat-like agility and flexibility that came through even in these simple motions and his hardened form so unconsciously displayed, were all like nothing she had seen.

'Okay... Well, God, please tell me some things about yourself

Artyn.'

Her mind was racing but she had no idea how to start. He grinned and looked down.

'I would lady,' he murmured, 'if I could stop looking at you.'

Sophia found herself blushing. Not because she was shy, but because he was so much of a man in a way she wasn't used to.

'Why... why are you staring?'

'Because you are so strange to me. You are like... something from a world beyond the waters, like the ladies that live below the lakes. You do not look like my women.'

'You're not exactly the norm where I come from either.' He laughed and then began to look serious. 'Do you think that I'm...' he appeared to search for a word, 'savage? A barbarian?'

Sophia shook her head immediately, though a day earlier if asked she would have said yes.

'No, you seem like a gentleman. I want to hear everything about you.'

'I don't know what you would have me say, lady.'

'Everything, anything,' Sophia said, gazing intently at him. She wished she had her clipboard. 'I want to understand, all of it. What life meant to you. How it's different to what life means to me. How much of what has gone before is unlike all I know. That's what I've been looking for in the dust Artyn, when I dig people's skeletons up. I'm looking to understand the past, the traces of people's lives.'

Artyn smiled at her, as though faintly amused by her passionate tirade. She looked at the delicate white line of a scar along the bronzed sinews of his forearm.

'How do you do it? Tell me that. As a warrior, going into battle, fighting, and killing. How does any human being pit soft, tearable flesh against iron blades and not die of fear.'

Artyn laughed outright this time.

'My body's not soft,' he replied.

'No,' she said with a faint smile. 'Not by comparison to mine, but by comparison to iron... well it's looking pretty squishy. What keeps you strong, don't you want to just run away?'

He shrugged, and picked up a stick with which to poke at the fire.

'I don't know, my lady. How can I answer? Being a warrior is just what I am. Fighting is what I do, what I was trained for. Running away is not an option because my people could die if I did that. What do you want me to say? Love? Honour? Pride? It was all of those things. But also it is just my purpose.'

He shrugged again.

'But you make it sound so natural to be that way, so easy. You've got to realise that for me I've never had to personally face naked blades, nor have I met anyone who's had to fight and die in the way you did. I want to understand why a warrior thinks he has to do those things.

'I try not to think at all. It's like playing music lady. You think, you slip.' He grinned widely. 'Except if you slip...' He made a gesture with his arm that seemed to indicate a very rapid but effective deathblow. He laughed at this gory fact of his life with real mirth, as though death were some kind of street parade. Sophia frowned, a little disconcerted. *Ah, I get it*, she thought, *he's mad as a hatter*. 'But,' he said, shrugging again. 'If you slip, you seldom know about it for long. You wake up in Annwn with your gods and your honoured ancestors. It is a better life than that of a bard. If he slips he loses his good name and is open to ridicule. Life is simple for a warrior, straightforward. I hope to do good and right. If I live I get to come home to my woman for another summer. If I die then everything is summer. Perhaps my name will be remembered for my bravery.' He paused for a moment and looked quizzically at Sophia, frowning but half smiling as though he just did not know what to make of her.

'But it seems to me lady that your world does not care over-much for things of the spirit.'

This time it was Sophia's turn to smile.

'My world doesn't know over-much about the life of the spirit at all, Artyn. I think they think it's something you can get at a Day-spa.'

Artyn didn't smile this time. He shook his head and got up to walk over to the wall of his hut, which he then leant against. After a while of thinking he sat down against the wall with his legs crossed and shook his head again.

'It is a wonder that they do not starve to death inside and dry up like husks that the wind can blow away.' There was a faraway look in his eyes as he uttered these very poetic words. Sophia was struck by a shadow of the profound melancholy that she associated with the Gaelic races, in him in that moment. It made her think of a long ago Brythonic England and gave that idea an authenticity it had not had for her before.

'Sometimes they do, Artyn,' she said, with a bitter little smile. 'But I don't want to talk about my world. I don't want to even think about it. Make me believe in your world, tell me more about this life of the spirit that is so real for you. I want to know what you felt.'

'I felt things too numerous to speak of, as does any man. I have so many things to tell you that are so much more important than me.'

Sophia shook her head, getting up and starting to pace back and forth in front of the fire.

'I don't think so Artyn. I think someone once said it to me, I can't remember. But I have this thought in my mind: that there are no unimportant things, they are all connected to other things that matter deeply.'

'All right,' he said simply, but with so much surrender and sincerity that it was painful. 'I was only just a man when the Romans came. I suppose it that where I begin. My people were Durotriges. My woman was a... a shamaness, I suppose, a priestess.' Each of his sentences were spare and yet laden with understated emotion. 'We were one of the last pockets of full resistance. The men were divided on what we should do. Resistance was the only thing I knew. When I looked at the land around me all I could see was resistance, our resistance mirrored back at me. It was all through the heat in my blood. Our Chief decided to fight but many were not pleased. I lived through the first encounter, but many did not. I saw my brother die. We had been surprised and it was rapid. They doubled back, sending some of their force to burn our encampment and sack the temple. It was that decision that saved me.' He paused. 'But it caused her death. Afterwards I found her still dying of the wound they gave her. She was the last of our wise-ones.

'While she died she told me and showed me secret things so our traditions would not be lost, things that I have kept inside me to this day, things that went into the grave with me and waited out the many winters that frosted my bones. I have not forgotten what she wanted me to remember. I will not let her die you see, lady. She can never be dead for me if I preserve her mystery. Mystery is a woman's heart,' he said with a sad smile. He looked at Sophia. 'Come we don't have much time.'

Frowning Sophia shook her head in incomprehension.

'Hang on, hang on, what do you mean, come we don't have much time? You tell me this amazing, terrible story and then you're just, like, well anyway, with that out of the way down to business...'

'What do you want me to say?' he asked flatly.

'I don't know!' she snapped. 'That you cried.'

'I cried,' he replied, just as flatly.

'That you're susceptible to normal human weakness like fear and maybe copping out or something.'

He looked at her for a long time with his arms folded, his face without expression. Then he moved as though disturbed out of his thoughts. 'I do not know what you mean by, copping out, but I am susceptible to normal human weakness like fear.'

Sophia was infuriated. There was nothing she hated more

than things she couldn't understand, especially when the thing that was so mysterious was something that was being hidden from her.

'Let me say this,' his voice was very low now. 'If there were some words that I know not of that could undo what was done or touch my grief with some measure of healing then I would say them. There are no such words so it matters not whether I choose to add tears to the telling.' He sighed and walked over to the fire.

'I guess I just want to understand how you coped.'

Artyn's expression changed at last, to crease into a smile with more than a hint of bitterness in it. 'That is easy: I didn't.'

His answer seemed to gut her for a second. Sophia couldn't speak. His understated statement of his pain was too poignant. Without realising she was doing it she moved toward him.

'I'm sorry,' she murmured, 'I've been cruel, thoughtless...'

'I'm not easily offended,' he said quietly. His voice and smile were soft but his hand firmly prevented hers from settling on him and showing sympathy. 'Please, don't pity me.'

13

'I wander by the edge
Of this desolate lake
Where wind cries in the sedge:
Until the axle break
That keeps the stars in their round,
And hands hurl in the deep
The banners of East and West,
And the girdle of light is unbound,
Your breast will not lie by the breast
Of your beloved in sleep.'
—W.B. Yeats

'I don't want to hit you,' he murmured.

'I don't care,' Seth replied, grinning at him, his eyes shining darkly. 'Come on, Christopher. I thought you wanted to be a warrior? That involved cutting people up with swords you know. This is just a punch in the face. But it's the reality.'

'I don't wan—'

'No one cares what you want!'

'Seth! Can I at least explain?'

'Explain what?' Seth's face was lit by moonlight and glistened with the sheen of sweat.

Christopher looked at him and shook his head. 'I care about you too much.'

'I didn't tell you to stop caring about me. I told you to hit me. It's just like with the rabbit.'

Christopher felt like he was about to cry. The response shocked him. He found he was still shaking his head. It felt wrong in his whole body and he was torn between his desire to please Seth and his own internal feeling that told him not to strike people he cared for.

'Christopher,' Seth sighed, standing back and crossing his

arms, 'I respect the fact that you won't be bullied or ridiculed into it. But you know what? You wanted to learn to fight. You thought you wanted to be an old-school warrior and you want to be able to protect yourself and those you care about. I can't do that without us hitting each other. So you're going to need to accept, that for you to serve compassion and rightness, protect the weak etc, you'll need to do violence.

'Think of it as one of those Zen paradoxes if you like. Do violence to preserve gentleness. Whatever! Just fucking hit me.'

Christopher nodded. It was like with the rabbit. Something hardened in him, snapped into place but it wasn't callous. It was about understanding and it came from the softness in him. With no anger or dislike Christopher punched Seth in the mouth with medium hardness. Seth stumbled slightly and his hand went to his face. Christopher felt sick to his stomach as soon as he saw the blood on Seth's lips. But Seth grinned at Christopher.

'Good, that was a decent punch,' he said, licking his top lip free of blood. 'I was beginning to think you were fucking soft.'

Christopher shrugged. 'Maybe I am. But last time I checked punching people you love in the face isn't normal.'

Seth raised his eyebrow. 'So you love me do you?'

Christopher smiled and rolled his eyes. 'Yes, you prick, of course I do.'

'Love you too,' Seth said, blew a sarcastic kiss to Christopher and punched him in the mouth.

The force sent Christopher staggering. He felt it jar his jaw and the dizziness of his brain impacting with his skull. Shaking his head he turned to look at Seth, a little shocked. Seth was looking at him very seriously now.

'I really do,' Seth said. 'It's a privilege to be involved in the first time you've hurt another man, and been hurt.'

Then he hit Christopher again. This blow impacted with Christopher's cheek and made him see stars; something he'd always thought was a metaphor. Its force settled in the base of his stomach and made his legs feel weak and heavy. But the image of the way Seth had looked at him as he did it, the respect and affection in his eyes, stayed with him for longer. After a moment he felt Seth's hand on his shoulder steadying him.

'That is an important first step. I'm going to teach you to fight now. But how you perceive violence and what you understand about fighting is a big part of the battle.'

Christopher dabbed at his mouth and they both laughed. Both men were feeling a little punch-drunk.

'I'm sorry I argued with you for so long.'

'Glad you did,' Seth replied abruptly.

'Why's that?'

Seth shrugged. 'Shows strength of character. If you didn't I would have thought you were weak and easily led. Blind-Freddy could have seen it didn't feel right for you. I just wanted to see if I could bully you into it, or whether you'd have to understand it first.' Seth slapped Christopher on the back hard. 'You did well.' He wiped his face. 'I told you the magic was always testing you.'

'This is magic too?' Christopher found himself continually awe-inspired by the scope and depth of what that one word encompassed in Seth's vocabulary.

'Course it is. Anything that makes the human spirit wake up and remember itself is magic, anything that thrills it, or tests it. Where blood is shed there is magic, where the hairs on the back of your neck prickle there's magic. Hell, where breath is drawn there's magic.'

When he rose early in the evening before the sun was fully set, Christopher would sit outside the run-down hut and watch it sink. His clothes were a little ragged now, and his hair was growing out into a shock of blond that more often than not fell in similar, not quite clean, clumps as Seth's. He had more than a couple of day's stubble on his face and the bruises from his training session were still healing.

As he did on many evenings Christopher had a notebook balanced on his knee. The hand that held the pen was grazed on the knuckles and calloused, but the pen moved with feverish pace across the page. Christopher glanced back and forth rapidly between his writing and the blood red spectacle of the sunset.

Every night Christopher worked hard physically. Every night he did rigorous magic training, honing his awareness and concentration. At the end of every night he would be trained in fighting. Seth said the whole process was making him ready to "go in" and that the exercise and combat was increasing his vital force. Although all men go to the Otherworld, not many men return, Seth explained. It wasn't that they were all prevented; they just didn't wish to leave. They were too much in love and their will was not in balance with their love. Christopher understood a lot more now. He knew that Seth was trying to make his will equal to his love. What he didn't understand was why he needed to go to the Otherworld when he summoned a spirit.

'Necromancy, the art of conjuration of the dead, is just bringing the Otherworld closer and yourself closer to it. You and the shade meet in the middle if all goes well, it is 'riding the Hedge', having one foot on one side and one on the other.' Seth explained.

So Christopher kept working hard. He exercised his ability to see what was beyond. He went through these exercises with a dedication seldom seen but in those who are deeply in love. Almost every hour he did the exercises that Seth had given him. Already he could see a new vital-force glow around animals and plants and people. Sometimes he saw elementals, small moving lights that appeared when he was alone in nature or looking up at the night-sky. But so far Christopher had not yet seen a human spirit he had only 'felt' the touch of that presence in his room that paralysed him that night. His eyes had grown distant with gazing at what was beyond things. Seth said it was a good sign and that it meant he would soon be fully open. He said that an occultist's eyes change as they can see more and you can watch them take on greater depth, and therefore more shadows and obscurities.

The night before they had gone into the woods together to a special tree stump that Seth used to make offerings to the spirit being he called the 'Black Huntsman.' A bowl of blood and milk had been prepared for him that they carried with them.

'Now we don't really want the Black Huntsman arriving here, that's not the purpose of the sacrifice. We aim to send it down to him in the Under-earth and it's best given our intentions that you do the offering.'

'Okay,' Christopher said, as the moss covered stump loomed ahead of them in the moonlight. 'How do I send it down to him?'

As they drew closer Christopher was able to see that the stump was littered around with clean picked bones and mossy segments of antler. It appeared that Seth had been working at that site for some time.

'Approach the earth-shrine and kneel down in front of it. You have to be down in your guts and balls, remember? Like I've told you. Not up in your head, down low. Stay like that until you feel your own blood tingling. Then start to think about the cavernous mouth of darkness that is the Underworld entrance in this place. Feel the opening there beneath you and simply think on the lurking black presence of the Lord of the Dead below. Will him the blood and milk, extend your awareness to him, tell him you wish to reach out to one from his realm and that when the time comes you wish him to release Eugene into your triangle.'

Christopher nodded to himself. Looking down at the pinkish stain that swirled in the milk in the bowl he held. Already just hearing Seth's words he was aware of the tingling in his blood and the feeling was no longer merely in his head. Without any more questions he went forward. Pausing before the tree stump, in a pale column of moonlight Christopher felt awash with the natural, innate religiosity of the woodlands. The sense of being in a green, night-time temple was so strong he knelt without even thinking.

The dewy wet ground began to soak through the fabric of his jeans and his knees sank slightly in the loamy earth. Immediately Christopher's newly primed senses began to feel he was sinking lower than the soggy ground had really given beneath his weight. Christopher felt like little goblin hands were reaching for him and deeper below, the awesome, bestial and chthonic force of the Lord of the Woodland himself, the King of the Dead.

Christopher held out his hands with the bowl of milk in them and mutely, in his heart rather than his head, asked the blessing that Seth had named for him. As soon as that desire came awake, raging like a newly disturbed insomniac in the darkness of his insides, he poured it out to the Black Huntsman below as he spilled out the milk. Christopher saw it seeping down to him. Almost immediately a heat filled him, a heady sudden heat that made Christopher feel he might faint for a moment. It reminded him of a more intense version of that feeling he'd had when he accidentally shed blood at Eugene's graveside. Yet now he under-stood the feeling better. It was the chattering dead, massing up close, just below the surface, reaching cold hands, gathered in the brambles, just out of sight. And somehow he knew they weren't just out there or under there, but they were *under his skin* also. As he lingered on his knees before the earth-shrine Christopher knew that the distance he would need to go to reach out for Eugene's hand had just become a little narrower.

He wrote it all down, poured out his desires, his moments of self-doubt, and his inglorious moments of petulant resistance, his triumphs and his insights. Today he wrote down what Seth had told him earlier:

He says that there will be no 'ifs' 'buts' or 'maybes' on the day. And afterward I will never have to ask 'what if?' I'll simply give it every-thing I have. That way I won't be around to know if something went wrong. Necromancy is an art that functions off people's vital force and it involves dealing with the God of Death. If he doesn't feel my sacrifice is worthy or if I make a mistake, I won't need to worry about feeling bad about it! That's how Seth operates, its balls-to-the-wall and down to business.

Christopher smiled as he closed the notebook. He liked the feeling. It was honest and simple. He was learning the wisdom that can only be learned when your own survival is on the line. It was putting his whole life in perspective.

'What will you say to him?' Seth asked when they were sitting around the fire that night.

Christopher sighed. 'I have no idea. How can anyone answer that until they're there?'

'I don't mean what exactly. I just mean, what's the balls of it? The guts of what you have to get off your chest?' Seth was leaning close to him.

As always intimacy with Seth contained affection and aggression in equal measures. Christopher found his challenging manner stimulating, and he was saying things he'd never thought he'd say to anyone.

'I wouldn't *say* a lot.'

'Would you want to touch him?' Seth asked.

Christopher nodded.

'Did you touch him when he was alive?' Seth asked, whittling at a piece of wood while he spoke.

'Ah huh.'

Seth nodded. 'You're a true obsessive like me then.'

'How so?'

'You don't have the normal story, you know? You don't have some special thing you never got to say. The unspoken I love you, the fucking deathbed confession gone wrong, bloody unshared kiss business. You just love him. And you don't want to let go.'

There was a silence during which Seth rapidly brushed some

wood shavings off his clothes and onto the floor. The stray cat that had started sharing the ruin with them rubbed itself languidly against Seth's leg. It rubbed in one direction and then the next, inclining its ginger head up to Seth to be scratched. Seth smiled at it ruefully and patted it.

He accepted it into his life the same way he accepted me, Christopher thought. *Just because he sensed its need.*

'Everyone forgets them, Seth,' he said after a while.

'So you want to be the one who remembers?' Seth asked. 'The resident psychic bone-house?'

'Eugene believed that when he died he would live on through me.'

Seth nodded. The expression on his face was grim. He put his whittling down.

'And he has, that he has,' Seth murmured, almost as though to himself.

'Do you see him?' Christopher asked, ignoring Seth's pregnant statement.

'Oh yeah,' he replied.

'Well?' Christopher urged impatiently.

'Well what?'

'You really are a bastard, Seth and I don't mean that in the way that flatters you.'

Seth laughed quietly. 'Your comments seemed a little laden with meaning, wouldn't you say?' Seth looked at him and all jocularity fell away from the situation.

'Christopher...' he sighed. 'With children and all young people who die before they finish growing up... it often happens with twins. One of the twins dies but it still possesses what we call a half-life through the other. It takes half of the vital force of the other and lives on, and lives things out through the living twin.

'What I'm trying to say Christopher is that your Eugene, he's not a child anymore.'

'But Sophia said she's seen him as a child or as a thirteen year old boy anyway.'

Seth smiled but it was still a bit grim.

'Oh, he looks like a young boy. Or he can do when he wants to. But don't be fooled by it. Eugene is not a child. He's the same age as you are and he's seen and done and absorbed everything that you have and possibly a lot more besides. You won't know what to expect from how he's grown up until you see him.'

14

'History is a nightmare from which I am trying to awake.'
—James Joyce

Sophia felt embarrassed suddenly, standing so close to Artyn and having been about to touch him. Moving back she made a few useless apologies. He didn't say anything in reply. Sophia noted that he didn't seem acquainted with the civilised art of talking for talking's sake.

Artyn's whole stance, the very independence of his masculinity seemed to reject her pity and seemed to almost reject *her* somehow. It was both threatening and alluring to Sophia. A thought came to her, sudden and unwanted, *what would it be like to go to bed with a guy like this? Is an old-school Briton warrior the 'wham bam thank you ma'am' type? Or was foreplay already around back then? Did they even share our custom of kissing on the mouth? Would his Durotriges priestess ever have gone down on him?*

'I do not know if I am making a mistake. But it is you that I want to give it to. What she gave me.'

'What is 'it'?'

Artyn sighed and rolled his eyes. For the first time he looked angry with her, as though this above all else tried his patience. Well they seem to use the same facial expressions to express exasperation, she thought.

'If I could tell you that, it would not be a Mystery.'

Sophia put her hands on her hips. 'So I'm meant to just say yes to whatever it is because it's some arcane mystery? Even if I don't know what it is? What if I don't like it? I mean you've dragged me into some other dimension and now you won't even do me the courtesy of telling me what I'm saying yes to?'

Artyn had half turned away but now he turned back and suddenly grabbed Sophia around the shoulders with his hands. It wasn't rough but Sophia cried out in shock.

'Woman, you talk too much!' he said, giving her a light shake of frustration.

'I have a name, thank you!'

'Yes, I know. Sophia, the way the Greek people say 'wisdom.' It is very beautiful. But you do not act with great wisdom now Sophia. You act like a silly, little girl.'

'Fuck you!' she cried, trying to pull free. Realising she couldn't she panicked and lashed out. She tried to slap him but he easily deflected her blow and moved his leg up to prevent her kneeing him in the groin. He didn't appear ruffled or surprised.

'Are you finished?' he asked.

Her lips pursed Sophia glared steadily at him. 'Yes,' she said quietly through clenched teeth. Pushing her back he released his hold on her. Her first impulse was to run at him and hit him again. But she had no wish to embarrass herself further. Her next impulse was to direct the baleful eye at him.

'Now a Mystery, Lady, is a Mystery. Respect it. Please. You will find it worth it. And if you don't you have no obligation to use it.'

Sophia took a long shuddering breath. She couldn't help thinking of her ex, Josh, who used to hit her. She hated being manhandled again.

'I think you are shopping in the wrong place for your girls, sweetheart. Because women in your century might have gone in for this muscle bound machismo thing. But it doesn't do much for me.'

He grinned at her quite unexpectedly. Then he took her arm.

'What?'

Before she could say anything else he pulled her toward him right up against his body. Taking her face between his fingers he turned her chin up toward him and kissed her.

Sophia made a sound of protest for a moment and then stopped. His tongue pressed into her mouth and her breasts were pushed up against the bare muscles of his chest. She felt her body surrender and it filled her with irritation for a moment. But then she was swept up in the hard male feel of him.

Almost at that very moment he released her, leaving her flushed and speechless.

'You talk too much, lady,' he said quietly.

That was an accusation Sophia hardly felt in the position to dispute. There were a few moments of silence before she felt able to speak again.

'Yes.'

'Yes what?' he asked in a weary voice.

'Yes to your Mystery.' Sophia's eyes felt as open as wounds as she let him look into them. Her hands trembled a little.

Artyn looked at her for a moment, as though he were searching for something in her gaze. 'You have the second-sight with your eyes but do you have those eyes in your heart also?' he asked.

'I don't understand what you mean.' Her voice was little more than a reverential whisper.

'Do you see only with your mind or can you feel things too?' he said, indicating his chest.

'It was always in my head before. But with Christopher...' Sophia paused, embarrassed suddenly at the realisation that she hadn't mentioned Christopher before.

'Christopher is your man?'

'Umm, ahh, yeah, sort of. I mean yes. Yes, I suppose he is.'

Artyn looked at her oddly, as though she were complicating a perfectly straightforward question.

'And you mean when you lay with him, you started to feel things?'

'Lay with him,' she murmured, musing on the term. 'That's kind of nice. What a shame we don't say that anymore. Umm, yes, when I lay with him I felt things that seemed to come from him, or were connected with him. It opened me up to feeling all sorts of things.'

Artyn nodded. 'That is the way of it. You share of your life essence, of your being. It is,' he said, looking down into the fire for a long time before looking back up suddenly, 'the best way to give something to someone.'

There was a brief moment where the implications of his statement began to sink in and Sophia felt a little blood suffuse her cheeks. His bright blue eyes were looking steadily at her. For a moment they reminded her of Christopher's eyes. Artyn was sitting casually with one arm resting on his bent knee, looking. She felt naked, as though he may as well have been looking directly between her legs. Clearing her throat she managed to say, 'Are you saying we need to have sex to do this?'

He simply nodded, as though he were not the least bit uncomfortable.

Again her mind flashed to images of Christopher but she pushed them away, fearing they would cloud her judgement. Was this the right thing to do? Could having sex with a ghost be considered cheating on Christopher? Was there even reason to consider herself Christopher's woman.

'It is of course ritual, you understand, rather than personal?'

Sophia blinked several times in incomprehension. 'I'm sorry, can you explain how rubbing your genitals against someone else's is not personal?'

Artyn looked at her for a moment before roaring with laughter. 'You have a very strange way of putting things lady.' He managed to get out in between laughing.

Sophia watched him laugh a bit more while she tried to be patient.

'You see,' he said eventually, still grinning. 'In ritual you are not fully yourself. You are your spirit-self, devoid of the everyday person. The rubbing genitals part does not matter, not like the rubbing souls part matters.'

'So through the sexual act you can give me the Mystery your woman gave you?' she clarified.

He just nodded.

'Did… did your woman give it to you like that?'

'Yes,' he replied. There was a short pause and then he said, 'Believe me, this does no wrong to your man, Sophia. Otherwise I would not be doing it. You will be behaving as a priestess not a woman.'

'I'm not a priestess.'

'You will be.'

Sophia nodded slowly to herself. 'What do I have to do?' she asked.

'You need to act as you do when you try to read a mind. Extend yourself toward me. Try to merge your power with mine.'

'So we're going to have sex and you want me to focus on your spiritual vibe?' she asked, with raised eyebrows.

'Yes,' he replied, with no obvious amusement.

'Am I allowed to get turned on or is that too personal?'

Artyn didn't seem to know what she meant for a moment but after appearing to think about it for a moment he laughed quietly.

'Let me put it this way Lady, I will find it very hard to do this if you are hating it. I'm not that sort of man.'

Sophia nodded as she examined his noble looking face in profile. 'You were very well born in your time weren't you?'

He nodded but didn't elaborate.

'You don't really want to do this, do you?' she asked, staring at him.

He looked up as though someone had stuck something in him. After a moment he regained his composure and looked away into the darkness. He opened his mouth to speak but didn't say anything.

'I'm sorry, I've upset you. I shouldn't have…'

He shook his head but still didn't speak. He got up abruptly and walked over to the wall, placing his arms against it and resting his head on it. He stood like that for some time. In that posture Sophia felt a deep sympathy for him and wished she dared go over and put her arms around him. He turned around then.

'Would you take your clothes off?' he said, his voice coming out very quiet.

Sophia saw the raw pain in his eyes but somehow it didn't discomfort her. She found herself not looking away as she pulled her top off over her head and unfastened her bra. Slipping her skirt down, she stood before him in only her underwear.

'It's all right,' she whispered. 'You don't need to explain.'

She took her underwear off and stood naked. He looked at her body for a little while before making a slight bow to her. Without knowing why she did it, she found herself making a light kind of curtsey.

'Lie down for me,' he said quietly, taking his cloak from off the nail in the wall and lying it down for her.

She did so. As she watched he knelt beside her and took out the dagger in his belt to put it off to one side. 'It is considered impolite,' he explained, before lowering his body down over hers. His groin came down level over hers, but he held the rest of his weight off her with his arms.

She closed her eyes as she felt his hand on her breast. While he touched her she noticed that his breath came in long even drafts, unlike the quick breaths an aroused man normally makes. It was more like meditation she noticed. She slowed her breath to try to breathe like that. But it was difficult; the sensation of his calloused hands working her breasts drove a breathy heat through her.

When his mouth closed unexpectedly over her nipple she moaned without meaning too and opened her legs further. She couldn't help wondering if she was meant to moan and she tried not too, as the long luxurious sucking continued. Taking deep breaths she tried to breathe the power gathering between her legs up her spine to the top of her head. Somehow she just knew that that seemed the right thing to do with it. But as though to let her know she could relax Artyn made a soft sound of pleasure as he reached down to touch between her legs.

Well this answers my question, she thought, *as his skilled and sensitive fingers explored her. Men did do foreplay in his time, and rather well too.*

'Relax lady,' he murmured, smiling at her as he leaned back and inserted his finger into her. 'It is natural and the Great Queen likes for us to enjoy it.'

Sophia smiled back at him and pressed softly against his hand. He knelt back after a moment to undo his trousers. She opened her legs wide and lay back watching him calmly. When he penetrated her it felt different to anything she had felt before. He took her completely in one thrust, which Christopher had been too gentle to do.

Along with a slight pain she also felt a dizziness that went straight to her head. With each of his thrusts the feeling became more intense. Very quickly she found she was beginning to become less aware of his body, which was really his subtle body but felt so real, something she didn't think she would easily forget. Then the sensation came that usually heralded the beginning of a trance state for her.

Visual objects started to blur together, with dots of colour and patterns that danced around the edges, they morphed and distorted and before long she started to flash on images that she knew came from Artyn. *It's like I'm drinking his thoughts,* she thought drowsily as it happened. She saw the image of a woman with long auburn braids over her shoulders. The image faded out like vision fades out when you faint, and then flared back stronger than ever. And with it the deluge... Some deep part of Sophia knew what this was; this was the power that she had been holding in check all her life, struggling to control, even when she didn't know what it was. Now it came down on her like the ocean...

...The temple. It was a passage tomb, like the Long Barrow, but the wall was set with the skull of a deer, and numerous human skulls. Ancestors, she knew them as though she'd known it her whole life. Those skulls were the dead shamans that they called on for aid. The smoke of the herbs and offerings tasted acrid in her mouth. She knew she was looking into the deep past, through the eyes of Artyn's own ancestors.

It took a while for the impressions to order themselves. Then she saw her naked body moving above Artyn's, the sweat on his skin glistening in the firelight. And she knew then how Artyn looked in the throes of real passion and how he looked at the woman he loved. Around her shoulders she saw the serpentine braids, treated in ochre and brushing her stomach as she pleasured him with a priestess' secret arts. She saw the cauldron being poured, blood and milk and herbs bubbling over the central fire. The women danced and a man kept a primal beat on the drum. The chant sliced through her like glass. She knew the words and she knew the stamp dance like her body had been formed out of these words and gestures. And then, so terrible, the flashes of agony as she died and died and died. It never seemed to stop.

She smiled at Artyn in their mutual passion and she saw the torc on his neck where the snake tried to bite its own tail. Leaning down over him she bit him gently on the lip. She knew he understood that they were like the snake; she saw his mystical adoration in his eyes as he looked at her, half unfocused with pleasure. Sophia heard herself speaking in their ancient Briton tongue and she understood herself. They were laughing.

Then the dying started again, the taste of blood...

'Artyn you must, you must there is no one to do it but you.'

And then his tears, they scalded her; she felt how they tore out of him. Sophia knew his grief.

Then she was in the temple again.

And Artyn made love to her, the most careful, painful love. She saw herself through his eyes then, the terrible wound that was killing her even as they lay together. He tasted her blood. And at the last minute she breathed the last of her life into him, shuddering with the effort of it, sending it home with her whole self. She breathed into his mouth, breathing fire like she was the dragon. And then her eyes glazed and he was still inside her while she died and he cried himself out while she bled out. She stared and stared at the sky, and never blinked again.

'Catrin.' She knew it was done. Felt how it all scorched its way into Artyn's soul and from Artyn's soul back into her.

'When it is safe Artyn,' she had said to him, 'give it to someone else.' The vision diffused through her whole body then and sealed it into her, down to the cellular level...

...Artyn's body felt cold and hers felt hot, it had swallowed his heat. His sweat was on her, she was wet and hot and dizzy. She opened her eyes. She expected to be gazing at the sky. But she wasn't. When she looked at Artyn his mouth was slightly open and his face was grey.

'Artyn,' she whispered, reaching up her hand to touch his face. She smiled. Somewhere in the back of her mind Sophia felt it. She knew she was her but she wasn't her. When she spoke it was not all her decision and her words surprised her, 'I love you.'

'Catrin,' he whispered.

'Don't try to talk my love,' her voice said in that strange tongue that was somehow so natural. 'You have done so well. Thank you Artyn.'

Sophia was struggling like a swimmer trying to reach the surface. She was almost there, trapped between two identities. But her eyes widened in horror when blood began to course out of Artyn's mouth and he started to choke on it.

'Oh my God,' she gasped. Artyn struggled to pull himself off her and free her from his body weight. When he did she saw the terrible wound. The sword cut that she had seen so many times in Artyn's skeleton. 'How did this happen?' she cried.

His breath was coming quickly with pain but he smiled at her.

'I can go to her now,' he managed to say, his voice coming out as a dry croak. 'I am back at my death. Thank you Sophia.... You really... are the... principle of wisdom.' Blood coursed out of him, running all over the floor, running onto her and he just got whiter and whiter... 'Give it to someone you love... keep it alive.'

He choked and more blood came out of his mouth. Then his face softened as he looked up at the ceiling. And she knew he could see the sky and that Catrin was coming.

When Sophia awoke in her body she was icy cold and trembling. Her first thought was that she was about to be sick. Immediately upon sitting up she dry retched several times. Taking deep breaths she managed to move her arms and legs and get the circulation moving again. Sitting in the darkness she rubbed her limbs vigorously and the nausea slowly started to fade.

'Jesus,' she kept murmuring, 'Jesus.' And while she rubbed herself she stopped every now and again to wipe the tears from her eyes.

15

'*Deep with the first dead lies London's daughter,*
Robed in the long friends,
The grains beyond age, the dark veins of her mother,
Secret by the unmourning water...'
—Dylan Thomas

Christopher and Seth were crouched side by side in the Long Barrow in the dim light of several tee-light candles that sat on the stone ledges of the barrow's interior. Around them was the echoing sound of water dripping steadily.

'What do we do if someone comes?' Christopher whispered.

The Neolithic monument gave off a similar atmosphere to a cathedral in that no one seemed to wish to raise their voice. Seth grinned at him.

'No one will come, trust me. I've worked this site for years. No one would dare when they see the candle light in here.'

Christopher shook his head. It was so strange to him that Seth had been practicing sorcery out here, only a few fields away from his family's home, for years and he had had no idea. He tried to imagine seeing the ancient site lit by a dim light at night, lit by an unknown occupant, and wondered if he would have approached? It seemed Seth had a point... With the thought that their privacy was pretty well assured Christopher set down the bowl of herbs he had been carrying, laying it on the sandy floor.

'We only have a little while before we must begin.' Seth observed.

Christopher nodded. This was his first practice session at invoking a spirit before the moment of truth when he would try it with Eugene. Nonetheless, he was well prepared.

Seth fingered the incense that Christopher had mixed, testing its consistency. It had the leaves of the yew, blackthorn, myrrh and marshmallow root 'We need one more ingredient for the incense.'

'What's that?'

'Blood,' Seth replied, taking out his pocket-knife and loosing the sharp blade inside. 'Your blood,' he added making a gesture for Christopher to give him his arm.

Christopher rolled up his sleeve immediately and offered his arm to Seth.

Seth smiled. 'You really do trust me don't you?'

'Yes.'

'Why? I can see no reason for it. I barely trust myself where other people's veins are concerned.'

Christopher shrugged. 'Call it a thing of unreason then.'

Seth turned Christopher's arm while they spoke, looking for a space where the veins were less intensely visible than they were on his wrist and hand.

'Does that mean you wouldn't prefer to do this yourself?'

'It does indeed,' Christopher answered with a smile. 'I imagine you're more experienced with blood-letting, so please.'

Christopher barely had the chance to finish his last word before Seth cut deftly and quickly into his arm. Christopher flinched a little with shock, even though it didn't hurt as much as he imagined. Then after a moment, as though his body had still been processing what had happened, a deep throbbing sting developed and Christopher felt the blood run out.

Seth held his arm over the bowl of herbs and allowed the blood to drip onto them and soak into the dry mixture. Breathing deeply Christopher watched the blood sluice down over his fingers. It felt strange. He both hated the feeling and was fascinated by it at the same time. Seth's fingers lightly stroked his arm for a brief moment, and Christopher was uncertain whether this was a comforting or 'milking' gesture.

He offered Christopher a cloth. 'Now staunch it with this. Press down hard.'

Christopher did as Seth said, and they both sat there in silence for a while.

As he pressed on the wound Christopher was more aware of his pulse, the movement of blood inside him and his heartbeat than he had ever been before. He glanced at Seth and noticed that the other man looked pale and his eyes seemed slightly unfocused, like he'd lost track of what they were doing. Christopher frowned. A strange compassion filled him. It was intuitive, instinctual, yet against all normal drives.

'When was the last time you drank blood, Seth? From a human I mean.'

'Your sister's I believe, my friend,' Seth said, sitting himself down against the stone wall of the cavern with his knees drawn up. 'Must have been months now.'

'Will you die without it?'

'Maybe. Given long enough I'd probably top myself. Without animal blood and being jabbed full of iron injections in a hospital, I think I would get sick, maybe eventually die, but long before that I'd just wish I had.'

'Is human blood better?'

Seth smiled then for a moment, showing his strong teeth. Christopher found himself thinking about how Seth's teeth walked some sort of extreme line. If a dentist examined them he would find them unusual, but not impossible, not freakish, not supernatural. They were merely on the extreme side of sharp, as some people's teeth are crooked and some have an extra set of canines that need to be removed or are missing canines altogether. Seth's head fell back against the wall and he looked up at the ceiling as if he was thinking, or tired, or both. Then he laughed.

'It's...God, it's like the difference between masturbation and sex. It's like the difference between iron supplements and a piece of steak. Yes, human blood is better.'

'I am bleeding quite a bit here. Why don't you drink mine?' His voice died away in the air and left a heavy silence.

Seth looked at him steadily after a moment but didn't say anything. He could not determine what emotion drove that stare or whether he had caused some kind of unmeant offence.

'I would like to do that,' he said after a while, and there was a strain evident in his voice to anyone really listening. 'But I don't know if I should.'

Christopher felt his blood soaking into the rag. He felt the blood resurge the moment he released the pressure he was holding on the material. In a heady sort of way Christopher wasn't sure if he didn't almost enjoy bleeding. Tentatively Christopher moved towards Seth and pressed his bloody fingers against Seth's lips. Seth's mouth opened almost as though it was an involuntary response. He licked the blood off Christopher's fingers.

Above his hand Christopher saw Seth's dark eyes looking up at him. It wasn't hard to read the expression in them; it was ravenous but there was also will power and self-control. Christopher just placed his bleeding arm in Seth's hands and continued to look at him. It seemed the most natural thing in the world to him, that when you sense another's hunger, especially someone you have come to care for, and it is within your power to satisfy it, you do so.

I think I understand you, Seth, Christopher thought in that moment, *I know what you mean about the hunger. We humans are comprised almost all of desires and needs. I crave Eugene's presence the way you crave blood.*

Seth pressed his lips down over the cut and Christopher felt him swallow the blood that ran out. Cold chills followed as Seth's mouth drew off his blood in a long, hard suck that seemed to strip his veins with its power. Christopher gasped quietly. Seth looked up at him again before taking another suck at the wound. He could feel Seth's tongue moving across his tender opened flesh and his teeth lightly graze it. It was clear to Christopher that he was holding back from using his teeth.

Then Seth pulled back very decisively and wiped his face several times. He sat back and looked up at the ceiling, as though he were either praying or did not wish to look at Christopher, or perhaps at his blood. After a moment he laughed.

'It's very sexual isn't it? I've never done it to a man before.'

Christopher didn't say anything, there didn't seem to be any need. He had never really been worried about social convention of that type. Seth pressed the material back over Christopher's arm and dressed the wound.

'That didn't disgust you did it?'

'No.'

Something vulnerable flickered in Seth's eyes for a moment before he looked away. He shook his head. 'You're a strange boy, Christopher.'

'Why? It made you feel better didn't it? Shouldn't that be all that matters?'

Seth laughed; it came out as a cynical sounding snort of air. He looked at Christopher and smiled slightly, an amused, gentle smile. 'Yeah, I guess it should.'

Christopher lay on Seth's bed beside Seth, both of them laying on their backs and looking at the ceiling like they had on the first night.

'What did she say to you?' Seth asked, in reference to the dead woman whose spirit they had evoked that night. Seth lifted up the stray cat that seemed to have made their shack his home and placed the ginger tom on his stomach so he could pet it.

'She didn't seem to know a lot about her past or about anything really. It was actually quite ghastly.'

Seth smiled and murmured, 'Ghastly.' I like that word, haven't heard it in years. Yes that's the Underworld, its heart of darkness. Oblivion. Or at least that's one aspect of it. Like Rosie Probert: '*I am going into the darkness of the darkness forever.*

I have forgotten that I was ever born.'

'What is that from?'

'Tut, tut, you Philistine!' Seth exclaimed, taking out a cigarette. 'That Christopher, my learned companion, is Dylan Thomas' *Under Milkwood*. That wonderful, drunken Welshman captured the entire inner life of a town in that radio play. And when he spoke of the dead, he spoke like a man who knows what it is to be haunted. ...*where the fish come biting out and nibble him down to his wishbone, and the long drowned nuzzle up to him.*' He threw out the quote in a very passable Welsh accent.

Christopher couldn't help a slight shiver. It was something about the word 'nuzzle.' He had a feeling that he himself had been so 'nuzzled' by the dead a few times now.

'Seth?'

'Yes?'

'Why did you think you shouldn't drink my blood?'

Seth sighed quietly. 'There are a lot of reasons. To be honest it's usually a sex thing for me, so it's a little more physically intimate than I was planning on getting.'

'Sorry. I seem to be good at missing all that stuff. It's Eugene's fault really. He seems to have destroyed my awareness of what normal intimacy levels are.'

'Don't be sorry,' Seth said, blowing smoke rings up into the air and watching them rise. 'It's one of my favourite things about you. Plus,' he shrugged, 'who am I to talk about normal? I'm a fucking vampire for the sake of the black hairy arse of the Lord of Hell!'

Christopher laughed.

'But I mean seriously, it's all just about where we decide to put our walls, our hedges, our fences... They don't really mean anything decisive, they're just walls. You just like to plant them pretty wide. Lucrece was like you.'

Christopher nearly jumped. It was the first time Seth had voluntarily used her name since he'd first told his story.

'She didn't really understand that other people thought there were walls at all, because she was a wild creature of the forest, forced to live in a walled garden. Consequently she just ploughed right through them without seeming to even realise it.'

'It's funny, I thought of you like that.'

'It is something I admire. I fell in love with that about her. I've tried to have as little bullshit in me as possible. I guess I've always hoped that I would get to have another relationship with someone outside of those boundaries. An 'outside the hedge' friendship, if you will. I only feel alive when I'm experiencing things that defy categorisation.'

Christopher nodded. 'I know just what you mean.' He looked over at Seth and then added. 'How well did you know her, Seth?'

Seth smiled sadly. 'Too well in all the ways you think matter at the time. Not enough in all the ways you realise matter later. It's funny,' he said, exhaling more smoke rings and turning his head to look at Christopher. 'You know, I think I get you and Eugene. There are so many different ways of falling in love. That's what people don't realise. It can be about characters and personality chemistry rather than physical chemistry. No sex to get in the way.'

'I never thought I'd meet a woman I could have that kind of chemistry with. I guess that's the curse of finishing your education at a boy's school. You fall out of the loop with girls.' Christopher replied.

Seth rolled over on his side to look at him more intently.

'Which is it?'

'Which is what?'

'Which one of them is it for you?'

Christopher frowned. 'Don't ask me that, Seth.' Seth stared intently at him and he added, 'It's too different. It's oranges and apples.'

'Why? Because of the sex?'

Christopher shook his head.

'It's more than that.'

'Then what?'

'I don't know. I just know it's different. Even if I did have sex with Eugene it would still be different, feel different...'

'It's still him isn't it?'

Christopher just shook his head.

'Don't, Seth,' he said quietly.

Seth reached over and squeezed his arm.

'Okay,' He stroked the wounded place on Christopher's arm for a second, as though to apologise for the poorly positioned squeeze, before suddenly, with all signs of compassion gone, slapping him on the arm as though he'd had an insight. 'You think your love for Eugene is higher because you didn't fuck him!'

'Do you mind?'

'See! That proves it. I used 'fuck' when you slept with Sophia and you never batted an eyelid.'

'He was thirteen and dying of a heart condition, Seth!'

'Don't be a prude! No one needs to get laid more than a dying virgin.'

'I'm not! I'm being... I don't know, a decent non-paedophile or something.'

'You really, totally are a prude! Listen to you. It was not as mere sublunary lovers love, but like unto gold to airy thinness beat.' Seth teased, sarcastically paraphrasing a John Donne poem they were both familiar with.

Christopher glared at him. 'I so do not think my love for Sophia is any less because we had sex!'

'Say it Christopher! Go on, *fuck*. Try it, you might like it.'

'I can say fuck just fine, Seth. It seems to be my carrying out of it or not that is attracting so much interest.'

'I just wanted to hear you say it,' Seth said, waving the curiosity aside. 'Okay, so why were you surprised to find a woman you could have real chemistry with?'

'I haven't experienced it before. The same reason, I would

imagine you were surprised to be drinking the blood of another man.'

'That's totally different. I have the opposite thing. You think lots of things *aren't* sexual, I think everything worthwhile is sexual. I'm just surprised that we can actually have a relationship of any intensity and I still don't feel like fucking you. You learn something new every day.' He shrugged.

Christopher sat up and faced Seth. 'But surely you can conceive of non-sexual intimacy. What about blood-drinking?'

'I already told you how sexual I find that. And I'm a little more biologically driven in who I get intimate with than you are. That's why even when I've been close to another guy I've never tried to drink his blood.'

'But isn't it more sensual than sexual?'

'What's the definition of that word?' Seth demanded.

'What, from the dictionary?'

Seth shook his head impatiently. 'Your definition.'

'Giving and receiving pleasure without one's genitals.'

'Or pain,' Seth smirked, 'if that's your bag.' He appeared to think about Christopher's definition for a moment before adding, 'so you'd say that sucking a woman's tits is sensual not sexual?'

Christopher laughed. 'Not with the genital response I get from it.'

'Or the response she gets from it. You're getting hard, she's getting wet, but it's just tits so surely it's sensual?'

Christopher shook his head. 'No, I think it matters what you're feeling while you're doing it, whether your mind is on sex. I mean women also feed babies with their breasts, so obviously people can do two entirely different things with the same part of their body.'

'So when does it start getting sexual for you? When you get a hard-on?'

'No. It can't be that, I've had a hard-on from brushing up against something, from adrenalin, when I first wake up in the morning, from just being eighteen... All these things can't be sexual.'

'Why not?' Seth asked.

Christopher rolled his eyes. 'The whole universe is sexual if we take your definition.'

Seth shrugged. 'The universe could do worse.'

'So you think my love for Eugene was sexual then?'

For some reason Christopher found himself wanting Seth to answer this question for him.

Seth poked at the fire and threw on some wood.

'I couldn't say as yet. You haven't told me enough about it. Tell me about your boy, Christopher. You've never really done it, not the way I did for you with Lucrece. Tell me the story of it, the things that cry out to be spoken of.'

Christopher nodded slowly. For a moment he wasn't sure it was possible even though he'd offered to do this very thing. So long had that story lived silently inside him, burrowing deeper into his marrow, he wasn't sure he could fetch it out again. So long had he tried to keep that story as still as possible because whenever part of it moved it hurt so much that movement now brought fear.

'Okay,' he began, 'I've never spoken a word of these things to anyone else. It seems fitting it should be you.' Christopher sat up on the side of the bed and Seth leant on the mantelpiece next to the antlers. Christopher took a deep breath and closed his eyes for a moment, and then he breathed out. With that out breath he felt something release in him. It was like a door flying open and breeze rushing in sending loose papers flying around a room. Dust went flying everywhere.

'The first thing I see when I close my eyes is Eugene when we were ten. He was new at school. His Mum Irene had just moved here and taken him from the Waldorf School in Devon to the one here. I noticed him not just because he was new and we were in small classes but because soon after he had taken a seat at a desk a few rows in front of me he turned around and looked at me. Not at everyone, as though he were looking around, but directly at me. I caught his gaze and he didn't look away. As soon as I saw his eyes I had this feeling... At the time I had no words for it. But I think it was what you would call 'Otherness'. He was like something from beyond the Hedge had taken human form. He just looked at me for a while, leaving me completely off balance, before smiling ever so slightly and turning back to the front. At lunch time that day he bounded straight up to me and said: "Hi I'm Eugene and I'm dying."

'Somehow the tragedy of that became instant for me. I was immediately wounded by that revelation, though of course, once again, I at the time had no explanation for why or how. But I was so excited that he picked me to talk to as if I was someone special, and then so utterly devastated by knowing he was going to die...

'He used to wear these horrendous knitted scarves his mum would make him in all these bright colours, and she wasn't even a very good knitter. Irene is a real dyed-in-the-wool Waldorf mum, or should I say an 'organic hand-dyed in the purest of local fleece Waldorf mum'. My mum doesn't do hand-made anything so I always remember Eugene and these bloody scarves. Even as early as ten he was quite a snappy dresser even though most of his stuff was second hand. Always picked his own clothes and would wear waistcoats and vests over button-up shirts. These god-awful scarves were his one concession to his mother's wants.

'We became friends immediately. I think when he told me he was dying instead of saying anything I just looked at him and bit my lip. It probably took me about a minute to say: "I'm Christopher". He put his head on one side and looked at me like he was worried he'd hurt me.

'I always had friends at school, I mean, everyone was a friend. It was that sort of environment. We were all in small classes with people we'd known since we were four or something. There was a lot of talented young people in that group but it was clear that Eugene was *brilliant*. His writing was way above my understanding at the time. But having been at a Waldorf school since the age of four I knew enough about music to stop and listen and feel impressed when I walked past the music room and he'd let himself in to play the piano. I played the guitar but I was never particularly gifted, not in those circles. So his accomplishment with the piano and cello was pretty intimidating. Not that I really got time to develop that intimidation about how gifted he was before he decided I was his best friend. I'd never had a best friend. And after Eugene... I just dropped off seeing any of my old school mates.

'Nobody talked about death at our school. Nobody except Eugene. Not to us kids. Most of us didn't see the News because we didn't see TV. So Eugene's blunt and somewhat perky statement about his impending death really affected me. I never would have called it falling in love; I didn't have a paradigm for that. Falling in love was something that men and women did when they were much older. But I guess I immediately fell in fascination with Eugene. Whenever he raised his hand to answer a question in class he would have my total attention. I couldn't wait for the lessons to be over so we could get outside and talk. He could make discussions about what was in his lunchbox sound like an epic tale.

'When I was at home and not with him I'd look forward to the next day at school so we could play and talk. I even worked out how to use the telephone for the first time so we could talk on the phone. We started staying at each other's places at least a couple of times a week and when we weren't together we talked online or on the phone almost all afternoon.

'I think after a while, with the familiarity, I started to not notice how strange he was. Like the fact he used to giggle when he was nervous or upset, rather than cry and that he would only cry when he was happy. That feeling of Otherness was just replaced by adoration I guess. When we were really little we played games and read books together. Eugene would invent on-going games that were acted out during the day so that the whole day became this story narrated by him. But I also remember it was hard and sobering from the first moment because from that first moment I knew I would lose him. A bit of childhood dies when you really come to understand something like that. Then there would be moments where it would become too clear. I remember him coming over funny at school one day and me practically catching him as he fainted. I was beside myself screaming for help from the duty-teacher...

'And then he would be in hospital for weeks at a time and they would operate on him. Mum was really good about it, I realise now. She would drive me in or drop me at the hospital or let me go home with Irene every day so I could be with him. I remember overhearing my mother describe it to my father as a 'friend crush' and 'totally normal'.

The doctors were trying to repair his heart but hoping for a donor heart for him. But he seemed to be the hardest person to find a match for; he developed an antibody response to every test every time we thought there was hope. And of course child sized hearts are always in short supply. He would always sit up in bed and be so cheerful. If ever he saw me looking anxious or down he'd grab my chin and make me look at him.

"Don't mourn for me while I'm here in the room, it's rude." He'd gin when he said it. He always reminded me of that over the years. That was his catch phrase whenever he caught me doing it. It wasn't until we were about twelve nearly thirteen that things became more intense. He had always been touchy-feely. Eugene was just like that. He was just this odd little creature... Not even a gendered 'little creature' to me really.

'He would leap into bed with me and give me cuddles and kisses on the cheek right from the start. But it changed. He started lying beside me without cuddling and taking my hand very solemnly. We would lie in his bed under the blankets,' Christopher spoke so quietly now, like whispering in a cathedral.

'He asked me if I wanted to listen to his heart beating. I did so and the emotions I felt in hearing it I couldn't describe. Its fluttering beat seemed the most precious and important sound in the world. If I could have willed it to keep on beating forever... I had tears in my eyes afterward. He asked if I wanted to see his scar where they had opened his chest up. I wasn't sure that I did, I hated thinking about them cutting him open like that, but in a way I did want to see. So I nodded. I couldn't help reaching out and lightly touching the pinkish, lightly purple flesh along the scar with my finger.

'He kissed me on the mouth for the first time then. It was only soft and lingered for a few seconds, I didn't want him to stop but I was far too shy to say so. Around that time it became common for us to say: 'I love you,' to each other. We were probably still twelve or just thirteen when we first really kissed each other.'

'With the tongue?' Seth interjected.

'Yes, Seth, with the tongue.' Christopher sighed. 'For quite a while sometimes. But I was always totally passive. He would stop eventually and just look at me, I don't know whether it was expectant, or whether he was checking he hadn't crossed some kind of line... He used to say he wanted us to share saliva so we'd stay a part of each other.' Although he had been intending to say more Christopher stopped there and swallowed down a hard, thick knot of emotion that was beginning to form in his throat. This was the first time he'd ever tried to explain these private parts of his relationship with Eugene to anyone.

'Sounds like your Eugene understood a thing or two. Saliva is almost up there with semen and blood when it comes to making a magical bond with someone, when it's done with intent anyway. So, did you have a hard-on?'

Christopher was bewildered for a moment by the change of

topic. He smiled and shook his head. 'I don't know.'

'Oh come now, don't be coy. Surely you know if your dick was hard? It's me, Seth. You can tell me, I have a hard-on almost all the time.'

'Yeah... Thanks for that image... In all honesty I really don't know. All I remember was my heart pounding and this intensity that was so strong that I forgot I had a body beyond my lips. I just know I didn't want it to stop. At the time I couldn't really imagine there was anything better that could happen. I can remember how he tasted. How he smelled. How I loved everything about his skin, his mouth... But I don't remember my own body...'

Seth smiled more gently this time. 'It's no wonder you're addicted,' he said.

'What do you mean?'

'To him. Eugene gave you your first transcendental experience. He was the first thing to ever lift you out of yourself, lift you out of your mortal casing and make you feel like you could see for miles. I understand. You were immortal with him.'

Christopher nodded quietly. He couldn't speak. It was difficult to even breathe for a moment. He had never expected this kind of understanding and he was afraid to move or breathe in case it broke the spell of the moment. There was a very long profound silence. Eventually Seth walked over to Christopher and patted him on the back.

'Do you want to tell me how it ended? If you can't don't worry about it.'

Christopher exhaled a breath that seemed to shudder on its way out.

'That part is so brief. So simple in a way... It was horrible like that. He was hospitalised when I was just fourteen and he was still shy of his fourteenth birthday. They were going to try another surgery to repair another hole. But he got really weak almost overnight. There were these terrible last minute blood tests to see if they could match him with a possible heart... But even if it had matched I don't know if he'd have survived the surgery. I was with him the whole time. He just wanted me to hold his hand. I wanted to feel it for him, the needles, the drip, and any fear he might have felt, all of it. But I tried so hard not to mourn him while he was still in the room.

'He was always so fearless, he put the rest of us to shame on that front. Toward the end he started talking about the afterlife more. Started saying that he saw people. That really freaked me out because I had heard that when you start seeing things you don't have much longer. I mean he always kind of talked about spiritual sorts of things and fairytales. But I just thought it was the poetry and books he read. It really ramped up toward the end. He would tell me his people were here, waiting for him, to take him back.

'When we got an opportunity with no parents around and the curtain drawn around his bed we kissed for the last time. Usually he kissed me but this time I had to kiss him because it exhausted him to sit up properly at that point. He put his arms around my neck and I could feel he didn't want to let go and I think if there was ever an adult sense of tension in what we were doing it was at that critical moment. We were definitely aware enough to be slightly awkward with each other.

"I love you so much, Christopher! Losing you scares me more than dying."

'I cried. My tears were running into our mouths as he kept pulling me back to kiss him more.

'I love you, Eugene, was all I could really say.

'And then he shut his eyes, screwed them shut really hard. I could see he was in pain and struggling for breath. I wanted to get a nurse but he held onto my arm and wouldn't let me.

"I need longer," he whispered. And for the first time I saw him cry when he was unhappy. I remember wishing I would die too.' "I just need a few more days," he said between clenched teeth.

'You will, Eugene, you will, I said. They're going to operate and everything will be... He shook his head vigorously and when he opened his eyes I stopped talking.

"No. No I don't. It's coming, Christopher. I'm cold. I always knew it would come. I never believed in any of the operations. I had them all for Mum and for you. So you could both have some temporary hope. I've always known I would die. I just hoped..."

'What did you hope? I asked desperately. I thought in some mad way that I could give him what he hoped for, wanted, somehow in that short time. I'd have done anything for him, absolutely anything, had I known what to do.

'There isn't time,' he whispered. There was a while where he looked like he might lose consciousness and I was terrified. The whole time on the verge of pressing the button to summons the nurse, even though he'd asked me not to. 'Just remember, Christopher,' he said, 'do everything that I can't do... for me.'

'He died three hours later. He was never as lucid as that again. I think they gave him some morphine after he admitted to pain. But he knew I was there. He squeezed my hand right before...while it happened, when his heart gave up.'

Christopher stopped. Tears had choked their way half way up his throat preventing further speech.

Seth just nodded slowly to himself, his dark eyes were full of rain clouds of dense sadness, as though the heartbreak of it was something he now shared also. 'Thank you. It was a privilege.'

16

'Time for you and time for me,
And time yet for a hundred indecisions
And for a hundred visions and revisions...'
—T.S. Eliot

The writing on the page before her was in her hand, yet she could not remember having written it. Sophia collapsed into the chair in front of the open book and stared. She had slept till late afternoon and she had awoken aching all over like she'd been at the gym. Touching the page of scribbled notes with her fingertips she began to read. The words didn't seem real, as though they had been written by someone else. Yet at the same time the words stirred deep feelings and memories.

Some time the night before, after she had awoke cold and stiff as though she had been dead rather than asleep, she found an empty diary and poured out everything onto paper. Sophia smiled as she touched the journal. It had been a gift from her family, what she thought of as the ultimate, we don't know what your interests are gift. It seemed fitting that it had come to be used for this aspect of her life, the one that they understood even less than any other.

Sophia read what she had written the night before, now with her mind a little sharper, and she was staggered by it. She simply knew that it could not have come from anything she had already known about iron-age religion or magical practices. Hell, she thought, what do we really know about it anyway? We archaeologists tend to be good at saying things like, this object is obviously of some kind of cult significance, probably used in some sort of primitive ritual. What does that say other than, we don't know?

Sophia read through her scrawled testimony that consisted of furiously written text and even pictures and diagrams. The pictures were of the rituals she had seen performed and sometimes of symbols. The diagrams were not of this earth; they were how the tribe had envisioned the world that comes after death, the realm that the priestess was expected to traverse at will. It was full of beliefs, practices, the poetry of their way of life, what they saw when they looked at the world and the meaning that they ascribed to events. It was, in short, a whole universe. All of this, thought Sophia, all of this beyond the silence of the bones... *What other universes lay buried seven layers of sediment down in the chalk and flint of this ancient land of ours?*

Finally Sophia closed the book and sat for some time staring out the window. Her loose locks hung down over her shoulders, her eyes were focused far away into the distance. She knew the reality of what had happened to her in her bones, but most of all in her womb. The realness of it was testified by the soreness between her legs, and at her inner thighs. Slowly she began to shake her head. She was tender in her body as though she had been with a man the night before, and she had before her the lost mysteries of an ancient Britannic tribe.

'Fuck,' she murmured to herself, rubbing her face and getting to her feet. 'Fuck. Fuck. Fuck. This coffee is going to have to be a strong one.'

When she arrived outside the New Age store Sophia stood looking in through the window. There was something puzzling about this place. She'd always known the crystal shop was there, she'd referred to it as Hippie Land or some other derogatory name only the day before. Now she found herself wondering if they stocked things that she needed. Nothing in the window reminded her of Artyn and Catrin's world and its raw paganism. This looked a bit like a gift-shop. She felt ridiculous.

Something tinkled as Sophia pushed the door open. A rather well rounded lady looked up from behind the counter over an equally large pair of reading glasses, and smiled at her.

'Hello, my dear,' she said.

Sophia smiled stiffly and ducked her head down. *What if some of my friends see me in here?* She thought. There didn't appear to be any one else in the store. She hesitated, went to move toward the occult books and then hesitated again. She had been distracted by the crystal-fountain-come-vaporiser that turned different colours as the crystal ball rotated in it and it puffed out its steam.

'Is there something in particular that you're looking for?'

'No!' Sophia all but shouted back, 'I mean... yes.' She added, trying to smile and look natural. Furtively she approached the counter and looked to both sides of her as though checking to make sure no one was listening. 'I'm looking for... witch things. Is this the right sort of place for that?'

The woman smiled. 'It is indeed. What sort of things are you thinking of? We have a great supply of Wiccan books. We have a good range of herbs over there. And then there's the ritual daggers, all blunted of course, and our range of cauldrons is all down there.'

'Any pointy hats?' Sophia tried to joke.

The woman didn't look amused. 'We have robes and cloaks.'

'Great. Okay.' Sophia began to back off and move toward the bookshelf. Then, she paused, indicated the large crystal hanging around the ladies neck, 'Am I going to need one of those?'

Sophia went from book to book. In half an hour she had covered everything from Faerie Wicca, to Eco-feminist Spirituality and all the way back to Cornelius Agrippa and his four rather long books on occult thought. None of it, not a piece of it, seemed to resemble the native British practices that she had had a privileged glance into.

'Not this,' she murmured, shutting another book. 'Or this.' She was so engrossed in her search for something that resembled what she had learned that she didn't pay much attention when another customer entered the shop. Out of the corner of her eye she noticed another woman take her place at the bookshelf and begin leafing through books. 'What the fuck?' Sophia muttered under her breath; as she put back a book that claimed to teach you all you'd ever need to know about cleaning your aura with crystals. 'That's all I need to know all right.'

'Hello Sophia.'

Sophia jumped and glanced guiltily over to see Millicent standing beside her.

'What are you doing here?' she said, in a hushed stage whisper.

'The same thing as you I suppose,' Millicent replied in a similar manner. 'Why didn't you contact me?'

'I didn't have anything to say.'

'Don't bullshit me, Sophia,' Millicent said, pretending to be engrossed in a book but edging closer to Sophia. 'I need your help.'

'With what?' Sophia replied, peering intently at a book that had something to do with finding out the star sign of your cat.

'Everything's changed since Seth came into our lives. Very strange things are happening at home. I've seen lights over the back fields, I've had strange dreams. Now Mum's having them too. She's hysterical and she thinks Christopher's going to die. Dad's on the verge of walking out on her if she doesn't see someone or get a new prescription or something.'

'What do you want me to do about it?' Sophia hissed, even louder than before. She heard the lady behind the counter shuffling around with her stock, but she could tell intuitively that she was listening.

'I need to know what's going on so I can do something to help Mum. I need to find Christopher and Seth. I already told you, Sophia. I know what you are, and I know that this is about magic.'

'Why don't you buy a book then?' Sophia said sarcastically.

Millicent seized the book from her. 'Don't patronise me!' She said, shaking the cat star-sign book in her face, 'Blind Freddie can see that this is bullshit,' she declared, rather too loudly. 'I need the real thing, and I know you're it.'

Sophia sighed in defeat. 'Okay. Okay. Meet me at my house at eight tonight, all right?'

When Millicent finally left Sophia picked up some juniper berries and some thyme with a mind to trying to recreate the incense she had smelt, and shamefacedly approached the counter to pay. Unable to look the woman in the face after Millicent's outburst she pretended to look at the stock whilst speaking. 'By the way, you don't stock woad do you?' The woman looked blankly at her. 'You know the bluish stuff in Braveheart?'

The woman shook her head. 'I don't know about woad dear, but you can probably substitute tobacco for that. Tobacco is ruled over by Mars, and Mars is the planet of war.'

Sophia frowned in incomprehension. 'Thanks,' she said, as though the lady had just spoken French to her. Slipping the herbs into her coat pocket she left the store rapidly.

It was nearly time. Christopher stirred in his sleep. He was starting to sense the onset of nightfall as he had always sensed the rising of the sun in the past. The roof dripped steadily but he felt warm under his blankets. He considered getting up, but something gave him pause. Instead he listened with his whole body in the gathering dark, with the tiny hairs in his ears, all the parts of him that had come alive in the silence that had risen in place of the noise of civilisation.

Frequently he would wake at dusk like this and just lie there, his whole body alive to the air, and it would seem like the world beyond this were just inches away. He would wait, explicitly hoping that, *that thing*, that had happened to him that had begun with sleep paralysis would happen again. It felt like the spirit-world were holding its breath... Where there had once been a mixture of excitement and dread Christopher no longer felt any fear. At a whisper he would tell the darkness that he hoped contained Eugene that he didn't care if it was terrible, cold, constrictive, dangerous... Whatever form Eugene came in, however he was able to contact Christopher, any and all of it was wanted.

Christopher would go through the events in his mind; the picture in his room that moved, his face changing in the mirror, the feeling at Eugene's grave after he bled on the headstone, the light flicking on as he descended the stair and the smell of hospital disinfectant, and finally the sleep paralysis and his covers moving... All of it together formed an undeniable picture; it confirmed that Eugene was still there somehow. And if that was the case, Christopher was willing to do anything to make contact with him.

Listening with his whole being as he was, Christopher jumped when he heard Seth's voice on the other side of the door. He assumed that Seth was speaking to the cat at first. Then, faintly, but unmistakably, he heard another voice answer him. The voice was female. Seth murmured a few words and there was a sound of movement on the old mattress springs, as though someone were turning over or sitting up. The woman's voice came again. It was clearer this time, a throaty whisper, very quiet but still fully audible.

'Not yet, Seth,' she said, her tone playful. 'It's not as much fun if I don't torture you a little.'

Christopher truly understood then what people mean when they say their blood ran cold. *She's here, and I can hear her.* In that moment what a ghost meant to him changed forever. Christopher heard light footsteps about the next room, like a child scampering. *What the hell is this?* He thought. Then there was silence. Sitting up in bed Christopher considered if he should go out yet but thought better of it. When the knock at his door came he jumped and then grinned at his own cowardice before clearing his throat.

'Come in.'

Seth opened the door and stood in the doorway without entering or speaking. The light from the fire and a few candles threw him into silhouette. Christopher could only see the smouldering tip of Seth's cigarette as he leaned against the doorframe and smoked.

'Did you hear her?' he asked, after a while.

'Yes.'

Seth appeared to nod. As Christopher's eyes adjusted to the new light coming from the next room he noticed that Seth's arm was bandaged from bloodletting.

'Still want to do necromancy?'

'Yes.'

'You trying to tell me you're not shit-scared?'

'No.'

Seth laughed and turned away. 'Up you get then, we have things to do.'

'Keep your fucking guard up!' Seth yelled. 'What's wrong with you tonight? I don't want to keep hitting you in the face but you keep dropping your hands.'

Christopher's fighting had been steadily improving. He had even been surprising himself sometimes at the body knowledge that his head didn't know was there till someone tried to hit him. But tonight his blood coursed freely out of his nose, into his mouth and out of his mouth to mingle with his sweat and run down the front of his shirt.

'Come on!' Seth shouted, taking another jab at him. 'What's the matter tonight, Christopher?'

'I don't know,' Christopher said, lifting his hands higher to ward the blows more effectively. His face ached and he had to keep blinking to stop his vision swimming. There was a weird hollow sensation low in his stomach and his brain throbbed. But

Seth made him keep moving, keep fighting. He kept saying, just a bit longer. Christopher shook his head to try to clear the buzzing sound in his ear. His stomach and chest were bruised and his ragged breathing hurt. But the training was starting to pay off because even in this state his body remembered things it had not known before Seth came along.

'Good,' said Seth, shaking his arms out from the blows he'd received on them. 'Good. You can stop for a while and clean up. Meet me in ten minutes at the fallen tree.' Seth went to go and then swung back around. Christopher had his hands on his knees and was leaning over dizzy with a bad stitch. 'Why are we doing this?'

'Cause I asked you to teach me to fight,' Christopher panted.

'But why are you learning to fight?'

'It's honing my Will to become equal to my Love?'

'There is that.' Then Seth was in front of him, grabbing him around the shoulders and taking Christopher's face in his hand; there was nothing playful about his manner now. 'But this, my friend,' he said, puffing also but grinning at Christopher with a manic intensity. 'Is so you never, never, compromise on those fine principles of yours and so you'll survive adversity.' He squeezed Christopher's bleeding face in his hand. 'You get it, my White Knight? This is so you don't have to sell it all out when push comes to shove. And believe me, if you want to really live a life, push can come to shove. It might not happen in your parent's world, but it happens. It's closer than you think, to you in particular, I fear.' Seth looked at him for a moment and kissed his forehead hard.

Sophia unpacked her new herbs, emptied them into glass jars with stickers and marked them. She had been clearing a shelf for her new occult items all afternoon. It seemed right somehow to mark the change in her with a change in her physical environment. There wasn't much equipment to accommodate, so when she was done she sat down to leaf through her notes again.

While she was reading it occurred to her that she should probably listen to her answering machine messages. The light had been flickering all day, telling her that she had message after message. Sophia felt a kind of inner peace she'd never known before and she didn't want the chaos of the outside world to intrude. Eventually the burden of habit became too much for her and she reached over and pressed the button.

'Hey Sophia,' said Becky's voice. Sophia pressed skip. Next was Tanya's voice.

'Hi Sophia, Becky says she's really worried and you won't pick up...' Sophia pressed skip again and the next message came on. She froze.

'Hey Sophia.' She shut her eyes and swore to herself under her breath. 'It's Josh here. Haven't forgotten me have you, sweetheart? I hope not because I'm in town. I want to see you. Just to talk. I know what you said but you just have to talk to me and then you'll understand.' There was a pause where she could hear him taking a breath. 'Well I guess you're really not home then. But I'm going to talk to you real soon, Sophia.' Sophia's finger hovered over the delete button and then pressed decisively down. In a flurry of movement she disconnected the machine altogether.

'Not now,' she said to herself through clenched teeth. 'Not fucking now.' She slammed her fist into the table and felt tears stinging their way up into her eyes. Getting up to pace frantically about the room she kicked a piece of inflatable furniture. *What is it about when you're really starting to find happiness that it seems to attract all the old demons?*

By the time the doorbell rang at eight Sophia had already disposed of the better part of half a bottle of Vodka and was sitting on her balcony with a spliff.

'Fuck,' she murmured when she heard the doorbell,

'Millicent!'

Having completely forgotten Christopher's sister she jumped up to try and fix her hair and makeup. I look like shit, she thought, confronting a mirror. She smiled sarcastically at her tear-stained reflection and tried murmuring a few practice runs of what she would say.

'Oh yeah, I'm great, great.'

A reckless sensation passed over her and she took a deep breath, breathing in a resolve to not care what anyone thought. With an air of abandonment Sophia went to the door and flung it open. The room behind Sophia was lit with candles and her hair was dishevelled. As she stood in the doorway Millicent just stared at her. For the first time since Seth had come into their lives Millicent looked knocked off balance. She opened her mouth to say something to Sophia but didn't.

Then eventually she smiled. 'Sorry, you just reminded me so much of how I saw you in a dream once.'

'Come in,' Sophia said, stepping back.

The other woman entered and they both just stood there in the uncertain light with the open door making the candle flames flicker. They looked each other up and down, as if they had to sum each other up all over again. Then Sophia closed the door calmly.

'Tell me about the dreams, Millicent, tell me everything.'

'I see you in a forest,' Millicent began, after Sophia had poured them both drinks. 'At least usually it is. Your face is painted black with clay or something. Seth is there too, but his face is black and bones hang around his neck.'

Sophia leaned over and topped up Millicent's drink. 'What else?' She prompted.

'There are lots of people, dressed in rags or primitive skins. The wind is wailing and it strips the sand back from something but I never see it.

'Mum dreams about Christopher. Mum's just...' Millicent

paused and looked at Sophia with an odd smile. It was quite an enigmatic smile and reminded Sophia of Christopher for a moment. 'Mum loved Christopher too much you see.'

'You mean like *too much*, too much?' Sophia said with a slight grimace.

Millicent just smiled and didn't look away or reply for a while.

'Mum loves Christopher *a lot.*' There was a sense of finality about the statement and then a feeling of change in direction. 'She's having the same dream about him over and over again. Dad thinks she's lost it and it's all Christopher's fault. He says he never wants to see him under his roof again.'

'Shit,' Sophia murmured.

Millicent nodded her agreement, had a drink and then looked back up at Sophia, this time with tears standing in her eyes.

'Dad says he has no son. Can you believe it? It fucks with me,' she declared with a surprising passion. Then she sighed. 'It's so stupid. I've always tried to be so sensible for them and now, when they most need me, it's not stuff a sensible girl can fix.' She looked at Sophia almost defiantly then, as though daring her to judge her. But Sophia just smiled sadly. 'I always thought avoiding passion was the only way to balance out how passionate Mum and Christopher are. You know Christopher, well Mum is just the same. They throw themselves into things with this abandon, like they'll die if something goes wrong with the person they love... And now, I guess the only way to help them is to follow them where they've gone.'

Sophia nodded. 'What does your mother dream about Christopher?'

'She sees Christopher come to her bedside,' Millicent whispered, her voice tight and thin, as though the words filled her with dread and she did not wish to tell them. 'There's thorns on his head and blood running down his face. He holds his hands out and they have wounds in them, like stigmata. And blood on his shirt. I mean, it's probably because her parents were religious. It doesn't mean anything.

'He tries to speak to her but Mum can't hear anything he says, even when he yells. And then his face turns peaceful like he doesn't see her anymore. He walks away from her and she wakes up.'

Millicent smiled grimly but Sophia couldn't look at her. A flicker of panic arched its way through her bloodstream like lightening. Slowly, slowly, with sickening intensity it settled itself into the very pit of her stomach as icy cold dread.

Millicent stayed the night at Sophia's and they talked till dawn. When the Vodka bottle was almost empty Millicent turned to Sophia with bleary eyes.

'You will teach me won't you?'

Sophia felt a quick rush of panic. *I am so in over my head here,* she thought. But she dug deep into the core of what Artyn had given her and when she did she felt the knowledge buzzing in her blood, slumbering in her bones. Out of it arose a certainty she had never had before about anything.

'Yes. I'll teach you. At least I'll show you what I have to give. I don't have the experience to do any more than that.' She paused. 'But I can't help you find Seth and Christopher, Millicent. I can't interfere with that. I can't explain it, but there's an understanding there between Seth and me. I don't want to go against that, it's kind of sacred. Like men's business or something. Seth will let us see Christopher when the time is right, or let us find him.'

Millicent looked away, not before Sophia was able to see the disappointment in her face. She shook her head in the way someone does when they think about it and decide they have few options.

'I have to find Christopher Sophia, for my mother's sake.'

'That's up to you Millicent, but I won't help you. Not yet.'

'When you invoke Eugene for the first time you mustn't do what I do with Lucrece.'

It was early in the night and the two men sat whittling, preparing the objects that Seth would sell at the coming market. Christopher was still learning these skills, for now he mainly applied oils and beeswax to the wood on the finished products.

'Why not?' he asked, looking up at Seth from his seat on the floor.

Christopher's appearance had changed significantly since he'd been at the ruin. He had allowed his beard to grow and his hair hung down around his face, long enough to tuck behind his ears. His cheeks had a hollowness about them and his frame was more wiry, all the bones and muscles had become visible through the skin. Any soft layer of fat that was there had disappeared, as though the land itself had blasted him back to his essential structure.

'Because I can control Lucrece, I don't need her in a Triangle of Art, outside a circle or anything.'

Christopher frowned as he polished the wood with stain. 'Eugene's been near me already, touched me, touched things in my room...'

'I know. I see him go in.'

After a short pause where he tried not to ask, Christopher broke and asked the question that sat so heavily upon him. 'What did he... look like?'

'Like a dead kid,' Seth replied brusquely.

'He wouldn't hurt me,' Christopher mumbled, almost under his breath. His tone did not carry any strong contradiction, but a certain gentle spirit of disagreement did sit pregnantly in the words.

Seth laughed quietly, as though to himself, at some private joke. He was sitting on one of the tree stumps, pushed up against the wall so he could lean against it. His face was partially obscured by shadows.

'Christopher,' he said carefully. 'I sometimes forget that you're only eighteen, you're so mature sometimes... We need to work through a couple of these Victorian Age concepts about the dearly departed that you're still carrying around. Eugene... how should I put this? Eugene isn't like your guardian angel or anything, okay? Love between the living and the dead is at its best a bit of a battle for survival, at its worst, a damned right massacre. To prosper in that battle you must never be under any illusions about the spirit's nature.' Seth broke off and looked away from Christopher briefly.

It seemed to Christopher that Seth's eyes settled for a moment on the air just outside Christopher's bedroom door. After a quick disinterested glance, Seth's eyes returned to Christopher.

'You make it sound so cold, the way you refer to him as "the spirit". Is that how you see Lucrece?'

Seth grinned widely. 'Damned right. She's a feisty little wench my girl. She'd smother me as soon as look at me, because she wants me with her of course. She waits for it, when I'm at my weakest, so that she might have a chance.' Seth laughed again.

Christopher couldn't help grimacing. It sounded a horrible state of affairs to him. To Christopher love was based on selflessness and profound trust. He didn't say it out loud to anyone but he was quietly ready to give his life in return for Eugene's if something like that was possible.

'Yes,' Seth added, as though he intensely enjoyed the fact. 'My beautiful dead woman is without mercy. What would that be *la belle morte Dame sans merci*? I can't remember the way the grammar works in French... Anyway,' he said, waving away the thought. 'The ghosts of all truly impressive hauntings are like that. And your Eugene is an impressive haunting. Eugene is what's called a 'revenant'; a type of powerful, very tangible ghost that sometimes forms when someone dies before their time or with certain energies not used up or terminated properly. I could tell you some things about revenants... but there's no point scaring you unnecessarily.'

Christopher didn't look at him. 'I'm not scared.'

'You should be!' Seth yelled suddenly. 'At the right time, and with the right situation available they can make themselves very tangible, very powerful. You don't have to agree with me,' Seth sighed, his anger suddenly spent. 'Or even understand where I'm coming from. But at least promise me that no matter what he says you'll never allow him into your circle.'

Christopher looked up at him. 'I understand you're trying to protect me Seth, but I know Eugene...'

'Bullshit Christopher! You knew a boy who is dead now! What exists now is a ghost, a revenant. And the same things hold true for him as they do for any other.'

'I don't believe you,' Christopher murmured.

Seth shook his head in exasperation.

'Don't then. But I'm telling you this: a revenant that can travel as far from his grave as Eugene is, without you even having his grave dirt on you, requires the life force of the living for that. The boy had just enough juice left in him to crawl out of his corpse and his grave on that first night and drag his revenant all the way up the road to your house. You set the perfect nest for him after that. He probably doesn't need to return to his grave to sleep. You are his resting place! If you think Eugene is just going to relinquish you for your own good because he loves you, you are even more sentimental than I thought.'

After his chores were finished Christopher sat down to write in his journal:

Today I think Seth and I had our first real fight. I've never been truly angry at him before. He yells at me a lot in training but I don't get angry about that. I know why he does it. I really meant it when I said I didn't want to hit him. No matter how many times he's hit me I've never felt like hitting him. But this I really hate. I particularly hate the things he says about Eugene.

I don't claim to know everything about Eugene or how he sees love, or how he sees anything in this new state he's in. And yet I know whatever he has become now I love him without conditions. I don't know what that will mean in practice, love is more like a dream that I've glimpsed and half remember, but I have a sense of what I feel it should be. I remember it from moments with Eugene where we touched upon the edges of something... something amazing. That feeling of wanting to suffer his pain for him, and how he covered up his pain and fear to prevent me suffering... Even though we were so young when we said I love you to each other, it meant we put each other first.

I think I am on the threshold of that amazing place again, with you, Sophia. And it makes me want to believe in it. I want to believe that love can make us rise above the lower impulses to selfishness or greed. And surely that applies even after we die?

Learning sorcery, being privileged to know some of the ways things work in the unseen, it does not succeed in reducing the mystery of a single thing for me. Sometimes I think it does for Seth. He says I'm an 'addict', as though that makes the persistence of love as explicable as heroin. And even if it explains it, can it ever reduce? I don't think so.

I believe I am in love again. And it's only when I think about that that I realise something that is even more disturbing than Seth's words. I realise how complacent I've been, how assuming. I assumed that you and I were involved in an attachment so mysterious that I could walk away and you'd just understand intuitively why I had to. In my immature way of thinking love is always meant to be I assumed nothing could possibly go wrong. But what if I lose you now Sophia? When you are the only thing that makes me want to live at all? What if my need to chase my past destroys my future? Seth says I can see you soon. I hope when you read all of this that you can understand, and perhaps forgive me my arrogance and immaturity.

Christopher closed his journal. He kept it for her, inscribing and breathing into it all of his hardships and all of his revelations. They seemed to flame and buzz with them, when he read over it.

The pages were marked with his sooty fingers and in some places smudged with dried blood. Placing the journal down Christopher suddenly sat still on his bed. A single candle stub lighted the room and the door was shut, but he knew he wasn't alone. It felt like something had suddenly sucked the majority of the oxygen out of the air. Holding his breath Christopher waited, neither moving nor breathing.

'Christopher.' He heard a faint whisper from behind him. It was only a breath of a word, yet every hair on his body recognised it. Fighting the impulse to swing around and look, Christopher whispered back his reply,

'Yes.'

For a few heartbeats the waiting was terrible.

'I am... still... *me*.' The words came out as though speaking required some enormous effort, like a mortally wounded person gasping out their last words; and yet it was Eugene's voice unmistakably. 'I have held... on.'

Christopher felt something cold lightly brush the back of his neck. The voice came from very close behind his ear now. He could feel the slight motion of air, like cool breath on his skin. Instinctually Christopher leaned back a little.

'How?' he whispered, tears stinging his eyes.

'For love... And for... the unsaid... and the time out of joint... not *yet*. I *love!*... I *heard* when the darkness... you say.. .don't... leave... me... Eugene. I *want*... Sometimes... before they zip me up... close. I *love...*'

17

'This spot, this hour is safe. Oh, vain pretence!
Man born of man knows nothing when he goes;
The winds blow where they list, and will disclose
To no man which brings safety, which brings risk.
The mighty are brought low by many a thing
Too small to name. Beneath the daisy's disk
Lies hid the pebble for the fatal sling.'
—Helen Hunt Jackson

'Sophia! There you are at last,' Sophia's supervisor said as she entered the lab. 'We have excellent news for you.'

'What's that?' Sophia asked, a little overwhelmed by all the excitement. She had hoped to slip in largely unnoticed after her absence and to avoid comment.

'We've successfully extracted DNA from Subject Twenty Two.' Sophia looked blankly at him.

'Twenty Two?'

'Twenty Two! Sophia what's wrong with you? Twenty Two, Twenty Two! Our find, your warrior friend,' he joked.

In his excitement Brian Evans failed to notice Sophia's involuntary blush. Unwillingly she looked over at the skeleton. He seemed so naked lying there with all those tags and numbers. She thought about laying a coat over him. It was terrible now. It was gruesome. It was *a body*.

'DNA,' she murmured.

'Yes! The local newspaper is all over it. They are calling for old families in the district to come in and give DNA swabs so they can see if Twenty-Two left any baby Twenty Two's. This is looking so good for continued funding.' Dr Evans rubbed his hands together as though already running them through the funding. 'This will show people why local archaeology is worth doing. And so much of this is due to your careful extraction of the find.

I want you to talk to the papers. The young, pretty face of local archaeology, it'll be great,' he beamed at Sophia. 'I don't think you'll have any worries about landing that fellowship now young lady.'

'That's excellent,' Sophia said quietly. Her outer vision was almost taken over by an inner picture of double helixes, unravelling and unravelling. The minute fragments of life, the code of his life. The tangible voyeurism of it, peering into the disintegrating building blocks of his individuality... She shook her head to clear it.

'This is great,' she repeated.

Sophia paused in her hurry to get home. On impulse she decided to bypass the town square. The market was on and it had attracted quite a crowd. Part of the market catered for those who came on pilgrimage to Salisbury's megalithic sites. The other part of it was for those who came on the more conventional sort of pilgrimage to the cathedral, under whose shadow the market place fell. Sophia couldn't help staring up at Salisbury cathedral. Though she had never been what you would call Christian it never failed to evoke awe in her. It was not so much a religious sensation, but a sense of awe at the grandeur of human achievement. What amazed her was that people with only wooden ladders, scaffolding and a primitive weights and pulleys system built a building of such dizzying heights. It went to show what human faith could achieve when mixed with human ingenuity.

But that feeling was something Sophia had always been aware of, especially when looking at the ancient engineering feats of places like Avebury and Stonehenge, which were the cathedrals of their day. *So in a way perhaps it's fitting*, she mused, *that in its shadow we have crystals, dowsing rods, Christ on the cross, crop circle calendars, rosaries and charms, all within arms reach of each other.* Sophia usually avoided this bustling crowd. Other people's faith had always seemed irrelevant to her and of little interest. But now she came out of curiosity, and also to see if anyone stocked things that she needed for her own spiritual pursuits.

She squeezed her way from stall to stall, scanning for what she wanted, her eyes never resting anywhere for long. Sophia didn't consciously remember that Seth had said he sold things at this market. And yet still she had come looking for something, and she didn't quite know what it was. The herbs she came looking for were forgotten. She was looking for something... It wasn't incense or crystals. She kept moving.

It was a deeply overcast day; the latent electricity in the clouds had created a pressure behind Sophia's temples that was fast becoming a headache. She rubbed at her arms. After the lab she had changed into a light shirt, now she wished she had brought a coat. This summer wasn't promising to be much of one, she thought.

She began moving towards the section of the market that was under a tarpaulin when she felt the first drip of rain. Once underneath it the noise from the chattering shoppers seemed to assault her more loudly and aggravate the pain in her head. Sophia stopped still among them, she was creating an obstruction but she didn't realise it or care. The ground seemed to have become uneven and the coldness was sickly now.

Him.

She would have known that sensation anywhere, the chill, that sensation of falling, half swooning. It was seductive, but sickening at the same time. It made her want to stay away and come close all at once. At first she saw him in profile through the crowd. He was sitting on a fold out chair in his normal black coat, sitting under the tarpaulin to ward off the little sun in the sky, wearing a pair of dark glasses.

Hello, Seth.

She sent off a strong greeting to him in her mind. It was almost a warning that she was near. It seemed fair play that she create ripples when entering his water-way.

Hello, Sophia.

The greeting came back to her. He did not move his head in recognition, but she felt his mind reach out to hers and acknowledge her. She could see that he had done so in every line of his body, though he never moved an inch.

Christopher.

The word came unbidden out of her, from her body it seemed. She felt him. She felt him in an altogether different sort of way. Her stomach fluttered and a heat started to course its way through her.

She moved forward as though she were unable to stay still. It was a compulsion; she was driven to at least lay eyes on him. There he was, sitting on another chair with his ragged clothes, ragged hair and beard and far away eyes. He'd lost weight and the beard and hollow cheeks made him look like some kind of heathen Jesus. He seemed to be looking at something else right through the crowd. She understood the changes she was seeing in him at a glance.

Then she looked at Seth again. He was looking directly at her. Over the top of his glasses Sophia met Seth's dark eyes that had her fixed with a very meaningful stare. He moved his head, in a very subtle but distinct 'no'. Sophia nodded once. It was just a dip of the chin to show that she had understood.

Not yet.

Okay, Seth, she thought to herself, *but it can't wait too much longer.*

Soon. Came the message from his eyes.

Sophia wrestled with her shopping bags when she heard the phone ringing, just as she was trying to get her keys out.

'I'm coming!' she yelled unnecessarily at the piece of electronic equipment. Dropping her bags in a pile by the door she picked up the cordless.

'Hello?'

'Hey, Sophia, it's Beck. Want to go out tonight?'

Sophia breathed a sigh of relief, and only then did she realise how much the sound of a ringing telephone was starting to terrorise her. *Must change my number tonight,* she thought, as she walked around her flat with the cordless pressed to her ear by her shoulder.

'Hey hon,' she said, stuffing some crisps into her mouth with the other hand. 'Oh sorry, I can't. Yeah I know, I've been so busy. It's work and... Of course we'll catch up soon. Yeah, Chris and I? Absolutely! Like rabbits, honey, you wouldn't believe it. No time to breathe let alone make phone calls. You know what eighteen year olds are like, want it all the time. What can you do? Look, love you hon, but I have to run. Okay, bye, bye now. Cheers, bye.'

Sophia sighed as she replaced the receiver and walked over to her shopping to grab a Weight Watchers meal she could throw in the microwave. She got a bottle of Diet Coke out of the refrigerator and nudged it shut with her foot on the way past.

'Now,' she said to herself out loud. 'Time to tidy this kitchen, get some actual food in the fridge and get my life in order.' But immediately after having declared her good intentions the microwave went beep to say dinner was served. 'Well, maybe after dinner.'

She took out her plastic enclosed meal and sat down cross-legged on the couch to eat it. I can't believe I saw him, she thought while she ate. The whole day was whirling through her mind, one thing after another. The night before, Millicent asking her to teach her, the DNA extraction, seeing Seth and Christopher... A few weeks ago it would have disturbed her to see him looking so dishevelled but now a new, deeper understanding had opened up in her. In fact, this new part of her was excited by what she saw. That part of her told her that what she saw was the beginning of wisdom, and the beginning of something else that she would never have dared to hope for; the possibility of being with someone else like her. She shivered at the thought. It was alluring and terrifying at the same time. *A male witch… Was that the right word?* She wondered. But words aside she knew what it meant, it meant the possibility for understanding.

The phone startled Sophia out of her reverie. Even before she answered it she swallowed down hard on her food and her mouth started to dry.

'Hello?' she said quietly.

'Hey, Sophia.' Her stomach tightened even further when she heard Josh's voice. 'It's Josh here.'

'I know who it is, Josh.' Sophia's mind raced. *Don't make him angry, but don't lead him on either,* she told herself. 'You didn't leave your number when you called.' She tried to sound casual, relaxed. But her hand was sweating on the plastic receiver, making it hard to hold it.

'Didn't think you'd use it.'

Sophia laughed off the suggestion and got up and walked towards her front door.

'There's no reason why we can't still be friends. We go back a long way,' she said, deadlocking the door and putting the chain in place.

'Yeah, we've got history alright. You and me can't ever be just friends though, Soph. We're more than that, always have been.'

Sophia glanced out the window, scanning the parked cars and the windows in the buildings across the road. *It would be just his style to be watching me while we talk,* she thought.

'So how did you get my number?' she asked, trying to make it sound like a light enquiry.

'A good friend of yours gave it to me. I have to see you, its important. I told her that.'

Sophia's heart was hammering so fast it hurt in her chest. Desperately she tried to fight the tremor in her voice. The insinuations behind his statement terrified her—he was always so good at that.

'Look Josh, I'm super busy right now. We'll have to catch up some time to say hi. Just give me a week or so to sort out all the insanity in my life right now, so I get a minute away from work. I'm just so swamped at the moment...' she laughed nervously. She could hear the shrill edge to her laugh that only ever came in when she was trying to joke her way out of danger.

'I don't think I can wait that long Sophia. And I'm not the sort of man that likes to be kept waiting.'

'Oh I know.' She laughed edgily. 'A week, maximum, I promise. A girl's got to work, you know?'

'A week, and then no more bullshit. I'll be around.' He put the phone down and Sophia stood for ages listening to the blips.

'Shit,' she whispered to herself under her breath, 'Shit! Shit! Shit!' she yelled, trying to stop the tears that came with the anger. She hated more than anything the fact that she always let him make her afraid. 'There was so much I should have told you, Christopher,' she said to herself.

18

'Old kettles, old bottles, and a broken can,
Old iron, old bones, old rags, that raving slut
Who keeps the till. Now that my ladder's gone,
I must lie down where all the ladders start
In the foul rag-and-bone shop of the heart.'
—W.B. Yeats

'Do you like the dawn?' Christopher asked, as they sat outside Seth's hut watching the very beginnings of the sunrise.

'It hurts my eyes.'

'But do you like it anyway?'

'Yeah, I love it.'

They sat drinking black tea and watching the early morning frost slowly begin to give way to the dark red that settled over it like an arterial gush. Next came the streaks of gold that made the frost turn to solid light, and then melted them away.

'What you have isn't normal Porphyria is it? ' Christopher remarked casually. Seth glanced rapidly at him, blinked and regarded the other man with a quizzical expression.

'Who said I had Porphyria?'

Christopher shrugged and sipped his tea.

'I'm just saying if you did then your skin would blister.'

'My skin doesn't blister so much as come out in a rash. But I don't keep out of the sun just for that. I keep out of it because it makes me feel ill. Who said anything about Porphyria?'

'It's the vampire disease, that's what they say at least. It's a congenital abnormality that causes anaemia and as a result, blood cravings. You can't go out in the daylight otherwise you come out in blisters.'

Seth looked at him for a while with a frown and then eventually said.

'I don't have Porphyria.'

'Did your parents have you tested for it? Were you ever taken to a hospital?'

'No.'

'Well how do you know?'

Seth sighed and shaded his eyes against the glare with his hand.

'What if I did, Christopher?' he asked eventually. 'What then? How would it matter? It's only a word, just like how vampire is a word.'

'There are treatments... It could make your life easier.'

'Treatments... Ah, yes, injections and tests and tablets. They could *cure* me could they?'

'Well... yes, I think so, or at least control the condition...' Christopher felt a little uncertain with the direction he had taken the conversation.

'Would they cure me of my night flights as well? Where I go into trances and leave my body to feed off victims in their sleep?'

'I doubt that...'

'And my urge to bite? This fundamental, powerful drive that I have to sink these sharp teeth that nature gave me into someone. That would be fixed with a few iron injections? What about the fact that I struggle to make friends because while I'm talking to the person I'm watching the vein pulse in their neck?'

'I don't know.'

Seth nodded to himself.

'I don't think medicalising something makes it go away, Christopher. If I told you there were injections you could take to cure your obviously destructive love for Eugene, would you take them?'

Christopher looked away quickly.

'No.'

'Well calling what's in my nature 'Porphyria' isn't going to make it go away either. There's more to what I am than an iron deficiency. It comes with a whole way of seeing the world. I doubt even the medical profession could cure me of that. Though God knows they'd probably have a good go at it.'

Christopher nodded, out of both tact and respect, he allowed the Porphyria topic to drop.

Instead Christopher watched the sun, his soul opened to it, drinking it in with joy. It felt like his chest opened to embrace its warmth and light. He hadn't seen the sun for so long, it really felt as if he had travelled to the Underworld and was about to re-emerge into the light of day. He had been preoccupied for days. Seth had been doing drills with him, taking him nightly into the West Wood, teaching him to hide and climb, teaching him to move through the trees. It didn't take long for it to make sense to Christopher, the way Seth could move so fluidly. It was all about being part of your environment. In this way magical and physical training merged. When you were part of the woodland you could move through it in a new way. Seth told him it was part of his natural heritage as a native of Britain. But for a few days it hadn't felt like that for him. He had been feeling at odds with everything since the night when Eugene's visitation had contradicted Seth's words.

His mind drifted back to their last training session and how he had started to think about Eugene half way through. Seth had been making him sit crouched on a branch for some time, waiting and listening to his environment, waiting for the right moment to jump down and catch Seth sneaking past. But all he could think of was a time that Eugene and he had been sitting in a tree only a few miles from that place. They had been facing each other talking when Eugene stopped suddenly.

'What?' Christopher had asked.

'Can you hear that?' Eugene said, and the expression on his face turned to one of intense seriousness.

'No. What?'

'The silence... Isn't it dreadful? All the birds have stopped singing.'

Christopher found himself listening carefully. Eugene inched a little closer to him. The day was sun-drenched and lovely but Christopher felt a rising chill. There was indeed a strange stillness in the air. It seemed more intense the longer he listened to it.

'What does it mean when the birds stop singing?' He asked breathlessly, staring into Eugene's wide eyes.

'It means They are near,' he'd whispered back urgently.

Christopher shivered.

'Who are 'They'?'

Eugene had only smiled mysteriously. And as he'd looked at Eugene his friend's face had appeared to change for a moment, morphing into something thinner with larger eyes.

'What do 'They' want?'

'Shh... They're whispering, Christopher... listen to them.'

Christopher couldn't hear anything except the silence, which was becoming louder and louder and almost constituted a booming sound.

'What are they saying?'

'They,' Eugene said, with a strange little smile, 'are whispering catches from Auden's *The Witnesses*.'

Christopher found himself leaning closer.

'Tell me what 'They' are saying.'

'They are saying, "Nothing is done, nothing is said, but don't make the mistake of believing us dead: I shouldn't *dance*."' Eugene murmured, staring into the distance as though he were indeed listening to a disembodied voice. And then he looked back at Christopher as if something had startled him. ' "This might happen any day so be careful what you say. Or do. Be clean, be tidy, oil the lock, trim the garden, wind the clock, remember the Two..."'

There was a pause where Christopher had felt like the very air around him was singing with motion and buzzing with presence.

'"We've been watching you over the garden wall, for hours.

The sky is darkening like a stain, something is going to fall like rain, and it won't be flowers."'

Christopher nearly jumped down from the tree and ran away, so strong was the irrational sense of horror that Eugene had conjured. But before he could think of such a thing Eugene grabbed him around his shoulders and threw his own body weight dramatically to the left. Before Christopher could steady himself, or Eugene, they both toppled out of the tree and landed with their limbs entwined in the leaves below. The fall knocked the air out of Christopher but his immediate concern was Eugene. Quickly he turned over to check on his friend, but Eugene was laughing and coughing intermittently, lying on his back in the leaves.

'Eugene! The shock could have stopped your heart!' he cried. 'It's not funny, you could've been killed!'

'Shh!' Eugene laughed, 'Listen, the birds are singing again.'

Back in the present Christopher felt his eyes burn with tears that wished to shed themselves but wouldn't as those images came to him. That day had been one of so many times that Eugene ignored his illness and took risks for something he thought was more important.

But there was more to why Christopher remembered that moment now. It was only now that he was being forced to realise what Eugene was. In the language of any people or any time; shaman, witch-doctor, sorcerer; these were the words they gave to people like Eugene. Sorcery had been a part of his nature, as natural as breathing. *And God he was good,* Christopher thought.

Seth had not only given him the words for it, but the knowledge to understand what Eugene was doing to him in those moments that loomed so large in his memory. Christopher knew now that to skilfully work the energies of the emotions was the very essence of spell-craft, and at that Eugene had been a master. For the first time Christopher felt that he had some idea of what he was up against.

Seth exhaled his cigarette smoke while he listened to Christopher tell him about his memory of Eugene.

'I told you, this is a war. You'll know it more than you want to by the end of this.'

'There's going to be an end?' Christopher asked quietly, his tone had a light irony to it.

'Everything ends.'

'Or does it just change forms?'

'Touché,' Seth replied, lighting another cigarette off his nearly extinguished one. 'But transformation always carries a kind of end within it.'

'If everything ends, do ends end?' Christopher grinned.

'Everything but ends.'

'How do you know that for certain?' Christopher asked.

'Because I have the whole of human history in my human bones, my friends,' Seth replied, with a long luxurious exhale. 'I've tried to train you to be ready for what my bones tell me about the future. And my bones tell me that trouble is coming. They tell me of blood and turmoil, revenge, and giantish forces stirring below the earth... There's a high-order magic around you, my friend. Some fate trying to manifest itself through you that I can't see the shape of... And I won't bullshit you, it's so big I'm afraid it's going to destroy you. I don't see its form so I've tried to make you a man ready for anything both magically and physically.'

Christopher nodded to himself. Somehow the information did not altogether surprise him. But it did make him start to understand and forgive Seth's harshness to him in training and his fearful approach to Eugene. After a while he looked over at Seth's cigarettes.

'Can I have one of those?'

Seth just extended the packet in his direction. Christopher

smoked with him for a while before Seth spoke again.

'Are you ready to go relic hunting?'

Christopher nodded slowly.

'Eugene's mother hasn't changed the room since Eugene died.'

Seth grinned.

'They're old, it's been a while since he's touched any of it. But still, given that fact it will be a gold mine in there. Good luck, this is going to be really hard.'

'Love you too, Seth,' Christopher said, smiling through an exhalation of smoke.

'So remember,' Seth added, 'Hair is the best other than blood. Clothing will do, but the more of Eugene's personal power it has on it, the better. And don't forget the grave dust.'

Christopher had not imagined it was going to be hard to take earth from Eugene's grave. Yet when he came to kneel beside it the idea of pulling back the turf with his fingers and delving into the black earth made him feel strangely queasy. There was strong magical charge in the soil of Eugene's grave, Christopher realised. It made him think about what Seth had taught about revenants and their need to rest in the grave. Given that it was daytime was Eugene down there in his coffin sleeping? The idea was disturbing, but once Christopher had his hands in the soil the feeling was more intimate than chilling. As Seth had instructed he asked Eugene's permission and waited for a sign.

The wait, though only short in reality, felt intensely long to Christopher. Finally after Christopher asked for a third time the wind got up so vigorously that it blew some faded artificial flowers from another grave onto Eugene's. Christopher looked down and saw they were fake daffodils, Eugene's favourite flower. He smiled to himself. That seemed to him to constitute a good omen. *Eugene had hoped to outlive the winter to see the first daffodils come up but the first one didn't break the ground that year until a week after we buried him...* Christopher tried to push the thought away. For most people daffodils are associated with hope, but the very sight of them always filled Christopher with sadness.

Still down on his knees he began to insert the silver coin under the sod. It was the traditional payment for taking grave dust and yet something felt immediately wrong. Almost franticly Christopher removed the coin and said to the air,

'Is there something else you'd prefer in return, Eugene?'

The feeling of wrongdoing had been so strong that Christopher was slightly breathless when he asked this question. The wind got up again and lifted Christopher's hair along the back of his neck. Nodding to himself Christopher took out his penknife and cut a lock of his hair for Eugene. Although he was unsure what Seth would say about this ad-lib deviation from tradition it felt a lot better to give Eugene his hair than an item of coin.

Taking another look around to make sure no one was watching Christopher cast himself down on Eugene's grave and buried his face in his arms and the grass. Closing his eyes he just lay there, breathing the damp, mossy scent of the ground and feeling the chill in the earth spread through his body.

Eugene's mother belonged to one aspect of Christopher's life and Seth to another. They were two branches that he was not eager to have touch. As he stood outside Irene's house in the daylight he felt as much a revenant as Seth had once appeared to him when they had first met at the flooded crossing, or as Eugene actually was. He was the ghost in this place.

Irene's house was a normal house, modern like his parents home though smaller, lightly touched by moss and damp. It had a neat row of conifers on one side, a neat lawn, and two cars for its two occupants. Really it was a very boring looking place. Yet there was something in the very stillness of it, the very calm that

belied the other invisible life of the place. Somehow it was more
eerie for its deceptive appearance.

Essentially Eugene was still here. Nothing changed. The
conifers were shaped but did not appear to grow. Eugene's
trampoline was still in the backyard, miraculously still in one
piece. It sat there for the daily use of a child who would never
grow up. And Eugene played here still. In this place it was the
living that were ghosts.

His mother used to say that Irene 'never really recovered'.
Then she would add the platitudes: who ever really recovers
from the loss of a child? Especially of one's only child... It would
be left there, an open-ended question, meant to add a sense of
tactfulness.

Christopher knew what it meant in reality. It meant his
mother thought Irene was nuts. Christopher was the only one
that saw Irene regularly and oddly, rather uncomfortably, he
came to doubt his mother's conclusions. Often it seemed that
Irene was privy to some truth that others didn't see. Something
that would have made the gossip mongers shiver.

'Christopher!' she said with a pleased smile, as she opened
the door. 'How have you been, my dear?' Irene stood on tiptoe to
kiss him on the cheek.

'Hello, Irene.'

'It seems like ages since I've seen you. Has it been ages? I
really can't remember. Come in and have some tea.'

He followed her in; taken aback that she hadn't even
mentioned the changes in his appearance. They sat down at the
kitchen table where they had always sat when he came to call.
Everything was the same except for one detail and when
Christopher saw it he froze. Unlike every other day he'd called
on Irene, the door to Eugene's room was open. The door lolled
uncomfortably open like the jaw of a dead person that hadn't
been tied shut for viewing.

'How have things been around here?' he asked, when Irene

returned with the tea. He had to be conversational otherwise he feared he would blurt out exactly what he'd really come for or say something about the door. *When they say she didn't change his room what do they mean exactly? Are his bedcovers still just how he left them?*

'Oh you know same old, same old... Martin is still away so much. I always thought he'd get out of the mines after... You know originally it was about the school fees,' she said, before suddenly changing the topic. 'I've just discovered a new friend in the German poet Novalis. Cannot believe I've only found him so late in life. He died when he was so young you know, and such fantastic work.'

'I didn't know that. What sort of work is it?'

She smiled, in that odd way she had, head on one side and eyes a little unfocused. It reminded Christopher of one of Eugene's smiles.

'Very spiritual, you know, my usual.'

Christopher nodded for a moment, rubbing at his beard. 'I've been getting very interested in spirituality myself. Looking deeper you might say. You know I've always been interested in the supernatural.'

Irene smiled. This smile was different, it kindled up from the depths of her and its warmth was the warmth of conspiracy.

'It's funny you should bring that up,' she leaned closer. 'I've been seeing this medium...' she spoke as though she feared someone would overhear, even though Martin was at work. 'She does séances.'

Just as Irene whispered this Christopher could feel the outward sighing of a released tension move the air. The door to Eugene's room moved slightly. Irene didn't seem to notice. Christopher looked deeply into the murky fenland secrets in her hazel green eyes.

'Do you talk to Eugene there?' He looked intently at her. Now he understood the phenomena that Seth called The Dance. It was when two people of occult interests are feeling each other out to see if they might confide in the other. Irene opened her mouth. He could see the flush of exposure in her face. But his heart beat hard too.

'You believe me...' she murmured. It had started as a question but before it was out she started to nod. 'Of course you do. I should have known it all along... He wouldn't have chosen you otherwise. It was like that with Eugene. He needs the person to be susceptible...'

'Yes.'

They were both looking at each other, nodding slightly.

'You do...'

'Yes.'

Irene laughed quietly, as though at some private joke and got up, wiping herself down as though grave dust had settled on her while they spoke. She held out her arm toward Eugene's room. 'You should...' she said, as though it were a complete sentence. Christopher nodded.

'I'd love to.' Although this was not at all true.

He did not immediately move towards the room.

'Yes.' Irene laughed lightly to herself, 'I'd love it too.' She picked up the tea tray and carried it toward the kitchen. As she went she said over her shoulder, 'Yes, you boys go and play. I won't interrupt you.'

Irene's words settled into Christopher like a cold sickness but they didn't get long to find their chill way to his bones because Christopher was already frozen to the spot. Through the open door to the hall that met the open door to Eugene bedroom, sitting on the bed and looking without expression at Christopher, was Eugene.

The room was just as Christopher remembered it. The cover on the bed was slightly rumpled; a few toys were out of the box. Eugene always refused to pretend he didn't still have toys.

Though Christopher couldn't remember seeing him play with them, even when they were younger.

It felt claustrophobically small to Christopher now, that young boy's room. The boy's room, full of objects that Christopher had outgrown, clothes that were too small, toys that had lost their appeal, and in the middle of it all the unmoving, unspeaking dead boy.

'Eugene...' Christopher murmured.

Just opening his mouth Christopher felt as though his tongue had thickened with dust. *If I let the air into this room* he thought, *would it all fall to pieces?* Eugene's eyes followed him around the room but he did not reply. Christopher's mouth felt dry now. It wasn't the air that made his mouth dry as he imagined. It was fear and some other emotion he had not words for. Judging by the way the image of Eugene seemed to repeat the same series of motions Christopher knew it was what Seth called an 'echo', something where an impression was left on the place that kept playing itself out. An echo was not really the person in their entirety.

On his knees, with clumsy fingers he went through drawers full of hideous, folded tee shirts. Every object was a fresh horror to him. He touched waistcoats and scarves of Eugene's that he remembered as though he'd found a severed head there and immediately withdrew.

Why did she do this? Why did she keep this shrine? How could she? How could she live like this, knowing his things were here? It made him feel physically nauseous.

It was the plush toys that Christopher hated the most. Each of them had the same eyes as Eugene, who wasn't really Eugene but a ghostly echo; empty and glassy. None of these things had Eugene on them, none of these things had been important enough to him. *Where was it? There!* On the shelf above the bed... It was Eugene's keepsake box. A black coffin shaped box with a skeletal hand hanging out the side. It was a kitsch little novelty item that looked out of place, a fragment of adolescence among a sea of childhood. Inside it, Christopher knew, Eugene kept the things that really mattered to him.

Christopher forced himself not to look into the eyes of the image of Eugene that he could feel looking right through him. *Had Irene created this thing? This cardboard cut-out of Eugene?* To get to the shelf he was going to need to get closer. But what was he staring at? *Is this a moment from the past frozen in time?* Christopher thought, *is he angry, waiting, what?* He couldn't even guess. If it was a moment from the past it was a moment where Eugene had simply sat and stared into space. All he knew was that the only way to get to the box was by leaning over the echo of Eugene.

His breath came faster as he edged closer. What would it feel like if they touched, he wondered? Would Eugene in the past somehow feel Christopher's presence? The prospect was hideous. Reaching his arm out to its full length Christopher felt gingerly with his fingers. His body was only inches from the echo of Eugene, which of course did not respond to his proximity. Swallowing hard and aware of a certain coldness he leaned further until his finger closed around it. Practically falling away Christopher took several steps back from the dead boy who sat looking at him with his catatonic stare.

Before he even opened it, Christopher knew what would be in the box. But when he did open it an unexpected jack-in-the-box sprang out with a clown smile on its face. Embarrassed by his small cry of shock Christopher smiled to himself. It was so like Eugene to mix the macabre with the amusing. He looked down to find what he was really looking for. Poetry.

He knew it would be there and it was. Underneath the lock of his hair and Eugene's plaited together, there they were, the folded pieces of silent paper. They were copies of poems that Eugene had written. As soon as his hands touched the folded paper and the twined hair a little shock of power went through him. Whether Eugene had meant to or not, a spell had been created in that little box. Christopher felt it as he disturbed it. The poems and the hair...

'I'm sorry,' he whispered without even meaning to. He slipped the papers into his pocket and left the room.

'Come around any time you like,' Irene said, with that quiet conspiratorial smile. 'It's good for Eugene, having you here, you can imagine how isolated it must get here sometimes.'

Christopher just stared at her. The feeling of sickness was only faint now, a far off nausea in the pit of his stomach. Her words shocked him so much he felt almost disconnected from the sensation and knew he would be processing some of this for days.

Irene laughed to herself again. 'Run along now, love.' She reached up to ruffle his hair.

Christopher shut his eyes. He did indeed want to run. He wanted to run from that unchanged room, from the blankness in Eugene's eyes and from the madness, for he now knew that's what it was, of Eugene's mother.

As he walked rapidly away from the house he felt afraid that the poems would somehow catch fire in his pocket before he could read them. He was afraid of that and he was also just afraid. It had been a while since he'd known that kind of fear. Christopher told himself that he was starting to run because he wanted to get back and read them, but really it felt like the open corpse-mouth of Irene's home were still gaping and attempting to swallow him.

Christopher's breath was ragged by the time he arrived at the ruin. There was still something unwholesome clinging to his clothes, his skin. But now he was shaking with adrenalin and it made him feel a little cleaner. It seemed as though the dust in Eugene's room had invaded his pores and he was trying to sweat it out. Again Christopher heard the sound of Irene's laughter. *Holy shit*, he thought, *'you boys play.'* He shuddered.

Christopher entered through the window of the ruin and walked straight into the room without knocking. It was not something he would normally have done but he was desperate to talk to Seth about what he had just experienced.

'Shit,' Christopher murmured to himself, spotting Seth asleep on the bed. Remembering what Seth had said about never disturbing him during the day Christopher began to creep past to his room. Before he reached the door he noticed something out of his peripheral vision that gave him pause. Seth seemed to thrash violently in his sleep and emitted a low growling groan. It was so convulsive that it worried Christopher; there was something of distress in Seth's face when he made that sound.

Christopher lingered uncertainly by the door. He watched Seth's fists working the bedclothes, his knuckles white with the pressure that he was exerting. Suddenly while he watched Seth's head straightened, his eyes opened and then rolled back in his head. *I should probably go,* Christopher thought, but his concern warred with this realisation. Seth looked so very pale and his breathing was so faint that it seemed practically non-existent. He moved closer and examined the other man's chest. It didn't appear to be moving at all. Seth lay completely and utterly still and appeared quite stiff.

Tentatively Christopher reached out a hand. He didn't want to intrude, but he felt obliged to place his hand close to Seth's nose and mouth to feel for breath. Not feeling any movement of air Christopher touched Seth's face nervously. He flinched in horror at how cool it felt.

Seth's eyes flew open and he moved so rapidly that Christopher hardly saw what happened. Before he could process the sudden movement an incredibly strong hand closed over his throat, crushing his windpipe shut. Christopher was unprepared for how utterly the whole body is affected as soon as the windpipe is closed. He tried to choke but couldn't. He only had enough time to realise that what he was looking at was fading out and that he couldn't fight. All he could see for that last moment was the blank expression in Seth's eyes, the mindless rage. Just as the darkness was about to settle over him and suck down all the colour and shape in his world, the grip loosened.

Collapsing forward Christopher gulped air and then choked on it, holding his throat and blinking the tears out of his eyes. As he looked up at Seth he saw the humanity infuse itself slowly back into the other man's eyes, he saw confusion there, and then concern. As though in slow motion Seth drew his hand away.

'Christopher?' he whispered. For a moment the sense of horror was evident in his voice and then he seemed to gather his composure. 'You possess two things innately, my friend,' he said, in a tone of quiet brusqueness.

'What's that?' Christopher croaked, as he righted himself and got up.

'An immense, almost impressive stupidity and weird luck.' He grabbed a handful of Christopher's shirt then and dragged him around to face him. 'Now get out of my sight for a while. And never touch me again when I'm sleeping. You got it?'

'I've got it,' he replied.

'Good,' Seth said, more gently now as he released him. 'Good. Now piss off and leave me alone. It would fuck me so hard if I hurt you, Christopher, you prize idiot.'

Christopher couldn't help smiling despite his bruised throat, because it wasn't until that moment that he realised how much Seth cared about him.

There was a ray of light in Christopher's room where the ancient masonry had crumbled away. Unfolding the paper carefully he held up the first poem to that light. His fingers were clumsy on the neatly folded paper. So precise, all of Eugene's folding, he thought. He felt anything but precise now, with the excess adrenalin moving in his system.

The poems were written on paper from a normal exercise book. Christopher smoothed out the paper that had last been folded by Eugene's hands five years ago. He knew when Eugene wrote them, it had not been too long before the end. Eugene had been on fire with creative impulses during that period. He was writing all the time and the things he saw and told Christopher seemed like poetry even when he was just speaking. And there it was, in blue biro, Eugene's neat but still slightly childish looking hand.

In a Dream

Last night I died,
and felt the wetness of grief
creep up my winding-sheet.
I stood in the church
near the organ
(Mum will want the organ)
the piling of flowers
muffled out my still
present death
for her.
–Numb
when they spoke of me.
–Numb
When Mum wept.
I looked up
At a stained glass angel
and the colours blazed more real
than this grey shuffling
this petty
and stifled pushing down
of light

'Jesus Christ,' Christopher murmured to himself out loud. 'He was a genius.' Somehow it was only now that Christopher realised, as an eighteen year old who was exceptionally intelligent himself, quite how extraordinary Eugene had been. The sense of unease and weirdness that Eugene had captured in that poem impressed him. But beyond that was meaning... Eugene's meaning, what Eugene had been trying to communicate. Like Eugene's mother earlier in the day, that part frightened him a little. Yet here it was, the voice, the answer from beyond the grave that he had longed for. Without hesitation he opened the next one.

Shiver

All the good poets are dead
it is required of us
for poetry's mortuary scent,
between the pages,
we need to shiver

So Eugene had understood that too, Christopher thought, how the obsession with the dead voice echoing out from the poetry of the long dead has a kind of magic about it. This was Eugene's echo reverberating out into the future... Hungrily Christopher's fingers took possession of the next piece of paper. The words in Christopher's mind had died away and he wanted to fill the world with Eugene's voice again, to set it free from off the page. His breath caught. He could hardly read, the words seemed to swim all across the page. *Will he speak to me?*

Dying to Tell You

I am scratching at the unspoken
like nails on a board,
like trying to scream underwater.

Gouging it out with my pen.
I am writing while I live
Writing to live
in a space with the space for me—
in a time with the time for me—
Making my argument with oblivion...
I am trying to tell you,
That which I cannot unword myself of
—divest my heart of...
I am dying to tell you,
That every scream, whisper, crush—
of ink on page—growing stain...
is only ever there
to be heard
by you...

Tears stood in Christopher's eyes. His fingers paused; it was the last poem, the last words, words that teetered on an abyss. After these would come the great silence. It was a hole Christopher felt he would fall into and disappear. He knew he would be falling forever into Eugene's silence.

To Christopher

This was going to mean everything,
I was told it before I knew you.
When I looked at you -collusion.
Instant.
I am known!
This was going to mean everything—
So that when they take back the layers
of skin and muscle and bone,
from my heart
in neat open-heart

surgery cuts
they'll find you in the holes
in me
and never mend them.
—When I take your hand
we'll burn each other
and I'll retract
first.
Because—
when I kiss your mouth I know It.
Dead men have words for It
in the language the dead speak
like reeds hissing
with whitest flame.
But I have none.
Not yet.
Maybe
I almost—
Another day or so—
Perhaps...
so terribly
so tremblingly
achingly
close.

This was going to mean everything...

Three suspension dots and a date two days before Eugene died...
And those 'Its' with the capital 'I's', Christopher knew that he
would be haunted forever by those little pieces of punctuation.

19

'Misery acquaints a man with strange bedfellows'
—Shakespeare

'No, you don't understand,' Sophia said impatiently into the phone. 'Calling the Police won't do any good. Restraining orders have never helped in the past. I'm getting out tomorrow. I just can't be dealing with this right now.' Sophia rolled her eyes. 'Are you crazy? You think I want him back at Mum and Dad's after last time?'

'Are you at least going to tell me where you're going?' Beck's voice persisted on the other end of the phone.

'Sorry Beck, no,' she said, her finger hovering over the button to cut her friend off, 'I don't think that's a good idea. If he finds out anyone knows where I am, he'll start trouble again.'

Sophia looked around at her flat, all packed up into boxes and bags now. Most of what she was taking was in a bag at her feet. This, she thought wryly, is the joy of inflatable furniture. When your stalker ex-boyfriend turns up unexpectedly, it all packs down nice and flat. My whole life packs down flat. Letters had been sent requesting leave, her electricity company had been advised and no forwarding addresses had been given to anyone. Sophia was preparing to make the final phone call. In a lot of ways this was the hardest call of all. Taking a deep breath Sophia keyed in Christopher's parent's home phone number.

'Come on, come on,' she murmured into the phone.

'Hello?' said Jane's voice.

Sophia breathed a sigh of relief.

'Hi Jane, it's Sophia here. I really need to talk to Millicent.'

'Sophia?' Jane paused for a moment, her voice sounded vague, almost as if she had to think about who Sophia was. *Hurry up, hurry up you daft old bugger,* Sophia thought.

'Sophia have you seen my son?'

'I haven't seen him Jane, no. But I know he's all right and he'll come home soon. I've heard from the person he's with. I don't know where they are though.'

'Oh,' there was a short pause, and then Jane said, 'I'd better get you Millicent. It sounds urgent.'

Yeah, you do that, Sophia thought, glancing edgily at her watch. After what seemed forever Millicent finally picked up. Sophia's heart beat hard, would Millicent be good for it? She didn't really know who else to turn to.

'Hello?'

'Millicent? I need your help okay? I can't explain now. But can you meet me at the Christian store near the Cathedral. Half an hour?'

'I'll be there,' Millicent said immediately.

Sophia smiled to herself and let out her breath.

20

'A tap at the pane, the quick sharp scratch
And blue spurt of a lighted match,
And a voice less loud, through its joys and fears,
Than the two hearts beating...'
—Robert Browning

Seth held the pieces of folded paper in his hands with his eyes closed. It didn't take him very long to smile and nod his head. He opened his eyes.

'These are perfect. He's all over this stuff like a rash. It's going to be easy actually. Eugene's waiting, he's ready... But are you ready?'

Christopher smiled his rueful, slightly crooked smile. He looked at the floor.

'As ready as I'll ever be.'

Seth nodded. He was crouched by the fire, poking the embers with a stick while he watched over Christopher's preparations.

'Seth? That weird sleep you were in earlier, what does that feel like?'

Seth laughed slightly, a deep bitter sort of laugh that was abruptly gone.

'That 'weird sleep' is me not being in my body, it's me in Flight. What's left here when I travel like that, well, it's not completely me. It's only my hunger, the part of me that's all beast.'

Christopher nodded, quietly studying Seth's profile. He had a tugging melancholy in his guts in those moments. He could sense something coming to an end. Christopher knew his time with Seth was coming to a close. As he was thinking this Seth suddenly looked up at him from under the shadowy blackness of his brows.

'It's my hungry ghosts Christopher, trying to pull me down.'

Seth passed the folded poems back to Christopher.

'Is there anything else I should know?' Christopher asked desperately. He wondered if this was indeed the last piece of instruction he would receive from Seth and he found himself suddenly insatiable for more of the other man's wisdom. Surely Seth didn't mean to stop teaching him as soon as this objective was reached?

'Speaking of hungry ghosts,' Seth muttered. 'You should know your boy's pretty special.'

'I realise that.'

'Good. I've seen ghosts that weren't ready to die. I've seen powerful ones that lifted things up off my desk and threw them across the room. But I've seen few like that kid. He wasn't only unready to die he was a sorcerously gifted adolescent who was unready to die, and who has been fed continuously since his death. And if I'm any judge of the finer emotions he was also in love, and perhaps hadn't quite had the chance to express that in the ways he wanted to—none of my business, but just guessing here. He's one of the most powerful ghosts I've ever seen. And there is something quite... different about him.'

Christopher frowned to himself. This growing awareness of what he just called 'the Otherness' around Eugene was a bit more disturbing to Christopher now that he realised his teacher didn't fully understand it either.

'So you don't know either? Why he was... different?'

'I have some ideas but... look, I think we need to keep focus here. Just remember, your compass round, your witch's circle is the black labyrinth of your deep mind, the unconscious parts of yourself. That's a liminal space where the border between Self and Other is misty indeed. Eugene has nested himself into that part of you and put down a root system. By putting him in that triangle you aren't trying to trap him, you are drawing him out of the unconscious realm, you are pulling him into manifestation but also into your own conscious awareness. What you are conscious of you have power over—just remember that.'

Christopher nodded. Seth had taught him all this already and yet he wanted Seth to keep telling him things just for the reassuring sound of the other man's voice. But Seth gave him a slap on the back that had a sense of finality about it.

'So what's with all this fannying about then? You're the one fucking this kitten, I just brought the butter.' Seth winked at him.

Christopher grinned. He loved more than ever Seth's ability to lighten a potentially tense moment. But when Seth opened the door to the unused room Christopher's heart pounded.

The door opened on darkness and draft. If he had seen a staircase Christopher would have believed he was really about to journey down into the Underworld. I'm ready, he thought, I'm ready for the darkness. *It has a cold appeal that pulls at me. But what do I do with my desire? What do I do with it when it's granted at last?* Christopher paused on the threshold. There was something both awesome and dreadful for him about this fulfilment of his heart's desire.

The room had a plain hard earth floor upon which Seth had drawn a chalk circle and the Triangle of the Art, which consisted of a chalk triangle with a circle inside it, was drawn in the north. Any equipment that Christopher would need had been laid out for him, including incense that they had made earlier which included Eugene's grave dust and a lot of Christopher's blood. He had taken a perverse pleasure in bleeding for that incense because it was for Eugene. Christopher turned to Seth.

'Thank you, Seth.' They both knew he meant for more than the circle.

'Don't mention it,' Seth grinned. 'Now good luck, okay?' He handed him the candle and closed the door behind him.

When the door clicked behind Seth, Christopher had a good look around him in the dim light. After a time he was able to perceive the skull and cross bones in the northern quarter of the circle. The skull was in the triangle, which was slightly outside of the circle. The only objects within the circle were a ritual dagger, which they had sharpened yesterday, the charcoal and incense bowl, and beside that a large, wooden hourglass. Christopher knew what to do with everything. He had bathed, dressed in clean clothes, shaved off his beard. The night before he'd gone out and found a three-way crossroad where three walking tracks met and left a meaty bone for the hounds of the Underworld, which Seth said would help to establish favour with the infernal realms.

As soon as Christopher entered the circle he positioned the hourglass. It was a sermon-timer, designed to keep time for fifteen minutes. This, Seth had said, was the absolute maximum amount of time that should elapse between the beginning of the encounter and the end. When Eugene arrived he was meant to turn it, and he should be gone by the time the sands had run their course. It was thought to estimate well the amount of vital force that an individual could safely give out to the world of the dead.

Christopher felt like he had to hurry. He lit the two black candles, and placed them behind him. *Good God, by the time I'm done here Eugene will be in that triangle...* But Christopher had been well trained. He did not allow his feelings of fear or excitement to get in the way of the conjuration. The ritual actions were done perfectly, the words all remembered. And while he spoke them he felt it all around him, the welling, oppressive energy of Eugene rising. It was all around him already, he knew, gathering itself like a miasma. In fact, as Seth had explained and was now very apparent, Eugene was as much pulling himself free of Christopher as he was from the world of the dead.

To Christopher's ears, trained on the Otherworld, the very fabric of the night seemed to whisper, creep and crawl. When he turned to the North, which was the final invocation, he knew he was nearly at the part he dreaded. Slowly, deliberately, he pinched out the first of the two candles, first the left one, then the right. And there it was; the darkness. The complete and utter blackness, that was so viscous and encompassing that Christopher felt it would have smothered out the candle flames anyway. *You tell me to trust in my own inner light Seth, but what is that little fire by comparison to the unfathomable darkness of love?* Christopher felt dizzy. It seemed that the earth beneath him had tilted and a counter-clockwise maw was opening in the fabric of the night. *Like a black hole in space,* he thought, *in space where there is no air.*

He crossed his arms across his chest in the pose of the dead and bowed his head. Quietly he whispered Eugene's name once. *There it is... The very night is aware of the rawness of it. The darkness jumps up at it like an animal.* He spoke Eugene's name again. It was louder and more confident this time, but just as naked. *And when I say it again, he will come.*

The incense smoke was beginning to swirl and coil, it seemed almost to be being sucked back into a vortex. Christopher's head was swimming with vertigo. He feared he would fall on his face across the floor and be sucked down into the opening. His head fell forward and the sensation that something was being pulled loose from him was so strong that the muscles in his back contracted and writhed with the effort. There was a sudden panic, as though to finish this evocation, to draw Eugene forth, would be to somehow lose him all over again.

'Eugene,' he said, one final time and spread his arms out into the crucifixion pose. Opening his arms like that seemed to release the last bind and it ached like loss.

There was an unutterable silence. Out of that silence, came a stirring in the invisible fabric, a rustle. Christopher's heart pounded so loudly he could hear it in his temples, banging frantic blood against his skull. It felt like the night-air inhaled then. Christopher kept his arms out. It was hard to believe in the circle, that such a thing, such a thing that Seth called 'a universal law', had any meaning in this place. But he called on the stark light within, drew it up, and made it pump out of him in offering.

'Welcome,' he said calmly, but firmly, 'I command you Spirit that you remain inside the triangle until such time as I should release you.'

There was a faint sound, as though a child were smothering a giggle to avoid being caught in class. The hairs all over Christopher's body rose. He could feel the roots of each of them buzz in their own particular follicles.

He could feel Eugene as if he had nuzzled up to him in the darkness. Fingers shaking and fumbling the first two attempts, Christopher finally struck the match. In his head he heard Seth's instructions from the day before. 'When you strike the match, do not allow yourself to lose composure when you first see it.' In this moment the word 'it' couldn't be displaced by the word 'Eugene' as Christopher shielded the flame in his hands against the sudden draft. And there *it* was. Out of the corner of his eye, the dark solid-looking shape in the triangle. Christopher lit the candles, and looked up. He drew his breath in. Less than three feet away, Eugene was crouched grinning at him, in the triangle, with his chin rested on his folded hands.

'Hello, my darling,' Eugene said. He looked as he had when he died except that his eyes looked unnaturally wide, like someone in a perpetual state of shock. 'You have bled a lot for me haven't you?' He said, looking down at the blood that was mixed with the incense, swirling up around him.

'Of course.'

Eugene did something with his eyebrows that denoted irony, but there was another emotion in his eyes that Christopher couldn't name. 'My, haven't you grown?'

I'm still on my knees, Christopher thought, but he couldn't seem to move.

'Please don't,' Eugene said, his blue eyes boring deeply into Christopher with a long, somewhat hard, stare. It was not the stare of a thirteen-year-old child by any stretch and Christopher found himself remembering Seth's warnings. Those eyes looked like glaciers to Christopher for a moment. And yet had Eugene's eyes ever actually looked like the eyes of a thirteen year old?

Eugene laughed then, and immediately his eyes became dancing blue flames as they had often looked in life. 'It's so touching.'

'I've missed you so much,' Christopher murmured, his voice cracking like he was going to cry.

'Did losing me hurt as much as it hurt me to lose you?' Eugene asked.

'You're a ghoul for asking.'

'I know, I watched,' he murmured. 'It was hell for both of us. Watching my own, almost unused body zipped up in a bag and taken to the morgue didn't hurt so much as seeing you rocking back and forth in the bottom of your closet. Or listening to my mother screaming... But do tell me anyway. You know I have to know everything about you, that I can't stay out of any of your secrets.'

Christopher let his eyes fill with tears openly, as he looked at Eugene, but he couldn't help smiling sadly. He was letting his friend see what he wanted to see after all, even if the desire he was satisfying was mildly sadistic, it was something he had to give him. Every year since Eugene had died Christopher had thought of more things he wished he could give or show to his friend. The only words that came to his mind were poetry.

'I felt a funeral in my brain, Eugene. And then a plank in reason, broke, and I dropped down and down—'

Eugene looked at him with something that looked like emptiness, or perhaps it was just vulnerability. For a moment it reminded Christopher of the zombie-like echo in Irene's home. Then something twitched around his mouth and he pressed his lips together like trying to close up a wound.

'God I love you, Christopher...'

'And I you.'

'When are you going to let me into your circle?'

'I'm not.'

Eugene raised one eyebrow.

'You're scared of me?'

Christopher looked at him, drinking in the sight of Eugene's eyes, with all their question and challenge. He shut his own eyes then and shook his head.

'Are you scared of me?' Eugene repeated. His lips were pursed and there was a slight frown on his brow. 'You don't trust me,' he said quietly and there was hurt in his tone. The sound of hurt went straight into Christopher and ached and writhed like the bound hands of someone who struggles for freedom until their wrists bleed.

'I trust you.'

'Then let me into your circle, Christopher, please! There isn't much time and I've never wanted anything like I want to touch you.'

Christopher got to his feet. It was as though his body and his heart made the decision for him. Eugene stood up too. It seemed so strange to be so much taller than Eugene. *If this is how I'm meant to die*, Christopher thought, *then so be it.*

Against all of Seth's instruction he reached out his hand, out through the circle and the triangle, and offered it to Eugene. Despite his resolution he jumped when the cold, solid feeling, young boy's hand, clasped his. And as Christopher looked down at it he saw Eugene's hand grow and harden into a fully-grown man's hand. He gasped and looked up as he saw Eugene's form stretch out to its full height, not much shorter than his own. The grip on his hand, which had already been formidable, tightened.

Eugene stepped into the circle and stood very close to him. Christopher could feel the cool movement in the air where Eugene's form seemed to inhale and exhale from the whole surface. Consciousness threatened to drain away from Christopher, as surely as it had when Seth had grabbed his throat. Dimly he knew that the extra pull on his own vitality was being taken to support this manifestation. It was almost more than he could stand. But he blinked and cleared his vision. He was looking at Eugene as an eighteen year old man; something he never thought would be possible. And he wasn't going to look away.

'Well? Do you like it?' Eugene asked, with his new deeper voice.

Christopher just stared and nodded slightly. Eugene smiled gently at him. His impish facial structure was still cute, but hardened somewhat by manhood. It looked, with that hardening, even more angular and elfish. Eugene's frame wasn't strong like Christopher's; it was elegant and wiry, entirely masculine but rather fine. Christopher felt Eugene's hand curl around his hand.

'How long are you going to stare for?' He whispered, drawing closer. 'We need to hurry, you can't do this forever,' he said, his mouth very near Christopher's ear. 'I'll drink you dry.'

'I hadn't been able to imagine you as a man,' Christopher replied. 'I suppose I knew it would never happen.'

Eugene laughed softly. 'Made it so easy didn't it? That's the beauty of death, keeping me a boy forever in your mind.' Eugene drew closer till their bodies were almost touching. 'I was never that child, Christopher. I was never a child at all.'

Christopher shook his head slightly, looking steadily into the other man's eyes. 'What *are you*, Eugene?'

Eugene laughed, in the throaty adult way he now had.

'The same as always, a being without age. The formal nightmare grief and the unlucky rose.'

Christopher placed one hand against Eugene's cheek and turned Eugene's face up to look at him. How strange it seemed to Christopher that this should be his instinct, to treat Eugene so softly and that Eugene would look at him so receptively; when before it had always been Eugene initiating everything.

'Can I kiss you?'

Eugene just nodded and wrapped his arms around Christopher's neck. Christopher couldn't even feel Eugene's coldness anymore. It seemed that he was becoming warmer, or that perhaps his own body temperature had cooled to meet Eugene's. Christopher touched Eugene's lips lightly, his own lips trembled and he hesitated. But Eugene's hand slid around the back of his head and his mouth pressed up against his eagerly. Slowly they kissed each other, with a mixture of just subdued violence and tenderness. Christopher didn't feel faint anymore. Eugene seemed to fill him, sustain him, and make everything feel right. Even if for a moment Christopher couldn't breathe, it still felt amazing. He paused.

'God... Please don't stop,' Eugene murmured his voice sounding breathless. Everything seemed to be spinning around him, but he could see tears standing in Eugene's eyes.

'I don't think I can do this for much longer.'

'Kiss me one more time!'

Christopher pulled him hard up against his body, kissing his face, his forehead, his mouth, kisses that would have left bruises on a living boy. Trying to kiss him as many times as he could before the agony of letting go. He felt the realistic graze of skin slightly roughed by shaving, and then the soft yielding flesh of Eugene's lips.

Then so suddenly, the light fell away and something swam downward in him. Something swept away the world and Christopher felt stillness like the grave. The last thing he heard was Eugene's breathless, tormented whisper.

'Please! I'm still not ready yet...'

21

'Once out of nature I shall never take
My bodily form from any natural thing
But such a form as Grecian goldsmiths make
Of hammered gold and gold enamelling...'
—Yeats

Seth gently lifted Christopher's wrist to take his pulse again. It was still slow and quiet. Sitting on the side of the bed, he examined the other man's face. Christopher was deathly pale, almost grey.

'You let him drink you down to your dregs,' Seth murmured, pulling a blanket up over Christopher. After rubbing his hands together vigorously he placed his right hand over Christopher's chest.

Seth shut his eyes, and when he did his inner Sight came on, sharpened by cutting off his daily sight like the instincts of a blind man. While Seth gathered his own life force to him Seth felt Christopher's energy. *Dear God*, he thought, *is it even possible for him to come out of it now? Even with everything I can give?* Medically speaking, Seth knew that Christopher was in a sort of cataleptic state. Magically speaking his spirit was missing because the vital forces of his body were so drained they could no longer support it. Seth intended, without hesitation, to give Christopher his own vital force in an attempt to tempt his spirit back to his body. Deep down Seth knew that it might be hopeless; the spirit had to want to come back...

Seth gritted his teeth. Giving out energy always hurt him and it made him hungry. When it came out of him, it poured from him like blood from an opened artery. He was capable of creating raw life force more abundant than most normal people could do in ten magical conjurations. Yet it ached his bones and made him shiver, it made him feel like he was starving and would lead to

269

him magically feeding on others. And yet Seth's power didn't even make Christopher stir. Seth pulled away and rolled over on the bed next to Christopher. His veins seemed to pull like hungry little mouths and he felt his inner darkness yawn and stretch, like something waking and about to prowl. 'I don't have time for that,' he told his own body out loud.

Seth knew his blood might be Christopher's only chance. It couldn't make him a vampire like in the movies, but it was the richest source of life force in anything. Somehow I need to make him drink it, Seth thought, sitting up dizzily. Irrationally he found himself taking Christopher's face in his hands.

'Wake up!' Seth gave him a little shake. If he was going to be made to swallow he would need to show at least normal reflexes. 'Wake up, damn it!' He yelled and slapped Christopher's face hard. Christopher's head lurched to one side and then came slowly back to its place, his eyes open but unseeing. Seth pulled out his pocket-knife and selected a place on his own arm.

He pressed the keen edge deep; he knew the sting, the deep sting that told you it was deep enough to really bleed. He had done it often enough that it held no fear for him. The wound felt hot for a moment, and then there was the rush of blood.

'Open your mouth,' he demanded of Christopher, using his fingers to force the unmoving lips apart. Seth pressed the wound down close, making it impossible for the blood to not run down Christopher's throat. 'Come on, Christopher, don't you dare give up on me, you stupid bastard.'

There was a brief reflex convulsion in Christopher's throat as he swallowed to avoid choking. Seth shut his eyes and pumped his arm to encourage the bleeding. Seth knew his blood was powerful, he just hoped it would be enough. Christopher swallowed twice and then three times and then his eyes closed and Seth's blood began to overflow and run out the side of his mouth.

Seth fell back against the bed in agony. He was nearly as

drained as Christopher now and his thirst was a burning Hell inside him. He knew if he bled any more he'd end up leaving his body and draining any person he could get near. Doubled over with the pain he lay beside his friend's inert body, clasping the wound on his wrist and bleeding on the sheet. Seth pressed his forehead against Christopher's ribs, listening to his heart.

'If you die I'll never forgive myself,' he murmured.

Seth felt then that Eugene was in the room, waiting, hovering succubus like over Christopher, and tempting him to go with him. *Filling him with the poisonous love of death*, Seth thought, *that's what the little demon is doing. Maybe Christopher is too good for this world. But let him make his mistakes*, Seth prayed quietly. *Let him have his glories and his disasters, his pathos and bathos. All the madness and splendour of being alive and young and in love. He's so vital; he doesn't belong in your world of gilded stasis, Eugene. He needs to yearn, and push and sweat, to cry and bleed. When's the last time you sweated? When the coldness of the death-sweat dried on your skin, after the last struggle and stress of it, of your heart not having enough life in it to keep the worlds apart, and then the squalor of life was behind you. And you sloughed your body off like a useless old glove that didn't fit anymore. But he's not like you. He's filled with a passion for our collective mess.*

'I don't think you know him as well as you think you do,' Eugene said, a quiet, well-enunciated and only slightly husky whisper from the corner of the room.

Seth glanced over and saw him sitting in a chair with his legs crossed and his head cocked on one side.

'Or me for that matter. But you have found some charmingly well worn in stereotypes to append us to. I'm meant to be Bosie, yes? Cold, vain, bound to favour artifice over nature, almost autistically disconnected? Unimaginably bad for the man I love... Yes?

'At least I know what I'm meant to be playing so I shan't disappoint you... But Christopher you have as the earthy and vigorous hero of the piece, rejecting the gilded stasis of art in favour of life's other messes... hmm. I don't know... I fear there is some narrative confusion here.'

I hope you're wrong, for his sake. Seth didn't have to speak. It was clear that Eugene could hear his thoughts.

Eugene raised one of his expressive eyebrows. Seth had to agree to Eugene's charisma. His blue eyes sparkled at times with a barely repressed mischief, or malice. Eugene's dimples and turned up nose presented a pleasing contrast with the regular irony in his expression and the poise of his posture. The razor-sharp mind that his verbal acuity emerged from seemed almost palpable in the room to Seth. Eugene's mind felt like a weapon capable of slicing the air.

'Why?' Eugene said, his voice still the grown up voice he'd been using since the conjuration, his form still reflecting more accurately what he truly was. 'There's so much trouble and suffering coming for him. I'm not sure I can bear to see him go through it. Why can you? So you can keep him here to stave off your loneliness and depression?'

Play your mind games in the kindergarten schoolboy. You're out of your league here. I'm not lonely, and I don't want to keep him here.

Eugene laughed as though he found something genuinely hilarious. 'Of course, I forgot. You brought him here out of your own good nature. What a nice man you are, Seth! So what do you really want for him? Would you prefer to see him out in the world being wasted on some job, married to that woman and submerged in connubial bliss? At least for a little while before Sophia starts punching out some screaming infants to ruin their marriage?'

There's more to love between a man and a woman than breeding. I can tell you that if Lucrece and I ever had the opportunity to create life together it would have been a damn sight more profound to me than, punching out screaming infants.

'That would have been sweet wouldn't it? You could have

peopled forth the world with little baby vampires.'

After what you did to Christopher tonight you can hardly talk.

'I love him! I would never hurt Christopher on purpose! Could you consider for a moment that I might be human enough to have held on for longer than I should have? That it might have been hard to stop when I've wanted him for so long? We still have feelings you know–the dead. No nerve endings to thrill to a touch or vibrate with pain but something like it, some dark feeling sense that is exquisitely sensitive. We feel pain. And this hurts like nothing I have words for! But despite it I want what's best for him, even if it's not what's best for me. Do you really think that woman can make him happy? Or understand him like I do?'

Jealous much?

Eugene looked down for the first time then and didn't look back at Seth again when he did finally speak. His sarcasm was so dry it sounded like total sincerity. 'No, not at all, Seth. It's perfectly lovely dying before you grow up and afterwards getting to watch the person you're desperately in love with in the arms of someone else. I thought I'd hang around to watch them screw because I just don't like myself very much.'

You'll have to excuse me if I don't weep for you. I have this thing against people who nearly kill my loved ones.

Seth turned his mind aside from Eugene's; the young man's words were filling him with a growing dread. It wasn't Eugene he was afraid of. It would have taken a lot more than Eugene to scare Seth. What Seth was afraid of was that Eugene was right. What if Christopher didn't want to come back? What if some terrible fate awaited him?

'You're a Romantic to the core of your damnable, suicidal soul.' He abused Christopher's inert form. But as much as Seth protested weakly against it, they were words of love. Seth knew he would never have come to love Christopher like a brother the way he had, if Christopher was not so stupid. It was a beautiful, noble form of stupidity that reminded Seth of a form of compulsive gambling. Christopher just didn't know how to love something a little bit. And neither did Seth. He reached for Christopher's hand and squeezed it hard.

'Stay with me,' he whispered.

22

'Where should we start looking?' Millicent asked, as they drove along the highway in her car.

'I figured we'd pull over near your place and trek out along all the paths until...'

'Until what?'

Sophia had to smile to herself at the seeming absurdity of her plan. 'Until I feel something.'

Millicent just nodded.

Wow, thought Sophia. *She's really got complete faith in that kinda stuff, and that I can do it.* Suddenly she felt ashamed of her own doubts. Sophia had so many more reasons to believe than Millicent, who simply took the matter on faith alone.

'You're completely committed to this aren't you?' Sophia asked, her tone curious but gentle. She looked at the other woman's profile while Millicent drove, at her jeans and sensible walking shoes. She wondered if Millicent had any idea how much of an enigma she was to Sophia.

'I've seen something out there, something that was no part of my narrow life. I don't know whether to call it magic, I don't know what it is. All I know is that the world has just opened up for me and I want to see more.' Millicent indicated right and pulled the car into the lane near the Penrose family home. 'I've left a note telling Mum I've gone to find Christopher. She won't find it till tonight.'

Millicent switched off the car engine and opened her door.

Grabbing her backpack she looked at Sophia as if to say "coming?" Sophia followed. She had made a genuine effort to dress sensibly, but her only shoes that weren't open toed, or left in the locker at work, were her knee high boots. She was wearing those boots with, what she thought of as, only a small heel, designer jeans and an open neck, button down shirt.

'What?' she asked defensively, pulling on her backpack. 'Problem?'

Millicent smiled. 'Not at all,' she said, still grinning to herself as she looked at Sophia's clothes. 'Come on.'

Millicent headed for the trail and Sophia went after her. Sophia had to admit with some embarrassment that it wasn't easy to negotiate the muddy trails in heeled boots. That was of course why she kept right away from having to walk on country trails when she wasn't on a dig and hadn't taken out her 'dig clothes'.

'Can you remember anything Christopher might have said about where Seth lives?' Millicent asked.

'Only that it's an old ruined cottage or something, patched up with wrought iron. At the time I was confused as to why I had to hear about some hobo.' Sometimes Sophia hated the irony of her life. 'It's always the fucking way,' she muttered under her breath.

'What's that?' Millicent asked.

'Oh nothing, just the tragi-comedy of my life.'

Sophia looked around them at the bleak landscape. She hoped that they would find Seth and Christopher soon. Something was making her feel jittery. It seemed that ever since she had even started to believe in omens, ravens had been following her every-where. She was fairly sure that wasn't a good sign. Their black wind-ragged wings seemed to haunt the grey skies, and their flat, black eyes regarded her from trees. It was as if they knew something. Sometimes she fancied they spoke to her. There was an old one that if it could speak would have said: I am ancient among the ravens and my forebears stripped the flesh from Britain's warriors on a hundred battlefields. Many are the stories

I could tell...

'I thought Christopher was mental actually, making friends with homeless people. I have no trouble admitting I'm a complete retard.'

Millicent laughed briefly and then stopped. 'What do you think Sophia? Left or right?'

Sophia stopped and shut her eyes on instinct. She felt the air with her mouth, smelling it, tasting it. It was like that sometimes, as though Artyn had awakened some animal part in her that knew things. 'Left,' she announced with a sudden confidence.

Millicent nodded curtly. 'I thought so,' she said. And they began to head left through some trees, pausing to climb a style.

While they were walking Sophia thought about what she was going to say to Christopher. Every dream she had had about him since he'd left rose in her mind with an aching clarity. His smile alone seemed to affect her sexually when she thought of it. She heard his voice whisper, I love you near her ear, in that breathless moment before he penetrated her. Her heart would throb almost painfully when she remembered that. Immediately the throb of passion was followed by a clench of fear, lest something happen to him. She didn't know why she felt so afraid for him. Sometimes the insides of her bones seemed all chalky as if there was really nothing of her, when she thought of losing him. For some reason Artyn's scarred body rose in her mind, and that look that his eyes had that had reminded her of Christopher. *God, please protect him Seth*, she thought to herself and she tried to send that thought out to Seth with all her might.

They trekked on in the same direction, roughly toward East Kennet, always scanning the adjacent fields for signs of any ruins Millicent may have forgotten, until they came to an intersection of two trails.

'Let's head uphill a bit,' Sophia said. 'It'll give us a vantage point of the surrounding area.'

'So,' Millicent said, as they were walking up the hill. 'What're you running away from?'

'Did you just fuck Seth, hon, or are you channelling him now?'

'What do you mean?' Millicent asked calmly, heading resolutely up the muddy incline.

'This whole blunt, I'm at peace with the world so I can afford to be really fucking honest thing.'

Millicent just shrugged and faced with no response Sophia sighed and said, 'I'm running away from my maniac ex-boyfriend, okay?'

'Surprises me.'

'Why's that?'

Millicent shrugged again. 'I don't know, I guess I just had this idea that you were really assertive. You know, the kind of woman that doesn't take crap from people.'

'I wouldn't start making me a role model if I were you,' Sophia snorted. 'I can't run my own life, let alone be an example to anyone else.

'My ex is danger,' she added. 'I have enough reason to be afraid of him. I don't normally let people push me around. Not when they're normal people, don't carry weapons and threaten my family.'

Millicent nodded and continued on. Then after a while she half stopped and turned.

'By the way, I'm nothing like Seth. Seth hides a complexity behind his bluntness. I've just discovered that I'm really quite simple. I figure there can be a dignity in that if you do it with sincerity.'

Sophia shook her head. *Bloody hell, she's so strong in her way*, she thought. It humbled her somehow. When they reached a copse of beech trees that heralded the beginning of Boreham Wood, Millicent paused to rest and look around.

Sophia saw something up ahead and walked on past her.

'What's wrong?' Millicent asked.

Sophia didn't answer. Up ahead, under a tree she saw a figure in white. Pushing aside a bush she realised it was a young woman, sitting against the tree with her legs drawn up and her arms wrapped around them. The girl, for she was that more than woman, was wearing something very flimsy like a nightgown and her long dark hair was hanging down around her startlingly pale flesh, so long it trailed in the dead leaves. Disturbingly she had no shoes, her feet were dirty and her nightgown was stained with mud. She looked like she'd been running through brambles and scratched her legs up and been caught in rain. *Has she been sexually assaulted or something?* Sophia thought. Something didn't feel right, but the girl looked young and vulnerable; Sophia hurried toward her.

'Are you alright?' she called out.

The young woman regarded her with huge eyes that gleamed like dark jewels in their shadowy sockets. There was no reply. Sophia could hear Millicent speaking behind her but she didn't notice what she said. Why was she talking to her when there was this poor girl here?

'Are you okay honey?' Sophia asked again, crouching down in front of her. The girl seemed waif–like, lost. Slowly, and unnervingly, she smiled and when she did Sophia felt the ground drop away beneath her. The familiar cold creeping started in the depths of her stomach. Leaping involuntarily to her feet and taking several steps back Sophia had to cover her mouth to avoid a scream. Her teeth were sharp like Seth's but more delicate. The girl just held out one elegant, white arm that bore several long scars along the forearm, pointing to her right and slightly back.

'If you're looking for Seth,' she said sweetly, in a very upper class accent, 'you will find him that way.'

'Thank you,' Sophia whispered.

'Who are you talking too?' Millicent asked, arriving at her side.

Sophia pointed under the tree but there was only the grass and the vagrant leaves that the wind toyed with. Shaking her head to clear the sense of disorientation Sophia recollected herself slowly.

'Seth's late girlfriend,' she managed to say eventually. 'And we have to go right, through the West Wood.'

After they passed the tree at the place where the three paths crossed and Sophia saw Lucrece, the landscape was suddenly crawling with ghosts. Sophia felt her skin prickle again and again and there was not a fellow walker that was not under suspicion of being a shade. The feeling intensified as they began to pass through the small copse that led up to the ruin. Millicent continued to walk ahead, purposeful and determined. But Sophia found herself slowing to almost a stop, as though sniffing the air to account for some atmospheric change she was sensing. Without warning an acorn hit her in the back of the head. She swung around. All she heard was a swoosh of branches and then the flash of Eugene's inverted face.

He just hung there by his knees and looked blankly at her, as though someone had hung his body upside down from the tree. She didn't mean to scream but the sound escaped her and she startled backward. There was a sound of laughter in the trees, getting further away all the time, almost as though a child were running through the treetops rather than across the ground. Suddenly up close again, like he was showing off now, she heard his voice like the wind hissing.

'Leave him alone, Sophia!'

With a deep breath she shook her head, turned and headed after Millicent.

Seth's dreaming seized him with unusual violence. His soul was whipped down in a whirlpool of darkness where his screams were drowned in blood and voices. So I end up here, he thought, glancing around at the library of Winthrope Manor. He was sitting looking out through the window into the garden. It was the same place that he'd been sitting when he realised that he would go to Lucrece. But it was not the room as he remembered it. There was mildew over everything, the carpet was mouldering and the window he was gazing out of was shattered. It looked like someone had put a rock through it. Why was that window shattered? He remembered so vividly that soft spring morning with the curtain billowing and how the realisation had come upon him that his life would be wasted breath without Lucrece.

Now, as he stood by the broken window, looking out, a blizzard raged outside, coating the world in white. Seth stepped back from it; the cold of the dream-snow, so real it stung his face. The window creaked open on its hinge, swinging wildly and then banging shut, before being ripped open again by the wind. It was too late to stop the decay of this room that had formed him, but he couldn't watch the snow coming in. Seth reached his arm out into the cold and felt for the window.

As he did something incredibly fast grabbed him, clinging on with its cold damp grip. He tried to retract his arm and scraped it against the jagged glass of the broken window. Abruptly before him, so close that no living person could have moved so fast, was Lucrece's pale face, surrounded by bedraggled wet hair.

'Let me in,' she cried, her voice forlorn and strange in the wind. 'Heathcliff! It's Cathy come home, I've been a waif these twenty years.'

'No!' Seth cried, pulling at his arm. He knew that in the story the man tried to carve the phantom's arm against the glass to make her let go. But Seth couldn't do that.

Suddenly the image dissolved before him. For a second it seemed that the mildew of the room was invading Lucrece also, in green and dark-green patches on her white skin, then she just melted away. All Seth could hear was his deafening pulse, the sloshing of blood in his arteries, minutely, specifically. And all he could see were the veins behind his eyes.

Then they were there. The ancestors, his hungry dead that sat among his cells like so many perching vultures on the branches of his double helix. A blood-moon was on the rise above him and he saw it all clearly now. The shaman tree, framed against the ruddy backdrop, the newly hatched vampires perched like demonic birds with their red eyes glowing...

'You are one of us, Seth,' something hissed. Seth knew that voice. It was the Mad One, the insane visionary with the filthy hair who had begotten someone who had had begotten him. The raving wild man's brain was so scorched by the magic that it was stark and black like a body pulled out of a peat-bog. He had terrified Seth as a child, with his leer, full of Neanderthal looking teeth of brutish power.

'It's your nature to bite,' he told him now. 'Look,' he said, pointing to the reddish moon. It seemed to Seth as he looked as though the black forms of birds or bats, or some hybrid monster that was neither were obscuring the moon. 'The red is the blood they spill when they suck from the tits of the Mother.'

Then Seth plummeted back to his body with a sickening thud. It was like a dream of falling, but more intense. He felt bruised and nauseous as he turned to look over at Christopher on the bed beside him. Someone is coming, he thought. Even before his brain was lucid and free of the blood-haze he imagined he could smell her. His animal instinct was to be angry like an animal whose lair has been invaded. But his human emotions were in such a state of desperation that he welcomed the intrusion.

'Are you scared Millicent?' Sophia whispered as they stood outside the window.

'A bit,' Millicent replied. 'I'm a bit afraid of how Seth's going to take this.'

'Me too,' Sophia admitted.

Sophia felt the cold sense of Seth's presence. It ran across the tops of the hairs on her arms and prickled. She feared it was something she would never get used to. There had only been one other like Seth, other than Lucrece. She had known even then that they were a kind of shaman, a creature that appears out of flesh as often as it does in flesh, a walker between worlds. Yet at the same time there was something different about these beings, something she found monstrous, and it was to be found in their flesh.

Either way she looked at it though, she knew they were not as they appeared in movies and in books. When she saw the first of them he had been coming out of a Gothic club in Nottinghamshire called The Pit and the Pendulum. It was the sort of place where you had to walk through a fake wall of books to use the bathroom. There was alchemic equipment on the bar, stuffed ravens and lots of vampire paraphernalia. Teenagers with dyed black hair and black lace gloves seemed to frequent it. She only came for the 'Seven Deadly Sins' drinks they served. Sometimes she picked up there and sometimes she came with friends. The night she saw him she was leaving alone.

As she stepped out of the pub she nearly ran into him. She only stood frozen to the spot for a moment, but it seemed an eternity passed. He had been standing on the sidewalk beneath the showy flaming torches, staring into the pub with his dead end stare. His eyes were either slate grey or navy blue, somehow she could never decide. She could not remember a thing about his features, despite the fact she had stared at him openly. Adrenalin had shot through her but still she didn't move. His pale face was washed out by the neon lights and his stare was the hollowness of something that went down a very long way. She fancied if you could throw a pebble down the tunnel of his stare you would stand and listen for some time before it would gutter out and leave an echo. Sophia knew him as a predator but somehow also as a person. A voice inside her head that wasn't hers seemed to speak to her without words.

'Pass on.'

And she had.

Now, staring into Seth's bloodshot eyes a similar darkness seemed to yawn and growl before her. Something was different in him, but something was different in her too now. She reached out to him, let him know with her mind and with her body language that she was no longer afraid of him. She needed to let him know, because in that moment, when she stood outside his house and saw the other one in her mind, an image of a real flaming torch had fallen between them. Seth seemed to acknowledge the fact with a nod and a grunt. You could see it in every line of his body that he knew; in history it had not always been his kind who had been the predator.

Seth showed them where to climb through the wall. They found themselves in darkness except for the light of a single, almost burned down, candle. Sophia's skin prickled again, but this time with a different magic. They were standing in a magic circle with a skull and cross bones placed in the North. Her head swam with the magic. The longer she looked at the skull the more it seemed to morph and take on different human faces. Realising what she was looking at Sophia walked over to the triangle that the skull was placed in and put her hands down on the ground as though looking for something lost. Only one word came to her mind: Christopher.

'Eugene drained him almost to death,' Seth said brusquely.

'What do you mean? What the hell are you talking about?' Millicent cried.

Sophia could hear the anxiety in her tone but couldn't fully take in the words she spoke. The magic of the place was altering her consciousness. She knew Seth was hurt somehow, and was scared for Christopher. They're both in trouble, she thought. And what was more, Eugene had been here in a way that she had never known a spirit to be anywhere. It almost felt like he was alive, the feeling was so human and physical...

Stepping forward Sophia took Seth's arm. 'Seth are you all

right hon?' she murmured.

Seth flinched back breathlessly from her touch and almost stumbled. 'Don't touch me.'

He let her see it with a naked sincerity, how much he needed blood and how much pain he was in. Her power welled toward him in sympathy; her whole life force seemed to shift in his direction.

'I'll help you,' she said, without even thinking about it. It just seemed so natural to offer what he needed.

Seth shook his head rapidly. 'No. Christopher... I mean,' Seth took a deep breath and seemed to gather his composure. 'Go to Christopher. He's through there. He needs you. You can bring him out.'

Sophia nodded. She ignored the logical voice in her mind that told her she didn't know how to do anything of the sort. 'Leave me alone with him,' she said. 'I'll do it.'

Seth just nodded, he understood without asking what she was going to do.

Millicent turned to Sophia. 'I'll take Seth into the other room with me,' she said calmly.

Seth shook his head. 'It's not safe to be with me.'

Millicent smiled with a great gentleness. 'I didn't come here to be safe, Seth.'

Christopher lay breathing shallowly on Seth's bed. His 'emptiness' was apparent to Sophia's subtle sight as soon as she entered the room. For some time she stood there at the end of the bed. Her eyes could not have portrayed the riot that was in her heart. Here he was after all this time... Yet at the same time, here he *wasn't*.

Here was his body and every feeling that clung to his form and flesh for Sophia. But his soul was held in thrall to a dead boy. She knew now that she would have to use all that Artyn had given her to go up against Eugene. Making Christopher wake up would be the easy part. Getting him free for good... That was another matter.

For now she knew what she had to do. Part of Christopher was in the Underworld, in the soul-life within things, within the ground, within the trees and springs. He was immersed in the All, entranced and entrapped. Sophia thought about the goddess Ishtar and her journey to free the soul of the young Tammuz. *But I'm meant to be Sophia, she thought ironically, the principle of wisdom Artyn said. I don't recall anything about Ishtar and resurrecting dying gods. Maybe I didn't read the fine print.* Sophia shrugged, *life is always messier than myth,* she thought. *We live between confused tissues of myth that intersect each other like haunted crossroads.*

Sophia moved to his side. She didn't know how she knew all these things, how she suddenly knew what to do. She just knew that all the ironies and instincts weren't just hers but those of every woman throughout time. From those ancestral instincts that knew more than she did she knew that reason didn't matter. Only this mattered.

Christopher's face had changed, it was harder, more rugged, and yet it maintained a boyish vulnerability in his sleep. Gently she stroked back his hair from his forehead and caressed his face. Something deep in her womb twinged. Leaning over him she began to carefully unbutton his shirt. She felt something in his shirt pocket and reached inside. It was folded paper. Unravelling it she began to read.

She hadn't meant to read it, not all of it. But there was something compelling about the dead boy's voice. Sophia nodded to herself. *I think I understand you now Eugene, you were like me.* She knew then, that Eugene had been able to see as she could see, she knew it as certainly as she knew her own magical nature. When she read his words they had weaved a distinctive spell. And she understood... *Poor Eugene,* she thought, he was on the very verge of adolescence, of love, of physical love maybe. And he died when it was all just about to blossom... No wonder he felt such frustration. He was acting out, but from the space of a very real injustice.

What she had come here to do seemed harder now. She knew she had bruised a place of intimacy between them by reading the poem. She sensed that Eugene had really loved Christopher, and that he therefore had a very real claim to him. She also knew what It was, and how do you interfere with someone's It?

'Because he's my It,' she said to herself, looking down at Christopher with a certain quiet determination, 'and you're dead Eugene.'

She undid the last few buttons on Christopher's shirt and pulled it open, revealing his naked chest and stomach. Softly, she climbed onto the bed and straddled him. Slowly, almost experimentally, she ran her fingers over the muscles in his chest and down over the light ripple of his abdominal muscles. It was intensely voyeuristic this feeling of having him there, helpless and unconscious while she touched and examined his body. She ran her hands over him, trying to memorise every contour of him with her fingers.

'Damn,' she murmured to herself in appreciation before remembering her spiritual mission. Leaning over him she undid her hair and allowed it to brush against his skin from his chest to his lower stomach. For some reason it made her think of Mary Magdalene unbinding her hair as she anointed Jesus. Leaning over him further she kissed his chest, tasting him with her tongue.

'I'm so going to wake you up, baby,' she whispered, running a hand up the side of his jeans to his groin. Good, she thought, he's dreaming already so he's half-hard in his sleep. Sitting back she undid the button and the zipper, opening his jeans. 'Come on darling, just a little harder, just a little more life and I'll fill you till you overflow.' With trembling enjoyment she took him in her mouth and began to coax a full erection from him. She herself had been hot and ready to receive him almost as soon as she'd undone his shirt. As she sucked him she undid her own shirt, pulling it off and removing her bra.

'There,' she said, standing up to remove her jeans and her shoes. When she was naked at last she climbed back onto him and closed her eyes. She pressed his erection between her legs and allowed herself to slide down over him until he was deep inside her. With a quiet moan she let her head fall back and began to move against him.

Closing her eyes she began to see it and feel it at the same time. It was as though her heart was opening like a golden flower, like a crack in the casing of her being was spilling out light.

Christopher felt like a shaft of hot light, rending her, tearing her open from heart to loins, so that she spilled light onto him like gushing tears. Her hands rested on his chest and they burned with heat against his cool skin. Her body rocked rhythmically, a measured ecstasy, like the whirling of the Sufi dancer. In her mind she chanted his name, over and over, stronger and stronger. Love possessed her and unfurled inside her. It felt like his cock became something that itself unfurled and sought, like the root system of a tree in the earth. It took possession of every part of her, drew from every part of her and the pulling that she felt was joy. Her body seemed to melt into love, love that poured out as water pours from an overflowing chalice.

Inside her skull she could feel her brain burning like it would lift off the top of her head and then she felt movements coming from him beneath her. In her state of exultation it seemed only natural that he was waking and pushing, and even when she felt the weak fingers running up her thigh she was not surprised. She was on fire and screamed in her head, the sound coming out as a gasp.

Yes, was all she thought, *that's right.* There were his hands on her hips, gaining strength with every time she thrust him deep inside her. There, after a moment, was his hand curling over hers. She saw his eyes open, she heard him make a sound, a gasp or a groan, right before her orgasm.

It happened with his hand in hers, her nails went into his flesh and his body came up against hers, holding her through it. Her forehead went down against his forehead and the light exploded from the top of her skull. She shuddered against him, unable to even moan. Christopher was still hard inside her, he looked up at her with blazing eyes. Sophia touched his face with trembling fingers. Instinctually she knew she shouldn't let him ejaculate but instead make him hold onto the power she'd given him.

'Hello, Sophia,' he said, and she saw the smile slowly spread across his face. It was like watching dawn break. Without meaning to she began to cry and he held her without speaking as the night fell around them.

Her voice came to him garbled as if her mouth was full of water.

'Millicent,' he murmured, but couldn't hear his own voice. Her pale, earnest face was near him, her hair was brushing him, it felt like it bruised his skin. Everything was hyper sensitised, touch, light, smell...Closing his eyes tightly he gripped onto her warm hand to steady himself. The world outside was tilting and draining away into his world inside. His mind seemed to be turning itself inside out and swallowing the world with his hunger, until he was destroying the world like the serpent that gnawed at the root of the world tree, like Fenrir at the end of the world devouring the moon and sun.

'Leave me,' he managed to say, turning away from her to the dry, cold of the stone wall.

'I can't understand what you're saying, Seth.'

He could hear her gentle voice but the only clear word was his name.

And here I am again, he thought, *in the testing ground of my personal Hell, my pit of the mind, where it happens again and again, my nightmare déjà vu.* Seth knew how deep he could go and the bottom of his endurance was close. He staggered and fell down on the bed. It felt like his veins held nothing but dust, his tongue had begun to swell like a dead man's and his teeth were made of chalk. Silently Seth formed a prayer, a desperate prayer for an end to it. He groaned and his fists closed on the bed as cramps began to wrack his body. Millicent's high-pitched sound of concern reached him but all he could do was shake his head.

I won't.

'You can't help it, Seth,' the Mad One said. 'Remember Rimbaud's *Season in Hell?* You have no moral sense, you are an animal.'

Seth just shook his head and rode the crest of the pain and back down into the swirling disorientation. He gripped on to the bed, made incoherent sounds and this time over came the tumult.

'Do you want to go down again, Seth?' Came the voice again.

No.

'Then feed.'

Seth managed to shake his head but when he felt the vertigo once again he tried to claw. He knew he couldn't stand it again. And down he went. The hunger of all hungers, because in this space all of his hungers become one hunger and all the hungers of the many-mouthed dead below became his also. It sucked him down and down, into the blackest chaos in his blood. He hardly knew who he was. And every time when the madness subsided and the pains slowly faded the ancestor would be there.

'Feed.'

Fuck off.

'But I can't, I don't really exist, Seth. I'm just the voice of your thirst.'

Something broke in Seth then. He grabbed Millicent and held her close to him. He had been speaking out loud but nearly incoherently. It wasn't the pain that was breaking Seth. It was the whirlpool. The whirlpool where his consciousness was dragged so rapidly through all things, all existences, all hungry things, that he forgot himself, forgot his own principles. And his principles were the one thing that Seth loved even more than he loved Lucrece. Without them there was chaos and terror. They were principles he would have died for, simply because he knew that without them he didn't exist. He clawed to hold onto those things as the vortex came again. His mouth tasted of iron. All there was, was the hunger. The whole universe was made of it, the Earth herself was a great devouring sow, The Mother of Bones, rending and gobbling down her young along with everything else. There is nothing but Her feeding...

Down it came, back into the place he hated most, the black place, the place where blood defined the very outer limits of space and of human nature. In this place blood was all that he wanted. Lucrece's dark eyes whirled into vision at breakneck speed and the roller coaster rounded a sickening corner. He was upside down, and then back around. Lucrece again, smiling insanely with her sharp teeth and her eyes full of chaos. The roller coaster in his inner fairground plunged into unutterable black. Seth doubled over on the bed. He was just going with the ride, letting it throw his body around like a rag doll, he had stopped caring. Seth was being whip-lashed to death in the arms of the universe. The lights and faces whirled by and his fear fell away from him, until it didn't matter what any of it meant.

'Coming into a new station at Lethe please disembark here for forgetfulness.'

The bite mechanism was just like the roller coaster in the end, a mechanism that breaks people, a machine with joints and parts but no mind. The silence wasn't even eerie. The pain and horror petered to a stop along with the ride and the whole fairground was quiet. All was quiet except for Seth laughing at the stars, stark black in the brain, howling and raving at an unheeding sky. Why had it all seemed so important only a moment ago? Seth couldn't remember. Ideas are flimsy, breakable as skin and artery. Ideas break down in the gut and the blood assimilates them.

Ideas are burnt down in acid and made flesh, vicious, innocent flesh. They are like food, they don't mean, they just are. It all seemed so clear. Seth was glad his delusions were gone. He ignored the heaviness that pushed on him from time to time with the thick, wet of his humanity. He didn't care about that feeling. He bared bloodied sharp teeth at it.

'The only thing that is real is The Hunger,' he said. The last thing he saw was Lucrece crouched before him grinning and he heard her chant as though her voice were in his mind now:

'This is the way the world ends
This is the way the world ends
This is the way the world ends
Not with a bang, but with a whimper...'

23

'*You will always be a hyena*'
—Arthur Rimbaud

Christopher got quietly to his feet in the dusky room. His shadow was enormous on the wall, it made Sophia shiver. It seemed to give visible form to the apprehension she'd felt on the way there, that something else, something bigger than both of them was at work in all that was occurring. It made her think of her very first premonition about Christopher bleeding and Jane's similar dream. He stood there for a while, stretched and then turned around.

'I think I know now what it must be like to die.'

Sophia just looked at him. She sat on the bed with her hair falling all around her naked body. In some way she couldn't articulate she was herself for the first time, at home in her own skin at last.

'I could see you as my wife, Sophia.'

'Really?' She smiled.

'Yes,' he replied. 'But I don't know if we have that long.'

There was no answer. Christopher knocked on the door again. *Should I wait?* Sophia had told him that Millicent was with Seth and he didn't want to interrupt anything. Despite this hesitation he urgently felt the need to let Seth know he was all right and to make sure Seth was too. Sophia had told him about the state she'd found Seth in and Christopher was worried. The bond that had developed between them, which Christopher could only express as brotherhood, pulled at him with a need to express his intense gratitude for everything Seth had done for him. Now, on top of everything Seth had already given him, he had probably saved his life as well.

Christopher knocked again. There was no sound within. He

looked at Sophia and she appeared alarmed.

'Go in,' she said.

'Are you sure we...'

'Go in,' she insisted.

Christopher opened the door.

The first thing that he saw was blood, blood on the floor, blood on the bed sheets. Bloody handprints on the walls and its ruddy brown was all he could see. 'Oh my God,' he said.

Sophia squealed and threw her hands over her mouth in horror.

Christopher raced into the room and saw Millicent lying half slumped over the bed bleeding from a messy gash in her throat. He went down on his knees beside her and turned her fully over.

'Sophia get me a towel!' he said, pointing to the stack.

Sophia grabbed one and threw it to him. He caught it as he felt for Millicent's pulse with the other hand.

'Is she... alright?' Sophia asked, as she knelt down beside them.

'She's alive.'

Lifting Millicent fully onto the bed and folding the towel into a serviceable square he began to apply careful pressure to the wound. Every time he tried to breathe or speak it seemed to catch in his throat, both because it was thick and because he was dizzy with the sudden adrenalin.

'Under the bed, on the nearest side, there's a first aid kit. Could you get it?'

Sophia nodded and quickly got up. 'I'll get some more light as well.'

Christopher sat there in silence with Millicent. Her face reminded him of a plaster death mask, one that captured a strange sense of peace. Handprints of blood were on the walls and the bedclothes, as though a struggle had occurred. Christopher felt sick.

Sophia set down another candle beside him and opened the

First Aid kit, passing him antiseptic swabs and bandages. As he took the sterile items from her he felt Sophia's hand on his arm for a moment. In a way that went beyond language and reason this blood that belonged to his sister was *his* blood.

'I swear to you he did not mean this, Christopher.'

'She's my *sister*, Sophia.'

When the bandage was in place and the bleeding seemed to have stopped Christopher wiped the blood off his hands on a rag and got up. Sophia watched him anxiously, waiting for some indication of what he intended to do.

'Sophia, I need you to stay with her.'

Before he had finished the sentence she was on her feet shaking her head.

'No Christopher. You need to stay here. We need to get your sister to a hospital.'

'How?'

Sophia paused for a moment and thought about it. It occurred to her with sudden panic that she had fulfilled the dare that Seth had given her and thrown her mobile phone in the river.

'I can't carry her out of here in the dark. We don't even have a flashlight here. And you don't have your mobile anymore, right?'

Sophia nodded. 'Where are you going?' she asked.

'After him.'

'Christopher don't do this! He's out of control. He didn't mean to do it. Please don't do anything you might regret.'

'I have to find him and stop him. If he's in the state you say he is I can't allow him to remain out there. He could do this again!'

Sophia swallowed hard. 'Do you think you can find him?' she whispered.

Christopher smiled without humour. He looked drawn and hollow to Sophia.

'That's the real question isn't it?'

Even in the darkness, lit by only a thin slither of moonlight,

Christopher could perceive the tracks leading away from the hut. As soon as he saw them he knew that Seth was not moving like himself but veering all over the place as though drunk. Nor had Seth gone to any effort to conceal his tracks, when he usually moved with such care through his natural environment.

Christopher ran beside Seth's tracks in a half crouched posture. The confused impulses in his body were reconciled in motion. His anger with Seth, his pain at this betrayal and his fear of what would happen when he found him, all fused into adrenalin. Blood flooded his muscles, causing them to swell and quicken. The veins stood out, carrying hot messages of emergency around his body. Periodically he dropped to all fours and examined the ground. With the benefit of Seth's teaching all he needed to see was a part of an incomplete track and he was on his way again.

The increased blood-flow to Christopher's brain was heightening his awareness, and with the help of the smothering darkness sound was amplified for him. Even his skin and hair follicles seemed to provide him with information. The night itself seemed to buzz. Then Christopher was in the trees. *This is where it gets hard*, he thought. There was a short rocky incline ahead that Christopher remembered, treacherous at any time, impossible in darkness. Christopher stood on the edge of that rocky outcrop. He knew without dropping to his knees to feel around that he stood right on the edge of it. His skin recognised it in the air. *What would I do if I were Seth? Would I be reckless enough at the moment to try and get down?*

Looking around him, feeling around him, Christopher found a branch above his head, it was thin enough to grip, but strong enough to hold a man's weight. Immediately he knew what Seth had done here. After backing up along the path Christopher moved toward the edge at about the speed he imagined Seth would have been travelling and at the last moment jumped, grabbed the branch and swung. His body swung outward easily on the supple branch and he let himself go as he felt his body swing to its maximum arch. For a moment he was falling and then he landed in a crouch in the leaf loam. The smell of wood-mould rose around him in the darkness.

The luminescence that the town lights gave the cloud cover, even out there, brought the faintest light to the floor of the slight clearing. In the dappled gloom Christopher perceived a pair of deep tracks, just a little ahead of his. Seth too had made that jump and landed in the same way.

Christopher proceeded quietly. The prints became few and far between now. A few times Christopher had to double back, feeling intuitively that he'd lost Seth's trail. After a while there were simply no more tracks, no broken foliage, nothing to indicate which way he had gone. The night around him was completely still. Christopher too stood still listening with his entire body, till every hair seemed to tingle with its own awareness. He closed his eyes and listened, the finest hairs in his ears were discernible too him, his very pores seemed to open themselves to the night seeking vibrations.

Christopher knew what he was dealing with. He'd watched Seth in the woods before. Seth moved like a wild animal, he was practically indistinguishable from a disturbed bird or a fox seeking its burrow. The only way to find Seth seemed to be to trust what Seth had taught him. Christopher proceeded without his eyes, moving in a half crouched position with his hands out. A bird called in the night and flew up. Christopher turned towards it and listened to the voices in his body. *My body knows Seth's proximity, he told himself, his scent, his presence, I can find him. But what do I do with him if I do find him? This man that I love like a brother and cannot hate...*

He squeezed his eyes shut, tried to squeeze those thoughts away, they were interfering with his perception. *Where would you go Seth? What would you do after something like that had happened? Are you afraid? Are you hiding from me, from the world?* Something ached in Christopher. It ached a little like identification.

Then a twig snapped in the night, echoing loud. *Seth*, he murmured in his mind, *are you near?* He headed rapidly toward the sound, but no more followed, only the settling of the leaves after a breeze and moist rising of the night mist. Soon Christopher reckoned he was close to the place he had heard the twig snap. He bent to look for tracks, but there were none. He knew from Seth's training that you always picked the ways with the most rock, hard ground, or springy leaves if you wished to not be tracked. *If I travel how Seth has taught me I have more chance of walking where Seth has walked,* Christopher thought. For a moment the thought brought an echo of another thought, a half remembered Native American Indian saying about not judging a man until you've walked a mile in his moccasins.

There was an immense discomfiture taking hold of him. He was beginning not only to question his right to hunt Seth, but to hear sounds everywhere. Branches around him seemed to move but did not. He was beginning to feel as though he were being slowly hypnotised, but whether it was Seth or the woodlands themselves that were bedazzling his senses he had no idea. Abruptly, there it was… The hairs on the back of Christopher's neck stood up. *I'm being watched.* He knew it in his marrow, though he could hear or see nothing. He turned toward the feeling and moved forward.

The air was almost too still in the trees. His blood banged in his ears, and even the movement of it in his veins was noisy. Beads of sweat were forming on his forehead while he moved so slowly. In a strange way that made his skin crawl Christopher knew that Seth was near and watching him from above. When Christopher moved he would think he heard something moving with him but it would stop when he stopped, move again when he moved. Pausing for a moment Christopher wiped the sweat away that had begun to run into his eyes and sting them. He looked around him and waited, but could see nothing but shadows.

For a moment everything was still, even the feeling of being watched was gone, and then something dropped from the tree. Christopher heard it land in the leaves but it was immediately away. There was only a movement of shadows, a trick of light, where he saw Seth seem to float away from him before the darkness swallowed the shape of him. Immediately Christopher's adrenalin shot back through the powerful muscles in his body which reacted with immediate movement. He was after him. He knew Seth was ahead of him even when he couldn't see him, even when the sound of him running drowned out the sound of Seth running.

He felt like his body took flight, as though his body took over. He was jumping fallen rocks, leaping down inclines and using branches to jump obstacles. Always there was the shadow ahead of him, and Christopher's whole being pounded to reach it. Then, unexpectedly, there was nothing, nothing but a single branch moving in the night. Christopher reigned in the desire to run and to give chase. Dropping to a full crouch. He listened, his breathing ragged and loud. Faintly, ever so faintly, he could hear another being breathing in the night. Perhaps he could more feel it than hear it. Jumping up he rounded the tree ahead, but Seth was around it already in a single agile leap.

'I've taught you well.' He heard Seth whisper, almost close enough for them to have touched, and then he was away again.

There was an ache in Christopher's chest that he could not mistake for fatigue. He wanted to feel it as tiredness, but it had begun in response to Seth's words and the note of sadness in them. What he felt was the urge to cry. Christopher wanted to run, wanted his body's motion to eat up his pain and consume his thoughts. But it couldn't, because up ahead, standing facing him was Seth. Behind Seth was a sheer rock face. Seth stood looking at him, clearly struggling for breath, as was Christopher. As Christopher drew closer he could see the dried blood on the other man's face and the sheen of sweat on his brow. With great effort Christopher looked into the dark subterranean place that was Seth's eyes and he saw the glimmer of the tears that stood in them.

'So what have you come to do, Christopher?'

Christopher opened his mouth to reply but couldn't. The tension pulled tight enough to make the air buzz.

'Stop you.'

Seth maintained eye contact, as long and as intense as a lover would. Christopher couldn't stand it and had to look away.

'Well you'd better do it then.'

Christopher moved forward. He was standing less than a foot away. They could hear each other breathing, smell the salt in each other's sweat. But Christopher did not move to grab him, or to hit him. Their gazes were locked in a way that was unbearable to Christopher.

'I do not understand the laws; I have no moral sense, I am an animal.'

Christopher stepped back and felt rising tears choke off his ability to reply.

Later Christopher would remember Seth slipping past him like part of the mist. He would never know whether he had imagined the slight pressure on his shoulder or the faint murmur that joined the breeze.

I love you.

Christopher's body had been convulsing with deep, quiet sobs that seemed to tear him apart. On one side of that feeling was what he loved, and on the other, what he knew to be right, and the pain itself was knowing that he could never relinquish either.

24

'The paths are rough.
The hillocks are covered with broom.
The air is motionless. How far away are the birds and the spring!
It can only be the end of the world ahead.'
—Arthur Rimbaud

As Sophia lit the last candle in the store she silently prayed that either Christopher or the dawn would come before it burned down. The idea of sitting in that draughty blood soaked room in the dark was nothing short of alarming.

Millicent stirred a few times as Sophia leaned over to tuck the blanket in around the unconscious girl. Occasionally she spoke to Millicent, but her voice sounded horribly loud in the quiet. It was only now that she realised she had developed affection for Christopher's odd sister. *God, what if she dies?* Sophia thought. She cursed the truth or dare game that had led her to throw her mobile phone in the river, not to mention what she thought of as Seth's 'Amish' living conditions. Seth, she figured, must have a fairly high opinion of his first aid skills. *Shame he didn't stick around to patch her up after dinner...*

Unable to do anything but wait Sophia looked down at the diary that she was holding. Before Christopher had gone he had given it to her, as though he had no idea that he was fulfilling all of her voyeuristic fantasies.

'Read it. I wrote it for you anyway,' he'd said simply.

Now it was a guilty feeling, this eroticised enjoyment of the object at such a time of crisis. She opened it almost with caution, as though something might spill out of it. She began to read, not in any particular order, but in an orgy of intrusion, flicking from one place to another.

I am only beginning to form a coherent idea of this man that I have

301

come to live with. It's been about three weeks now. We watch out the wee hours of every morning together and I am coming to know him in a way that I have never known anyone, except perhaps Eugene. Seth is so mysterious and yet he's completely what he appears to be at the same time. I don't understand him yet. But I study him I suppose. Not in a freak-show sort of way but because in the darkness of this place he is the only other, the only mirror of the self. I know now that I want the friendship of this man as I have wanted few things in my life.

Everything that's happened between Sophia and I seems to have happened in a dream. I feel, and I have felt since I met her, quite helpless. It seems I am caught up in a kind of dance that I lack full control of. My actions are no longer limited to my sense of self. When we slept together I was totally confident. Not because I had some false belief about my sexual prowess, just because I couldn't have any pretensions with her. I was just myself and there was a confidence in that honesty. It's strange this calmness that's coming over me. I feel like it's her, somehow, that's worked this transformation on me, but I doubt I could explain that claim.

Sophia flicked through more pages.

I want to know more about Lucrece, but I dare not ask him. When I try to I imagine what his pain must be, I can't. How could I disturb it for my idle curiosity? To have lost her so violently, by her own hand, it must have been unimaginable. It made me begin to think about the day Eugene died. I realised then how I've blocked so much of that day from my mind. It's only now, confronted with Seth's pain as a mirror that I'm forced to see how I fell apart. I hadn't thought for years about how I locked myself in my closet for hours and just lay there in the dark, afraid I'd scream if I moved. I didn't want anyone seeing it. It was my grief, it belonged to me and Eugene.

Sophia flicked nearer to the diary's end, wanting to know what had transpired recently:

Everything just got easy all of a sudden. My body just got hard I guess. It's learned to shake things off. I feel like physically I'm up for anything but mentally I'm still tearing myself apart. Seth has turned his back on this world to live for a dead girl. I can't do that. I know that now. Because Sophia is in this world and the more time passes the more I realise how much I want her and how good she makes me feel. But I know when I see Eugene I'll fall straight back into that again. The only way I can go to Sophia is when I've seen Eugene. My determination is sealed, if I can see him, look into his eyes, and still choose life, then I will be ready to be with her. Until then I'm disaster...

Millicent stirred and murmured Seth's name. Sophia closed the journal quickly and looked over at her. A faint smile clung to Millicent's lips, as though she were dreaming pleasantly. To her surprise Millicent weakly fumbled for her hand.

'Seth,' she whispered.

'It's me, hon, Sophia.'

Millicent's eyes flickered. 'It's okay,' she said. 'Everything.'

Then she lay still, her breathing returning to its previous deep regularity. Sophia felt the overwhelming desire to begin to cry. A spirit of sadness seemed to have entered by the door as a mist and settled about them like a pall. Pressing her hands to her face Sophia succumbed to a little sob. Somehow the night itself had a soul of melancholy, which called out to her in the quietly moaning wind. It spoke of past sadness, and whispered darkly of future loss. It was about Millicent hurt, Lucrece dead, Eugene dead, Artyn and his priestess murdered so long ago... It was all of the immense mass dead of the land that was beneath her feet. It was the sadness of a land whose very chalk hills were the powder of bones.

'How do you do it?' Sophia whispered aloud, to no one in particular. She just wanted to know how anyone who would answer coped in their own way with the tragedy of life. She felt a cool draft caress the side of her face. It was so subtle, a breeze through the cracks in the masonry. But she knew she wasn't alone. Nervously she swung around and had to suppress a scream. Lucrece was standing in the corner, looking at her with her arms folded. Her dark eyes seemed like vortexes in her pale face; it seemed that they could pull Sophia down in a death roll, if she looked for too long.

'You have to be crazy,' Lucrece said quietly, in her hyper-feminine, well-enunciated voice, which was as reed-thin as her pretty bones.

Sophia stared at her. *What a creature she is*, she thought, shaking her head in wonder. It did not surprise her that this girl could have captured Seth's imagination as she had. Softly Lucrece moved forward stirring the air. Irrationally Sophia wanted to leap up and throw the chair between her and the girl's spirit but the other woman smiled slowly at her, revealing her unusual teeth.

'Don't try to run away.'

Sophia swallowed hard, unnerved by the use of the word 'try'.

'You had a question, Sophia.'

'I was just talking to myself.'

'That's the first sign of madness you know,' Lucrece said, with that smile again. 'Looks like you don't need my help.' Lucrece sat down against the wall. She sat as she had sat against the tree at the crossroads. Her legs lolled a little apart and her underwear was visible, her head hung to one side.

'My man loves your man,' she said after a while.

'Yes,' Sophia agreed.

'That's what matters. That girl isn't like us. Not like you and I or Seth and Christopher.'

'She's a good person,' Sophia said, without even really meaning too.

Lucrece looked blankly at her, as though this concept did not compute.

Finally Sophia had to break the discomfort of her stare by speaking. 'What should I do?'

Lucrece looked down slowly and then back up. She stared at Sophia from under her brows, her lips hung slightly apart as though it were too much effort to restrain their sensual torpor.

'Don't you realise yet? It doesn't matter. Nothing does.'

Then she smiled and wasn't there anymore.

Pulling her coat tightly around her and checking protectively on Millicent Sophia felt a certain comfort from the peaceful look on the other woman's unconscious face. Not knowing what else to do she opened the journal again and turned to the recent pages.

I just went to see Irene. It was so macabre I still can't shake the crawling sensation from my skin. And I can't shake the pain behind my breastbone since I read his poems. That terrible sense that he was waiting for something, needing a little longer to live to express something… It lingers with me, that sense of his frustration and how I'd give anything to be able to answer it.

Sophia took out the poems that had been slipped into the journal and began to read them. It wasn't voyeurism anymore. For Sophia this was no longer the ordered voyeurism of archaeology, the unearthing of the secrets of others, the storage of them in specimen containers, it had become instead a respectful need to understand Eugene. She opened them carefully.

Christopher came with the first hints of the dawn. Sophia's candle had almost guttered out and Millicent was sleeping deeply. In the semi-dark Sophia's eyes had adjusted so that she began to perceive the beginnings of dawn through the gaps in the wall. He came so quietly that she didn't hear him until he opened the door. His hair was damp with sweat or dew, and dirt clung to his hands and knees. Immediately he went to Millicent and looked down at her. Sophia thought it best not to enquire what had transpired between him and Seth just yet.

'How is she?' he murmured.

'The same,' Sophia replied, placing Christopher's diary in her pocket. 'She came conscious once and told me everything was all right. She asked for Seth. Other than that she seems to be in a very deep sleep.'

Christopher nodded. 'We need to get her to a hospital. I need you to get my car or Millicent's and drive it up as close as you can while I carry her down to it.'

'No problem,' Sophia said, getting up and pulling Millicent's keys out of the other woman's top pocket. 'It'll take me about half an hour or more.'

'Don't follow the trails, head due West until you cross White Horse Trail. Just jump the fences and keep your back to the sun till you reach the trail then head down it to the road.'

Sophia nodded rapidly, buttoning her coat as she stood. As she headed for the door she felt his hand on her arm and turned around. He pulled her up against him and kissed her mouth. Sophia's heart sped up at the brief contact and her body heat quickened so abruptly it made her dizzy. It shocked her to find that the dirt and sweat on his body did not repulse her or even lessen the thrill of feeling his body against hers.

'I can't believe I'm letting you kiss me when you're sweating,' she muttered.

Christopher laughed. 'Neither can I.'

'I think I must be turning into an iron-age woman after all.'

'Sophia?' Christopher said, and she paused. 'What were you thinking when I came in?'

Sophia smiled faintly, almost enigmatically. 'I was thinking of something Lucrece said to me.'

'What was that?' he asked.

'She told me that nothing matters. Do you think that's true?'

Now Christopher smiled at her in a similar manner. 'No, I

think everything matters.'

'I think perhaps nothing does.'

'Maybe it's the same thing.'

As she slept Christopher tenderly stroked Millicent's forehead.

'I'm sorry, Milly,' he said quietly. The sense of condemnation for having done nothing when he found Seth added to his sense of guilt and responsibility. Seth's words resounded in his consciousness as he sat there. Leaning his head against the stone wall he sighed deeply. 'I am mistaken in handing you over to justice, Seth,' he whispered. The hospital would ask questions, the Police would be contacted... What the hell would he tell them? Christopher cringed when he imagined Seth hunted, captured, held by the authorities and worst of all: medicated, as he feared most. The idea was horrible. Yet... it was all too clear to Christopher now that Seth was ill. It didn't matter whether you called it anaemia or vampirism, at the end of the day Seth had bitten his sister. He hadn't just bitten her; he'd ravaged her throat in a state of total lack of control. For him to have done so without her screaming for help it must have involved him having his hand over her mouth. *He needs help of a kind I can provide.*

Millicent suddenly moved then, breaking him out of his reverie. Something caused her to jerk suddenly as though she were shocked.

'Shh,' he murmured and tried to hold her still but she thrashed in his grip. He lay almost against her, trying to keep her still with his body weight. As he looked down at the bandage a fresh red stain began to seep through it at the joins. 'Shit.'

Sophia ran. At first she walked briskly but some increasing adrenalin seemed to build in her as she walked, moving her into a jog. Then she began to run. She didn't question the impulse. All she could hear was her breath and her heartbeat as she leapt over styles, scrambled over fences, tearing her clothes, and ran through bushes with her hands shielding her face. After a while she slid in the mud and fell heavily. Get up! Something in her head screamed, and she did. She raced down the hill, using tree branches as traction with her hands, sliding, then running again.

He applied another swab and taped it down. Christopher's breath was coming fast now. He was so afraid of the moment when he would lift her and whether the bandage would hold the wound together. For a moment he considered leaving her and trying to get to a payphone. Something tightened like it would break in his stomach and he winced. He couldn't do it. In his mind Christopher told himself it was because he couldn't leave her. But deep down he knew it was as much about protecting Seth as it was his sister. Silently he hated and condemned himself utterly, and yet hate as he would the loyalty held fast and tight like a knot in his gut.

'I'll get you there,' he whispered to Millicent.

Sophia collapsed covered in mud and sweat. For a brief second she lay against Millicent's car before scraping back her wet hair from her eyes and opening the door and jumping into the driver seat. She quickly readjusted the mirror and the seat. She didn't need an explanation, her body had told her to run and she took it seriously. Once she was in the car she started to think again, driving rapidly along the road she worked out quickly how she could best drive up onto the embankment as far as possible without getting bogged. Pulling to a stop she wondered desperately, could Christopher really carry Millicent that far, especially having recently been cataleptic?

He slid his arm under her gently and braced to lift as slowly as he could. Before he lifted her he had tightened the drawstrings on her anorak and tied it so that only her nose and mouth were visible. This held her head in place. He managed to get her out into the air without disturbing the bandage. As he turned he looked at the sun. There was no way Sophia would make it back any time soon. He knew she went to the gym regularly, but her shoes were impractical and she wasn't used to the terrain, nor did she know the wound had opened. So Christopher found her tracks in the mud and began to follow them as slowly and carefully as he could.

At last she was satisfied that the car was as close to Christopher as she could safely get it and she got out, locked the door and began to run up the hill. Sophia felt ill now, her temples pounded with the exertion and she was afraid she was going to be sick. But some resolve had hardened in her on the way there and she gritted her teeth when she fell again and got straight back up. She dragged herself up the slippery slope using her hands on the rocks and bare earth.

Christopher struggled over a stile with Millicent. His muscles were burning with trying to hold her dead weight still. Gently he leaned her weight against the fence to allow himself a couple of breaths to rest. His vision was starting to swim and he couldn't wipe his face to stop the sweat running into his eyes. Only now did he feel a residual weakness from the conjuration and having been drained by Eugene. Then he saw something moving out of the corner of his eyes. Downhill from him was a woman running and stumbling towards him at a frantic pace. *Sophia?*

At first it seemed unlikely she could have got back so soon. Then he saw it was indeed her. She was covered in mud and her hair had escaped from its restraint. Shutting his eyes Christopher breathed a quiet prayer of relief and gratitude. As he opened them he saw her all but collapse in front of him, panting for breath, her face red and running with sweat.

'Are you all right?' he gasped, struggling for breath himself.

She held up her hand to indicate that she couldn't talk right now, but instead reached into her pocket and pulled something out, holding it out to him in her tremulous hand. When he looked down he saw Millicent's mobile phone. He wanted to throw his arms around Sophia and hug her or simply weep with relief.

'You won't... get her... down there without... dropping her,' Sophia panted. 'Too steep, too muddy. Need rescue helicopter...'

Gently Christopher lay Millicent down on the grass and undid the parker. Pulling back the hood he looked down to check the bandage.

'Oh shit,' he said quietly, as they both looked down at the bandage that was soaked with blood and inside the parker hood which was also pooling with blood.

With clumsy fingers Christopher managed to dial the right numbers and he heard his voice say 'ambulance.' He answered the questions mechanically, with the last part of his brain that was still functioning beyond the exhaustion. In that moment he really felt how conjuring Eugene had drained him, he felt his run through the woods after Seth, and he knew for a fact he couldn't pick Millicent up again without risking passing out. When they asked him where he was he looked helplessly around at Sophia.

Sophia, still unable to speak, thrust an ordinance survey map into his hands and pointed to the spot. Christopher gave them the coordinates and pressed the button to end the call. After a moment they collapsed on the ground together and said nothing for a long time. Eventually, as though out of a dream, Christopher heard the sound of the rescue chopper a little way off.

'We found her like this,' he whispered to Sophia. 'Out on the trail. She went off on her own and we went looking for her. We found her like this, out on the trail.'

'Of course,' Sophia replied.

25

'Dying sun, for one day more
Your beacon light has beckoned forth
All viviparous holocausts
Of the cult which men call love.
And now as you feel your strength fails
Before the wild night falls
You come to bathe the alcove
With one last wave of martyred blood.'
—Jules Laforgue

'Of course I was young and dumb at the time,' Sophia said, taking a drag of a tobacco filled cigarette, something she had given up years ago.

A pallid dawn was creeping across the sky. One of those sickly, cruel dawns that rises on those who have had no sleep and shows their pale faces and the dark marks under their eyes. The hospital grounds were almost deserted, but for one other furtive smoker.

Sophia exhaled cigarette smoke. 'I mean, I suppose I may as well tell you now. We've got nothing to do but fucking wait anyway,' she muttered, scraping at the pathway with her boot-heel.

Christopher just nodded. He was seated on the bench beside her, his elbows leaning on his thighs, his head hanging down.

'I started dating Josh when I was about fifteen. He was weird. You know the type. He liked to be seen to be disturbed, took drugs etc. Well my parents...' she laughed ruefully and took another drag of her cigarette. 'My mum's like your parents, well not quite *that* middle-class, but my dad's Greek Orthodox so that brings in other factors. I was into the bad-boy thing, and the whole emo, I'm too sad to even try and stay-alive kind of vibe. I wanted to be seen with him, but you know what it's like, good

Greek girls don't put out. So he dumped me.' She laughed again and Christopher took her hand in his.

I hope you don't let go of that hand Christopher, she thought. I couldn't bear it now. 'He broke my heart, well, in the way most people mean when they say that as teenagers,' she added, realising it probably didn't mean the same thing when she said it that it meant when Christopher said it about Eugene.

His hand was still there, grubby and strong, much larger than hers.

'At the time it seemed like all that mattered in life. So I became a slut. I slept with so many men Christopher. I couldn't name them for you. It didn't take long before Josh was looking back in my direction...' her voice trailed away for a moment and she became apparently preoccupied with the horizon. 'It was a matter of mixed success though. I got myself into some big trouble.'

And then without meaning to she squeezed her eyes shut tight and tears stung them. She felt Christopher squeeze her hand.

'Whatever it is, Sophia, it's not too big for us to handle,' he said quietly. Both of them looked up when the nursing sister beckoned to them to come back inside the hospital. Sophia threw away her cigarette and Christopher was on his feet in a second.

The nurse told them that Millicent was going to live and was in a stable condition. She'd been given a blood transfusion and they were replacing her fluids with a drip, other than that she was conscious but tired. Christopher only closed his eyes briefly and moved his lips in a silent prayer of gratitude.

'Thank you,' Sophia managed to whisper to no one in particular.

Christopher's mother had been notified and would be arriving any minute and neither of them felt like facing her questions.

'Come on, Christopher,' Sophia said, taking his arm. 'Let's go back outside.'

Christopher had a dazed look about him, as though the electric lights and movement were dazzling his senses. He had after all spent months in the dark and silence of the woods and the ruin. When they were finally outside in the semi-quiet Christopher said,'Tell me about it all.'

'About what?'

'About you.'

'It's not really relevant. I just had that whole deathbed confession feeling going on. But she's going to live now right? It's okay.'

'It's not okay. What if there isn't another chance like this?' He grasped her urgently and she immediately shook herself free.

'Stop it!' she cried, then whispered more quietly and gently. 'Stop it darling, you're scaring me.' She laid her head against his chest for a moment so that her ear was level with his heart. 'I can't lose you.'

His hand alighted over her ear and he was about to say something but before he could she pulled away so she could fumble for a cigarette.

'You don't even know what I'm going to tell you.'

'It doesn't matter,' he said with a faint smile. 'Remember? Nothing matters. Except this.'

Sophia smiled too and let go a long, slow breath.

'I always knew he was a drug dealer,' she said firmly. 'But I swear to God I didn't know that he killed people. By the time I realised that part, well... I was already in deep.' Her hands went involuntarily to her face then, as though the story itself were straining to get out and causing her pain. 'There was this guy I knew... Josh reckoned it was him who grassed them up to the cops for something. I don't know. But the guy disappeared. No one ever found out what happened. I panicked. That was the first time I tried to leave him...'

Christopher squeezed her hand again when she paused, as though he were letting her know he was still there.

'What happened then?'

'Oh, he hit me of course, I told you about that, but this time he threatened to kill me if I tried to leave.' She sat there for a while, smoking. 'Well I tried to leave anyway. I started a life for myself in another county.' She shook her head bitterly and tears coursed down her cheeks. 'I thought I was pretty smart, covered my tracks really well and all that. But then I get a call from my mum and dad's place.'

'Shit,' Christopher said softly.

'Shit's right. Mum was on the other end in tears, scared out of her wits, saying Joshua was there and made her dial my number. So I said to put him on the phone. Fuck I was angry Christopher, but I was sick with fear too.'

'Did he hurt them?'

'No. He's too smart for that. He just insinuated his threats. He's really insidious and scary in action. I think there's something seriously wrong with him. I lost it and started screaming, don't you dare hurt my mum! So he says, tell me where your new address is then and they'll be safe. Of course I gave it to him and he left to go there immediately. Only problem was mum and dad called the cops the moment he left the house and when he got there the cops were waiting.'

'So he thinks you turned him in?'

She shook her head and threw away her spent cigarette. 'I don't know what he thinks. But I know he ended up in the nick for a bit. Either way, my options are pretty limited right now. I have to leave town again.'

Christopher shook his head. 'No. No you don't.'

'What do you mean 'no.' Surely you don't think you're going to take him on? We're talking knives and guns here, not the gentlemanly art of pugilism.'

'You can't spend your whole life running away from him. For the time being we'll go to my parents. He's got no way to trace you there. Even your friends don't know where my parents live.'

It felt to Christopher like someone had peeled back the layers on his heart to its core and within it he found a strange quietude. His emotions were still there, surging with oceanic chaos but at the centre there was a calm, a readiness. It was something to do with that time between times where he had not been in his body. He couldn't remember what he saw or did after Eugene took him but something of the world beyond the hedge had stayed with him leaving an eerie sense of fatefulness in everything he did.

When he stepped back into the hospital waiting room to check on Millicent's progress he found his mother waiting for him. There was something about the pinched quality of her face that shook that quiet centre in him, even threatened it.

My God, he thought, *she's aged since I've been gone.* A stab of guilt assaulted him as he walked toward her but he forced it away. *I didn't do this too her*, he told himself. *It's not my fault that she made me the source of her life. I had to live eventually, had to remove it from her whether I meant to or not.* Then his real tenderness for her came, not guilt driven tenderness but natural and deep. He strode rapidly towards her and took up her frail form in his arms almost as though he meant to lift her.

'Christopher!' she cried. 'Oh my God, Christopher, what's happened?'

'It's okay, Mum,' he said. 'It's all going to be all right now. Millicent is in recovery now. She was hurt out looking for me in the woods.' He managed to say these words with such an unwavering sense of conviction that he could see they carried some weight with his mother.

'Thank God you're home now. It doesn't matter why,' she murmured. 'It doesn't matter. I don't need to know what's been going on. Just as long as my babies are safe.' Her voice cracked and she began to cry uncontrollably in Christopher's arms.

Millicent was sitting up in bed. Her neck was bandaged with just a large plaster now but she still had the drip in to replace her fluids. She hadn't noticed Christopher yet but he could hear her saying:

'I don't remember anything, except something jumping on me. It was hairy, like a big dog. Then I lost consciousness.' Millicent glanced up briefly and they made eye contact. There was a quiet understanding, something conspiratorial between them. Christopher didn't fully understand her decision to lie for Seth, but he loved her for it with all his heart.

'I just can't believe that she was attacked by a wild dog and that it didn't leave any other marks on her,' his mother insisted on the way home in the car.

Sophia sat silently, looking out the window. Christopher had her hand tightly in his, he could feel that her palms were sweating. He didn't find it any easier to lie than she did, yet somehow, because it was his mother, he knew doing so was his responsibility and must be managed well.

'Well I guess we won't know till the pathology reports come back,' he said. 'But don't you think she'd know better than anyone what attacked her? How could she make a mistake about something like that?'

'I suppose so.' Jane sighed.

Christopher could tell his mother was not content, for all that she said it didn't matter. Sometimes she is just too intuitive for her own good, he thought. Then he experienced an eerie sensation. It seemed to come to him from her body, like osmosis, through some invisible membrane that still connected them like an unseen umbilical cord. *She knows that I know*, it told him.

Later that night when Sophia and his father were asleep, Jane drifted quietly into the room. He was pouring a glass of water at the sink and she stood beside him while he did it. He didn't look up. He felt the cool tip of his mother's finger run along the edge of his wrist near his forearm. 'What?' he asked, before he looked down at what she was touching.

Almost thoughtfully she ran her finger over the scar on his arm where Seth had cut him for ritual and he had cut himself again in the same spot for blood for Eugene and that second cut was still scabbing over. His instinctual reaction was to pull his arm away and cover it secretively, it was after all something deeply private.

'That looks like quite a deep cut,' she said. Staring into space as she spoke.

'It's nothing,' he replied, pulling his arm away.

'You weren't with Sophia,' she said suddenly.

He opened his mouth to reply but she stopped him, hushing him as though she were listening intently to something just beyond the normal range of hearing. Christopher narrowed his eyes. All right then, he thought, what was she listening too? He began to turn up his own senses. Shutting his eyes he concentrated on his hearing, until the very quiet buzzed. He felt, as he had felt in the woods, how the air tingled on the hairs on his arms and inside his ears.

Gradually he became aware of something, and then something else. First the house's soul, breathing, fighting against the landscape around it, yet permeated with that other life whether it wanted it or not. He had become aware during his time with Seth how we can listen far more than we choose to. The earth all around them possessed its own phantom acoustics. The Long Barrow was a great almost ultra-sonic boom that stretched out forever. Over the top of that Silbury Hill in the distance sang to the barrow in a silvery high tone and Avebury blended with that, like the dusk note of a cello. If Christopher listened even harder it all became one symphony of sound through which threads and tendrils of human whispers mingled.

He realised that his mother had begun to listen to the land, and now she couldn't stop listening. It felt cold in the house all of a sudden. He heard his mother drift past him again. Is she mad? He thought. If she's mad, am I mad? Then she said to him quietly,

'It's all right Christopher, I won't try to find him.'

His breath caught in his throat and he nearly choked on it. But his mother was gone, ascending the stairs and leaving him alone in the humming gloom.

Christopher and Sophia had come alone to the hospital. They had waited until Jane had left before they went to see Millicent. When they entered Millicent was sitting up in bed reading The Sun. She put her newspaper down and smiled. Christopher came straight to her side and kissed her on the forehead. He saw that she was reading an article about her own attack, an article that asked: *Strange Beast in the West Wood?*

'How are you feeling, Milly?' he asked, tenderly patting her shoulder as though checking to see that she was indeed there.

'I'm fine, a bit bruised, but fine.'

Sophia leaned over and kissed her on the cheek.

'Hi Sophia, thanks for coming.'

Christopher sat down on the bed close to his sister, as soon as he did so she leaned in closer.

'He totally lost it Christopher, it wasn't him. His eyes weren't even seeing me. It was temporary loss of responsibility if ever it occurred. He just... he went mad with hunger.'

'What happened then? Do you remember it?'

'He grabbed me and one of his hands was over my mouth and he bit me. I passed out with the shock for a bit. I only remember a flash of him... feeding off me.'

Christopher shuddered and shook his head slowly to himself.

Millicent squeezed his arm. Her pale blue eyes were filled with sadness and concern at the same time. 'You have to help him.'

'How can I help him? I don't even know anything about his condition. He needs to see doctors and have tests done, but he'd never consent to that. There's only one person who could help him, and she won't for her own reasons.'

'Who's that? Lucrece?'

'Ah huh,' Sophia answered for him. 'She'd rather have him for herself, if you know what I mean.'

'Then there really is nothing we can do,' she murmured, staring blankly down at her discarded newspaper. 'I could never compete with her.'

'No, the living can never compete with the dead.'

Sophia's words hung in the air, pregnant with uncomfortable meaning. Nobody moved to refute them and so they remained until Millicent sensed the need to dispel them.

'I'm tired,' she said, turning her head toward the window. 'I want to sleep now.'

Respectfully they both withdrew.

'I love you, Millicent,' Christopher said.

'Thanks, Christopher,' she replied, without looking at him.

When they were in the hospital corridor Sophia glanced desperately over at Christopher wondering what he was feeling. Before she could glean anything or enquire he spoke.

'Do you think, Sophia,' he said, holding the door open for her, 'that when you love someone you love their entire nature? Or do you think people love what's best in someone?' Sophia smiled slightly. This question is obviously completely hypothetical, she thought.

'I think there are different types of love.'

Christopher sighed deeply at that. 'Seth always said that as my teacher he loved my 'original self' more than he loved my every day self.'

'I think it's human,' she said, with conviction.

'What's that?'

'I think it's human when you love someone for everything about them.'

'But otherworldly when you love what's best in them and want that for them?'

Sophia nodded as she pulled her coat on. It had got cold. When they had arrived the parking lot had been full and they'd had to park down the street. Now it was all but empty. The dull-orange lights of the parking lot reminded her of the nightmare of their initial arrival with Millicent.

'So is it human or otherworldly?' she said.

'Is what?'

Sophia rolled her eyes but didn't comment on what she regarded as a typically male attempt to pretend they weren't talking about Seth.

'Your love for Seth.'

'As much as I wish it was otherwise I think it's completely human.'

Sophia nodded, she had thought as much. They turned into the street where they had parked the car and began to walk along the footpath. She felt sorry for Christopher in the situation with Seth. It seemed that for once her Second Sight had been a mercy, allowing her to be aware of the predator in Seth from the moment they met. She had known him as dangerous from the first moment she set eyes on him, but decided he was worth taking a risk on.

Christopher had got to know Seth as a person first, and that, she knew was exactly the solace Seth had sought in Christopher. The fact that Christopher had seen him as a person had spawned a great loyalty in Seth. Sophia doubted anyone had ever loved Seth as innocently and blindly as Christopher had. No doubt that was only increasing the pain that Seth was now experiencing. Not for the first time Sophia found herself aware of the cruelty that can exist in suffering the love of the pure of heart. That was when she felt Christopher's hand close more tightly on her arm.

'What?' she murmured, but her body already knew before her mind did. She felt the signs of sudden stress coming from

Christopher's body. She felt danger. Through his fingers she could all but feel the sudden rush of adrenalin and increase in his pulse rate and her own pulse responded in kind.

'Don't walk faster,' he whispered.

She wanted to run as soon as he said that, otherwise she was sure she would collapse under the burden of panic. Christopher was holding her firmly and she was glad of it, for she had now perceived the sound that Christopher had noticed earlier. Slow purposeful footsteps following them. They were the kind of footsteps that someone does on purpose to let you know they are coming, slowly.

At that instant Christopher stopped and her head swam with a sudden sensation that this scenario had already happened, not once but a thousand times. It was like a nightmare she'd already had but could not remember the ending of. Christopher turned around. She stood beside him, her eyes widely darting about, searching the darkness. Christopher was aware of something in the darkness, she could tell by his fixed gaze. Nothing seemed to surprise her about this situation. She even recognised those footsteps, they had been coming for her for a long time it seemed. Sophia knew what these instincts were that were coming alive in her, they were the instincts of prey.

'We should go into the light,' she said, her voice shaking audibly.

Christopher shook his head.

For some reason she trusted his judgment utterly, his readiness was evident in every line of his body. Her body trusted his even when her brain was telling her to run and to panic. She wished she could make her breath come out more quietly. Then she saw Josh as he stopped, just within the reaches of the nearest streetlight.

'Hello, Sophia.'

His words affected her as though someone had fired a starter's pistol. Every part of her screamed run! Christopher's hand locked down over her arm. Hadn't she been told this sort of thing with vicious dogs as a child? If you run it just antagonises them. *Fuck,* she said to herself as she looked at Josh. His blue eyes had a cold sparkle in them as he smiled at her. It could have appeared playful but she knew better. It was a detail her mind had forgotten. All at once he was so familiar; she felt her own self-destructiveness must have created him out of the ether, so perfect did he appear for the task.

'Just leave me alone, okay? I didn't mean for anyone to grass you up I...'

'That doesn't matter now, sweetheart,' he said casually, as he walked toward them. 'That's all in the past.'

She remembered everything then, in those six steps it took him to close the gap between them. She remembered his personal magnetism, the live wire of sex and danger that this man had been. She remembered how he managed to intimidate her the way he did because she could sense the breathless presence of his violence and his utter unpredictability. It could all be read in his very swagger.

'So who's the kid?' he asked, grinning at her as though they were meeting over coffee, as though he had not stalked her, threatened her parents, followed her car and waited there on that deserted street for her. 'Picking up at the local high school these days?'

'Why don't we discuss this later?' Christopher said then, his voice steady and reasonable sounding.

Joshua turned toward him melodramatically as though surprised to hear him speak. 'What?' he asked, as though genuinely unable to understand him. ' How old are you anyway?'

'Nearly nineteen,' Christopher replied. 'Did you go to school with Sophia?'

Joshua smiled even more broadly. After a moment he broke out into a quiet chuckle. He stopped abruptly. 'I feel like I should clap. Diversion technique they call that don't they, crisis management or some shit? Let me guess, first year psychology student?' Josh turned to Sophia grinning. 'You've really made this fun for me this time.'

Sophia felt a sick sensation settle into her stomach, spreading into her legs so that they trembled and she wasn't sure she would be able to walk. Joshua stepped towards Christopher and examined him.

'Josh, please,' she said, her voice tight and frightened. There was a blatant touch of begging in it. It horrified her how obvious her love for Christopher felt in that moment, as though a great glaring weakness were hanging out for Josh to see. Clearing her throat she tried to put more force in her voice. 'Can we talk about this later, on our own... over coffee? Like old times.'

Joshua laughed without humour this time. 'Coffee,' he said to himself, as though it were the punch line to a joke only he understood. Without any warning he yelled, 'Coffee would have been great, Sophia! Before you started fucking moving counties to get away from me!' Turning back to Christopher he looked him over again, almost thoughtfully. 'No. It's a little late for coffee.' He looked Christopher in the eye for the first time. 'So, you're the latest in the small nation of men Sophia's fucked. And so many of them not me...'

Sophia snapped then and yelled, 'Josh you threatened my mum!'

'Whinge! Whinge! Fucking whinge Sophia!' he yelled at her again. 'Fucking worked though didn't it? At least you've got some fucking loyalty to someone.'

He took a step toward her. Christopher quietly placed himself between them.

'Oh,' Josh said, making eye contact with Christopher again.

Oh no, Sophia thought. She knew that look when she saw it. It was the look of Josh gearing up to hurt someone.

'Christopher run!' she sobbed suddenly, not able to hold it

together any longer. He shook his head very slightly and moved Sophia back from him with his arm.

'This is getting interesting.'

Sophia shut her eyes for a moment and swallowed deeply.

'So what's this protective bullshit? Is she yours is she?'

'No,' Christopher replied. 'But she's not yours either. You need to move on, Josh, because this has to stop here.'

'Christopher!' she gasped quietly, horrified by his words. She could feel the violence in the air cresting, and she could feel them running out of options.

'It has to,' he added. 'Because it will never work out if you've got to be always watching to stop her running off. You don't want to live like that. There are heaps of women out there who—'

Joshua laughed abruptly then, in that unnervingly humourless way of his. 'I've already told you,' he said quietly. 'The psych shit isn't going to work schoolboy.'

Sophia detected the movement of his hand before she even saw the metal flash in the streetlight. She screamed. 'Christopher! He's got a knife.'

'Keep back, Sophia,' Christopher said.

Automatically she did as she was told. She was too frightened to make her own decisions at that point. She watched with horror as Josh flashed the knife across Christopher's line of vision, trying to distract him, dazzle him with its glare. But Christopher seemed to be looking directly at Josh, not paying any attention to the weapon at all. It was all so slow, the way they moved around each other. She couldn't breathe until Josh slashed the air near Christopher with the knife and she squealed, breaking the tension for a moment.

'Good reflexes,' Josh grinned, and lunged for him suddenly.

Sophia threw her hands over her face as she saw the knife go very near Christopher, slicing the material of his shirt. It seemed that Josh had overreached, was slightly off balance for a second. Christopher moved left, stepping behind Josh's foot. For a moment they were too close for Joshua to use the knife and it seemed that Christopher had the arm with the weapon. Sophia heard only the sound of utter shock, before the knife clattered to the pavement.

In a second the feeling of weakness left Sophia, sudden empowerment coursed through her as she ran forward, darting in and grabbing the knife. She was prepared to stick it in Joshua if she had too, brandishing it in her two hands, her eyes dancing from one of them to the other, ready to kill in Christopher's defence.

But somehow it was all over. Joshua's body seemed to twist oddly, as if his elbow shouldn't have gone that way, followed by a horrible pop-squelch sound. Christopher swept his legs from under him and she saw Josh fall to his knees. The grunt of pain that he made was slightly tardy, following the injury. There was hardly a moment for him to realise the break before Christopher's knee connected with his face. Joshua tried to get up, holding his bloody nose with his hand but Christopher kicked him to the ground. Sophia stared in disbelief and horror, until Christopher grabbed her arm.

'*Now* run.'

When they got to the car Christopher got in his side and told Sophia to lock the door. They drove rapidly without speaking until they were out of the town and on the country road, then without warning Christopher pulled the car over.

'What's wrong?' Sophia cried.

'My hands are shaking,' he said, holding them up to demonstrate. He laughed nervously. 'I've never been in a real fight before.'

Christopher's words somehow released the full extent of fear that Sophia was still holding and she began laughing too, crying a little at the same time and embracing him feverishly. With her hands she caressed all the parts of his warm flesh that she was so relieved were not wounded. 'Oh thank God,' she whispered.

'Thank Seth,' he said. 'He taught my body how to do things that my brain doesn't even remember.'

Sophia could tell that Christopher wasn't relieved. Slowly she pulled back from him and they sat there in the darkness for a while, as it dawned on her what they had done.

'Oh God,' she murmured. 'He's never going to let us go now.'

'He was never going to let you go anyway.'

'What are we going to do?' she asked, closing her eyes and letting her head fall back against the car seat. 'He'll never let you get away with what you did tonight. He has a pretty serious reputation to uphold. And you broke his bloody arm. He can't exactly conceal that. He'll never forget it.'

'Unless I kill him,' he said, his voice lacking expression.

Neither of them spoke.

26

'Blood was flowing
in Bluebeard's house, in the abattoirs,
in the circuses where God had set his seal to whiten the windows.
Blood and Milk flowed together.'
—Arthur Rimbaud

Back at the house Sophia sat down on Christopher's bed watching him examine Joshua's flick-blade. 'Do you know how to use that thing?' Sophia asked.

He nodded. 'Enough.'

'Did Seth teach you how to deal with guns?'

He didn't answer her, so she reached out to him and took his other hand.

'I wish I could go to my flat and get my work numbers off the phone. Seth's little dare about throwing out my mobile has turned out to be a whole lot more trouble than it was worth. I don't have a single phone number on any bit of paper. All of them are on my phone back at the flat. I can't even really go back and get the last of my stuff out.'

'Why not?' Christopher asked, running his finger along the edge of the blade. 'I think it's the best thing to do, better than waiting for him to find me.'

Sophia reached for him, her eyes filling with uncontrollable tears.

'Above anything I don't want him coming here.'

'Jesus Christ, I'm so sorry,' she whispered.

'What for, love?' he said, stroking her cheek.

'What if something happens to you? I could never forgive myself. I should never have come anywhere near you.'

He placed his fingertips over her mouth. 'Shh, I've got no regrets. No matter what happens, there's no regret.' When he kissed her she kissed him back passionately, but she could not agree.

Christopher made love to her more slowly than he did the first time. There was controlled fire in it, a slow-burn fire. As he looked into her dark eyes he felt a strange vertigo, as though they hid a great depth and he would fall into them. With every thrust he affirmed what he had told her and did so joyously. *I've been more alive with her than I ever would have been again,* he thought. Every detail was heightened by the thought of death; every feeling took on a hyper-reality that was almost maddening. When he thought she would start to cry he'd come down over her, thrusting deeply between her thighs and murmured to her. 'Nothing matters, Sophia.'

'Everything matters,' she murmured back.

There was an absurdity to it, Christopher thought, the things that seem to matter at a time of crisis, and the things that don't. As he headed along the A4 into Salisbury, he couldn't play the radio. The trivialities of the talkback and the advertisements seemed offensive now. After Seth's prediction that one of them would not survive the summer their already dire situation seemed direr to him still. *When you don't know how much time you have, you tend to think more about how you spend it,* he realised. *What if he's not even there?* It didn't matter either way, because he knew now that he and his death had a kind of relationship. He'd been able to feel it ever since Eugene had taken him over the hedge for that short time. There was something coming. He had known it ever since he woke up. Almost as if Eugene had tried to warn him and he'd half forgotten the warning. Christopher realised that at some level he'd felt it ever since Eugene died. It was only to be a matter of time, somehow. Part of him was already in the ground. There was no way he could stop his death or hurry it, so why be afraid? There was an hour that Fate had allotted him and he saw no reason or purpose in quarrelling with Her.

As he drove in silence he remembered what Seth had said about the moment of crisis. He smiled to himself as he turned into the road that Sophia's flat was on.

'Don't worry, Seth,' he said aloud to himself. 'I'm ready.'

He hoped that if Seth ever found out about what happened the night before and what was at that time still in motion, that he would feel proud, that he'd feel satisfied with all he had taught Christopher.

When Christopher got out of the car there was no one around. He slammed the car door and headed for the stairs to Sophia's flat. When he unlocked her flat he found the bag she had told him was still there and some notes that had been pushed under the door by worried friends. "Call me!!!!" was written on one of them. Christopher pocketed it and began to look for her disconnected cordless phone that she said was on the counter. When he switched on the torch he had brought with him he found papers scattered all over the floor and that the address was not where she'd left it.

'Shit,' he muttered. He didn't like the idea of Joshua having Sophia's phone which still had her addresses in it. There was no sign of forced entry though, so he wondered if she'd made a mistake. After a fruitless search he took what he could and headed out the door and down the stairs. He reached the car, opened the passenger's side and threw the bag in the back. Going around to the driver's side he opened the door.

Maybe it had been paranoid, assuming Joshua would be watching the flat, he thought. He was about to put the key in the ignition when he paused thinking he heard something. Suddenly the passenger door opened and someone got in. He heard the click of the handgun's safety coming off.

'Don't move a muscle,' he heard Joshua's voice say. 'Keep both hands where I can see them.'

Christopher felt the cold tip of the gun as Joshua pressed it hard against his left temple.

'Seriously, don't try and grab it. You're a quick fucker,' he whispered near Christopher's ear. 'But you ain't that fucking quick. I guarantee your dashboard will be wearing your brains before you can even touch me.'

Christopher just smiled faintly and leaned back in his seat, both his hands resting on his thighs.

Joshua frowned slightly, dissatisfied with the response. He pressed the gun harder against his head. 'Now take me to where you've taken her or I'll blow your fucking brains out.'

Christopher didn't move, he just kept looking out the windscreen as though thinking deeply about something.

'I'm not going to hurt her or anything. I only want to set the record straight with her. Everyone's treating me like this is my fault. It's that little slut who started the whole thing, all right? Now start fucking driving.'

Without saying anything Christopher turned the key in the ignition and started the engine. The car kicked over immediately and soon they were heading along the main road.

Joshua leaned back a bit but kept the gun facing in Christopher's general direction. After a few minutes on the highway Christopher indicated and turned the car right into a less well-populated road. Joshua looked around him. 'This better be where you've taken her.'

Christopher did not reply. He took another right turn into a small lane with no streetlights. Having lived in the area since birth Christopher knew every bit of land and byway of this place. It was clear by Josh's confusion and rising stress that he did not. They drove on in silence. No actual thoughts passed through Christopher's mind in that time. It was his body that knew what to do, his body that he trusted. His body was alive with hyper-awareness in those moments.

There were no other cars on the road, the only sound was Josh's breathing. Christopher could hear it, rapid and shallow, almost smell the other man's adrenalin. His own breathing came slow and deep. Christopher indicated again and turned off onto a lane so narrow that only one car could pass at any given time. There were no lights along its way and it did not appear to be going anywhere intensely populated.

'Did you hear me mother-fucker? Where are we going?'

'You didn't think I'd have left her somewhere easy to find did you?'

Josh didn't answer; he just pushed the gun closer to Christopher's head again.

Out of the corner of his eye Christopher could see that the gun was shaking slightly. After another minute or so he indicated again and made another turn. The tarmac had completely disappeared now and they were heading along a dirt lane into the woods. As the lane got thinner the trees seemed to reach out to embrace them and brushed against the windows. Without warning Christopher suddenly drew the car to a halt and turned off the engine.

'What are you doing?' Joshua said, thrusting the gun tip against Christopher's head. 'I should blow your fucking brains out right now. You've even brought me to a convenient place to dump the body.'

'Do you want me to show you where she is?' Christopher replied, reaching for the door handle. When the light came on inside the vehicle as Christopher opened the door the two men could see each other properly for the first time. In a glance Christopher took in the plaster cast on Joshua's right arm, his lead arm, and that he was awkward with the gun in his left. Christopher also noticed tiny, almost unperceivable beads of sweat breaking out across the other man's forehead.

'Get out slowly,' Joshua ordered, getting out of his door and walking around to Christopher's side.

But Christopher didn't move slowly. In a sudden rush he swung open the car door and threw himself down behind it. The gun discharged and blew a hole through the door beside him, but before Joshua fired again he was on the other side of the car. Another bullet hit the tyre beside him causing the air to rush out from it and flatten it. Christopher dove into the bushes to buy himself time. Putting his fingers to his mouth he made a special whistle. It was a sound that Seth and he used to alert the other one to potential danger. It also alerted Joshua to where he was so he had to move fast.

Joshua spun around at the sound and fired into the bushes. A bullet went whizzing through the undergrowth, and was followed by a strained silence.

'I'm gunna riddle that bush with bullets in a minute so you may as well get the hell out here where I can see you.'

But Christopher wasn't in the bush anymore. The noise of the bullet had given him just enough cover to creep quietly back around the car.

'I'll give you three seconds,' Joshua said.

Christopher was watching Joshua as he stalked the parameter of the tree line. His hand tightened around the knife, he held his breath. Looking at the terrain Christopher knew he couldn't sneak up behind Joshua, he was going to have to move a little bit each time he spoke or fired.

'One!' Joshua yelled.

Christopher moved closer.

'Two!'

Closer again.

'Three!' he shouted, and began firing bullets into the bushes. During the noise of the bullets Christopher leapt, throwing himself on Josh. As though with some kind of developed instinct Josh felt something at the last moment and swung around.

Instead of burying itself in Josh's back the knife slashed the side of his throat instead. Christopher withdrew slightly to try and plunge the knife into the other man again in grim determination. As Josh fell he managed to turn and hold Christopher's body weight off him just far enough to get the gun between them. As they crashed to the ground Joshua discharged a bullet into Christopher's chest.

Christopher's body was thrown backwards by the first bullet and Joshua quickly corrected to fire a second. Christopher's body slumped down against the car.

Joshua staggered and fell near the bushes. He looked up to see Christopher's body slide down the side of the car, leaving a bloody smear along the window and door.

'Fuck,' Joshua's voice swore in the darkness as he clutched at his wounded neck. The blood was spurting out between his fingers. The wound was on the same side as his broken arm and as the shock began to wear off the pain was becoming sharper and sharper.

But there was something more compelling than the pain, or even his concern about the blood loss he was suffering. It was the need to make sure Christopher was dead. Josh fumbled for his gun in the leaves with his one good hand. He winced as he did it, but the hate and rage burned too deep for him to heed his body. Picking up his gun he limped over to where Christopher lay inert beside the car. Joshua looked down at him. Everything he saw as he looked at Christopher made him hate him more. He seemed to represent something to Joshua, something that made him feel threatened and jealous of everything he imagined Christopher to be.

'Still breathing,' he muttered, lifting the gun and aiming it at the young man's chest. He pulled the trigger. Nothing happened. 'Shit,' he swore again. The gun was empty of bullets. Stopping to load another cartridge Joshua thought about where he would shoot him.

Four in the face, he thought, *mess up his pretty features for his family when they have to identify him*. He could just imagine what the family was like. *Proper and stuck up, no doubt, think they're better than me. That would fucking teach people to mess with Josh*, he thought. When the pistol was loaded he held the gun at arm's length again and aimed it at the unconscious man's head. He paused.

Something prickled at the back of his neck, and he had grown used to listening to that prickle in prison. He couldn't hear anything, but when he moved to look around him, he thought he heard something else. Something was moving as he moved... The sound stopped when he stopped. It reminded him of an animal moving in the trees from when his dad took him shooting as a kid. Joshua turned back to Christopher, thinking he had disturbed a fox or squirrel. But there was another noise that was closer. As he turned back and looked in the opposite direction he almost got to see what dropped on him. He was thrown to the ground with such crushing force that he could hardly even scream when his broken arm was smashed into the earth.

Something was on him, something fast and very strong. He tried to push its face away as he heard it growl and bury its teeth in his throat. With a strangled, wet, half-scream Joshua wriggled his gun arm that was firmly pinned to the ground. Twisting his hand he shot wildly at the thing, missing it. With one last, final effort, he twisted desperately and fired again, hitting the thing, once, twice. Joshua felt its blood but he never had time to see where he'd shot it because his jugular vein was torn almost completely out of his neck.

Sophia's body began to twitch as she lay on Christopher's bed. It had been nearly two hours since he'd left. She didn't feel she had any choice or any better plan than to try trance. She had considered getting her car and going there but Christopher had made her promise to wait at the house for him. But she had a way now to find out what was happening and still stay at the house.

Everything spun for a moment, there was the familiar feeling of half sickness, half numbness. Then the vision flashed before her with an urgency that none of her visions had ever contained before. She saw herself running through the woods screaming Seth's name.

'Help!' She was screaming. From somewhere she heard Seth's voice in her head, dusky and deep, invading her softly, like vapour.

'What is it, Sophia?'

'Christopher!' she cried. 'You have to help him, Seth!'

She couldn't remember what happened next. There was chaos. She thought she was screaming but no sound came out. A flash of blood darted across her consciousness. What's happening? I can't see! Finally the whirling speed of the vision slowed and she saw Christopher standing up ahead. Bursting into a run she went to him, crying with relief. But his facial expression... Something was wrong with him. He looked so blank, and then he just turned and started walking away. Why couldn't he hear her?

'Christopher! Come back!'

But he didn't. He stepped through the mist and it closed behind him, enveloping him and hiding him from her view. Sophia didn't stop running; she headed right into the mist, calling his name. Once inside the dense soupy fog, she stopped. She couldn't see Christopher and everything was white. Well, she thought, he came in here he must be in here somewhere.

'He is,' said a voice she knew.

Eugene stood in front of her with his arms crossed. The mist seemed to part around him, as though it moved at his will, or he contained a heat that burned it away. But this was not the child Eugene, it was Eugene as a young man, the same age as Christopher. *Oh my God, this is death*, realised Sophia. *This mist is death. Christopher is in here and Eugene wants him to stay.* Her eyes narrowed on Eugene. She had not had time to really own her new power, to sum him up from the fresh vantage point of it. Now she stood before him without her fear of ghosts.

'Get the fuck, out of my way.'

'No.' There was no expression on his face or tone in his voice, just this simple refusal to comply.

She let it happen, let her power well out of the darkest, deepest recess of her. Sophia felt a fire run over her skin, till her eyes themselves burned and her skull felt like it would explode. She grabbed him, intent on pushing him out of the way or rending him with her bare hands but she pulled back in shock. His body felt so cold it burned her hands.

He laughed at her. 'Just learning sorcery are you?' he asked, with a smile that showed his dimples, and then he threw her hard against the ground without even touching her. She flew through the air and landed some ten feet away with a thud that made it feel real. 'I'm afraid you won't be able to just shove me about. It's a little more complex than that.'

After a moment of suffering the illusion that she was winded Sophia got straight back up. *I can't be winded I'm not in my body!* She told herself firmly.

'You're not taking him, Eugene!'

'I am afraid it isn't me taking him. It's the gunshot wounds that your ex-boyfriend just gave him. Do you know how badly hurt he is? I won't help you put him back in his body so he can be in agony. Every hurt that alights on him is as real as my own pain to me. I'm not sure how love works for you, but personally, I don't want to watch him choke out on his own blood. I've done that whole slowly dying thing and it's nothing to write home about.'

'He wants to live and if you really loved him you'd let him go!' Sophia cried.

'That is such a charming cliché. It must be your intellect he likes about you. "If you love something set it free, if it comes back it's yours, if it doesn't, it never was." Did you get that from a Hallmark greeting card? We could try that approach if you like. Despite what you believe of me I've no wish to do anything to

Christopher against his will.'

'What are you talking about? You're the one trying to stop me seeing him because you're too scared to see who he really wants to go with.'

Eugene raised one eyebrow and looked at her quizzically. 'Actually, the only thing I was trying to stop you doing was pushing me. I appeared here with the intention of letting you know what had occurred. But, all right, let's do it this way.'

'What way?'

'The, if you love something let it go cliché.'

Eugene stepped back and made a mock bow in her direction. As he did the scene around them changed. Sophia felt dizzy at the sudden change and the detail that it contained. *He is a master of illusion*, she thought. *Everything I'm seeing except perhaps for Christopher's behaviour and my own, is inside of his mind, something he is creating...*

Sophia and Eugene were standing about twenty feet apart suddenly and she could see Christopher standing in the clearing mist between them on a green field. The green was brighter and richer than anything she had ever seen. Indescribable light seemed to permeate everything and yet come from no single source. It created every glorious hue of colour, all awash with just enough shadow to make the columns of light majestic. There were flowers of every possible shade. Roses larger than any she had seen, the air smelt of their perfume. It was the most exquisite thing she had ever seen, she wanted to weep from the sheer beauty. It was as though they were standing in the middle of a painting. Christopher was standing among it, looking toward Eugene.

'Christopher!' she cried, but he didn't respond. She screamed his name again but he didn't seem to hear her. Her voice was lost in the air as if a nonexistent wind were taking it and distorting it. He looked up finally and seemed to see her. His expression was calm, he smiled gently, sadly, but did not come to her.

Then she watched Eugene say Christopher's name and she saw Christopher go towards him. For a moment her heart faltered. Why did she want to take Christopher away from this sublime vision before her and put him back into a wounded, broken body? Was Eugene right? Was this cruel of her?

Eugene was close enough to her that she could see the emotion on his face as Christopher came toward him. She saw him screw his eyes shut tightly as they held each other. Sophia didn't think she'd ever seen two people hold each other like that. They held on to each other as though the other were their salvation, as a dehydrating man would guzzle at water... The way they cherished and needed one another was clearly entirely mutual.

She could see Eugene's lips moving desperately near Christopher's ear as if he were confiding something that had to be said quickly.

Sophia's hands went to her face, she felt them press hard over her mouth. It was so terrible to see because when she looked at Eugene with Christopher, how he looked at him, touched him, she knew that however spiteful he'd been to her, Eugene genuinely loved Christopher as few people love in this world.

In despair she watched Eugene kiss Christopher and then pull back from their embrace. Lingeringly he squeezed Christopher's hands. She saw the passion in the way Christopher touched Eugene, his unwillingness to let go, the agony there was for him in letting go. Then Eugene turned and came walking towards her.

'So you won,' she whispered.

'There was never a competition, really,' he replied, there was no expression in his tone.

She had expected him to gloat but it seemed he was just stating a fact. The tears scalded her eyes though they weren't real tears, scalded her heart. She shut her eyes tight; it hurt to breathe without him, to think about living without him now. She opened her eyes she wanted to ask Eugene if she could say goodbye, but she couldn't speak at all. She saw that Eugene had turned his face away from her and that something appeared to be wrong. Was he feeling guilty? Was he able? She walked around him, trying to see his face while Eugene pressed his hands over his eyes. For the first time since she'd seen him in his adult form, his body language looked like that of a boy. But when she came close he pushed her away with one hand, not looking.

'Take him. I'll help you do it.'

Sophia's eyes began to widen in disbelief. She was too afraid to believe, she suspected some sort of cruel trick. 'But I thought—'

'Hurry. He doesn't have long.' Later she would remember seeing, after Eugene helped her remove Christopher from the mist. After she'd grabbed him and pushed him back into his body, Eugene weeping silently into his hands.

Materially it had only been a second where his eyes had opened but it seemed slow and strange. It had been so dark in the woods and the white light where he was blinded him. Christopher felt wet around his shirt but didn't know why. He couldn't feel anything. He shut his eyes and let the trolley take him away from Eugene. The moving away hurt so much it wasn't possible to feel anything over that pain. It had felt so good in the other place, as though they might finally have time for all that had been left unsaid and undone between them.

The only thing now was light after light passing above him and people running. There seemed no hurry to Christopher so he couldn't understand. He moved his head weakly from side to side, trying to free it from the thing that was pressing over his nose and mouth. For a brief moment a middle aged woman's face came into his field of vision and he heard her say,

'You're going to be all right, sweetheart.'

He wanted to tell her that it wouldn't be, it couldn't be all right. The moment his hand and Eugene's had separated nothing had been all right since then, there was only this cramped confusion. It was all too late, for everything...

...After the darkness came the white room. It was very quiet except for the humming and beeping sound just outside of his full awareness. He felt the need to sit up and get out of bed. *Sophia must be worried*, he thought, *with all these people panicking*. It was necessary to let her know he was all right, and to tell mum...

'Lie still,' he heard a familiar voice say.

Relaxing back into his flesh, Christopher felt as though he were settling back into something a little cold that he'd forgotten about. He wasn't altogether pleased by the sensation. There was a little jolt of pain, a strange constriction, the awful half-awareness of something up his nose and down his throat. Desperately he wished to rip it out so he could swallow properly.

'Seth,' he whispered.

'Yes, Christopher,' the other man's voice said with a deep tenderness that surprised him.

He felt Seth take his hand and wanted to ask him why he was acting so weird. And how did he get here? Somewhere something twinged in him, a distant desperation, a distant unease.

Seth squeezed his hand. 'Don't try to talk.' Christopher heard him say.

'I can't see you,' Christopher said, trying to pull Seth closer, only to find he couldn't turn his head. Then he saw Seth's face above him, very close to him. Seth's hand was on his face, squeezing it slightly.

'You're going to be fine. I just want you to know...'

Christopher was confused as he looked up into Seth's eyes. There was a smoothness to Seth's face, a flawlessness that wasn't usual. He might have asked a question but Seth didn't give him time.

'You've got a talent for life, a fine talent. And you're strong enough to be everything that's waiting inside of you. You've got the imagination to find all the possibilities that life holds, and to squeeze out the last drop of all of them.'

Christopher tried to hold him there but Seth somehow managed to avoid being held and was sitting back off to one side.

'And you're the best friend I ever had. You're like a brother to me. And what I hope more than anything is that you remember above everything else the best things we shared. The hard shit too, but the living of it all, the real stuff. You're one hell of a man, Christopher. It's been an honour.'

It seemed Seth wasn't holding his hand anymore. Something seemed to interrupt. For a moment the ceiling seemed closer than it should and he could hear people hurrying and frantic shouting. He saw machines and bags of blood being loaded onto chrome stands around a bed. All the people in white seemed to be obsessed with what was taking place on the bed, so he looked too.

He knew it was his body lying there, his bloody shirt being cut off him and all those stick on heart monitors on his chest. They had both of his arms out at his sides, supported by two stands with blood-coloured tubes going into both of them. His face was scratched across the brow by brambles and his hands were filled with his own dried blood. It seemed so strange to see himself like that, surrounded by blinking screens and still having plant matter through his hair. Everything else looked white and clean except for him.

I'm going to die in this white clean place, he thought. It was an irony but not one that concerned him too deeply. Then hard and strong he felt Seth's hold on him again.

'Come on, lad.' He heard the other man's familiar brusque tones, the old hard loving he knew so well.

'That's more like it,' he whispered. 'The way you were talking before you'd think someone was dying.' He tried to smile.

'You've seen the stellar radiance of death, but you don't want it yet! You're not ready to want it yet.'

'Why not? You do,' he replied, feeling like he was running his fingers through cool water, creating languid ripples.

'I'm not looking for peace. Death is something different for each of us and I never needed to look for it. Death is something I am already.'

Seth's voice was fading again. The white room seemed very far away, all in the blink of an eye. Christopher was standing on one side of a stretch of water. He saw Eugene for a moment, silhouetted against the sky. Eugene turned his head slowly as though he knew he was being watched. *He's so elegant,* Christopher thought as he smiled to himself. *He knows it too. To think he never grew up...*

Something pained Christopher; Eugene's face seemed so desolate. It seemed to contain the kind of stark despair that is beyond tears. But then he looked at Christopher and smiled, his dimples appeared in his cheeks and light darted into his blue eyes: He threw up his hand and waved...

...'Clear!' Christopher heard the man's voice dimly. *It's just like when Eugene died,* he thought. He remembered how Eugene's body had buckled off the bed on that last horrible day, just like his was doing now and there had been the same flat-line. That sound... The shrill cry of a heart monitor no longer picking up a beat...

'When I first saw you,' Seth whispered. 'I saw so much light in you I thought you were the kind of man who falls in love with either life or death. But I know you won't choose death now, because you've seen another way to live. And I know you won't take the easy way out now, you're too brave for that.'

'Clear! Again!' The heart monitor sprang into life. 'We've got action.'

For Christopher the entire room seemed to be pounding with nothing but his heartbeat. In his ears pulsed thick, hot blood. Behind his eyes pulsed moving blood. All through the pain his heart beat and he smiled faintly as he felt it, heard it, was overcome by the flooding tide of it. And with each beat he said it again 'yes', 'yes', 'yes.'

'Goodbye for now,' he heard Seth say. For a moment he saw that smile that Seth only ever gave in moments of extreme levity, the one where he forgot to cover his teeth. In surrender Christopher fell into the arms of the needles, the tubes and machines, and his torn body. *Okay, let's do it*, he thought.

Sophia had never run like that before. Not even when Millicent was hurt and she'd thought her heart would burst then. This time was different. There was no feeling in her body. She had driven so fast luck alone had prevented her crashing the car and then she was running. She was there among the ambulances and chaos before they had even fully taken care of the situation. As soon as she had come to in her body she had called an ambulance and got in the car.

She drove as close as she could to the West wood and then headed for the place she had seen in her vision, right near Seth's hut. It was the ultimate test of faith in her ability, but it never occurred to her not to make that call. If she was wrong the price would be embarrassment, if she didn't make the call and she was right the repercussions could be deadly.

She got there just in time to see the body bag closed. As though in a dream she told them that she knew the man, that she could identify him. They looked at her like they suspected she was crazy.

It all happened around her, not to her. Over and over she just shook her head at the police officer and murmured that she only knew that Christopher was her boyfriend and that Josh had been stalking them. Christopher had gone to her flat that night and that was all she could tell them.

Never had she felt like this. Never had she known this complete lack of concern for what people thought of her. Her hair was matted and damp. Like a mad woman, barefoot in the rain and covered in dirt, she stood there before all of them. She didn't care. They would not even tell her what was happening and she felt wild and on the edge.

'Where the fuck is he?' she demanded of the nurse in the hospital waiting room. 'I have to see him.'

Her face was tear stained, her nails were broken and dirty and she still had no shoes on. She stood there in the corridor and sobbed. It seemed like someone had turned the sound down on the world. People stared at her and whispered things but she didn't hear them.

'What are you fucking looking at?' she yelled at a passerby.

'I'm sorry, Miss, I'm sorry,' the nurse said, trying to extricate herself from Sophia's grasp.

'What do you mean you're sorry? Are you trying to tell me he's dead? Is he fucking dead?' She screamed and everyone looked at her. The hospital administrative staff stopped working on account of her.

'I don't know okay? We're really busy here. I think he's still in surgery.'

Sophia felt the security guard's gentle but insistent hand on her upper arm and pulled away from it. She turned to the kind looking Indian gentleman who had come over from the waiting room seating to offer her his support.

'I just want to see him, I don't even know if he's alive.'

Despite her attempts to pull away the man was half holding her up and half holding her in his arms.

'I understand what you are feeling, Miss. I really do. My son had a terrible car crash only two years ago and they would not tell us a single thing for what felt like hours.'

'Is he okay now?' She sniffed.

'He is all right now, yes,' the man said. 'They are always okay, it is us who are not okay.'

Sophia stood with Jane and they both stared at the movement of the second hand on the clock for an hour. Jane looked so pale that Sophia was afraid she would die herself. But Jane didn't seem able to talk. She just stared straight in front of herself. Sophia couldn't stand it. She got up and stalked towards the doors that said, hospital staff only beyond this point. Sophia pushed the doors open and poked her head around. There was no one there so she scuttled rapidly along the hall in the direction of the sign that said 'surgery'.

Finally she saw a surgeon coming out of another room from between two plastic flap doors that closed behind him. He was peeling off his plastic gloves and pulling off his facemask. For some reason she felt certain that it was Christopher's blood that this man had on his gloves.

Her heart stopped for a moment. The man did all these things in a slow, exhausted way. He was not in a hurry. It was the slowness of a tired man who had just saved a life, or the slowness of a man who had just lost one. There was no discernible difference in body language that answered this question. Sophia bit her lip as he peeled off his last bloody glove. He turned toward her and appeared to get a shock to see her there.

'After Christopher Penrose?' he asked.

Sophia nodded, biting hard into her lip. There was hardly a moment in between but it was eternal, then the doctor smiled wanly and nodded his head. He rubbed his face and exhaled long and slow. Sophia laughed and burst into tears. The doctor smiled too. He was too sleep-deprived and distracted to ask her to leave.

'Is he your husband?' The surgeon rubbed his red-rimmed eyes as he looked at Sophia.

'No.' She beamed at him. 'But he will be.'

The doctor nodded thoughtfully. 'Yes,' he said. 'He will be.'

'Thank you.' She sobbed. He patted her shoulder absently as he walked past.

'It's weird,' he said, almost to himself as he was about to walk away. 'He died on the table twice. It was the last attempt I was going to make to use the defibrillator and something just told me, do it, this kid's a fighter. And I was right...' His voice trailed away. 'I've got to get some sleep.' He half laughed, 'I'm starting to see people. People who aren't there.'

'Know the feeling,' she murmured.

The surgeon walked away down the corridor and Sophia slumped against the wall, her legs going from under her. She sat against the wall gathering herself for a while. After a few moments she got up and ran toward the direction that the sign saying 'recovery' pointed.

She ran so she could get close to him before they stopped her. There were people everywhere, people saving lives, people succeeding, people failing, people waiting. People elated as though they had a second chance at everything, and other people who had just had the one they loved taken to the place in the hospital that doesn't have a signpost.

'Thank you, Seth,' she whispered. Sophia stood back against the wall to let a trolley go past.

'Hey! You shouldn't be here!' Someone yelled at her but had no time to say more. Shaking her head she ran down the hall towards the doors where doctors came and went at a more leisurely pace and pushed past some nurses talking about what had just happened. It was only now, in her relief, that she felt her intense, bone-aching fatigue. She was going to have one look at Christopher before she collapsed. She had to see with her own eyes that he was fine.

As she threw open the door to recovery a man in a long, black coat slipped out as she slipped in. Sophia looked at him distractedly for a moment and caught a glimpse of familiar dark features. He winked at her and then he was past her. Swinging around Sophia did a double take and scanned the moving people.

Pushing her way back through the people and trolleys, she

thought she could see him, walking ahead occasionally, walking slowly and meditatively though the busy halls even though she was running and not catching him. At the waiting room she raced breathlessly up to the counter.

'Excuse me!' The woman looked up at her frazzled, but still holding onto her patience.

'Yes Miss?'

'Did you see a man come past just then? A man in a black trench coat, dark hair, dark eyes, medium height?' The woman nodded quickly.

'Just went past. If you hurry you'll catch him up on the stairs. He left with a young woman with dark hair.'

The tiny hairs on the back of Sophia's neck and up her arms stood to attention, she was already staring off into the distance and suddenly not in any hurry.

'Thank you,' she murmured. She turned to walk out through the doors and out onto the front stair. She found the street and the parking lot empty, except for some dead leaves that the wind played with.

'Hey, Sophia,' Christopher whispered.

Immediately she came closer to him. 'Hello, Christopher.'

Christopher felt her kiss his face. He smiled weakly as he looked at her. Tears were standing in her dark eyes. He wanted to reach for her and take her in his arms. But he was impeded by the drip and the fact that he wanted to keep looking at her like she was in that moment.

'How do you feel?' she said.

'Like I've been under water and this is the first breath I've taken.'

'You've been unconscious for a long time. One of the bullets grazed your lung.'

He shook his head. 'No, I mean since Eugene died. I feel like this is my first real breath since then.'

Sophia smiled. Light seemed to pour in all around her. He couldn't see if it was the morning sun rising from behind the hospital curtains around the bed or the electric lights above, but to him it seemed that a radiant sun disc danced and shimmered behind her head. Somewhere in his mind he seemed to remember he had once had a dream like that. But he couldn't fully remember. Christopher smiled too.